THE EDUCATION OF A GRINGO

THE EDUCATION OF A GRINGO

H. R. DeArmond

White & Wilkinson

Dedicated to Janette . . .

the love of my life.

Dear Reader: There are several lengthy conversations in this book that are being held in Spanish. Even though they are written in English, they are italicized and printed in bold in order for the reader to recognize that Spanish is being spoken at that point in the story.

Part I
Late 1950s – Late 1960s

"El Camarón que se duerme se lo lleva la corriente"
— From a Mexican folk song

Chapter 1

"Look out, he's got a knife," someone yelled. Jimmy looked at the guy facing him and saw the glint from the headlights on a shiny six-inch blade. Behind it was a large surly Mexican.

Jimmy wasn't normally a violent guy; he didn't go looking for trouble and usually tried to avoid a fight. But on this evening, he was infuriated that a carload of Mexicans had pulled up and thought they were going to crash their going-away beer bust. Not happening, Jimmy thought as he picked up a three foot long two-by-four.

"You can leave now, or I'm going to take this two-by-four and bust your greasy skulls and then shove that knife up your ass," screamed Jimmy. Then he looked at the tall skinny white guy beside the Mexican and added, "and you're next, you skinny bastard."

Mexicans were not invited and they were not welcome. White boys and Mexicans just did not mix in the fifties and sixties. Mexican was the nicest term used to describe them. Even though none of them were actually Mexicans, they were all at least third-generation in the United States. In fact, many of them did not speak Spanish.

But a carload of Mexicans had come, and they wanted some of the beer or they would cause trouble. This was a bad mistake on their part. They had underestimated how many white boys there were, and how unafraid of knives they were when armed with a two-by-four and fortified with beer. So, after a round of threats and an exchange of insults, the Mexicans left.

Jimmy was startled to have seen a white boy with the Mexicans. He asked Lonnie, "Who was that white guy with those Mexicans?"

Lonnie replied with a sneer, "He's Charlie Goodman. He's just like 'em, lives with 'em. Hell, he's even married to one of 'em."

"That's sickening," Jimmy replied. And back to drinking beer they went. But Jimmy could not quite forget the incident. He continued to wonder how a white boy got so involved with a damn bunch of low life greasers.

****

It was one of those warm, sultry, San Joaquin Valley, California nights. The kind that causes sweat to trickle down your back into your butt crack. But Jimmy and the boys didn't mind. They were very content to be gathered in a friend's barn drinking beer.

The reason for the gathering was the imminent departure of Lonnie. He had graduated high school and joined the Army. In the pre-Vietnam era, the United States military was a safe place to learn a trade. Lonnie preferred joining because he could pick his specialty. The alternative was to wait to be drafted and assigned, to who knew what.

On Monday, Lonnie was off to the Army induction center in Oakland, CA. The boys wouldn't be seeing him for a while, so they had to send him off in style with a beer bust.

Some of them were 21, the legal drinking age, and some

weren't. But all were welcome to pull the handle of the pony keg and partake of the refreshing amber liquid. They weren't too concerned about underage drinkers getting in trouble. The two police officers in the town were usually willing to look the other way, unless they were causing a problem. They definitely were not causing a problem. This group of young men were sitting and drinking, telling stories and insulting each other as men and boys do when they are bonding.

Chapter 2

He was Jimmy to his friends and Jim to his parents, unless they were irritated with him, in which case, he was James Andrew. But by whatever name, he was the first-born son of Okies. He was a first-generation Californian.

Jimmy was a big kid; he had his growth spurt at twelve. By age twelve, he was 5'11" and 120 pounds. Now, as a high school student, he had matured to a solid 6'1" and 170 pound young man. He loved sports, singing in the choir and playing his trombone in the band. In fact, Jimmy loved just about everything except the studying part of school. He would much rather have been out roaming the countryside than studying. He wasn't stupid; he loved the outdoors and was just a bit lazy.

Jimmy's parents had left Oklahoma to escape the grinding poverty brought on by the depression and the Dust Bowl. They made it to California in time for Jimmy to be born in Richmond, California. There, Jimmy's dad found work in the Kaiser shipyards when he was only seventeen. But as fate would have it, his dad was drafted shortly after his eighteenth birthday. After basic training, he shipped out to join the war in the Pacific. He participated in the invasion of Okinawa, and subsequent occupation of Japan. Luckily he returned with only psychological damage.

Mom and Dad always wanted to return to Oklahoma. They did not like the fast-paced California life or the people who looked down on them and called them Okies.

They were inflamed with anger when Jimmy told them why he had a black eye. "Jerry and I were walkin' out by the railroad tracks, and we saw a big pile of dog poop right on the railroad. Jerry said, 'It looks like Okies have been here. You know they're dirty and stupid. They'll shit right out in the open like a dog.' I said you take that back and say you're sorry. My mom and dad are Okies and they would never do that! But he wouldn't say sorry, so we got in a fight."

If anything, incidents such as this increased their desire to return to Oklahoma. However, Oklahoma was still locked in the throes of depression, and no jobs could be found. They decided to carry on until things got better, then they could return to Oklahoma. They soon moved out in the country to a place more like their small town in Oklahoma. The town of Perryville was still California, but the people were much nicer than in the city.

When they moved to Perryville, it didn't take long for Jimmy to make friends and to discover there was a group lower on the pecking order than Okies — Mexicans. He decided right then not to let anyone know where his folks came from, and he soon joined in the degrading talk about Mexicans. Instead of his own abuse sensitizing him to the pain of others, the self-absorbed boy piled on with the rest. His favorite joke became, "Do you know how a Mexican knows how to put his drawers on in the morning? Yellow in front, brown in back."

But even when his audience laughed and snickered, Jimmy couldn't help but feel a bit uneasy and remember the fight over the dog shit slur.

****

Jimmy's ethnic education began very slowly. Like most

important learning, it started with trying to answer some questions.

He was a boy in a small town in the San Joaquin Valley. He had very little exposure to Mexicans. There were a few U.S. born, of Mexican descent, in the community, and they mostly kept to themselves. Many of them didn't even speak Spanish. There were some braceros who were allowed into the U. S. for a specified time to work in the fields. There were those called "wetback" who had entered the U.S. illegally, also to find work in agriculture. The wetbacks were a shadow group who stayed out of sight as much as possible for fear of being deported to Mexico.

Jimmy didn't have much exposure to Mexicans, but he did have Mexican food once as a teenager. His college prep track in high school required a foreign language class. It was a choice of Spanish or French, so Spanish it was. The teacher, Señor De Leon, was a great guy. He had been taken prisoner by the Germans during World War II, and he was always telling how the German guards would correct the English of the American soldiers. Señor De Leon said, "The guards knew better English than most of my cellmates." He urged his students to acquire knowledge of other languages and cultures. This led to a field trip to Joe's Mexico City Café in the big city of Stockton, California, population 144,000.

All of the students were very excited when the big day came. They boarded the bus at 4 p.m. at the school, and were transported to Stockton to eat at Joe's Mexico City Café; they had been schooled in how to order and were assured the waiter would speak only Spanish. It was a wonderful experience for them to learn that anyone actually spoke Spanish outside the classroom. The students stumbled through giving their order to the very patient waiter. It really didn't matter what they said, since they were all having the same thing, one enchilada with beans and rice. Even if they incorrectly ordered ensalada con fritos y arroz (salad with fried and rice), as one nervous girl did, they still got one enchilada with refried beans and rice, and a nice smile from the waiter.

"How did you like eating ground-up cat?" a friend asked Jimmy at school the next day.

"What are you talking about?" Jimmy replied.

"Don't you know that Mexican restaurants catch stray cats and grind them up to make their food? That's why they put all that sauce on it. My dad told me so," Jimmy's so-called friend said.

"You're crazy," Jimmy said. But as he walked away, he had questions. Señor De Leon would not eat cat? He wouldn't take us to a place that did this, would he? he thought. Jimmy decided the answer was no! He's a very nice man, and he is not mean. No, he wouldn't do that. He is a good Mexican.

Chapter 3

Renaldo was born into poverty and raised in the state of Michoacán, Mexico. He lived with his wife and two children in a small house and worked the farm fields near his tiny village. He had no electricity and the household water was supplied by a trip to the community well each morning. He plowed the fields with a mule using a forked branch, cut from a tree, as a plow. As he turned over the rich soil, he yearned for something more in life. One evening he spoke to his wife, Conchita, of a serious matter, unlike their usual conversations.

"I heard some exciting news today, my queen," said Renaldo.

"What was that?" asked Conchita.

Renaldo explained, *"The North Americans are recruiting more laborers to go there and work in the fields. They promise food, bed, and good pay, more than I can ever make here."*

"Where will the children and I live?" she asked.

"You would have to stay here, but I would send you money from my pay to the Western Union Office every month. I would only be gone for six months, then I will come back. We can save money, and when we have enough to buy a little farm, I will go north no more."

"We will do as you say, my love," Conchita said.

Renaldo began gathering his documents the next day. He knew he needed a birth certificate and one or two letters testifying to his good character. The birth certificate was not a problem. His *abuela* (grandmother) had made it her business to gather birth certificates for all her grandchildren. Renaldo kept his in the metal box where he and Conchita kept their special papers and the little money they had saved.

Renaldo knew he could get one of the character references he needed from his priest. ***"Why are you here, my son?"*** the Priest asked.

"I want to work in the north," Renaldo said. ***"They won't let me in without letters that say I am honest and a good worker."***

"You are honest, a good worker, and a good husband and father. I have seen how you work and care for your family. I will give you a letter that says all these things," the Priest confirmed.

"Thank you, Father," Renaldo replied.

"Receive the blessings of the church," The Priest said while making the sign of the cross. ***"May you be protected and successful in your journey."***

After a payment of twenty pesos, the Mayor provided Renaldo with his letter of approval. Renaldo had everything he needed to board the bus for the check station on the Mexican side of the border.

There were sad farewells and tears as Renaldo, who had never been outside his little village, left for the border. After a very long and tiring bus ride, he and twenty others arrived at the check station just twenty miles from the U.S.-Mexico border. Renaldo was shocked to see more than a hundred men lined up to have their documents checked.

Renaldo waited for eighteen hours before his name was called. **"Documents, please,"** the official said. Renaldo handed over his two letters and birth certificate. **"Okay, show me your hands, palms up,"** the official demanded. As Renaldo held out his hands, the official took them and felt the tough raised calluses. **"Good, good,"** he said. Renaldo received a stamped document and was directed to another waiting area.

Feeling dizzy and faint, Renaldo sat on a hard bench, and for fifteen pesos, he bought a plate of beans and rice and some water from a traveling vendor. Someone hollered, **"Wake-up, the bus is here."** Renaldo shook himself awake, and for a minute wondered where he was. He soon remembered, refreshed from his meal and sleep, and got in line. It was a comparatively short ride to the American side of the check station, where papers and hands were once again checked.

The major check was yet to come. Renaldo and his fellow applicants were given a thorough physical exam and then subjected to what he would remember as one of the most degrading experiences of his life. They were stripped of all clothing and required to walk through a narrow hallway where they were sprayed with DDT, a powerful, and soon to be illegal, insecticide.

Renaldo was willing to bear the discomfort and humiliation for his family. He thought of them as he went through the rigors of the selection.

After the four-day journey from his village, he was put on another bus that drove off into the night into a strange land.

Chapter 4

Johnny was a second-generation American of Mexican descent. His grandparents had fled to the U.S. in 1915 to escape the constant fighting in Mexico. The long revolution was waged to end the dictatorship in Mexico, and to provide a better life for its citizens. But, while the fighting continued for ten years, many left Mexico, the Martinez family among them.

Johnny loved living on the family farm. His six-foot frame was well suited to work on the farm. He could be seen most mornings milking the one cow the family kept for their own needs. Johnny's dark black hair was pushed up against the cow's flank, and Johnny could be heard gently talking and sometimes even singing to her. He loved animals, all animals, especially his two dogs, Mutt and Jeff, who were his constant companions around the farm. With a twinkle in his dark eyes, he'd call out to the two collie-mixed brothers, "Come on boys, it's time for a run!"

Johnny's parents were born in the little town of Perryville. They were people of the land, and over time, they were able to save enough money to buy a small farm just outside of town. They made a modest living by selling produce, grown in the rich loamy soil of their twenty acres, from a stand by the road. Often a local grocer would shop with them, buying lug boxes of peaches, tomatoes, and squash.

Johnny's duties would increase during the planting and harvest seasons. During planting, he would get up at

5 a.m. and go immediately to the fields behind the family house, where he lived with his mom and pop and sister. They would begin early to plant tomatoes, watermelons, and zucchini squash. By 8 a.m., he would have finished his planting, showered, and had his breakfast of frijoles and corn tortillas. Then he would walk a mile to catch the school bus.

He loved school, even though he knew he was different from the other kids. He learned his difference the very first day of kindergarten, as roll was being called. The teacher struggled to pronounce his name. "Jewan," she said in her best phonetic extrapolation of Juan. But Juan didn't answer, and kept looking around to see who Jewan was. Finally, the kindly teacher walked over to him and said, "Aren't you Jewan?"

"No, Miss Holly, my name is Juan." With a startled look on her face, she said, "Okay, we will call you Johnny from now on."

And so the difference was made clear to him. At home he was Juan, and at school he was Johnny. As his school years passed, his classmates continually reminded him that he was a Mexican. They did this in large and small ways, some intentional, others not.

Even so, he loved school. He loved the math, the reading, the baseball, all of it. He did wonder, from time to time, why all the pictures in his reading books were blond boys and girls. The contrast when he looked at his caramel-colored face in the mirror was striking, but that didn't stop him from excelling in school.

Perhaps one of the most shocking reminders of his difference was when he was in high school; he asked Jamie

Struthers to the prom. Jamie asked her parents if it was okay and was told, in very direct terms, that she was never to date a Mexican. She was disappointed; Johnny was a handsome boy and she had seen how kind he was. But Jamie was an honest girl and, as painful as it was, she told Johnny the truth about why her answer was no.

Johnny was perplexed, "How am I ever going to get a date," he mumbled to himself, "The only Mexican girl in school is my sister."

Chapter 5

Jimmy labored on and enjoyed his last days of high school. He was glad when it was over. He knew that he was going to college. His parents always impressed upon him that a good education was the key to a better life.

From the time he was old enough to understand, his mom would always tell him, "Get yourself a good education and you won't have to work as hard as we do, son. Remember, an education is something no one can take away from you."

Jimmy's mother helped to give him a great start to an education by reading to him every night before bed. By the time he was five years old and ready for kindergarten, he had heard *The Adventures of Tom Sawyer* and several other classic children's stories.

Now, as Jimmy prepared to leave for college, his dad assured him that they would help with finances as much as possible. Jimmy knew he would have to work to help with expenses, but it was possible to finance a college education with a minimum wage, part time job in the 1960s.

As Jimmy left for San Francisco State College, he thought about his prior education and knew that he had coasted a lot of the time. To his surprise he passed the college entrance exams and had been admitted. He vowed to work harder in college and do better.

One piece of learning was firmly set in his mind, and

the whole community had helped to teach him this. Every brown person was a Mexican, and Mexicans were lazy, dirty, ignorant, and thieves. He did have a bit of trouble reconciling this lesson with what he saw. Señor De Leon was a quiet, gentle, neat, kind man who had served his country in WW II. The braceros worked sunup to sundown and were never in trouble. Johnny Martinez was always neat and a top student. Jimmy finally decided that there were a few good Mexicans, but most were like the community said.

****

Jimmy was the first person from his extended family to go to college. He was the hope of his family for a better life. The burden was on him now to carry out his parent's dream of a better future for their children. His extended family from California to Oklahoma and Tennessee were watching, helping as they could, and hoping for Jimmy's success.

Move-in day at the dorm was a great and joyous day for Jimmy, albeit a little sad for his parents. They would miss their oldest child. His mom and dad had agreed to pay for the first and second semester, and after that Jimmy was expected to get a part-time job to help with expenses.

Jimmy was without a car in San Francisco, but no matter. All he needed was located on campus or in the Stonestown Shopping Center, a short walk away. Venturing further into the city was made easier by the excellent system of streetcars, buses, and cable cars. In fact, his first trip off campus was on the 19th Avenue streetcar which eventually arrived at the Powell St. cable car turn-round. Then he took the cable car over the hill to Fisherman's Wharf. There he found this wondrous store called Cost Plus, which had exotic items from all over the world. He bought a little carved teak elephant for his mom for Christmas and a reed mat for his beach day sunning.

Life in the dorm went well for Jimmy. His roommate and he shared a 10' x 12' room with two beds, two desks with lamps, and two closets. There was just enough room to pass between the beds to a window overlooking the parking lot.

Jimmy couldn't study too well in the dorm. It was male-only in those days and consequently, always had a lot of activity and noise. Jimmy usually took an evening walk up the hill to the library where he pored over his textbooks.

Jimmy wasn't an outstanding student, but to be fair, it was because he had never put much effort into studying. It was a surprise to everyone, himself included, when he was able to pass all entrance exams required for college, including the writing exam. So, he enrolled in English 101, instead of the bonehead English class taken by many of his high school classmates who had much better grades.

But now, laziness and disregard of studying was not an option. He had the whole weight of his extended family's expectation riding on his shoulders; he was determined to be successful in college. Therefore, he threw himself into his studies. What caught his attention most was the study of history. He chose it as his major in preparation for a teaching career.

Previous to college, Jimmy had never heard anyone utter a word against the United States, its political policies, or historical actions. But now, he heard those things almost daily. In his class on the Westward Movement, the professor lectured at great length about genocide carried out by the United States Army against indigenous people. Jimmy was told, in the lectures about the Civil War, that Abraham Lincoln wasn't really very interested in freeing the slaves; he just knew it had to be done to preserve the United States. He was taught that Thomas Jefferson wasn't really such a great man because he owned slaves.

All this talk about abuse of one group by another caused Jimmy to think about his sociology class lecture on ethnocentrism. The professor explained that every ethnic group on the face of the earth perpetuates the idea that it is the greatest and best of all ethnicities in the world. "It's only when ethnic groups are in close proximity and one group gains power that problems begin," the professor explained. He continued by saying, "Power is gained by one or more of these four factors: greater population, better technology, more wealth or more knowledge."

The professor cited several examples of ethnocentrism gone amuck. The enslavement of Africans by Anglo Saxons and the enslavement of indigenous people by the Spanish, were two examples given. The current process of discriminating against Black people, by pushing them into inferior positions and the murders of Assyrians by the Turks were two other painful examples. He finished with the murder of six million Jews by the Nazis as the greatest example of ethnocentrism in the history of the world.

The Professor ended the class with a story. "An astronaut was sent up and circled the earth several times in his space capsule. When he returned to earth, he had a dazed look. 'What did you experience?' his officers asked. 'I have seen the face of God,' he answered, 'She is Black.' Give some thought to how you feel about this story. We'll talk about it next time." He finished and dismissed class.

It wasn't long after this lecture that Jimmy was in a math class where the topic of the historical development of math was being discussed. The professor very eloquently described the struggle through the ages to develop systems to quantify and describe the world around us through math. He spent a great deal of time talking about the different number bases, and how the system used in the U.S. was base 10.

But what really caught Jimmy's attention was when the professor described the ancient Maya of Mexico and their math. They were the first people in the world to conceive of the null set, or as he put it in plain English, the concept of *zero*. He continued with a description of Maya astronomy and their method of mathematical calculations using base 20. Their calculations resulted in the production of a calendar more accurate than our Gregorian calendar. The Maya calendar was so accurate it did not require a leap year.

Jimmy went away from this class shaking his head. Mexicans are smart? Jimmy questioned. Finally he was able to reconcile that even though the Maya were very brilliant, their society had collapsed. He had always been told that the Mexicans of the present were lazy, stupid, and dirty. Now he learned that the indigenous people of Mexico were brilliant. He thought long and hard about ethnocentrism. The Maya were brilliant, and now the United States and its founders were bad, according to what he was hearing at college.

Chapter 6

Renaldo did not like being away from his family for so long, but it was necessary in order to get the money to make a better life for them in the future. In his bunk at night, he stared at the dark and dreamed of the time he would buy a little farm in Mexico, and his family would prosper and be happy there. For their sake, he was willing to endure the poor living conditions and isolation in El Norte (the North).

A typical work day for Renaldo would be 8 to 12 hours in the blistering sun with temperatures sometimes cresting the century mark. Now, in the spring, he was using the short hoe to cull out the weeds near the tomato plants. His back ached from bending over all day, and he felt like he was in an oven. But he worked on, always telling himself, "This will end when I have enough to buy the farm and move back home." The fall would come, then the grape cutting time would arrive with the cooler weather. The only major discomfort then would be cuts on the hands from the curved grape-cutting knife. It was difficult to cut each bunch of grapes from the vine quickly without cuts to the hands. An occasional wasp nest added to the potential pain of grape cutting. The insects, with their painful stings, sometimes made nests in the vineyard. If a grape worker was not wary and disturbed the nest, those vicious wasps would come boiling out and attack.

In the evening, Renaldo returned to a barracks with fifty bunk beds, top and bottom, filled with braceros. One light bulb, hanging from a wire, gave just enough light to find the way to the toilet in the dark. The facility was originally built to house Okies, during the Great Depression of the 1930s. It was one of the few places in California where a facility had been provided for the Okies. Most of the Okies had camped out, as shown in the "Migrant Mother" photo taken by Dorothea Lange in 1936.

After a long work week, Renaldo and his coworkers were able to relax on Sunday. "*Oye Beto* (Hey Beto), ***let's take a walk to the cantina*,*"* Renaldo would say to his friend every Sunday. Then he and Beto would set off for the two-mile walk to the cantina on the edge of Perryville.

The cantina was a little bar and grill run by a second-generation American of Mexican descent. Pablo had seen a market niche when the braceros arrived and quickly took advantage of it. He established his "cantina" specifically to serve the braceros. He supplied the otherwise unavailable menudo, tacos, and pozole, food that the braceros loved. He had plenty of cold beer, sometimes Tecate, for them to wash it down. It was an oasis, with hints of home, to the tired and often lonely workers.

Chapter 7

"Yeah Pop, I'm going to graduate from high school next month and I want to go to college," said Johnny.

Pop replied, "Yes *mi hijo* (my son), I know. You do good in school, but we can't afford for you to go to school anymore. We need you here to help with the farm. It costs money to go to college, money we don't have."

"No Pop, I checked into it. It will only cost $100 a year to go to Junior College in Stockton. I can get a part time job and live at home to help with the farm. What do you say, Pop? Can I do it?"

"Let me think about it," Pop said.

"Thanks Pop!" Johnny said excitedly.

That very evening, Johnny's parents had a long conversation about Johnny and his school.

"*Mi amor* (my love), you know he is smart and he does well in school. Why not let him try this college?" said Mom.

Pop explained, "Yes, but I don't want him to get his heart broken when he gets out of there, and they still won't give him a good job because he's Mexican. It's better that he stays on the farm."

"Oh *mi amor*, he is a strong boy and smart. He will find his way. Times are changing. You see on the news that they changed the law. They can't refuse him just because he is Mexican!" Mom pleaded.

****

Mom packed Johnny a lunch of a burrito and a peach from their orchard, and off he went for his first day of college. He was the first person in his extended family to attend college. Pop and Mom had their misgivings, but they were proud of their son.

The compromise they reached was a good one for all. Johnny would take a reduced number of classes and still be able to work the farm. It would take him longer to graduate, but he knew he could do it. He loved school and knew he would be successful.

Chapter 8

Hilario was on fire with ambition and he rightly saw that his time was now. The 1964 Civil Rights Act had opened the door to opportunities for him. He was smart and aggressive, and he was pissed off. He chafed at the years of being called a beaner, a greaser and worse. Now was the time he would right a thousand past wrongs.

Hilario was ready, willing, and able. He had assumed a leadership role in the Chicano movement, and was actively pursuing more opportunities for himself and others like him. His 6-foot, lean muscular frame accorded him immediate attention. His mahogany skin and dark mustache immediately identified him as a Mexican. His agile mind and dedication assured him a leadership position. He marched every time there was a march. He rallied anywhere and everywhere there was a rally.

He was the voice of dissent in every college class he attended, no matter what the subject. Hilario was even able to disrupt his class on the History of Art, by loudly questioning why famous Mexican muralist, Diego Rivera, was not included as a study topic. He loudly claimed racism and discrimination as the cause of the omission.

Every outburst gained new followers. He was a leader, and he knew how to touch the nerve which set his fellow Mexican-American students atwitter. Hilario was constantly preaching and explaining the politics of racial discrimination. He was the de facto Chicano recruiter, and he was good at it.

Hilario was a good soldier and then a good officer in the army that formed *El Movimiento* (The Movement). He had attended the Denver Conference where *Plan Espiritual de Aztlán* (Spiritual Plan of Aztlán) was born. His innate leadership ability and intellect, coupled with his persistence, prepared him to be the community force he would become.

Chapter 9

"I'll be back in time to help with picking the peaches," Johnny called out. He gunned the old '54 Chevy pickup and headed for his new adventure.

History 104 would fulfill a general education requirement for the Associate of Arts degree that Johnny had in his sights. He thought it sounded interesting; *A History of the Southwest United States from Coronado to 1950.* was the course title.

Professor Hendrickson was describing the reasons for the Alamo and the eventual wresting away of Texas from Mexico. As he droned on, a student from the back of the room raised his hand.

"Yes, Mr. Jiminez?" asked the Professor.

"Aren't you going to talk about the Treaty of Guadalupe Hidalgo?" questioned Hilario.

"Yes, Mr. Jiminez. I am but not this class period," replied Professor Hendrickson.

"And are you going to talk about how the United States has never held up its end of the deal?" Hilario inquired.

"Well, that is a matter of opinion Mr. Jiminez. But yes, we will discuss the treaty next week."

Johnny was amazed and shocked on a couple of levels, by this interchange. First, he was amazed that there was another Mexican-American in the class. Then, the fact that

Hilario was willing to speak up and challenge the Professor shocked him; this was a new experience for Johnny.

After class Johnny caught up with Hilario as he walked to the cafeteria.

"Hey, what were you talking about in there about this treaty?" asked Johnny.

"Got a minute? Come on in the cafeteria, get a cup of coffee, and I'll tell you," answered Hilario.

Over cups of strong, black, bitter cafeteria coffee, Hilario held forth on his view of the treaty and what it said. "When Mexico gave all of the Southwest to the U.S. to end the war between them, the treaty said Mexicans could stay and keep their land. They could even be citizens of the U.S. if they wanted. If not, they could remain Mexican citizens but live legally in the U.S. Also, Spanish was supposed to remain the language of the Southwest.

"But look what happened. Whites came in, took the land, said we were foreigners and had to speak English. Now they call us beaners, greasers, cholos and make fun of us. They take the good jobs and leave us the grunt work.

"We settled the Southwest and they came and took it. Now they treat us like shit. Look at you, Johnny. Is that your name? No, it's Juan, isn't it? They want you to be like them but not quite as good. Just a nice quiet little Mexican boy who puts up with all their shit. You don't even speak Spanish, do you Johnny?" Hilario hissed.

"No, my pop told me a long time ago that to get ahead, we have to speak English," answered Johnny.

Hilario emphasized, "Yeah, well, the whites keep trying to stamp us out, but some of us aren't going to put up with it anymore. If you're ready to stop being a second-class citizen, come with me next Saturday. We'll go to a meeting where you will learn a lot about *El Movimiento*."

"Okay, what time?" Johnny inquired.

"2 p.m. Meet me here and I'll take you," said Hilario.

"See you then, Hilario!" Johnny exclaimed with excitement.

Chapter 10

Jimmy woke to the *"oohhs and aahhs"* of the foghorn off the coast. He listened to the bells of the floating buoys as they began to sing out their warning to the ships to keep clear of the rocks and shallows, which would surely destroy them. Three years into college, he was really on his own now. Living in the small studio apartment on 48th Avenue, he was supported by his furniture delivery job.

The furniture store manager, in the Stonestown Shopping Center, was only too happy to hire a strong young college student. Jimmy spent twenty hours a week helping to load and deliver merchandise. He was glad for the job. It gave him enough income to pay school expenses, his rent, and other living expenses. It also allowed him to move out of the dorm and finally have some privacy. Although he adapted, he did not enjoy the communal life of the dorm, and now he was free of it. He was truly on his own in San Francisco. What could be better?

The lack of a car was not a problem at all, now that he knew his way around the city. His job in Stonestown was a short walk from the college. He caught the bus at 46th and Judah for a quick 15-minute ride from his apartment to the college. On the weekends, he took it to make connections all the way to Fisherman's Wharf, on the opposite side of town. Also on the weekends, Jimmy liked to take the short walk through the tunnel under the Great Highway, which opened to a beautiful vista of the Pacific Ocean. On a clear day, he could see the thirty miles from the beach to the

Farallon Islands, site of the 1863 Egg War. The short war was a quirky slice of California history. It amazed Jimmy that groups could fight so viciously over seabird eggs.

Often on his beach walks, Jimmy would be joined by his, across-the-hall neighbor, Daniel Watson. Daniel was also a student, but he attended the private Catholic school, The University of San Francisco (USF). Even though USF was much more expensive than San Francisco State, Daniel did not come from money. He had served in the United States Marines and was supported, in part, by the G.I. bill. The rest of his costs were met by scholarships and his 15-hour a week job at the University Library.

Daniel's 6'3" frame gave him a stride that made it difficult for Jimmy to keep up. Often, as they did what Daniel called the "pep step," Jimmy would find he was looking at Daniel's blond hair in the distance. He had to trot to keep up. With his size, blond hair and piercing blue eyes, Daniel reminded Jimmy of how he visualized an ancient Viking.

As they walked, they talked about many things. There was some talk of school and girls and parties. But for these two serious fellows, the conversation often moved to the changes taking place in society.

"There was another protest and sit-in at State last week," Jimmy commented.

"Oh, what was it this time?" asked Daniel in a disgusted voice.

"Black students and supporters were protesting the poor coverage in the school paper of their last meeting," answered Jimmy.

"Pretty damn ridiculous," said Daniel.

"Oh, I don't know," replied Jimmy. "There does seem to be a big deal made out of every little gathering of any group — lots of coverage, even photos. But the Blacks seem to always end up with little or no coverage."

"If they would stop wasting time sitting on their butts protesting and get to work studying, maybe they would get somewhere. I'm amazed at the number of whites that join their protests," Daniel spouted with force and feeling.

"Oh, I don't know," said Jimmy. "The Blacks seem to always get the short end of the stick no matter what they do."

Daniel was only three years older than Jimmy, but he had seen a lot more of the world and was very bright. Jimmy tended to listen to Daniel's opinions. But very often he did not agree and felt compelled to say so. They walked and talked in this way often and sometimes disturbed each other with their divergent views.

Chapter 11

Renaldo was again plowing the fields trying to eke out a living for his family. It was hard — so much work and so little return. His days as a bracero were just a distant memory now. The work in the U.S. was hard; he was not well treated and he missed his family, but the pay was more in a day than he could earn in a week at home.

Some of Renaldo's neighbors who had been braceros before, had defied the law and gone back into the United States. They did this even though the bracero program had ended in 1964. They told him it was difficult getting in but once they were there, the work and pay were good.

Guillermo, his neighbor, had come to visit just yesterday. *"We are going next week back to Texas,"* Guillermo said. *"We go to the border, then at night swim the Rio Bravo. Then we are in Texas. We go to work in Edinburg the next day. A big farm there, they always have work. Now they are planting. We plant, irrigate and harvest, then come home. The farmers want us there. They can't get enough gringos to do the work. Most of them are too lazy."*

"What happens if the Migra (U.S. Border Patrol) catches you?" Renaldo asked.

"They take us back across the river, then let us go," Guillermo explained. *"We wait a couple days, then take the bus to Rio Bravo, swim the river again. It's a game to the Migra. Everyone knows they have to have us to do the*

work, or they will have no crops. But they have to pretend to try to keep us out."

"They don't put you in jail?" Renaldo asked with surprise in his voice.

"Well maybe overnight to wait for the bus. But the jail is good — good food and good bed. We just rest, it's like a hotel. Come with us," Guillermo urged. *"You work six months, come home, have money to live all year."*

That night at dinner, Renaldo was restless.

"What bothers you, my love?" his wife, Conchita asked.

"I talked to Guillermo today. He says we can sneak back into the U.S. and they will give us work. Just like before when I was a bracero."

"Yes, but not like before, because the Migra will be chasing you," Conchita said.

"Yes, but Guillermo got caught and they just took him back across the river and let him go. Two days later, he was back working in Edinburg."

Conchita asked the same question that Renaldo had asked Guillermo the day before, *"You mean they don't put you in jail?"*

"No, the farmers want us and the Migra don't want to fill up the jails with us. They bring us back to Mexico, and we go back to the farmers. I want to go, Conchita. I know it will be hard like it was before, to be away. I will miss you and Jesús and baby Andrea. But here, I barely make a living by working hard all year. There, I can work

six months, and we can live better all year. I need to go my love."

****

It was decided. Renaldo went with Guillermo to the city of Rio Bravo. They swam the swirling waters of the Rio Grande, with strong quick strokes, on a moonless night. Years of field work had equipped them with muscles and stamina that made the swim a pleasure, not a chore. As they sat on the Texas bank and dripped dry in the muggy night air, Renaldo stared up at the stars, and missed Conchita.

Guillermo was true to his word; they were at work planting Brussels sprouts the next day. They stayed in a small house the farm provided. It was a much better place to stay than the barracks were when Renaldo was in the bracero program.

Renaldo stayed out of sight of the townspeople, except for his trips to Western Union. Once every two weeks, he would walk into the little town of Edinburg and wire money to Conchita. She used some for living expenses, but most of it she saved in the little metal box under the floorboards of their house.

****

One day, after a long six months, the bus pulled into his little town and deposited Renaldo. Renaldo missed his family terribly. He didn't think he could go away again and leave them. Baby Andrea was already walking and Jesús was big enough to play fútbol.

Renaldo had a solution, but it would be a difficult and maybe, dangerous one. He had met a man in the town of

Rio Bravo who offered, for a fee, to take Renaldo and his whole family across the river. A friend on the Texas side would take them in his pickup to the farm where Renaldo worked. The farmer was very pleased with Renaldo's work, and said he would make him a crew chief. He would even give him a little house for his family while he worked, if he would come back the next year.

Renaldo was soon back into the rhythm of his home life and was loving it. But he knew he had to go back to Texas. The only doubt in his mind was whether he could take his family. That night, he had a discussion with Conchita.

"I want you and the children to go with me when I go back to Texas next year," Renaldo said adamantly.

"But what would we do with our house here? Won't it be dangerous, and what if they put us in jail?" Conchita asked nervously.

"It will be fine. Your uncle will take care of the house here. We'll come back in December for Christmas and stay until March. They won't put us in jail. The worst that will happen is that they take us to McAllen and back across the river," Renaldo said convincingly.

"Oh my love, I am worried," Conchita replied. *"I've never been away from home before."*

"It will be fun. You'll see," Renaldo replied, although he was worried too. *"We will take a bus to Rio Bravo. Then a man there will take us, in his boat, to Texas. His friend will give us a ride to the farm, and we will have a house right on the farm. Then I can work and not miss my family."*

"*Alright my love, you know what is best. We will go as you say,*" Conchita conceded.

Renaldo was not as sure about his plan as he appeared. He didn't want Conchita to worry, so he maintained his confident appearance. He knew he couldn't be away from his family anymore. It was the best of some difficult choices. Only time would tell if it a good choice.

Chapter 12

Johnny loved college. He had always been a good student; he loved school from day one in kindergarten. His parents had preached to him to do well in school as far back as he could remember. Now he was a college student, the first person in his extended family to be one.

Johnny loved college even more than the other schools because he got to choose what he studied. Not everything was open to choice. There were certain state requirements, but there was a large area of study left from which he could select courses.

Johnny was unaware of the structure of a college curriculum until he was trying to enroll. His college counselor advised him that for the first semester, he should choose something familiar for his electives.

"Perhaps you should consider Chicano Studies," the counselor said.

"What's that?" Johnny asked. "I've always thought Chicano was a bad word."

"Not anymore. Chicano Studies is the study of the history of contributions that Mexican-Americans have made to the United States," explained the counselor.

"Okay, that sounds good," Johnny replied.

****

Saturday came; Johnny and Hilario met in the parking lot of the college at 2 p.m.

"Ok, are you ready for this, Juan?" Hilario said excitedly.

"Yes, let's do it," Johnny replied.

Hilario started off driving down Pacific Avenue and was soon in South Stockton.

"Where are we going?" Johnny asked.

"The *Pachanga* [party] is in the Barrio. You'll see," Hilario answered.

They parked in a large dirt parking area, next to a baseball field with a slightly dilapidated backstop, covered in graffiti.

"Okay, here we are," Hilario said with some excitement.

Johnny found himself staring at a crew of brown faces setting up a portable stage in left field. In fact, there were brown faces everywhere. Many of them were wearing Mexican-made sarapes and sombreros. Most were speaking Spanish, or at least the California dialect of Spanish.

Johnny was overwhelmed. He hadn't seen this many brown faces since the family reunion in Los Angeles when he was five. There was a carnival atmosphere in the air. People had spread out blankets and were drinking beer and soda and eating. Kids were running in every direction, chasing each other and playing.

Soon the stage was up and the call went out to come and see. A man with a bandana tied around his head stepped onto the stage. Oddly enough, he spoke to them in English. "This skit we are about to do is called 'What's in your bag?'" He immediately took off his bandana and put on a man's dress hat. Speaking in perfect East Coast English, he imitated a businessman making a real estate deal. Next, an actor took the stage in Chinese garb, and in broken English, talked about making shark fin soup. And so it went, through all ethnic and racial groups in California.

Finally, the initial actor took the stage in a sarape and began to speak rapidly in Spanish, which Johnny did not understand, and to imitate a zoot suit kind of walk. He ended by saying loudly in Spanish and then in English, "We don't have any of that stuff in our bag. We have a brown bag. We are Chicanos, and we need to act like it. Don't let them turn you into a gringo or anything else. We are Chicanos from Aztlán, *La nueva raza [the new race].* We are brown and beautiful."

Cheers rang out from left field to home plate. Johnny was on his feet cheering wildly. He had never been with such a group, all like him and proud of it. He felt pride well up in him, and he stood tall, cheering until his throat was sore.

After a little visiting, a little dancing of the cumbia, which Johnny just watched, they left. Hilario spoke first, "Well, what did you think?"

"It was great! Terrific," Johnny said enthusiastically. "I've never seen anything like this. But why did he call us Chicanos? I always thought that was an insult."

"It was. People call us all kinds of names — greaser, beaner and Chicano. We are proud of our heritage. We embrace it; we are born here but descended from the magnificent cultures of Mexico, the Maya, Olmec, and the Aztec."

"Oh yeah, I see that. It's good to be with our people," Johnny said.

"Right brother!" Hilario shouted.

"What about Aztlán? What does that mean? He said we were from Aztlán," Johnny asked.

"That is the mythical home where the Aztecs originated. Since we are their descendants, we come from there too. We are rejecting everything of the white world. They have shut us out, made fun of us, discriminated against us, rejected us, and now we reject them. There are more of us now. We have greater strength, and we use it to reject the whites and go our own way. We no longer try to be like the cavacho," Hilario finished with great excitement.

"What does cavacho mean?" Johnny asked.

"It means the same as gringo but with more power, more hate," Hilario answered.

Johnny was taken aback by the edge in Hilario's voice when he talked about gringos. There was something in it that went beyond dislike. The word Hilario had used, *hate*, probably described it best.

Johnny was not happy with the way he and his family had been disregarded, but his pop had always counseled against hating. "Hate only leads to destruction," Pop had told him. "It destroys you from the inside, and then it causes you to hurt other people. I won't hear of it in this house."

"So, what did you think of that Veronica chick, huh?" Hilario asked while chuckling. "She was giving you the eye."

"I don't know. When I tried to talk to her she started

answering me in Spanish, so I just walked away," Johnny answered.

"Well, she is definitely a Chicana. You get your shit together. Start coming to the rallies, and she'll come around. Oh yeah, learn to do the cumbia. You got to dance vato, the chicas like that," Hilario said with a laugh.

"Ok, thanks for the ride and the rally. I'll see you in class on Monday," Johnny replied.

****

Monday was an eventful day, starting with the class discussion of the treaty of Guadalupe Hidalgo. After Professor Hendrickson's lecture on the treaty, Hilario raised his hand and started to talk.

"Isn't it true that the treaty allowed Mexican citizens living on the land taken by the U.S., to become U.S. citizens and to continue to have Spanish as their language?"

"Yes, that is true," Professor Hendrickson replied.

"Then why are we treated like foreigners and discriminated against? We're citizens too! The U.S. has never honored that treaty, and it still doesn't. We face discrimination every day," Hilario exclaimed.

Professor Hendrickson stood silently staring at Hilario. "Yes, while it is true that the U.S. has been slow in responding to violations of the treaty, I am not aware that discrimination is sanctioned by the U.S. government. In fact, the Civil Rights Act of 1964 stipulates just the opposite."

"Yeah, well, it's happening. We get the short end of the stick every time," Hilario spit out.

"For next week, read Chapter 26 on the Westward Movement. Class dismissed," Professor Hendrickson finished.

Hilario grabbed Johnny as they walked out. "Let's go have a cup of coffee," he said.

They had cups of bitter, black coffee just like in every college cafeteria in the country. Even though it wasn't good coffee, it held what most students needed – caffeine.

"Did you see that old gringo squirm when I questioned him?" Hilario asked.

"Yeah, he seemed a little uncomfortable," Johnny replied.

"Well, he should be. He knows this country has screwed us and still does," Hilario proclaimed. "Don't forget the rally this Saturday, same time, same place."

"Okay, see you there," Johnny replied.

Johnny walked slowly between two WWII Quonset huts that served as dressing rooms for the athletic teams. California was not into building new college facilities.

As Johnny turned the corner, he almost ran into Veronica. A guy Johnny didn't know was just turning and walking away. Johnny spoke first. "Hi Veronica."

"*Hola Juanito, cómo va?*" Veronica said.

Johnny asked, "What does that mean?"

"Wow, Spanish 101," Veronica said. "'How's it going,' is what it means. That gringo that just walked away knows more Spanish than you do. But he thinks because he knows a couple of sentences, I'll go out with him. I wouldn't date a gringo if he was a United Nations translator. Now you

Juanito, that's a different story. The blood of the Aztecs runs in your veins, and I can teach you what you need to know," Veronica said with a coquettish smile and flip of her long black hair.

Johnny watched her walk away. A very nice rear view, he thought. She was beautiful — her shoulder length black hair, dark eyes, flawless bronze skin, a wide sinuous mouth and a smile made him feel weak in the knees. But even though she had just invited his attentions, he still felt an outsider in her group. It wasn't the discrimination he had felt in high school, the rejection of his person. It was a nagging thought that in her view, he wasn't quite as Chicano as she would like him to be. Wow, he thought, I wasn't white enough before and now I'm not brown enough. I'll die an old maid or whatever they call lonely disappointed old men.

****

It was Friday afternoon, and Jimmy was on his way to the Post Office. Just coming out of the door, he saw a familiar face. "Hello Johnny. How are you?" Jimmy asked.

"Hey Jim. I'm doing fine," Johnny replied.

Jimmy asked, "What have you been doing?"

"I've been going to the Junior College and working at my folk's place," Johnny answered.

"What's your major?" inquired Jimmy.

"Chicano Studies," replied Johnny.

"What's that? I thought Chicano was a bad word," commented Jimmy.

"Yeah, it was. We call ourselves Chicanos because we

want to let people know we're together as a people, and their hateful words don't bother us," Johnny explained.

"What do you study in Chicano Studies?" Jimmy asked.

"It's all about learning the past and the future for people like me, who are born here but are from Mexican descent. You know, we have not been accepted, and now we don't want to be part of the melting pot. We are going to be ourselves and stick together," explained Johnny.

"Sounds interesting, it was great to see you Johnny. Best of luck," Jimmy said.

"Yeah, thanks Jim. By the way, my name is Juan," he said in a curt tone.

Looking a bit startled, Jimmy said hesitantly, "Okay Juan. See you later."

After Jimmy mailed his letter, he was a bit unsettled by his encounter with Johnny, or Juan. There seemed to be a sharp edge to his voice as he described Chicano Studies. His voice was harsh, especially when he announced that his name was Juan. Jimmy wondered what Juan would study in Chicano Studies that could possibly help him in getting a job. On second thought, Jimmy knew Juan would do okay; Juan was always a smart guy and got good grades, so he'll figure it out.

****

Saturday, Juan pulled into the dirt parking lot. Another rally was already in progress. A young Chicano that he didn't know, was on the stage at the microphone. "The gringos have disregarded us. They have oppressed us, and they have abused us in every way. And now it's our turn.

There are many more of us now, and it's time for them to pay for what they have done. We must show them their reign of terror is over." The crowd cheered! The man spoke in slightly accented English but with an edge that caused every word to cut like a knife. He was an attorney from San Francisco, Juan was told. He would defend any Chicano involved in acts of government defiance.

The young attorney continued. "They call us beaners, greasers, and take away our rights. They deny us jobs and dignity and put us in the lowest part of society. They deny us the right to speak Spanish in a land that was ours before they stole it. Starting tonight, we will even the score. We meet at 7 p.m. and we march through downtown."

Juan wasn't too sure he wanted to be part of a march, but the attorney's words had inspired him. With Hilario's urging, there he was, ready to march. The protest march started at the intersection of the two busiest business streets in Stockton. It was a gathering of young people, much like a football homecoming rally, except with an edge. A sea of young brown faces chanted in response to their leader. ***"What do we want?"***

The crowd answered, ***"Justice!"***

"When do we want it?"

"Now!" they shouted.

Down the middle of the street, they marched two-hundred strong, stopping traffic and continuing their joyous choral chant. Soon the police began to arrive in riot gear. They stood respectfully by on the sidewalk as the marchers passed. Juan was smack in the middle of the crowd and feeling good about being with a group of like-minded people. It wasn't right, what had been done to them. Justice demanded that they be given the same opportunity and respect as any other citizen.

All at once, Juan's thoughts were interrupted as he saw a guy in front of him launch a brick, just like throwing a football pass. Only the receiver was the windshield of a police cruisier. The windshield shattered and chaos broke out. Juan saw rocks now flying through the air like a flock of Starlings. He was surrounded by the sound of plate glass windows breaking.

The police then waded into the crowd with batons swinging and marchers scattering. Some ran away, but to Juan's amazement, he saw several marchers coming out through the broken window of a clothing store, arms loaded with clothing.

Juan saw Hilario try to stop them and make them put the clothes back but, they shoved him aside and kept going. A white man in a shirt and tie reached for Hilario, then took a swing at him but Hilario was too quick. Stepping aside, Hilario punched the man in the face and then kicked him in the groin and ran away.

Getting over his shock, Juan followed Hilario's lead and ran. He took off like a hundred-yard sprinter, ducked down an alley and came out two streets away. From there, he carefully made his way over to his pickup and drove home.

****

"Let's get a cup of coffee," Hilario said in a demanding tone after their Monday class. "It's your turn to buy."

"Alright, I'll get it," Juan replied.

Over cups of coffee, they dissected Saturday's march.

"I didn't expect the looting and fighting," Juan said.

"I didn't either," Hilario agreed. "But you know what the gringos say: 'you have to break some eggs if you want to make an omelet.'"

"Yeah, but I saw you fighting. I think you broke that store owner's eggs," Juan said with disgust.

"He started it. He took a swing at me," Hilario said defiantly.

"Yeah, but he was just trying to protect his store," Juan said.

"Well, so was I. I was just telling those thieves to put the stuff back," Hilario said defensively.

"I know, I saw, but he didn't know that," Juan explained.

"I'm going to teach you a little Spanish right now. **'Sin Lucha no hay triunfo.'** Do you know what that means, Juanito?" Hilario asked.

"You know I don't," Juan said with exasperation.

"It means 'without struggle there is no triumph.'"

"Yeah well, robbing somebody's store is not what I would call a triumph," Juan said adamantly.

"You really don't get it, do you Juanito? We have to make a bold statement. We must let the gringos know we're not going to take it anymore," Hilario exclaimed.

"I'm not a thief," Juan replied.

"Oh yeah, I know. Robbing that store wasn't part of the plan. Those guys weren't part of our group. I've never seen them before. I think they just saw a chance to steal," Hilario said with contrition.

Juan walked away feeling a little better about the event but still with some misgivings. Whether the thieves were part of their group or not, the thefts still reflected badly on the march. The thefts probably just reinforced the stereotype that Mexicans *will steal.*

****

The first year of college was ending; Juan was poised to make the Dean's List. He had studied hard and stayed away from any more marches or demonstrations.

After Juan's second absence, Hilario had confronted him. "Missed you at the march last weekend."

"Yeah, I had a term paper due, had to get it done," Juan replied.

"You got to make this a priority, vato. We are gonna change this country," Hilario boasted.

"Maybe so," Juan retorted, "but I've got a lot at stake here. I plan to transfer to a four-year college, and I need a scholarship to do it. I don't have the money. To get that scholarship, I need good grades. And if I get arrested, like some of you did last week, I'm sunk."

"Now you're beginning to talk like a gringo, like you don't care about La Causa," Hilario said bitterly.

"No, I do care. I plan to finish college and be a teacher. That way I can help the cause, by being an example of a successful Chicano," Juan said proudly. "By the way, why did you start saying gringo instead of cavacho?"

"Because no one understands the word cavacho around here. It doesn't matter what I call them; I still hate them," Hilario answered.

"Well, I don't hate them," Juan shot back.

"Johnny, you're beginning to make me think you're a coconut," Hilario spat.

"What does that mean?" Juan demanded.

"Think about it! Brown on the outside and white on the inside. A coconut!" Hilario replied loudly.

"Well, you can think what you like! I'm going to get a good education and have a career," Juan said defiantly.

****

Juan was true to his word. When first-semester grades came out, he made the Dean's List with a 3.8 grade point average. For the next three semesters, he was on the Dean's List, GPA ranging from 3.8 to 4.0. His hard work was rewarded with a scholarship that would cover books, tuition, and about half of his living expenses for his final two years of college. He knew that he could make up the rest with part-time work. Because of his family's low income, he was eligible for a job on campus.

Juan was in the Junior College bookstore selling his used textbooks back, when he ran into Veronica. "Hi Veronica."

"Hola," Veronica replied. "I hear you're leaving town."

"Yeah, I'm starting San Francisco State in the fall," Juan said. "How about you?"

"I've got another year here, then I don't know," Veronica replied.

"How about you and I have dinner sometime before I go?" Juan inquired.

"I gotta be straight with you, Juan. I don't date coconuts," Veronica said dismissively.

"Oh, okay. See you around," he said as he turned and walked away.

Part II

Late 1960s – Late 1970s

"The human species always divides itself into us and them."

— Tony Hillerman, Mystery writer, World War II combat veteran,
proud son of Oklahoma, and recipient of
the Navajo Tribe's Special Friend Award.

Chapter 13

Jimmy had just graduated with a B.A. in History. He intended to be a teacher at some point, but just then he wanted to see the world.

His graduation party was a gala affair; every relative he had in California came. It was held at a restaurant at Fisherman's Wharf. It was a proud day for mom and dad and a host of transplanted Okies. One of their own had graduated from college. There would be many more college graduates in the family, but Jimmy was the first.

Jimmy's date to join Uncle Sam was cancelled because he failed the hearing test; a draft classification of 1-Y meant he could only be drafted in the event of a declared war. He was a little saddened not to do military service. He had planned to see the world while he served his country. Most likely the only part of the world he would have seen was Vietnam. He was still in the mindset of youth that told him others might be killed but not him.

Still his desire to spread his wings and see the big world was strong. Jimmy did a little research and hatched a plan. He would work and save some money and go to Europe. The Stonestown store put him on full time, and his money hording would have put Silas Marner to shame. Even at the very low wage of $2.50 an hour, within seven months, he had saved enough that he estimated he could travel Europe for a year. There was the no-frills, Universe Airlines, which flew out of San Francisco International for $175 to Copenhagen round trip; return ticket to be scheduled and used within 365 days of departure. Then there was the wonderfully informative book by Arthur Frommer which explained how you could travel in Europe for $5.00 a day.

****

So it was that one foggy San Francisco August day; Jimmy caught a bus for the airport. He had bid farewell to his family just two days before, said goodbye to work associates and his landlord, and he was on his way. He would miss his little apartment on 48th Avenue. He loved it there with the sound of the fog horns, but he was off to see the world; that was very exciting.

The flight over the top of the world was relatively uneventful. He saw the sun set and rise within the space of 12 hours as they looped over the North Pole. The little Danish grandma with a small mustache who sat in the seat next to Jimmy was sort of interesting. She smoked small black cigars that smelled a lot like a burning bale of hay. But other than that, she was very pleasant.

Jimmy was so excited when he landed in Copenhagen — his first time outside of the United States. Well, he had been to Tijuana once, but you could throw a rock to the U.S. from there. Jimmy planned to splurge and take a cab from the airport to the hotel reserved by the travel agent. After that, it was buses, trains, Arthur Frommer hotels, and youth hostels.

Jimmy arrived at the small Copenhagen hotel, checked into his room, and immediately took a two-hour nap. After that he was off to see the city. He couldn't help thinking of the irony, seeing this city name, Copenhagen, on chewing tobacco cans in the United States. He was somewhat disappointed as 1960s Copenhagen looked a lot like 1960s San Francisco. He had hoped for something more exotic. But he was not disappointed for very long.

Early that evening he followed the Frommer map and found the Tivoli Gardens. A marvelous place — Denmark's answer to Disneyland. There he met Carl and Emil. These two young men were his age and were partying it up after graduating from Carpenter School. They were on their way to a night club and off Jimmy went with them. Their English was impeccable, and they were a hoot. He had a great week with them, and then they had to leave Copenhagen to go to their homes.

"Come and visit me in San Francisco. I'll show you around the city and California," offered Jimmy.

Carl stared at his feet and then replied sadly. "We could never do that. We would have to save for many years to be able to afford such a trip."

That's when it began to sink into Jimmy what a powerful economy the United States had and how strong the dollar was. Carl and Emil knew that the Danish krone wouldn't go very far in the United States.

With fond goodbyes, Emil and Carl went north and Jimmy headed to Amsterdam. He loved it there and loved the prices. $2.75 a night for a room with a hearty cheese, ham, bread, and jam breakfast. After a month long stay in Amsterdam, his next stop was Heidelberg. The evening he arrived the fog was so thick he walked into a light pole while looking for his hotel.

He did finally find his hotel by walking up to within 6 inches of each street number until he found the right place.

For the price of $6.00, he had a meal in the small restaurant and a room for the night. Jimmy had just snuggled down into the feather bed when he heard a loud kick on the door and a shout in German. This was followed by the same voice slurring the words but clearly saying, "Come out American. I will kill you." For at least one German, WW II was not yet over. But, of course, Jimmy did not come out of his room.

The next morning, Jimmy needed toothpaste, so he went off to the pharmacy. The clerk, a young man about his age, inquired, "May I help you?" in flawless English.

"Yes, I need some toothpaste," Jimmy replied.

"We have mint or plain Colgate," the clerk advised.

With that, the clerk and Jimmy began to chat. Jimmy learned that the clerk was going to be a pharmacist but he had to work at the pharmacy while waiting two years for a place in the University. Wow, thought Jimmy. I was half way through college in the amount of time he has to wait.

Proceeding on his way, Jimmy caught the train for Dachau. He had read of the atrocities that had taken place in the Nazi concentration camp, but being there made it all too real. People treating other people as if they were cattle headed for the slaughterhouse was all he could envision. Seeing the "no man's land" strip of ground where prisoners were shot for sport convinced him it was time to move on. Jimmy was shocked and disturbed to the point of depression that such things could have been done.

****

The city of West Berlin was still rebuilding from the

destruction of World War II. The city was already vibrant and bustling. He enjoyed being there very much. Taking in a cabaret show one evening gave him great delight.

Jimmy got a rare chance to take a bus tour of East Berlin and saw quite a difference from the West. Drab apartment buildings with broken windows were everywhere. Several once stately mansions lay in ruins, the result of allied bombings.

The bus made no stops, and no one was allowed on or off. As they passed back through "Check Point Charlie," Jimmy could look straight down the barbed wire topped fence that divided the city. No wonder the communists needed a fence to keep people in that awful place that was East Berlin.

Every time that an escape attempt from East to West Berlin hit the news, Jimmy remembered the devastated East Berlin, enclosed by the ugly, menacing wall. But he thought mostly about the abused downtrodden people who lived behind the wall, yearning to be free. They could see the Promised Land just beyond the wall but were not allowed to go there. Needless to say, Jimmy's eyes were opened to realities he had never given much thought.

****

In Italy, Jimmy saw the magnificent ruins of the Roman civilization. The derogatory word 'Dago,' used where Jimmy grew up, did not seem to apply to the builders of this amazing place. Words more like brilliant and ingenious came to mind.

In Spain, Jimmy was taken into the home of a Spanish family and given a wonderful meal of paella. He had set up a system to have his money wired to various American

Express offices throughout Europe. When he arrived in Barcelona, the money had not arrived. He was sleeping on a park bench and eating very little. The kindness of the family was overwhelming. Even though they spoke very little English and he knew almost no   Spanish, they managed to communicate.

Jimmy traveled to every non-communist country on the European Continent and experienced the various cultures firsthand. He was staying in youth hostels and hotels that cost less than $5 per day and therefore was thrust into the parts of the communities where blue-collar Europeans lived. These were not neighborhoods normally visited by American tourists. He was so impressed with the marvelous European cultures. He was amazed and delighted by the language ability of the Europeans.

An experience at the information booth at the Rome train station stood out in his memory. The young woman in the booth could not place his ethnicity and first addressed him in French, then she went quickly to Italian. When she got no reaction, she finally switched to Spanish. When Jimmy said he was an American, she addressed him in only slightly accented English.

Jimmy didn't quite make the year in Europe; his money ran out about day 345. He could have stayed. He was offered a job in the recreation department on the U. S. military base in Frankfurt, Germany, but he declined.

It was time to go home. Jimmy left Europe with a head full of wonder at all the beauty and grandeur created by the many cultures there. He also left with a very strong feeling of being so lucky to live in the United States, and with more than a little trepidation about what he was going to do for a living when he got home.

Chapter 14

Johnny worked hard on the family farm all summer. There was hoeing weeds around the melons, spraying the peach trees after an attack of boring beetles, and irrigating all the crops; he did them all with his usual good humor. Before he left for school in mid-September, he helped with the tomato and melon harvesting and helped his sister with the fruit and vegetable stand.

Johnny was very hesitant to leave his family. This little farm and vegetable stand were their livelihood. But Mom and Pop both assured him they would be fine. All that was left was the harvest of the late peaches, and they would be able to handle it. Johnny insisted until they agreed that he would come home the last two weekends of September to help with the peaches and the roadside fruit stand.

After a summer of scorching hot ten and twelve-hour days, Johnny was ready for a change when move-in day at the dorm arrived. Mom and Sister gave him tearful goodbyes and he and Pop pulled away in the family pickup. Johnny's pickup had been sold to offset his first semester share of dorm charges. His scholarship was a good one but only covered about half of his living expenses. He knew he would not need a vehicle in the city. One of the many great things about San Francisco was its wonderful system of public transportation. Also, there was a Greyhound Bus for transportation back to Perryville.

Johnny had a job waiting for him as an on-campus parking lot attendant. This income was needed to offset his share of the second semester dorm charges. It was his hope that he could locate less expensive housing for semesters thereafter.

As Johnny and Pop crossed the Bay Bridge, his excitement grew. He could look to his right and see the city skyline. The cylindrical shape of Coit Tower stood out like a beacon to a new world. The salty smell of San Francisco Bay rose as the fog hovered in the air. The 99-degree temperature of the San Joaquin Valley now plunged to 63-degrees as they entered the city and started west on Fell Street.

Johnny thought with amusement of the Mark Twain quote, "The coldest winter I ever spent was a summer in San Francisco." How true, Johnny thought. After my summer, I'm ready for some cool weather.

As they pulled into the parking lot in front of the men's dorm, Pop remarked, "This looks like a concrete cracker box." Johnny agreed as they parked and entered the building where he got his room assignment from a student desk clerk – Room 302.

"Let's go up and take a look," Pop said.

"Up the elevator, third floor, turn left, two doors down, west side of the building," the desk clerk instructed.

The door stood open to reveal a small room with a mirror image on each side. A bed, a desk, and a small closet were on each side of the room with a three-foot walk way between them. Johnny walked to the window and looked out on the top of a parking garage and to the left, a grassy football practice field.

"Well, looks like it's got everything you need, mi hijo," Pop said.

"Yeah, a place to sleep and a place to study. That's about all I need," Johnny agreed.

"You go ahead and pick a side and get settled. I'm going to go," Pop said.

"I'll go down with you," Johnny said a little sadly.

They walked slowly to the pickup, both reluctant to say goodbye. Johnny saw what he thought might have been a small tear in the corner of his dad's eye as he started the truck and waved goodbye.

Johnny was in that odd state of youth, excited but sad, missing family already but happy for his new adventure. He hurried back to Room 302 and picked the bed on the right side and began to put his clothes in the tiny closet.

As Johnny hung up his last shirt, he heard a key turn in the door, and in walked his roommate with flaming red hair; his hair was flowing down to his shoulders. He was a small man, about 5'8", probably 150lbs, and very wiry.

This new roommate took one look at Johnny and burst out, "*Oye vato. Qué pasa?* (Hey dude. What's happening?)" As he stuck out his hand he said, "Glad to meet you, man. I'm Herschel O'Brien from Los Angeles. I'm a sophomore this year. What about you?"

"I'm Juan Martinez. I'll be a junior this year." Just at that point, Juan realized he was no longer Johnny. It was a new world; he was truly Juan now.

"I'm pleased to meet you, Juan. Looks like we'll be seeing a lot of each other. Pretty close quarters, huh?" Herschel said.

"You're right. Do you speak Spanish?" Juan asked.

"Well, I'm from L.A. man, so you gotta speak a little just to get along. You speak it, am I right?" Herschel asked.

"No, not really. I never learned," Juan replied.

"No problem, man. I'll teach you anything you really need to know. Gotta go get the rest of my gear," Herschel exclaimed.

Johnny was overwhelmed with this red-headed dynamo, yet he was pleased with their first meeting. In truth, he had been a little concerned about what his roommate might be like.

Herschel was back soon with a small gym bag and what looked like a surf board. "Are you a surfer?" Juan asked.

"Oh, for sure. Surfing is my life. My parents think I'm up here because it's a good school at San Francisco State. But I'm really here because the surf off Half Moon Bay is primo. I'm going to go out and take a barrel ride on one of those epic waves. Don't get me wrong. I do enough studying so Mom and Dad will support my surf habit," Herschel proclaimed.

"Is that your surf board? Looks kinda short," Juan remarked. Juan had never actually been surfing, but he had seen it on television.

"Oh, no man, this is a boogie board. My surf board will be here next week with my brother. Gonna keep it under the bed," Herschel advised.

"Okay," Juan said. "I'm glad to meet you. I'm done putting my things away, so I'm gonna take a walk around the campus. Catch you later."

"Alright, don't be late for dinner. 5 p.m.," Herschel advised.

"Okay, see you then," Juan said as he was walking out the door.

Chapter 15

It was a beautiful Christmas. The nine days of Las Posadas were wonderful. Jesús was now old enough to walk in the procession each evening. The hymns, scripture readings, treats, and mass were all a great joy.

Renaldo loved Mexico and his people so much. Sooner than he would have liked, it was time to leave for Texas again. This time would be very different though. This time, his family would be going with him. This fact was both a source of joy and of anxiety. Many disaster scenarios flitted through his head and threatened to cause him to go to Texas without his family. To Renaldo, not leaving was not a choice. His family had to have the income from Texas.

It was a Tuesday in mid-March when the family waved goodbye to Uncle Gustavo and boarded the bus. It was a long and fairly uncomfortable ride, but after two days and three bus transfers, they arrived in the tiny town of Rio Bravo, Mexico, the south side of the Rio Grande River.

They checked into a small boarding house which had one big room for the family of four. Renaldo went to find Manuel. True to his word, Manuel was ready to ferry them across the river.

"In two days," Manuel told Renaldo, *"it will be the dark of the moon. I will come for you at the boarding house when it is midnight. I will call my friend, Hernan, across the river to meet us just before I pick you up. He knows where. You will pay me 500 American dollars when you*

and your family get in the boat. You will pay my friend 100 American dollars when you get in his pickup. He will take you to his house until just before dawn, then he will drive you out and leave you at the farm."

"Okay, I understand," acknowledged Renaldo.

When the much anticipated night came, it was indeed dark. There was no moon, and the million or more stars winking down from the inky sky gave little light. Manuel tapped lightly on the door at just past midnight. They all filed silently out with their little bundles and one suitcase and got into Manuel's sky blue 1965 Chevy ¾ ton pickup. Conchita and Andrea sat in the cab with Manuel. Renaldo and Jesús and the suitcase were in the bed.

The short drive to the Rio Grande River was soon over. Manuel stopped in a pull-out usually used by fishermen. There, tied to a willow tree, was his fishing boat. Pulling the bow of the boat onto the small beach, he directed Conchita and Andrea to the middle seat and Jesús to the back seat. Then Manuel brought a fishing rod from his pickup and put it in the boat. Climbing in behind it, he went to the back seat beside Jesús.

"You may hand me the money now," Manuel said. Renaldo did so. He then directed Renaldo to push the boat back and jump in the front seat.

Soon they were drifting downstream. *"Grab the paddle in front and paddle hard on the right side,"* Manuel directed Renaldo. As Renaldo paddled on the right side of the boat, it turned toward Texas. Manuel began to furiously paddle on the left side until the boat was on the Texas side of the river current.

They drifted silently along, like a downed log floats

in the current. Finally, Manuel saw what seemed to be a fisherman's lantern on the Texas shore. To all appearances, Manuel and his crew looked like they were trying to snare some of the delicious Rio Grande catfish.

"Paddle hard right side," Manuel directed as he began to paddle on the left. ***"We head for that lantern. When we get there, throw the man the bow rope."***

Hernan expertly caught the rope and pulled the bow up onto the muddy little beach where he was "fishing."

"Okay, everyone out," Manuel whispered.

Hernan helped each of them out of the boat and directed them to the weed-covered embankment where a white Chevy pickup was parked. ***"Okay, up this trail,"*** Hernan was saying, ***"and get into the pickup, front and back."***

As the pickup pulled away, Renaldo could hear the small five horsepower Johnson outboard on Manuel's boat sputter to life. There was no need for quiet now; Manuel was just another fisherman trying to reel in a tasty meal.

It was a short drive to Hernan's riverside house. He invited them in and directed them to comfortable overstuffed chairs and a couch. ***"We will leave in three hours while it is still dark. I will leave you at the farm just before daylight. The farmer will be up by dawn and you can get your house then,"*** Hernan explained.

"Yes, that's fine," Renaldo said. ***"We will take a nap now. Here is your money, Hernan."***

"Oh, thank you," *Hernan replied.*

No one slept. It was just all too new and exciting and a little scary. They did rest and close their eyes. In the silence,

Renaldo couldn't help but wonder if he had done the right thing, bringing his family here.

When it was time to go, they trooped out into the pickup, and down the road they went. Life begins early in Edinburg, Texas. As they pulled in front of the workers' family housing area, there were people sitting around even though dawn was a good thirty minutes away.

They unloaded their meager belongings from Hernan's pickup. As Renaldo stood there watching, Hernan pulled away. He wondered if his anxiety was how Mary and Joseph felt. But this was no Posada; there just had to be room at this inn for them.

Chapter 16

"Hello, Hilario. I'm Miguel Delgado. I'm the new academic counselor here. Thanks for coming in. I asked to see you because I see you're graduating this year with your A.A. and wanted to check with you and see what you plan to do."

With a bitter tone, Hilario replied in Spanish. *"What I plan to do is keep telling my people's story and not letting the gringos screw us like they have been doing for almost two hundred years."*

"Okay, well you have an opportunity to be a real force for change, but you have to channel that energy so you focus and really make a difference," Señor Delgado responded in articulate well-educated Spanish.

"What do you mean?" Hilario asked.

"Well, you have been heard and people are aware, but this is a democracy. Things only change when laws and rules change. How will you focus your energy to help those changes take place?" Señor Delgado finished in English.

"Oh, change will take place alright or we will burn this town down," Hilario replied in English.

"Well, that would be a change, but not one that would do anyone much good," Señor Delgado said calmly. "Look, we need smart people like you to get in positions in the system where you can change it. I've looked at your grades and heard enough about you to know that you are one of those people. I've got a proposal for you. There's a B.A. program at Sacramento State that is for Chicanos only. It's paid for by the federal government and will give you two years of free college education, plus living expenses and you wind up with a B.A. I'd like to recommend you for the program. What do you think?"

"Well, I don't know. I never thought I would do any more school because I don't have money to pay for it. I work twenty hours a week now to pay for Junior College," Hilario answered.

"This wouldn't cost you a dime. Here's some literature. Take this and give it some thought. I need to know if you're interested by day after tomorrow."

"Okay, thanks. I'll let you know," Hilario said.

Hilario walked out of the office in a daze. His only thought about the end of his two years at J.C. was that he would get a full-time job. Now he had another choice. But two more years of school! He didn't know. Even though his grades were okay, he didn't really love school, just knew that more education was a way to get ahead. He would sleep on it and make a decision tomorrow.

That night Hilario did not sleep well. He was plagued with dreams of himself in a school room. The teacher called on him, but he didn't know the answer and everyone laughed at him. He woke with a start. It was 5 a.m. but he couldn't go back to sleep. He lay there thinking about his choices. One path was to get a job, make some money, get a nice new car and some new threads. The second choice was more school but this time with students like him. The second choice was what he decided. Just once in his life, he wanted to go to school where he wasn't the odd one.

At 10 a.m., Hilario knocked on Señor Delgado's door. "Come in. Good morning Hilario. Do you have good news for me?"

"I hope its good news. I want in the program," Hilario said proudly.

"That's great news. You will make a wonderful addition to the group. Let's get some paper work filled out right now, and I'll move it along," Señor Delgado said excitedly.

Two weeks later Hilario received a letter scheduling him for an entrance interview into the program. He thought a lot about it and was now very interested. He wanted this and was going to do whatever it took to get into that program. Two years of free college plus room and board. This was his ticket to bigger and better things.

****

In late July, Hilario was at Sacramento State, waiting in the outer office for his interview. "Hilario Jiminez," the interviewer called. "Please come in."

Hilario was offered a seat facing a three-person interview panel. Interviewer #1 was a middle-aged, gray-haired Latino man. Interviewer #2 was a young, slightly pudgy, Latina woman. Interviewer #3 was a young muscular Latino man with fierce, piercing hawk-like eyes.

The older gentleman introduced himself and the other panel members. "I'll begin. Why do you want to be a part of this program?"

"Because I want to finish college, and I have no other way to do it. I want to study with a group like me," Hilario responded.

"Okay, next question. What do you envision yourself doing after college graduation?"

"The same thing I have been doing, advocating on behalf of my people for better opportunities. To see that we get our piece of the pie and aren't continually shut out because of who we are. I'll be able to do it better with a college degree," Hilario answered enthusiastically.

"Okay, thank you," interviewer #1 said. And so it went for 45 minutes; one question after another until Hilario's psychic energy was spent.

Exhausted but happy, Hilario felt very good about his answers and the positive body language he was seeing from all three of the interviewers.

Hilario was correct in his assessment. Ten days after the interview, he received his letter of acceptance. Classes would begin the day after Labor Day, two weeks ahead of the regular college schedule. He was to report August 25th for a room assignment in the dorm and could move in as soon as the 26th.

Hilario was elated. He knew this for the tremendous opportunity that it was, and he was going to grab it with both hands and hold on. He was working odd jobs, buying some new clothes for the school year, and saving a few bucks to have some spending money.

Chapter 17

Juan walked up the hill from the dorm to the quad with its speaker platform. Past the gym, across to the library he went, then paused and looked through the locked glass door. He knew he would be spending a lot of time there. He continued on the huge circle of the campus. Past the art department, he stopped to look at the half-finished sculptures in the yard, and to admire the huge mobile hanging from a tree. He then went back around, past the Quonset huts, where snacks were sold. Juan completed his walk back at the dorm dining room where he ate a filling, bland, well-balanced meal.

Herschel asked Juan, "How is it you don't speak Spanish?"

"My family has been in the United States since the 1920s. My parents were born here. This is our country now, and my parents stressed that speaking English is the way to get ahead here," Juan replied.

"Yea, gotcha. Look at me! I'm the product of a Jewish mother and Irish father. I was born here but Dad is from Ireland and Mom from New York. Dad speaks Irish and Mom speaks Yiddish and I don't know either one. My Dad kinda told me the same thing as yours. English is not only the language of the U.S. – it's an international language so learn it and learn it well," Herschel finished.

****

The alarm went off at 7 a.m. and Juan rolled out of bed while Herschel slept peacefully. Down to the shower room he went, soap on a rope, shower, shave, and out the door by 7:30 for a walk up the eucalyptus-lined hill to an 8 o'clock class. The History of U.S./Mexican Political Relations, his first class at State.

Walking into the classroom, Juan was immediately struck by the fact that five out of the fifteen bright young faces were brown. Better yet, three of them were brown and female. The professor began to lay out the process by which California and the Southwest became part of the United States. He explained the background politics of the change and passed briefly over the Treaty of Guadalupe-Hidalgo. The lecture ended and it was question time.

Juan raised his hand and asked, "Isn't it true that the treaty held several provisions that the U.S. never honored? Like allowing residents of those areas to maintain Spanish as their language."

The professor's answer was cloaked in lots of verbiage, but was a yes. He continued on to explain that the concept of "Manifest Destiny" drove the U.S. to negate the rights of indigenous people as well as former citizens of Mexico. From sea to shining sea resulted in much warfare and bloodshed. The professor dismissed the class and promised to take this up during the next class.

"Wait up, Juan," a female voice called. Looking over his shoulder, he saw a young woman from his class approaching. "Hey, I liked your comments in the class. You sound like you know what you're talking about. Got time for a cup of coffee?"

Juan looked at his watch and said, "Sure, I don't have another class until eleven."

"You have me at a disadvantage," Juan said as he shoved a quarter into the coffee vending machine. "You know my name, but what is yours?"

"I'm Marina Lara," she answered.

"Well, Marina, I'm buying. Cream and sugar?" Juan asked.

"Yes, both please." Marina smiled.

Another quarter inserted, the cream and sugar button pushed, and soon they both had a steaming cup of stale watery coffee.

"Are you a history major?" Juan inquired.

"No. I'm an English major. I just took the class as an elective. I'm from San Diego and just curious about Mexico-U.S. relations. The change when you cross the border to Tijuana always amazes me. Such a poor dirty country. What about you, are you a history major?" Marina inquired.

"No, like you, I'm an English major but with a history minor. I'm a junior," Juan continued. "And you?"

"Yes, I'm a junior too. I spent two years at San Diego State but just needed a change of scenery; my folks agreed to let me come here in the fall. My aunt lives across the street in Park Merced. I'm staying with her while I go to school," Marina explained.

Juan looked at his watch and said, "It's almost time for my class. I don't want to be late on the first day. It was nice to meet you, Marina."

"Yes, nice to meet you too, Juan, and thank you for the coffee," Marina said with a smile.

"You're welcome," Juan replied, also with a smile.

Fall transitioned into winter and winter to spring with hardly a change in the climate. There was a little rain in the fall, a little more rain during the winter and spring. Of course, the chilliest season in San Francisco was summer with its fog and wind.

****

By summer, Juan was back home in Perryville. He had a very successful school year. He made the Dean's List both semesters and had a ball doing it. He and Marina were not exactly an item, but they had spent time together and were getting to know each other. One of their favorite outings was to the zoo. They agreed that their favorite attraction was the talking Mynah bird.

"See English is the universal language. Even birds speak it," Juan said laughingly.

"Yes, I know," said Marina, "but I still want to learn Spanish. It's the language of my ancestors. My aunt said she would teach me."

"Yeah, I agree," said Juan, "I'm going to learn too, but meanwhile, I'm focused on graduation."

Chapter 18

"Hello, my name is Dr. Romero Sifuentes. If you get a cold or break a bone, don't come to me. I'm not that kind of doctor," he said as the class laughed. "However, I do hold a doctorate in political science and an M.A. in United States history. I'm the Director of this special pilot program, and I'll be teaching some of the classes.

"You'll notice that I'm speaking English." As he transitioned to Spanish, he said, ***"The reason is that I have spoken at length with each of you twenty-two students and the level of Spanish ability varies a great deal. It is better that we instruct in English.***

"Everyone here is a fluent English speaker. Spanish, not so much. However, we will provide some individualized instruction in both Spanish and English for those who need it. I will teach one hour per day in college level Spanish. This will be difficult for some of you to follow, but it will be a repeat of an earlier lecture, so you will not miss any content.

"This is a rigorous academic program which you are about to undertake. You will be expected to work hard and keep focused on the goal of attaining a B.A. The people you see seated behind me are instructors and tutors who will help you toward this goal. If at any time you are not feeling successful in your study, I ask that you contact me directly.

"Each of you has been chosen because the selection

committee determined that you have the ability to obtain a B.A. but were probably not going to because of financial or other constraints. Welcome to your new world. *Bienvenidos damas y caballeros!* (Welcome ladies and gentlemen!) We begin!"

****

"Okay, everyone let's settle down and get to work," Dr. Sifuentes said. "We have broken you into small groups so you can strategize. You will have to present your plan tomorrow. Let me read the assignment again. 'Develop a political strategy that will promote and sustain equal education opportunities for ethnic and racial minorities.'"

"Let's brainstorm for a bit. All ideas are valid. I'll write them down," Hilario's group leader said.

Student #1 said, "Change college entrance exams. They discriminate against minorities."

Student #2 offered, "More financial aid for minorities."

Hilario spoke up, "Keep college records of minority enrollment and close the college if the percent of minority students isn't the same as the percent in the population."

Student #3 offered, "Have colleges fund a position to go to the barrio and recruit students."

After some debate and discussion, the plan was developed and a group member chosen to present it. A summary was written as follows:

- We propose to develop and promote adoption of legislation that would accomplish the following objectives.

- Change the current entrance test requirements

for California State Colleges and Universities so they are more appropriate to the life experience of California's minority students.

- Provide financial aid for minority students to attend four years of California State Colleges and Universities.

- Require California State Colleges and Universities to recruit minority students.

- Require California State Colleges and Universities to keep records of the number of minority students enrolled and the number who graduate.

The proposal was well received by the class and instructors. They considered the points well-made and the content, if enacted, would give minority students an equal opportunity. Hilario held out for a more punitive measure for the Universities that didn't comply, up to and including, losing accreditation. The rest of the group was unresponsive to this idea and insisted on toning it down.

Hilario kept insisting. "You ask for the moon, you get a star. You ask for a star, maybe you get a flashlight. We have to go big to have room to work. We got to shock them! And let me tell you, we have the gringos on the run now. Ever since Affirmative Action started, all you have to do about anything you don't like is say the people who do it are racist. No proof is needed. Just say it, it works." The group listened but was not convinced.

Hilario was fired up. He was loving the constant daily interaction with like-minded people. Even though he was much more aggressive in his solutions then most of the students, they were all focused on the same outcomes. They wanted more equal opportunity in education and employment for minorities and cessation of the racial and ethnic stereotyping so prevalent in society.

To these goals, Hilario added in his mind an overlay of humbling and punishing the gringo society which had committed such gross discrimination against him and his family. He did not give voice to this desire but it was always there, underlying every action he suggested. His peer group had a few who agreed and supported Hilario's positions, but the majority were more modest in their approach.

Some of the group had been willing to follow Hilario's lead when it involved mocking, chanting, and taunting officials. Now that they were actually developing political strategies that might be put into practice, they were more hesitant and careful.

****

"What about Hilario? It's important that this first effort be a success in order to have a continuation of federal funding," Dr. Sifuentes said during the staff's weekly meeting. During these meetings they checked both the academic and social progress of each student.

"He's doing fine academically. Not at the top of the class, but doing okay," Maria the tutor replied. "He is a rabble-rouser though. It seems that he not only wants to change the structure of society, but he also wants to get some sort of revenge on society for all the past insults and wrongs committed."

"Okay," Dr. Sifuentes replied. "Rabble-rousers are sometimes needed. We just have to teach him how to channel it in an effective manner."

Chapter 19

Life was good for the Preciado family in Edinburg, Texas. They soon adapted to the rhythm of life there. Their lives were ruled by the needs of plants. Plant them, irrigate and weed them, harvest them, and return to Mexico. At the next growing season, do it all again.

After years of the seasonal life of intense hard work, followed by months of rest in Mexico, Renaldo was ready to venture out to look for new opportunities.

Renaldo had been talking to a friend from work who had just gotten back from California. The friend explained, *"You can work all year if you're willing to travel. Go out to California in April; they are planting lots of crops then. You find work there every day from April until the middle of November. The crops they grow, like grapes, need lots of workers; grapes can't be picked with a machine. Then go home and enjoy Christmas. Start again in Texas in January and work until time to go to California. You've got a good pickup now, so you can make the drive. And you have your papers, right? The ones the forger in Edinburg made for you? You can drive back and forth across the border with your family, no problem. You know they don't look too hard at papers. The United States really doesn't want to keep us out. They want our hard work. The gringos are too soft and lazy to do what we do."*

"Thank you," Renaldo said, *"I'll think about what you have told me."*

That night after the children were asleep, Renaldo said, ***"Conchita, my love, I think we should go to California this year. I heard they have lots of work there from April through the middle of November, then we go home until January and then work in Texas, January, February, and March. Then we leave for California in April. They have better housing there too. California has housing just for farmworkers.***

"I know the farmer here in Edinburg has been good to us, but the work is getting slow. More and more machines doing the work and more crops that don't need us," Renaldo finished.

"Yes, I know," Conchita said. ***"We will do what you think is best. But when will we have enough money to move home?"***

****

It was with some trepidation that they left Edinburg the next April and headed for California. Renaldo's coworkers had all told them that McKinley was one of the best places to go. It was a major farming region in the San Joaquin Valley of California. California provided good housing at a nominal fee, and there was plenty of work during the growing season.

During the last leg of the journey from Edinburg, Renaldo pulled the pickup off Highway 99, down Highway 158 to Highway 33, and headed north. He had driven all night while the children slept in the newly acquired camper. As the sun rose and hit Conchita with its first rays, they saw a city limit sign announcing McKinley, and then a line of pickups.

Renaldo pulled into the end of the line, parked, and walked up to the pickup in front and said, *"Is this the line for housing?"*

"Yes, this is it. Go up to the front and get papers from the man and fill out as much as you can. It will go faster for you," the man replied.

"Thank you," Renaldo acknowledged as he headed up the line.

When they got checked in, Conchita said she was glad they came. Even though the house wasn't beautiful or very big, it did have an air conditioner in the window. The weather was hot, but it was not nearly as humid as Texas.

The house was small, but it had everything they needed, except a washing machine. It did have its own clothesline and there was a coin laundromat just down the street. All things considered; they were happy they had come. Now it was time to find some work.

Finding work was no problem. On his first day there, Renaldo got up at 3:30 a.m. and went to the spot where the Farm Labor Contractor picked up workers. Renaldo's next-door neighbor explained to him, *"You don't have to look for work. Just come out, be there early. If you have callouses on your hands, the contractor will take you to the fields. After that, if you want to drive your pickup to the fields, it's okay."*

Before dawn, Renaldo was sitting on the bench waiting for the contractor to come, as workers began to drift into the area. The van showed up, Renaldo went to the driver and said, *"I'm ready to go to work."*

"Let me see your hands," the driver demanded. Renaldo

displayed his hands, palms up. ***"Nice calluses. Where have you been working?"*** he asked.

"Texas," Renaldo replied.

"Okay, get in the van. If you can stand Texas heat, you'll do fine here," the contractor said.

****

Conchita got the children up at 7 a.m., washed their hands and faces and gave them tortillas and refried beans for breakfast. She would add some scrambled eggs to this the next day after visiting the local market.

Conchita looked at the clock with some nervousness. She had been told that the children had to go to school or the authorities would come. So, at 8 a.m., she walked them over to the school, not knowing what she might find there. Would it be a welcome or a sneer? Would they speak Spanish or not? Andrea was 6 years old now and Jesús was 11, they had to go to school.

Conchita saw a sign as she walked up to the school that said "Office." She knew that meant "oficina," so she knew where to go. As she walked in, a bright-eyed young secretary chirped, *"Buenos Días, bienvenidos (*Good morning, welcome*)."*

"Buenos Dias," Conchita replied. She was grateful to have someone to talk to, so she asked, ***"How are you today?"***

The secretary replied, ***"I'm fine, how are you?"***

Conchita smiled and said, ***"We are good and happy to finally be here."***

"Have you traveled far?"

91

"Yes, from Texas," Conchita answered.

"Well, you will find lots of people here from Texas. Some from Weslaco, McAllen, and Edinburg."

"Oh, we are from Edinburg," Conchita interjected.

"Good. You will find lots of people from all around the Rio Grande Valley. You will have lots in common with them. Are you here to enroll your children?" the secretary questioned.

"Yes," Conchita replied. *"They told me that they have to go to school. I am worried because they don't speak English. Andrea has never been to school, and Jesús has only been a little bit because we move a lot. He went to school in Mexico and a little in Texas, but he only knows a few words in English."*

"Well, don't worry because he will learn a lot," the secretary said firmly. *"The teachers don't speak Spanish, but I help them and we have some teacher aides who speak both. Don't worry, they will learn. Now, let's get some paperwork filled out."*

Paper work completed, it was time to leave the children. Conchita walked Jesús down to Room #6 and he marched right in like the little man that he was.

With Andrea, it was different. Her first entrance to school was not a happy one. She clung to her mother and cried big tears. It broke Conchita's heart to do it, but she knew that school was a good place for Andrea. With the teacher aide comforting Andrea, Conchita walked away looking at the sidewalk with tears welling in her eyes.

Conchita walked back to get Andrea at noon. As she approached, she saw Andrea happily playing in the yard of her classroom. All were giggling and shouting in various degrees of Spanish, English, or both.

The bell rang just as Conchita arrived, and Andrea and the others lined up and went back into the classroom. They did so in perfect formation just like so many little soldiers. As they walked home, Andrea was full of stories about her new friends and all the fun things they had done that day.

Jesús came in after his class had finished. He was a little less enthusiastic than Andrea but said he liked the teacher. Some of the kids were stupid and called him a wetback, but most were nice. Most of them spoke Spanish and he was going to play fútbol (soccer) at the school on Sunday.

Finally, Renaldo was home and the family was together again. After his shower and dinner, they all talked about the day and their new home. They were seasoned travelers now and used to new places. They all thought this place was okay.

Chapter 20

Jimmy was welcomed back to his folk's home in Perryville with open arms. Even though his Dad was against his going to Europe, he was happy to see him back. Jimmy wasn't thrilled about going home and moving into his old bedroom, but he was broke. Or as he would say, "financially embarrassed." He knew, and they knew, it was temporary.

Jimmy was qualified as a teacher and found a California teaching position the day after he arrived home. Thumbing through the list of teacher openings in the Stanislaus County Office of Education, he found two positions. One was in the town of Lodi and the other in the tiny farm town of McKinley. He called them both and got an interview at McKinley for the next day.

As he drove through the open countryside to McKinley, Jimmy was awed by the beautiful green open farm land of the San Joaquin Valley. He realized this land could practically feed the whole nation. The Sierra Nevada Mountains to the east and the coastal range to the west framed this beautiful fertile valley.

After a 45-minute drive, he arrived at last in McKinley. What passed for a town was really simply a wide spot in the road. It was a small collection of businesses all geared to serving the surrounding farms. There was a small grocery store, a farm implement repair shop, a loading dock for railroad cars and a bar and grill which offered 4 rooms for rent on the second story.

A short block from the "town" was the school. It was a nice enough looking building. Early 1950s construction with a flat roof and stucco siding, painted pea green in the fashion of the day. It was constructed in a U-shape with office, teacher's room and cafeteria at the bottom of the U facing the road, four primary classrooms on one leg of the U, and four grades (fourth through sixth) of classrooms on the other leg. The middle of the U boasted a walkway all the way around the U, and a lawn filled the rest.

As Jimmy looked through the open end of the U, he could see what looked to be about five blocks worth of small houses, duplexes, and mobile homes. He was told this was all housing designated for farmworkers. It looked a little run-down to him, and he began to wonder what kind of community this was. He was about to learn the answer.

The interview was conducted by the principal of the school, Mr. Charles Campbell, a parent, and a teacher. They started by telling him that the school served 225 children; 200 children came from the farmworker housing and the remaining 25 were bussed in from farms in the school district. They asked him about his education and student teaching experience, and his philosophy of education. Then they began to ask of any experience he had working with poverty families, especially Mexican-Americans.

"I did do part of my student teaching in the Mission District in San Francisco where there are some pretty poor families. I think some of the students were Mexicans, but maybe they were Mexican-Americans. My philosophy is just to give kids assignments to do that are a little harder each time and make them stretch a bit. Don't let them get lazy; make them try to reach a further goal every day," explained Jimmy.

Then there was a walk around the schoolyard at recess. That is when Jimmy discovered that 90% of the kids at the school were *Mexicans*.

Jimmy began to worry right away. He'd never been around more than two or three Mexicans at a time in his whole life, except when he went to Tijuana. How could he possibly work with these kids? About that time, a chubby little boy who looked about 8 years old came over, grabbed Jimmy by the hand, and with a heavy accent, said, "You gonna be my teacher?"

When Jimmy looked down, he found himself staring into the most sparkling blue eyes he had ever seen; those eyes in that chubby, happy, little brown face were striking. "I'm not sure but when I find out, I'll let you know. What's your name?"

The little boy replied, "My name is Rafael. What's your name?"

"Mister Welch is my name, Rafael," answered Jimmy.

"Okay, Mister Welch," Rafael acknowledged as he ran off to play tetherball.

Within an hour of arriving home that afternoon, Jimmy got a call from the principal offering him the job. It probably wasn't his insightful answers to the questions that got him the offer, since he had no actual paid teaching experience. More likely he got it because of the lack of applicants. Not many teachers were interested in going to a little isolated country school to teach a group of poor Mexican kids.

"I have an interview on Wednesday in Lodi. I'll let you know one way or the other by Friday," Jimmy said.

"Okay," Principal Campbell replied.

That evening Jimmy thought long and hard about his choices. It was a pretty dreary place out in McKinley, and the pay scale was very low. But he'd traveled a good part of the world this last year and seen lots of cultures and learned something from each of them. The kids he saw on the playground were quite foreign sounding and looking. He decided to try it! He couldn't forget that nice little boy Rafael. If they're all like him, this will be a dream job, Jimmy thought.

At 10 a.m. the next morning, Jimmy called Lodi and cancelled the interview. At noon, he called the McKinley School and accepted the offer. Principal Campbell directed him to come in at the end of the week to fill out the employment papers. School starts the day after Labor Day. "I'll be there tomorrow," Jimmy replied.

****

It was Labor Day and Jimmy was nervous. He worried that he was going to a place filled with Mexicans. What if they're like the ones at the party? What'll happen if they catch me alone? Will they mug me? Then the image of the friendly little Rafael came into his head. No, they'll leave me alone because I'm a teacher.

But Jimmy continued to stew. What if the parents don't like me because I'm white? What if they turn the kids against me? He went on and on with his anxious thoughts, back and forth. It will be okay. No it will be a disaster. Thoughts of the near gang fight at Lonnie's beer-bust loomed in his head, only to be shoved aside by thoughts of the friendly staff and children at the school.

Finally, it was time for school to start. The day after Labor Day was when school children all over California started a new school year. The traditional date of school opening was always the day after Labor Day.

Jimmy had been working hard to get his classroom set up and now was the moment of truth. The bell rang and 30 fifth and sixth graders walked into his classroom and found a seat. The new teachers always got the mixed grade classes.

"Good morning. I'm Mr. Welch. I'll be your teacher this year. Welcome, we're going to have a good time and learn a lot," Jimmy said nervously. He looked out at a room full of brown faces, all with black hair and suddenly felt out of place. He had grown up with lots of negative ideas about Mexicans and was now wondering why he put himself and these children in this position. He quickly remembered his anxious thoughts about meeting new people from different cultures in Europe, and how uplifting it was to get to know them. The thought calmed his anxious mind.

"Before I pass out the textbooks, let's get acquainted a little. As I call your name, please raise your hand then tell us the name you go by, if you have a nickname, and also tell us a little about what you did this summer." They all looked at each other and giggled. "Okay, let's start with Carlos Alvarado."

"My name Carlos Alvarado. I like be call Carlitos. Last summer I go with Popi to work in the fields. Pick strawberries, apricots, cherries, peaches."

"Thank you, Carlitos. Next is José Alaniz."

"My name is José Alaniz. Last summer I went with my dad to work in the fields. We hoed weeds in the tomato fields, picked peaches, cherries, plums and watermelons."

"Thank you, José."

"My name is Jesús Preciado. I worked with Popi in the tomatoes," Jesús said in clear Spanish.

Someone in the back of the room shouted "Oh, a *mojado!*" The classroom erupted in laughter.

"Okay, someone help me out here...what did he say?" Jimmy asked.

José piped up right away, "He said his name is Jesús and he worked last summer with his dad in the tomatoes."

"Why did everyone laugh?" asked Jimmy.

"Because Roberto said Jesús is a wetback. You know, he swam the river to come to the United States," replied José.

"Okay, that will be enough of that kind of talk," Jimmy warned.

And so it went down to Angelica Yarto. The day went rather smoothly considering there were three kids in the room that spoke no English. There were eighteen more who spoke a variety of English that, by and large, did not have past tense verbs or any adjectives. There were nine who spoke standard English, some with no accent, and some with very little accent. Of course, two of them were white girls who spoke no Spanish.

At the end of the day, Principal Campbell called Jimmy to see how the day went. Jimmy explained that the day went well; the kids were cooperative, but it's going to be a bit of a problem teaching those who don't understand English.

"Yes, I understand," Principal Campbell said. "We have quite a few non-English speakers this year. We're in the process of hiring some bilingual aides. I'll assign one to you for part of the day when they're hired. Meanwhile, get José to help you. His mom and dad speak English and his English and Spanish are very good."

When Jimmy got home that afternoon, the first thing his dad asked was, "How was your first day of school?"

"It was okay but a few difficult things. There is a kid named Jesus in my class and one named Angel. Neither of them speaks English."

With a grin on his face, Dad said, "Well, you should be pretty well taken care of with Jesus and an Angel in your class." Jimmy and his dad both knew it was going to be quite a job, but he would find a way to make it work.

Jimmy further explained, "The students come to school looking really nice, hair combed and clothes neat. I always heard that Mexicans were dirty. There are twenty-two boys in the class all 10 or 11 years old, and every one of them spent the summer working in the fields.

"There's one girl who is 13. She should be in the eighth grade, but the principal explained that she went to school in Texas and Texas doesn't do social promotion; they hold kids back until they catch up with the rest of the kids. This poor girl went to four different schools last year; no wonder she can't keep up."

"Well Son, it's your job to see that she gets up to where she needs to be. You know, Mom and I have always told you that getting a good education is something no one can ever take away from you. We didn't have a chance to get an education; just like those Mexicans out there, we had to go to work. But I'm glad you got your education and now maybe you can help them do the same."

"Thanks Dad. I'm going to do my best," promised Jimmy.

****

Week four—time was flying fast for Jimmy. He was learning every day and loving it. One thing Jimmy learned right away was that he was just as foreign to these kids as they were to him. Rafael (Rafi), being only a fourth grader, was not in his class, but Rafi didn't miss a chance to talk to him on the playground.

One day as Jimmy was on yard duty, Rafi ran over and greeted him with a cheery "Hello Teacher." As they walked along, Rafi began to probe and try to find out about the new teacher.

"You got a wife, Mister Welch?"

"No Rafi, I don't have a wife. I don't even have a girlfriend," replied Jimmy. Jimmy could see the wheels turning in that little head and the perplexed look on his face. An adult young man with no wife just didn't make sense to Rafi. It was completely out of his realm of experience.

Struggling to understand, Rafi went to the next question, "You got a mother?"

"Yes, I have a mother."

The relief on Rafi's face was palpable. The final question was a hoot and Jimmy had some fun with it.

"Do you let farks, Teacher?"

"Oh no, Rafi, I would never do such a thing," Jimmy answered.

"Not even when you was a little boy," Rafi questioned.

"Not even then," Jimmy affirmed.

Ring, Wow, saved by the bell, Jimmy thought. Who knows what the next question might have been?

Each day was a new learning experience for Jimmy. He was enthralled with learning about a culture he never knew existed, and he didn't have to travel to Europe to find it.

At the morning recess, Jimmy was chatting with Ofelia, one of the bilingual teacher aides.

Jimmy said, "Rafi has lots of questions, and one of them was very odd. He asked me if I have a mother. Doesn't he know everyone has a mother?"

"Yes he knows," Ofelia replied. "When he found out you didn't have a wife, he just wanted to know if you had a mother to feed you and take care of your clothes and other things you might need."

"What do you mean? I can do all that stuff myself," Jimmy said in a surprised voice.

"Yes, but in our culture, the woman is responsible to do those things. If not the wife, then the mother or perhaps a sister. It's changing some but not too much," Ofelia explained.

The bilingual teacher aides were very helpful in introducing Jimmy to the culture. But the children were his very best informants.

****

One bright October day, Jimmy noticed Leticia crying on the playground and asked what was wrong.

"La Llorona is coming for me tonight," she cried.

"What is La Llorona?" Jimmy asked.

"You don't know what is La Llorona? She is a lady. She get mad at her husband because he only love the keeds and not her.   She take the keeds to the reever and she drown them so the husband he will love her. But he don't love her; he tell her to find the keeds then he will love her. He ride away on his *caballo* (horse). She go to the reever and she drown herself. Now she cry at night a lot but still look for the souls of the keeds.

"She don't find them because they in heaven. She think if she find her keed's souls, God let her in heaven, but she don't find them so she cry a lot at night and look for keeds. Sometimes you hear her at night. Then she catch other keeds and drown them too, and she try to get into heaven with the souls of them," Leticia explained.

"Why do you think she is coming for you?" Jimmy asked.

"Because she come at night and brother, Pablo, say he will open the windows tonight so she can come and get me!" cried Leticia.

"Don't worry. I'll talk to Pablo. I promise he won't open the windows," Jimmy said calmly. After sniffling a little longer, Leticia skipped away to enjoy a tetherball game.

The story of La Llorona helped to consolidate Jimmy's growing awareness and understanding that he was among people who had a distinct culture that varied quite a lot from the dominant culture in the United States. Of course, ghost stories abound in almost every culture. Perhaps it's an effort by people to try to understand what actually happens after death. Who knows? Jimmy thought.

The fact that La Llorona was so different from any ghost story Jimmy had ever heard stuck in his mind. It helped him consolidate his understanding that he was among people now whose world view was somewhat different from his, and he wanted to understand it. He believed that if he better understood the traditions and beliefs of the people, he would be a better teacher of their children. He had spent a year in Europe among people who had cultures very different from his. But if he had learned nothing else, he learned that they valued their children and wanted the best for them, and so did these Mexicans.

The searing heat of September gradually melded into the placid month of October, and Jimmy began to feel more comfortable day by day. José had done a masterful job interpreting and Jesús was well on his way to finishing the first half of the California State Department of Education math text for fifth graders. Jesús was far ahead of all the other students and seemed to need very little explanation of math concepts. Even with the *new math*, which relied on students understanding the *why* of math, Jesús was able to solve all practice problems with very few errors.

The experience with Jesús crushed a long-held belief that Mexicans just weren't smart. Jimmy had thought that since they didn't speak English, they were not smart, and anyone with a Mexican accent was not smart. But these kids were very smart, and Jesús was a brilliant mathematician.

Jimmy's bilingual aide took over José's interpreting duties, but Jimmy continued to work with Jesús on math and introducing him to English. Jesús' progress in English was a little slower than his math, but he was definitely coming along.

José was a great student, and it wasn't just because of his fluent English. He was a curious and very bright kid. Jimmy was sitting at his desk when a paper airplane floated lazily by and made a 180 degree turn before landing softly on the floor.

Jimmy inquired, "Who's playing with paper airplanes?" José raised his hand immediately. "José, you know this is silent time to work on your math problems or read."

"Yeah, but it flew real good, Mr. Welch" José said proudly.

Jimmy suppressed a chuckle and replied, "Yes it flew real good, but its silent time now. You stay in at recess and we'll talk about this."

The recess bell rang and José remained in his seat. "Tell me why you thought it was okay to be flying a paper airplane during silent time, José?" Jimmy inquired.

José proudly explained, "I was finished with all my math and reading. I even did the next assignment in the book and I was bored."

"I get that but you know you can't disturb the other kids. Are we clear on this?"

"Yes, Mr. Welch," José said.

"Are you interested in airplanes?" Jimmy asked.

"Yes, I want to fly one and be a crop duster some day!"

"Well then, I suggest that you buckle down and pay particular attention to your math and science. I'll ask the library van person to bring some books on flying. When they come next week, you can check one out. Okay, go out and get some fresh air," Jimmy finished.

****

The days passed quickly, and Jimmy grew more comfortable in his work with each passing day. Then controversy struck.

The sixth-grade social studies curriculum focused on Latin America. On the previous Friday, the reading assignment had been about Mexico. The textbook author had made a clear point of saying that most Mexicans were of mixed Spanish and Indian descent. Mestizo he called them. Now on this Monday discussion of the reading, Carlitos eagerly raised his hand, "My Popi say we not Mestizo; he say don't want teaching like that."

Jimmy wasn't too sure how to respond, so he just said, "Okay Carlitos, thank you for letting me know that."

At recess, Jimmy went right to the office to check with Principal Campbell.

Chapter 21

"Someone called for you today. I left a note by the phone," Mom said.

"Okay, thanks," Jimmy replied. Just home from school, he went to his room and changed out of what he called his "uniform." White shirt and tie, and on cool days, a sports coat. The school district had a strict dress code: dress like a professional, act like a professional. Jimmy didn't like having a dress code, but one month into his new job, he wasn't going to try to buck the system.

Jimmy picked up the message and was quite surprised. Daniel Watson, it read, his college friend and neighbor. He had left a phone number and the message, "Please Call."

"Hey Daniel, good to hear from you. What's up?" Jimmy asked.

"Just calling to say let's get together. I'm still at the University of San Francisco going for an M.A. in Political Science. I've gotten up in the world a little. I got a full ride scholarship for two years. One semester is an unpaid internship with a public agency. How about coming to the city this weekend? I've got a new apartment with a little more room and a nice big couch for your sleeping pleasure. We can drink a little beer and walk on the beach. You know how beautiful the weather is here in October," Daniel said very convincingly.

"Give me the address and some directions," Jimmy enthusiastically agreed.

"Great. See you about noon on Saturday. I'm looking forward to it. I'll have a cold one ready for you!" Daniel said.

"Who's Daniel?" Mom asked, unable to restrain her curiosity.

"He's a guy I knew in college. I'm going to spend Saturday night at his apartment in the city. It's really beautiful up there this time of year. There are lots of warm sunny days and cool evenings. He lives out by the beach. Should be fun," Jimmy explained.

"Have a good time," Mom said.

Saturday couldn't come soon enough for Jimmy. He was up and out on the road by 9 a.m. which was pretty early for Jimmy on a weekend. He arrived in the city a little early, so he drove to the old neighborhood on 48th Avenue. Nothing had changed in the last few years; he was glad of that. On the way to Daniel's 36th Avenue address, Jimmy drove through Golden Gate Park purposely, just to see the buffalo. He was always intrigued that the city had its own small buffalo herd of eight in a three-acre enclosure. A bit of the Wild West, Jimmy thought.

"Hello, Jim. Glad you could make it," Daniel said. "Come in." After a brief tour of the new apartment, Daniel lifted two Coors Lights from the fridge and handed one to Jimmy. As he pulled the pop top off his and deposited it in the trash, he said, "These pop tops are a nuisance. People throw them all over. I stepped on one on the beach last week and cut my toe. I'd rather just use a 'church key,' like we used to."

"Count your blessings," Jimmy said. "I don't have any beach to walk on." They both chuckled.

"So what's happening with you?" Daniel asked.

Jimmy explained about being rejected for military service, going to Europe, and now being in his teaching job.

"I wondered why you dropped out of sight. Guess you were in Europe," Daniel mused.

"Yeah, I liked it there but ran out of money. I probably could have gotten a job on a military base and stayed, but I wanted to get back home and get started on a career," Jimmy explained.

"You say the school where you are is Mexican farmworkers?"

Jimmy replied, "Yes, 90%."

"Are they illegals?" Daniel questioned.

"I don't know what their immigration status is; it's not a school registration requirement," Jimmy answered.

"It should be," Daniel retorted.

"What I know for sure," Jimmy said, "is that they are all hard workers, doing some nasty jobs for low wages."

"Yeah, but probably getting paid a lot more than they would in Mexico," Daniel replied.

"No doubt," Jimmy agreed, "but still low wages and hard work, for here."

Daniel proclaimed, "You know I've often wondered why Mexicans come here. They work, they live here, but they don't assimilate. Other groups come and after a generation or two, you can't tell them from anyone else. Mexicans come, they don't learn English, just keep speaking Spanish. They continue on with their holidays and way of life, as if they are in Mexico. They act like they don't want to be part of the United States," Daniel concluded.

"I don't know what to tell you about that, Daniel. I really don't. I'll give it some thought. Meanwhile, let's hit the beach!" Jimmy proposed.

"Okay, let's do it," Daniel agreed.

It was a great weekend going to all the old places. Walking on the beach by the Cliff House, a trip through the arcade at Playland, pizza at the old place on upper Judah; it was all wonderful fun.

With profuse thanks to Daniel, Jimmy drove away. But all the way home he thought about the question Daniel had asked. Why didn't Mexicans blend in?

No sooner had Jimmy left than Daniel was cracking a book. He had a paper due in two weeks and had chosen the topic of presidential politics just before, during, and just after the Civil War.

Daniel was a great fan of Ulysses Grant and was looking for some explanation of why his presidency was so corrupt. His reading of the General's life resulted in nothing but respect for him. Daniel wondered, how did he allow the corruption and outright thievery that took place under his watch as President?

Daniel didn't know what had happened, but before this paper was finished, he would know. He was every bit as tenacious as the General had been.

Chapter 22

"Yes Jim, I know about it. Carlitos' dad paid me a visit and complained about you teaching the kids that they are Mestizos," Principal Campbell said.

"But it's in the textbook. I'm just teaching what's in the State adopted textbook," Jim said.

Principal Campbell began to explain, "Yes, I know. Let me try to explain as I understand it. In Mexico, the indigenous people, the Indians, are the lowest social class. It's very much like what happened here. The British invaded America and took the land from the Native Americans and made them lower class. The Spanish invaded Mexico and took the land, subjugated the natives, and made them lower class. The word Mestizo has been used in Mexico to designate a lower-class citizen, one of mixed Spanish and Indian blood. The similar term that has been used here in the United States is half-breed, to designate a lower-class person who is of White and Indian blood. The major reason for the difference between the historical numbers of mixed-race population in the U.S. and Mexico is that the English brought women with them. So, only a limited number of the men had children with Indian women. The Spanish did not bring women. The Spanish were conquistadors and came only to pillage, claim the land, and take anything of value back to Spain. Consequently, the Spanish soldiers did have children with the native women on a large scale. The result is that many, if not most, of modern-day Mexicans are of mixed blood. It is my experience that many of them would prefer to be thought of as Spanish. But here in McKinley, we don't mention Mestizos or talk about it. My advice is to just drop the discussion about Mestizos and move on to Central America."

Jimmy walked away with another lesson learned. There was so much he didn't know about the people. Just like the countries he visited in Europe, they had a different culture and history. They would like to be thought of as Spanish, but Jimmy had been to Spain; the people there didn't look much like these Mexicans. The cities in Spain sure didn't look like Tijuana. Jimmy thought, I'm going to do what Principal Campbell said and just drop any discussion of race in Mexico and move on to Central America.

The Teacher's Room at the McKinley School was like every school in one regard and that is that the teachers talked about the children. Jimmy was eager to learn all he could and would often engage an older teacher in conversation.

Mrs. Holiman and her husband owned one of the largest farms in the area. She was a crusty old gal in her early sixties with gray hair and a little wider than she once was. She was born in the neighboring town and had lived in the area of McKinley all her life, except for four years at college. This day the conversation turned to the impending departure of many of the families.

"Yes, they'll start to leave soon. The work will run out, and they'll leave for the next place. Most of them will go to Mexico and Texas along the border. A few live here all year, but most leave," Mrs. Holiman said.

"But there are a whole lot of houses here. What happens to them?" Jimmy asked.

"Oh, they're owned by the local housing authority,

and they just board them up until the next growing season when the workers come back. Didn't use to be this way. No, we had the braceros. The government would bring just the Mexican men here. The wives and kids would stay in Mexico and not get dragged all over the country. It was better then, didn't have all those kids coming and going from the school. But a lot of people here wanted to keep those braceros out."

"What do you mean? Didn't the farmers need them to do the work?" Jimmy asked.

"Well, sure they did. In 1964, when the bracero program ended, half the strawberry crop was lost because there was nobody to pick them."

"Why did the government stop the program?" Jimmy asked.

"It was those agitators. They were trying to unionize the farmworkers, and they couldn't do it with all these foreign workers here. With that bleeding heart, Lyndon Johnson, in office, they finally put an end to the bracero program." Mrs. Holiman continued, "Now we have a few farmworkers that are legal residents with green cards. But they can't do all the work, so there's hundreds of illegals, wetbacks they call 'em, because a lot of 'em swim the Rio Grande into Texas. Then they make the farm work circuit. When growing season is over, they go to a state where it's cheap to live and nobody bothers them."

"It seems like if they were here illegally, they would be picked up and shipped back," Jimmy said.

"Well every now and then the immigration authorities, *"La Migra"* is what the Mexicans call them, pick up a few and ship 'em to Mexico, but that's just for show. We don't have enough people in this country willing to do farm work to get the jobs done. They never got much of a union formed, so wages are still pretty low for farm work. And you know, farm work is back- breaking work," Mrs. Holiman said.

"Why do the Mexicans come here then and risk getting deported to do low-paid hard work?" Jimmy asked.

"It's because they don't have a choice. There's no work for them in Mexico and if they do get a job, they're paid next to nothing. It's just like the Okies were before them. They come here and do this hard work because they're desperate; there's nothing for them back home. I heard you say your family came here from Oklahoma. I'll bet it wasn't to look at the California poppies," Mrs. Holiman exclaimed.

****

The days rolled by pretty quickly. It was mid-November and things were going well. The children were learning and seemed happy. Even the non-English speakers were making good progress, so it was quite a shock when Jesús came up to Jimmy after school, carrying the math book he had loaned him.

"I bring book," Jesús said.

"You can keep it as long as you need it," Jimmy said.

"No, I bring book we leave," Jesús said.

"You're leaving?" Jimmy said in a shocked voice.

"Yes, we leave. No more work here, we leave," Jesús explained.

"When are you leaving?" Jimmy asked.

"We leave morning," Jesús responded.

"Can I come over to your house and talk to your dad?" At least Jimmy had learned that the dad in the family was in charge, and he knew not to ask to talk to the mother.

"You come," Jesús replied.

"Okay, you tell him I'll be there in a little while."

Jimmy was distressed. Jesús had become one of his star students in just ten weeks; he had mastered most of the fifth grade math requirements and was soon to start on the sixth. He had learned enough receptive English that he understood pretty much everything said to him, and he could respond with simple sentences.   Jimmy wanted to talk to mom and dad about Jesús' education and tell them of his distress at Jesús leaving.

Jimmy went directly to the teacher's room and found Ofelia.   "I need your help," he said.

"Okay, what do you need?" Ofelia asked.

"I want you to go with me to Jesús' house and translate for me," Jimmy said.

"Okay. Lets' go," Ofelia agreed.

It was a short walk from the school to the farmworker housing. As they arrived, Jimmy was surprised at the look of the house. Not much more than a plywood box. Maybe 30' by 20' with a swamp cooler hung on the side. Mr. Preciado and family were busy loading cardboard boxes into their 15-year-old pickup truck.

When Jimmy and Ofelia arrived, the family stopped and looked apprehensively at them.

Ofelia said, *"Buenos Tardes. Comó estan?* (Good afternoon. How are you?)"

"*Muy bien* (very well)," replied Mr. Preciado. He was a muscular man about six feet tall, maybe 180 pounds with a black bushy mustache. He looked a little nervous as if he had been caught in the act of doing something wrong.

Ofelia quickly told Mr. Preciado that Jimmy was Jesús' teacher and wanted to talk to him before they left. Mr. Preciado turned and said something to Jesús' sister, and she soon had set three chairs under a tree in front of the house.

Ofelia introduced them. They had the limp brief handshake that Jimmy had learned was typical of Mexicans. Mr. Preciado beckoned them to be seated.

Jimmy stated that he wanted to talk to them before they left. "Your son, Jesús, is one of the best students in my class, and he is making lots of progress. He has a gift for doing math. He's at the top of the class. And he has learned enough English in just a little while to be able to communicate. I was just wondering if there was any way you could stay here until the school year is over so Jesús can finish the year." As Ofelia translated this, a smile crept over Señor Preciado's face.

"*Un mil de gracias,*" Señor Preciado began. Ofelia translated into English. "***A thousand thanks for coming here to speak to us about Jes***ús***. He's a good boy.***" At that, Mr. Preciado called his wife over and the daughter brought another chair. After introducing his wife, Conchita, Mr. Preciado continued, "***Jes***ús *** is a good boy and a hard worker. We're glad to hear he is doing well in school. I'm honored that you came to my house to try to help my son. My wife and I think of the teachers of our children as second parents. We thank you for your care of him.***"

"Thank you, Mr. Preciado. I appreciate what you are

saying and I will always try to do the best for your children. Can you stay here though so Jesús can continue in school?" Jimmy asked.

"With regret, no. That we cannot do. We have to have work, and there is none here. We are going to Texas or maybe Florida to look for work."

"I understand. Will you come back here again?" Jimmy asked.

"Oh, maybe next year when growing season starts we will be back."

"Will you be able to get Jesús in school where you go?" Jimmy inquired.

"Yes, we will put him school," Mr. Preciado answered.

"Good. I have a letter that I wrote that you can give to his new teacher. It just tells the teacher about how he was doing in each subject. And here, I want Jesús to have this math book; he can keep it. With this, he'll be able to practice math at home. He is very good at it. Have a safe trip," Jimmy said.

"*Vaya con Dios* (Go with God)," Ofelia said as she and Jimmy slowly walked away.

Chapter 23

Dr. Sifuentes was saying, "There is a general election coming up in California this November. There are several candidates and propositions on the ballot that will greatly affect us. I know some of you guys thought a proposition was something you said to a *chica* (girl). But in this case, propositions are proposals to change California laws and regulations. How do we win elections?"

"Stuff the ballot box!" someone shouted from the back of the classroom. As the classroom erupted in laughter, Dr. Sifuentes said, "Hard to do these days, so why don't we do it the old fashioned way and get the votes."

Dr. Sifuentes explained that people needed to be registered to vote. He went through some dismal statistics of the small number of people who actually voted in elections, followed by even sadder statistics of the small percentage of eligible voters who were registered to vote.

"Your assignment in your groups this week is to develop a process to get people registered to vote and to ensure they actually vote. And of course, we are only interested in registering those who see things our way.

"Your instructors and tutors will provide you with demographic data and information that you will need to develop your group plans. They will be available to help with your questions and provide suggestions, but the plan will be yours."

****

"Okay, the area we were given is about 100 miles to the south," Hilario was saying in the morning group meeting. "We need to lay out a plan to visit all the Mexicanos and Chicanos and get them registered to vote. And don't forget to explain what they should be voting for and against. There are six of us, so we will work in pairs. Those that don't speak good Spanish will go with one who does. The area we are going to work has two little towns, one is McKinley and the other is Harpersburg. The rest of the population lives on farms. That's another reason for going in pairs, to take care of each other in these rural areas. You know that the ballot is printed in Spanish now, and here is some literature in Spanish and English to explain the propositions," Hilario said as he held up voter pamphlets.

"Be sure people you talk to *understand* which way to vote on the propositions and which candidates to select. Don't leave them wondering which box to check. We have two days to do this. We have a van with a driver from the college. Meet in front of the dorm tomorrow at 8 a.m. We will return at 10 p.m. and do the same schedule the next day. Questions?"

"Yes. Why are we working 8 a.m. to 10 p.m.?" one group member asked.

"So we can get those that are working and talk to them after work. This is the main part of the harvest season, and the farmworkers will be in the fields from 5 a.m. to around 5 p.m. The commute is two hours each way," Hilario explained.

****

They were ready and eager to go forward and affect

the outcome of this election. They piled into the van and arrived in McKinley at 10 a.m. Hilario, his partner, and two others got out while the last pair rode on to the smaller area of Harpersburg.

Activity was pretty slow until 5 p.m. They were able to talk to some store clerks and truck drivers during the day, but the crowd came at around 5 p.m. They contacted the farmworkers as they arrived at their housing and as they went in and out of the store. The student workers, who were not fluent in Spanish, were at a disadvantage as all the conversations were in Spanish.

"Hola, cómo va? (Hello, how are you doing?)," Hilario said to a dusty sweaty man parking his pickup.

"I'm fine. How are you?" he replied.

"Doing great. Do you have a minute so I can talk to you about an important election?" Hilario asked.

"Okay," the man said somewhat reluctantly.

"We need to vote down some propositions on the ballot in November," Hilario said enthusiastically.

"Oh wait," the man said. *"I thought you were talking about the tenant council election here for the housing. I can't vote in the election. I'm not a citizen and I won't be here in November. I live in Harligen, Texas."*

"Okay. Will you take these papers and give them to anyone you know who can vote?" Hilario asked.

"Yes, I will do that," the man said kindly.

"Thank you," Hilario said.

This was a scene that was to be repeated over and over with all the student organizers in Hilario's group. "We interviewed over a hundred and twenty people during two days. We gave handouts to all of them and explained about the election. Sixty-five of them told us they were not eligible to vote. Several others acted very nervous when we were talking to them. They may be undocumented. The ones who can vote listened and agreed with what we said."

"Thank you for your report, Hilario," Dr. Sifuentes said. "The next report please."

The reports were all very similar from those who were assigned farming regions with no large towns. There were few eligible voters and lots of nervous people who probably thought these students were working with the Migra.

Hilario was very bothered by the lack of eligible voters and asked to meet with Dr. Sifuentes. "Yes, Hilario. You wanted to see me?"

"Yes, I have some questions. We didn't find very many people who are eligible to vote, so how are we going to make any change in the election? We might as well not have bothered," Hilario said frustrated.

"Don't be discouraged," Dr. Sifuentes replied. "Even though they can't vote, they are counted in the census. We have still been able to avoid having the citizenship question asked when the census is done. Even though they can't vote, they still help us get votes.

"Politicians are all about getting re-elected. From the first day they take office, they are planning their re-election. They look at us and they see, for example, that we are 20% of the population in their district, and we vote as a block. 'I better support causes that they want so they will vote for me next election,' they think. They don't know that the eligible voters in that 20% are perhaps 8% or less. Who tells the politicians what the causes are they should support?"

Dr. Sifuentes answered his own question, "Not those folks you interviewed out there! No, we do! We tell them what to support and threaten them with loss of votes if they don't do it. And guess what? They fall in line.

"So don't be discouraged. Those farmworkers are helping us get what we want even if they can't vote. I'll admit, it's a little underhanded, but I never feel bad about manipulating politicians. First of all, many of them are people with huge egos who want to be in charge and will do most anything to get re-elected. And more importantly, the politicians have supported a system which allows poor desperate Mexicans to slip into the United States. They do this so employers can have a pool of cheap labor and make more profits. Just remember, it's important that we never allow any official survey or census to count how many of our people are eligible to vote. That includes avoiding, at all cost, asking a citizenship question on the census.

"It's not only our ability to 'guide' politicians that is helped by the number of Latinos that are counted, but we move up on the Affirmative Action scale too. So, if you and a gringo apply for a job, you are going to get it. Why? Because politicians will vote to support racial discrimination in our favor as long as we keep them convinced that we can deliver the votes. As long as they get re-elected, they believe that we helped that effort.

"And think of the even broader picture. These unfortunate folks that our government lets slip in with hopes of exploiting them are very poor. They also have only a few years of education. Their kids go to school, not knowing English, and they don't do well in school.

"So they drag down all the statistics on income, on school attendance, and high school graduation rates for Latinos. Then we go to our politician friends and use these data to explain why they need to vote for us to have preference in jobs, in education funding, in college placement, in government subsidies. How do you think we got this program you're enrolled in?

"But remember, all this depends on never counting who is eligible to vote and who is even eligible to be in the country. We are simply taking advantage of the fact the gringos wanted to let poor Mexicans sneak into the country to take advantage of their labor. They know they will work hard and cheap. They too, do not want much clarity about whether the Latinos being counted are here legally. They will help us to avoid accurate counts. Meanwhile, we all profit from the huge numbers of our people allowed to sneak into the U.S."

It was this day that Hilario decided his destiny was to be an elected official in California's government. And from that day forward, every move he made was calculated to advance his political career. He would get elected, and he would put down the gringos and raise up Chicanos. If that was done on the backs of poor Mexicanos, so be it. His course was set.

Chapter 24

The summer went fast. Juan had long days working on the family farm, every day except Sunday. Things were going financially well for the family. Juan's school job as a parking lot attendant paid for all costs not covered by his scholarship with a little spending money left over. Tourist traffic had picked up passing through Perryville, and sales at the fruit stand were terrific, up 80% according to Pop.

Herschel stopped by on his way to Los Angeles for the summer. He and Juan had become, not only roommates, but friends.

"Cool," Herschel said as Juan showed him around the farm. "I've never actually seen where peaches grow. And those watermelon bushes, that's something!"

"No, those are black eyed peas. The watermelons grow on those vines over there," Juan corrected.

"Oh yeah, I see now," Herschel replied.

****

When time for the fall semester arrived, Juan was a seasoned veteran, no need even for a ride. He took the Greyhound Bus from Perryville to the 3rd and Mission terminal, got off, and caught the M streetcar right to the campus. One suitcase was all Juan needed, and he lugged it from the 19th Street stop, across the quad, and down the hill to the dorm.

Herschel and Juan got bumped up to the fourth floor for the new school year. They could see Lake Merced from room 404 and were loving the view. Herschel left his surf board at home; he was actually taking an interest in school.

Juan was not only looking forward to a new semester, he was looking forward to seeing all his friends from MEChA (Movimiento Estudiantil Chicano de Aztlán [Chicano Student Movement of Aztlán]). He was approached last semester by the President of the San Francisco State Chapter of MEChA.

"Hello, Juan," the President said. "I'm Gilberto Ramirez. I want to invite you to a MEChA meeting next week on Tuesday night."

"What's MEChA?" Juan asked.

"It's a student organization of many affiliated colleges and organizations. We advocate for the rights of Chicanos," Gilberto explained.

"Oh, I'm sorry. I don't think I want to be a part of that. I had a bad experience in Stockton when a riot broke out," Juan said.

"I know. I heard about that, but we have adopted a non-violent approach to change. Yes, we do sit-ins and sometimes marches, but if any of our members become violent, they are out. You know, Juan, some of the rioting had to happen to get people's attention. Those in power never change by gentle persuasion. We have their attention now, so we continue to push for education reform and civil rights for Chicanos. We do whatever it takes short of a riot. How about next Tuesday? Come and see," Gilberto finished.

Juan did go and was pleased to see that Marina was a member. He was encouraged to hear members speak out against the same kind of insults, neglect, and discrimination he had experienced. He knew he had found his niche in *El Movimiento*.

When Herschel heard about the political action and non-violent demonstrations of MEChA, he wanted to join the group. Juan asked Gilberto about Herschel becoming a member.

"No, we don't want members who are not of Mexican descent. We're trying to overcome that old idea of the melting pot that we all get molded into one. That only works if you're white. You get put in the melting pot and you become an American. When it came to us, someone turned the fire off under the pot. Even though your parents and mine were born here, they still call us Mexicans. We are not Mexicans; we are Americans. My dad fought in World War II to defend this country. But they see our brown skin, call us Mexicans, and don't want us to have the rights of Americans. We think of America not as a melting pot but as a salad. All the parts of a salad make up one salad but you can recognize each part, and they are all important. We want to be recognized. When we march or do a sit-in, Herschel can come but he can't be a member," Gilberto exclaimed.

"Okay, I understand. I'll explain it to him," Juan said.

****

"So you see Herschel, that's the reason you can't join. Do you understand?" Juan asked.

"I understand that your group is as racist as the people

you protest against. You say that race or ethnicity shouldn't affect anything but now I see MEChA discriminating on the basis of ethnicity," Herschel replied.

"I'm sorry you feel that way, Herschel. I hope you don't hold it against me," Juan said.

"Oh no. I know you aren't a racist. I'm just sorry your group has taken a stance that shuts people out because of their ethnic origin. Don't worry, Juan, you and I are good." Herschel smiled.

****

Juan's last year of B.A. study was good too, very good! He participated in MEChA and even became vice president. He and Marina became close friends but stopped short of a romantic relationship. He made the Dean's List again. As Mom and Pop sat in the Cow Palace at his graduation, they heard some words they didn't understand attached to their son's name, Juan Martinez – Magna Cum Laude.

Soon after the graduation parties were over, and promises to keep in touch were made, Juan started packing. One promise, to keep in touch with Marina, he knew he would keep. They were close friends and members of MEChA. She was going home to San Diego and wasn't sure what she would do next. Herschel had decided to make more effort in school and had one more year to do it. After Herschel's graduation, he planned to chase the perfect wave off the coast of Nazare, Portugal, then live in Ireland for a while with his dad's relatives.

Chapter 25

As Jimmy pulled into the school parking lot, he was greeted by Jesús. "Good morning, Teacher. You see I learn some the English?"

"Hey that's great, Jesús. It's good to see you. When did you get back?" Jimmy asked.

"We come here yesternight," Jesús answered.

"I'm glad to see you back. I'm going to see Mr. Campbell right now to be sure I get you in my class. Okay?" Jimmy smiled.

"Sí, it okay. I happy we back. My Popi want talk you. You come after school?" Jesús asked.

"Sure, I'll come to your house. I'll bring Ofelia so she can help me talk to Popi."

Jimmy went directly to the teacher's lounge and found Ofelia preparing some mimeograph test papers. "Good morning, Ofelia. I saw Jesús this morning. He asked if I could go to his house after school. He said his dad wanted to talk. Any idea why?"

Ofelia replied, "Yes, I saw that Jesús was back. I have no idea why Mr. Preciado wants to talk to you."

"Can you go with me? His dad's English is pretty minimal, and I don't trust my Spanish either; it's a work in progress. Can we go right after school?" Jimmy asked.

"That would be best. I don't think Jesús' dad will have started work yet since they just got here last night. I'll meet you after school," Ofelia confirmed.

The day went by quickly. There was so much to do with administering the end-of-year achievement tests and enrolling all the new migrant children that arrived. Before Jimmy knew it, the last bell was ringing and it was time for the visit to Jesús' house.

Ofelia and Jimmy walked the few short blocks to the migrant housing complex and easily found Jesús' home. Jesús' mom and dad were still unloading their things from the pickup and getting the house in order.

The whole neighborhood was buzzing. In many ways it reminded Jimmy of move-in day at a college dorm. The housing had just opened, and all of the 35 units would be occupied by the end of the day. Occupants had come from various parts of the country. Like a college dorm, occupancy was seasonal and was strictly controlled with little input from the occupants.

Unlike a college dorm, the opening and closing dates were determined by the agricultural seasons and could vary year to year. The housing was dedicated for migrant farmworkers only and usually opened mid-spring when the planting and soil preparation was at its height and closed late-fall after harvesting was complete. This housing was greatly coveted by migrant workers as an alternative to living two or three families in a small rental apartment. Or even worse, living in a tent in the county park.

Jesús' father, Renaldo, looked up from his work and greeted Jimmy and Ofelia with a big smile.

"***Hello, welcome to McKinley***," Jimmy said. He had

learned already it is not the Mexican way to jump right into the reason for meeting. He asked through Ofelia how the trip was, inquired about the family in Mexico, and how the pickup was running.

After a rather lengthy discussion, Ofelia said, *"Jesús said you want to talk to Mr. Welch."*

"Yes, I do. I thank you, Mr. Welch, for teaching my boy English. He helps me a lot to talk to American people. He loves school, and I want him to get an education. He studies a lot when we are traveling, and he is really happy to get back to school. And now I know it is helpful to know English. I want to ask you; will you teach me English?"

Renaldo looked at Jimmy with a sincere look of longing on his face. Jimmy could feel and see the great desire to learn. He knew the feeling of wanting to talk with people and being unable to speak their language. Without a moment of hesitation or any thought of how this would be worked out, Jimmy said, "Yes, I will!" with emphasis and a big smile.

Ofelia chimed in, *"That's really good you want to learn English. I'm glad to hear it. It will help you and your family a lot."*

"Yes, for many years I wanted to move back to Mexico when I made some money, but now we want to try to stay here. I want to find a job with a farmer here so my family doesn't have to move. I know if I learn English, I have a better chance to stay," Renaldo said.

"You are very right about that, and it will help your whole family. Mr. Welch is a good teacher; he will help you," Ofelia replied.

"Okay, let me do some planning, and we'll come and visit again and set times for English lessons," Jimmy said. Ofelia translated and Renaldo exclaimed, "*Muchas Gracias. Hasta la vista* (Thank you so much, see you).**"**

As Jimmy and Ofelia walked back to the school, Ofelia said, "That's really great that he wants to learn English. I think there are a couple of others that want to learn too. Would you be willing to do a small English class?"

"Yes I would," Jimmy exclaimed. "If they want to learn, I will certainly honor that by helping them. You and I both know that if they want to stay in this country, they won't make much progress without learning to speak English."

****

Back in the car on the way to Perryville, Jimmy enjoyed the beautiful view around McKinley. The green rolling foothills in the background were a striking counterpoint to the flat level fields. The tan furrows, soon to be planted with green tomatoes, stretched out for miles in every direction until they ran against the cool orchards of apricots and peaches.

The very next day, Jimmy was on it. Meeting with Mr. Campbell, Jimmy said, "I have a request from a parent to teach him English, and Ofelia tells me there are about three others that also want to learn. Do you have any objection if I use my classroom and have the parents come one night a week from 6 p.m. to 8 p.m.?"

"No, I have no objections. In fact, I'll see that you have some coffee, water, and snacks to offer them. You know, soon they're going to be working from about 5 a.m. to 5 p.m. or sometimes later. They're going to be tired and need a little *pick me up*," Mr. Campbell replied.

"Thank you very much. I'd like to start next week, if that's okay?" Jimmy asked.

"That's fine. You let me know the day and I'll have the snacks and drinks ready for you," Mr. Campbell said enthusiastically.

"Okay Ofelia," Jimmy said as he entered the classroom. "We are all clear to start adult English. I'd like to do it Tuesday night from 6 p.m. to 8 p.m. starting next week. Will you pass the word to Renaldo and the others you mentioned?"

"Yes, I'll do that. Jim, I need to ask you something though. You don't speak that much Spanish. How are you going to be able to teach them?" Ofelia inquired.

"I'll be using a method where they have to memorize English conversations and repeat them. Its immersion, and they have a great opportunity because they're living in an English speaking environment. They'll get the meaning of what they are memorizing from pictures and films that I will bring. I would like your help for the first class to explain how I'm going to teach. You can see the first lesson and see how we do it," Jimmy explained excitedly.

Jimmy knew he only had a few weeks of school left, but he hoped to have Renaldo and any others to learn enough that they would be hooked. He also thought that if they get over the embarrassment of speaking English, they can practice with people they meet. The embarrassment was a problem with him too. He was very hesitant to speak the little Spanish he knew and thus did not practice or improve.

****

Tuesday came soon enough, and it was time to test out

the immersion method. He had told his folks he wouldn't be home for dinner and had brought a ham sandwich with him. Six p.m. rolled around and Renaldo came meekly into the room.

Renaldo had faced many dangers and hardships to be in the United Sates working to support his family. But this schoolroom held one of the most fearsome things he could imagine. His experience with education in Mexico was not positive. He had attended four years of elementary school in his rural town. Those years were spent in a multi-age classroom with a teacher who made regular use of the paddle and shaming. One of her favorite sayings, was *"A E I O U el burro sabes mas que tu."* The sound system of the Spanish vowels fit nicely with the phrase "The donkey knows more than you" and she used it liberally.

Ofelia arrived just behind Renaldo and with her was another would-be-student, Tiburcio Cruz. Jimmy welcomed them and offered coffee and snacks. Mr. Campbell was as good as his word; they had coffee, water, finger sandwiches, carrot sticks, and oatmeal raisin cookies.

Ofelia was very helpful to interpret Jimmy's welcome and explain that they should have a snack and soon class would start. The coffee and snacks were well received and consumed. At 6:15 p.m., Jimmy said and Ofelia interpreted, "Let's get started."

Jimmy began by explaining the teaching strategy he would use. He gave each of them a book that was full of illustrations and descriptions of common items found around the house, the grocery store, the doctor's office, and the post office. "We will use these books to learn the names of these things and to memorize the conversations you see there." Ofelia translated his foreign sounding words into Spanish, which was familiar to the two men.

"We will use no Spanish after tonight," Jimmy declared. "Everything will be in English. You will find that soon you will be able to ask for what you need at the store or anywhere. You will see. We will meet here from 6 p.m. to 8 p.m. every Tuesday. From one Tuesday to the next, you can learn more English by practicing the things you learn with people you meet. Any questions? Are you ready to begin?"

Renaldo told Ofelia he had a question. He could only read a little in Spanish and none in English. He asked how he was going to read English. Jimmy responded that first they would be practicing only listening and speaking. Learning how to understand and then produce the words in English. Reading would come later. When Ofelia translated, both men smiled.

"Okay, let's begin. Look at page one," Jimmy said as he held up his book and pointed to the 1 on the page and said again, "Page one. Listen" as he held his hands cupped around his ears. Then Jimmy pointed to each object on page one as he pronounced the names. "House, car, bicycle, dog, cat." He repeated each item several times then he said, "You repeat," as he made a motion with his fingers flaring out of his lips to indicate speaking.

They continued in this manner until the end of the session. Both Renaldo and Tiburcio could repeat all the names of the objects, with an accent to be sure, but well enough to be understood by an English speaker. Jimmy knew that they would be able to follow when he transitioned them to repeating full sentences and finally to reading the sentences.

Chapter 26

"I would like to visit some other families of kids in my class. Will you go with me?" Jimmy asked Ofelia.

"Sure," Ofelia replied, "I'll be glad to."

"How about we go see José's folks next week? I'd like to visit when the kids are doing good rather than just when they're in trouble," explained Jimmy.

"Okay, yes I can go next week, but you don't need me. José's family speaks English," Ofelia offered.

"I'd like you to come anyway this first time. They know you; they don't know me. Is José's family leaving soon?" Jimmy asked.

"No, they live here all year. José's father has a green card," Ofelia answered.

Jimmy was glad of this answer. It was difficult to keep "learning continuity" when the children arrived in the spring, around April or May, left in the fall, around October and November, and returned the next spring.

"What about Mr. Preciado?" Jimmy asked.

"No. I'm not sure, but I don't think he has his papers."

"Doesn't anyone check to see if they are here legally?" Jimmy questioned.

"No, the farmers need them to come and work. Nobody

wants to have the immigration pick them up and take away their workers. The agriculture around here would be in trouble if all the illegals left. The crops wouldn't get planted or harvested," explained Ofelia.

****

Jimmy was still living with his parents. The teacher salary of $4,500 per year didn't go very far. He needed a new car. The old clunker he bought from the wrecking yard for $200 wasn't going to last much longer. It was missing on one cylinder and the other five were losing compression. Even a modest new automobile would cost a year of his teaching salary. He didn't even have enough after saving for three months for a decent down payment on a car. He continued living off the fat of the family and planning his budget to get a new car and then his own place. He would like to live a little closer to McKinley School and be on his own.

One night at dinner, he opened the conversation by saying, "I went to visit one of the families a while ago. They were taking their kids out of school and moving on to find work in the fields somewhere else. Pretty hard on the kids."

Mom replied, "Yes I suppose it is. You should ask your cousin, Jackie, if you want to know."

"What do you mean? I thought you all had relatives to live with and just came from Oklahoma and stayed here," Jimmy asked.

"We did, but your Cousin Jackie's family didn't have any place to stay. He was just a boy in 1937 when the family left Oklahoma and started for California. They had an old Model A with bald tires and about $10 in their pocket.

They got as far as Tucumcari, New Mexico and blew a tire. Lucky for them, your Uncle Albert knew a man there, and he let them camp on his place while Uncle Albert worked at a gas station for a week in exchange for a tire.

"When they finally got to California, they came into Arvin, outside of Bakersfield, and got there just in time to find a campsite. They set up their tent and got right to picking fruit. When that work ran out they went over to Nipomo, on the coast, and got in a migrant camp and picked peas and so on. They spent the next two years following the crops up and down the State of California. Jackie went to about 5 different schools in a school year.

"Nobody wanted the Okies to stay once the crops were picked. If they tried to stay in camp, the Sheriff would come and run 'em off. Albert told us about a time, someplace around Salinas, where they had camped and were picking lettuce. After the season, they had no place to go, so they just stayed there.

"It wasn't but about a week when the Sheriff pulled up and told 'em to be gone by the next day. They packed the next morning and just drove around camping here and there until they found work again.

"Jackie never would have got an education if they kept that up. Lucky for him and them that they came up our way, and when the Kaiser Shipyard began building ships in 1940, Uncle Albert and Aunt Shirley both got jobs there. They finally got an apartment in Richmond and had a place to live close enough to walk to the shipyard.

"When we entered the war in 1941, Uncle Albert was drafted. The shipyard had to pick up production then because we were in the war. Aunt Shirley and a lot of other women went to building ships. They were 'Rosie the Riveters.'

"Jackie went to Nystrom Elementary School and graduated from Richmond High School. He did really well in school. Lord only knows how, after the start he had," Mom finished.

Jimmy still wondered how things would turn out for Jesús if the family continued to migrate. He thought a lot about Cousin Jackie and how much his experience was like that of Jesús. Jimmy realized that a person doesn't have to be a Mexican farmworker to be abused. You just have to be poor and without any means to help yourself. Then society will be okay with you wandering around looking for a way to feed your family while your kids are not getting an education. It's sad to say, but the war was a lucky thing for Cousin Jackie. Jimmy wondered what it would take for Jesús' family to stop chasing the crops. Hopefully, not another war.

****

Thursday came around, and it was time to visit José's family. Jimmy was looking forward to the visit; José was his top student. After class let out, Jimmy and Ofelia made the short walk to José's house. Ofelia did the introductions, and Mr. and Mrs. Garcia seemed very happy to meet Jimmy. They spoke English with only a slight accent. Mr. Garcia said, "Welcome to our home. We are happy to meet you. Please come in and have a seat."

The Garcia's lived in a small yellow house with stucco siding and a flower garden by the entrance. These more permanent houses were reserved for farmworkers who did not migrate.   The permanent seasonal farmworkers had a longer work year and were usually employed by the same labor contractor each year.

Jimmy and Ofelia sat on a couch that had seen a little wear but like the rest of the house was immaculate. On the wall, Jimmy saw a photo of John Kennedy and a painting of Jesus with a crown of thorns. He was to see this decorating theme in many more farmworkers' houses over the years.

"I'm glad to meet you too," Jimmy said. "I want to tell you how well José is doing in school. He's the top student in my class. He always gets his homework done, and if he has questions, he asks and we get them cleared up. He's very good in math, and his English is just about perfect. Before Ofelia got here, he helped me with the students that didn't speak English."

"We are glad to hear that. We always speak English to him at home because we want him to speak good English. We tell him, 'In this country, English is the language.' When he goes to his grandparents, they speak Spanish to him so he keeps both languages."

As they walked back to school, Jimmy questioned Ofelia about why Mr. and Mrs. Garcia speak English so well.

Ofelia explained, "He came here as a bracero right before the program ended, and one of the farmers he worked for helped him get a green card and gave him a permanent job. He's very smart and is now studying for the citizenship test. They're buying the house they live in. He's a foreman now for the big multi-national agriculture company over by Kelsoville."

"What's a green card?" Jimmy asked.

"It's a permit that allows him to be a permanent resident in the U.S." Ofelia answered.

"How did he learn English so well?" Jimmy inquired.

"Mr. Garcia went to school in Mexico and learned a little English there. Do you know Mrs. Holiman?" Ofelia asked.

"Yes, she's one of our teachers," Jimmy replied.

"Her husband was the farmer who helped Mr. Garcia get the green card. Then Mr. Holiman helped him enroll in adult school to learn English," Ofelia explained.

"I've noticed that most of the other parents speak only Spanish. Why don't they learn English?" Jimmy asked.

"For most of them, it's because they don't plan to stay here. They only want to save some money and then go back to Mexico. They dream that they can buy a little grocery store or a small farm with the money they make here and live well in Mexico. I know people that have been here ten years and don't know English because they are always planning to move back to Mexico. Sad, but most of them are never able to do it. They go to Mexico every year around December and stay a month or two, then they come back. When they talk about family and good times, it's always Mexico they're talking about. They want to live there, but most can't save enough to make their dream come true. All the farmers and businesses around here have someone to speak Spanish to them so they never have to learn English to get along," Ofelia explained.

As Ofelia finished, Jimmy's thoughts drifted back to the annual trips of his youth to Oklahoma. They were joyous times with family. Jimmy loved his grandparents, and they loved him. It was so much fun going fishing with Grandpa, swimming in the community pool where his mom and dad had swum as children, and on the warm summer evenings, listening to the adults in his extended family, tell stories of the family history.

And the food, things he would never have in California — fried okra, fresh black-eyed peas cooked in bacon, crispy fried channel catfish straight from the river, pecan pie, and strawberry Nehi soda. Yes, Jimmy understood what it was like to be separated from the place and the people you loved by economics.

****

Fall morphed into winter, and the rainy days were followed by blinding fog from December through March. Jimmy continued to try to learn all he could that would help him to be a better teacher to his class; kids he now saw as in great danger of not getting an education. By December tenth, his class had dwindled to eighteen children of permanent residents. The migrant children had moved on.

Jimmy's parents' early admonition was, "Get a good education. It's something no one can take away from you, and you'll have a better life." He knew what they said was true, and he wanted to be sure he gave the best education he could to those in his class. He tried to learn all he could about how to best teach this group of individuals so foreign to him.

****

Spring finally came and with it the warm weather, abundant wild flowers, and migrants. It was growing season; there was work to do and they were back. Jimmy's class now swelled from eighteen to thirty-four with at least

141

five that were Spanish-only speakers. He had to hustle to find enough textbooks and paper and pencils for all of them.

Jesús was back in the sixth grade now. He was not speaking much more English than when he left. Jimmy was very glad to see him. He had taken a liking to the boy because he tried so hard. Jimmy knew this boy was gifted in math and could do very well in all subjects with the right instruction.

You don't have to speak English to be smart. This was a new concept to Jimmy. Ethnocentrism is a real thing, he thought as he remembered his stereotype-busting sociology professor. The professor was right; ethnocentrism is a real thing and it cuts us off from lots of good and smart people in the world. It cuts off not only the ethnic majority, but the ethnic and racial minorities as well. The minorities are also afflicted with its power to separate people. They just don't voice their prejudices as openly as the majority.

Jimmy was just getting the new class well organized when he got a message from the principal to come to his office after school. Oh no, what could be wrong? Finally the last bell rang and lots of happy kids poured out of the classrooms while Jimmy made his way to the office.

"Come in," Principal Campbell said. "I've got an offer I want to make to you." Jimmy hoped the relief he felt didn't show on his face. "There's an institute being sponsored by San Francisco State this summer. It's for teachers that work with primarily Mexican-American students. Interested?"

"Yes, I'm very interested," Jimmy replied.

"You would go to class one day a week for six hours and study the Spanish language and Mexican culture.

This program starts a week after school gets out until July 3rd. Then you would be taken to Mexico and placed with a family until the third week in August. You would be brought back to California just in time to be able to prepare for school opening. Now, are you still interested?"

"Yes. I'm beyond interested. I would love to do this; I just don't know if I can afford it?" Jimmy anxiously replied.

"Not to worry. This is being done through a special grant to the college. I'm recommending you, and if you are selected it will be at no cost to you. I do want to warn you though, the family you will be placed with will be in a rural part of Mexico. This isn't a vacation to Acapulco. Most of the Mexican farmworkers that come to California are from very rural farming areas of Mexico, so you will be placed in a similar rural area. It's possible you may be in a home without electricity or indoor plumbing. Still interested?" Mr. Campbell asked with a giggle in his voice.

"Absolutely!" exclaimed Jimmy.

"Okay, I'm sending your name to the district office as my nominee. Complete this application and return it to me by day after tomorrow."

****

It was a beautiful late spring day when Mr. Campbell called Jimmy into his office to tell him that he had been selected for the institute. Jimmy could barely contain his soaring excitement. Jimmy was doubly glad now that he had saved enough money for a down payment on a new car. He not only needed it to make the 30-mile drive from Perryville to McKinley, but now he would need it to make the weekly drive of 140 miles round trip to the San Francisco State College. The Chevy Nova wasn't anything fancy, but it was reliable and would get him where he needed to go. Jimmy definitely was not a car guy. It was just transportation, not an extension of his personality.

The days went by like a runaway train. Jimmy was completely engrossed in how to teach thirty-four fifth and sixth graders, eight of whom spoke no English. Jesús was back, and that pleased Jimmy greatly. Jesús had not been to school since he left last year. On the upside, the math book Jimmy had sent with him served Jesús well. He could solve most of the problems on the worksheet pages Jimmy provided. Jimmy was sure Jesús would test at about the seventh grade level in math even though he was only 11 years old and in the sixth grade.

****

June rolled around much too quickly, and it was time for the school year to end and his adventure at the institute to begin. It was also time for most of his fifth and sixth graders to go back to work in the fields. These were not summer jobs to earn money to buy things they wanted. No, their labor was devoted to supporting the family. Every penny they earned would go into the family budget to buy necessities.

Jimmy had learned a little Spanish from the kids during the year, and so he bid them '*hasta la vista* (bye, see you).' They giggled a bit at his thick gringo accent but replied 'hasta la vista. *Vaya Con Dios* (Go with God).' They chorused because he had told them he would be traveling to Mexico during the summer. He left school that day full of sadness and excitement. He had grown to love being with the kids but also was very excited for his new learning opportunity.

The week between the end of school and first institute

day seemed like it would never end. But finally the day arrived, and at 6:00 a.m., Jimmy started the drive for San Francisco State. Even though the highways were not great, the traffic was very light. He estimated that the 70 mile drive from Perryville to San Francisco State would take about two hours.

Jimmy was excited for the institute but also for the chance to go back and see the campus where he once roamed as a student. The institute was being held in the Humanities Building, Rooms 101 and 102. He knew exactly where the rooms were. He had taken The History of American Ideas in Room 101. He also knew where to find free student parking on Font Blvd. His 6:00 a.m. departure should have him parking at around 8 a.m. and making the 10-minute walk to the classroom to arrive at least 20 minutes before the 8:30 a.m. start time.

Just as he planned, Jimmy arrived in plenty of time to get settled into a student desk chair in Room 101. It was a good feeling to be a student again. Jimmy had loved his student years and was looking forward to another great learning experience. He looked out the window at the fog-shrouded library building and thought to himself, this is a typical San Francisco summer day. It was a day much unlike the 80-degree day Jimmy had left at 6:00 a.m. in the San Joaquin Valley.

A middle-aged, well-dressed Latino man entered the room and began speaking, "Hello and good morning. My name is Dr. Hector Suárez. I am the director of the institute. You have each been selected by your school district and the institute committee to participate in this program. Congratulations on being part of this pilot group."

Jimmy paid close attention as Dr. Suárez introduced

himself. "I'm a professor at San Diego State. I was born in Tijuana and educated in the San Diego public schools. My family moved to San Diego when I was a child, and I was raised there with summers spent in Tijuana with my Tía (aunt) Juana and Tío (uncle) Ricardo. I'm pleased to be here and looking forward to a wonderful learning experience for all of us."

Class had finally begun. After each of the 20 students introduced themselves and put on their name tags, Dr. Suárez continued, "I'd like to start by outlining the next two and a half months. Please open the packet on your desk to page one, titled *Schedule*. Let's go over it. You will attend classes on Wednesdays from 8:30 a.m. until 3:30 p.m. with one hour for lunch and conversation. From 8:30 a.m. to 11:30 a.m. on each of our meeting days, you will be learning how to speak Spanish. We are doing this so you may better participate when you go to Mexico. We will be using the audio-lingual method of teaching which means we will be using the language, not talking about it. There will be a thirty minute time period from 8:30 a.m. to 9 a.m. in which we will speak English and answer any questions you have about Spanish. You will be expected to use the tape recorders which we will issue to you to listen, to repeat, and to memorize each week's lesson.

"At 11:30, lunch will be provided in Room 102. At 12:15, we will open the partition between Rooms 101 and 102 and we will be joined by 15 Mexican-American college students. These students have been selected from several colleges and universities. They're all seniors and will be beginning their teacher training in the fall.

"Their purpose in being here is twofold: first to help you learn more about the experiences of Mexican-Americans in the schools, and secondly for them to learn about Mexico and Mexican culture along with you. None of them have ever been to Mexico.

"At 3:30, we will dismiss so those of you commuting out of the city, can get across the bridge before the back-up starts.

"That covers the schedule until mid-July. On July 12th we will board a bus for Mexicali, Mexico. Those of you from the Valley will board in Stockton. Those staying in the city will board in front of the men's dorm here at State.

"We will travel by bus to Mexicali, Mexico where we will board a train to Mexico City. From there you will be taken to the homes in the countryside where you will spend the next month. On August 14th we will meet in Mexico City and board the train for the return trip. Are there any questions?"

There were no questions as everyone sat stunned by the immensity of what they were about to experience.

Into the Chevy Nova at 6:00 a.m. the next Wednesday, across the Bay Bridge, down Fell Street through the park, and finally down 19th Avenue to Font and a great parking spot. Jimmy walked into the Humanities Building Room 101, settled in just in time, as the Spanish teacher, Señor Girón, walked in and introduced himself. He was a distinguished-looking gentleman in his early fifties. He was about 5'10" with a small thin mustache and curly jet black hair. He had a smooth coffee and cream complexion with very few signs of aging. It was rumored that he had been an interpreter at the United Nations and now taught at the Defense Language Institute in Monterey, California, but he said little about himself.

Señor Girón began in English by explaining that his teaching method required students to memorize dialogues and then practice using them in class. "Pronunciation and word usage will be corrected as we practice in class. This is the last English you will hear from me unless the building is on fire."

He immediately began in Spanish, ***We will begin on page two with José and María talking. Everyone listen to me as I read the dialogue.*** He put his hand behind his ear to indicate listening. ***Now as I read each line, you repeat it.*** He then put his hand in front of his mouth and made a motion like throwing kisses to indicate that they should speak.

Jimmy was familiar with this method. He had read about it and used it in teaching Renaldo and Tiburcio. But watching Señor Girón helped Jimmy learn a great deal more about how to use it.

The students quickly learned the words for listen and speak. It went well for the rest of the almost five week session. Students would memorize the written dialogue. Then they spent the first part of class correcting pronunciation and word use by copying Señor Girón. Finally, the last half of class was spent taking the parts of the dialogue and repeating and responding to each other, as if doing a play. They were learning in this intense Spanish-only environment, and they all felt eager to try out their new found language ability.

Jimmy experienced profound empathy for Jesús and mono-lingual students like him. Jimmy knew that at times Señor Girón was saying something important, but he just didn't get it. It was just noise with no meaning. He couldn't help but think of Jesús and how he must feel the same frustration of wanting to learn but being unable to understand what was being said.

Lunch everyday was a continuation of instruction. On the first day, it was tacos, Mexican style which means the tortilla is soft. The class was presented with a buffet of corn tortillas, chopped cilantro, diced boiled chicken, diced tomatoes, and green salsa. One of the Mexican-American students Sylvia, demonstrated and explained the proper way to make and eat a taco.

This was an exotic food to the 20 teachers and students. The only tacos known to Jimmy and his crowd were at Taco Bell, and Perryville didn't even have a Taco Bell. Jimmy was shocked to learn that crispy tacos did not exist in Mexico. The food delivered at the Taco Bells, at that time, was only vaguely Mexican. A taco, like they were eating, was only to be had at a few small Mexican restaurants in the Mexican part of large towns. Of course in Los Angeles and parts further south, closer to the U.S.-Mexico border, such food was more available. But this was Northern California and the teachers and students were feasting on this new strange and delicious food.

Immediately after lunch, the afternoon session on Mexican culture began. Dr. Suárez did this section himself. It seemed that he was hesitant to let anyone else do what he obviously felt was the most important classroom part of the institute. His instruction in this part was in English to ensure that all of the teachers understood. There were also five among the Mexican-American students who did not speak Spanish.

Dr. Suárez was an imposing figure; he was about 6'

and 195 pounds. He appeared very physically fit. He had piercing, almost black, eyes under bushy gray-speckled eyebrows. His shock of black hair was also speckled with gray and was combed straight back with no part. His small thin mustache was kept neatly trimmed. He dressed in slacks and a sport coat with a white shirt and conservative brown tie.

Dr. Suárez had been a Professor of Humanities at San Diego State specializing in Latin American history and culture for over 25 years. His voice was soft; he seemed a quiet and kind man. But as the students soon discovered, he was all business, and his business was ensuring that they learned the Spanish language and Mexican culture.

He began his lecture this day by telling a story from his high school teaching days. "A seventeen-year-old boy named José was always getting into trouble, fighting and cutting school. He was about to be expelled, so I asked the principal if I could speak with him and try to help him stay in school. The principal agreed, and José was directed to meet with me twice a week after school. We would talk about any issues he was having and work them out. During the course of several meetings, the reason he was having problems became clear.

"First, he complained about being treated like a baby. He was from Michoacán and had been in the United States only two years. He was obviously smart because he had learned to speak English pretty well in two years. When I asked him how he learned to speak English, he said, 'watching television and listening to people.' But when he left Michoacán, he was already being treated like a man and had the expectations of an adult assigned to him. However, in the school he was treated as a teenager. He found this treatment to be demeaning and insulting, and he rebelled against it.

"During several more meetings it finally became clear that he did not like being told what to do by the women teachers. I understood this because in Mexico, men are in charge; women are to follow their directions. In a family, a younger brother is not only allowed but taught to give his older sister directions. But he is also required to look out for her and protect her.

"It became clear very soon that José was a victim of a clash of cultures. All of his upbringing had taught him that he was a man and that women were to follow the directions of men and should stay in the background and be protected. Over time I was able to help him understand that he could maintain those beliefs and act on them in Mexico, where people held similar beliefs. At school, in the United States, he would have to modify his behavior. He was a smart kid and he said, 'Okay, I will do it and then when I make some money, I will go back to Michoacán.'

"I told you this long story to emphasize that there are several areas where Mexican and United States culture differ. Women in the U. S. do not think they have the freedoms that they should have, and they are probably right. But Mexican women have far fewer freedoms. In Mexico today, women are to be cherished, protected, and in the home cooking, cleaning, and making a nice place for the husband and children. Men are to protect women and provide for them so they have the means to provide a nice home.

"I know it's always dangerous to make generalizations about people, but what I'm trying to do here is alert you to some possible problem areas you may encounter in dealing with students and parents who have beliefs foreign to you. It's no secret that Mexicans and Mexican-Americans in the U.S. have faced discrimination. There are many ways in which this has been purposeful and deliberate. But what I plan to do here is point out some ways in which there may be clashes that are not intentional, but are the result of cultural differences.

"And while we are on the topic of discrimination, let me caution you college students. I know you have never been to Mexico, but when you go there, you may find another kind of discrimination. When you have been born here in the U.S., many Mexican citizens don't think of you as Mexican. They have a word 'Pocho' which they use to describe people of Mexican descent who are born and living in the U.S. They think of you this way even if both your parents were born in Mexico."

Dr. Suárez continued in his quiet voice. "Those of you that speak Spanish, the Spanish you use is often different than is used in Mexico today. The Spanish of California has incorporated lots of words from English with a Spanish accent. We are having you travel to Mexico so you can see the beauty and grandeur from which your ancestors came. But if they refuse to accept that you are Mexican, ask them this, 'If a dog has pups in an oven, are they pups or are they muffins?' Enough about that. Let's move on."

Jimmy was startled as he listened to this discussion. He was shocked that Mexicans would not think of these brown students in the room as Mexican. Why not? Everyone in the teacher group thought of them as Mexicans. Then too he was disturbed to think of these college students as being discriminated against in the U.S. and also in Mexico. He knew people in the U.S. discriminated against them but didn't know people in Mexico did the same. That's a tough situation, Jimmy thought.

Jimmy was puzzled too about Dr. Suárez's comments regarding cultural clashes. He had never thought of things that way. He just thought of Mexicans in the U.S. as ignorant, awkward, and trouble makers. But that point of view was changing dramatically and quickly.

Jimmy thought that the sociology professor, Dr. Goldman, was really right about ethnocentrism. It's alive and well in Mexico too. But quickly, his thoughts turned to his own extended family and how they were treated in California. That wasn't ethnocentrism. They were all people from western European countries. They were white, not distinguishable in looks from other Californians. It was something else that drove entrenched Californians to treat the Okie arrivals so badly. It was because the Okies were poor, powerless, and spoke a dialect of English slightly different from native Californians. They were abused by employers and society in general because they did not have the choices that having money provided. They could not fight back.

Could it be that Mexicans abused other Mexicans for the same reasons? That they were poor and had no power. The realization that there were so many parallels between the California Mexican families and his own family hit Jimmy like an NFL linebacker. California Mexicans don't speak the same kind of Spanish that Mexicans in Mexico speak just like Okies didn't speak the same kind of English that California people spoke. Jimmy had even seen an 'Okie vocabulary list' which was given to 1930s social workers in California.

Okies had been poor as many California Mexican immigrants were poor now. Okies were migrant farmworkers and suffered many of the same problems now experienced by Mexican migrant farmworkers. Okies in the early days banded together, tended to live in neighborhoods together and talked a lot about how and when they were going back to Oklahoma, just as many California Mexican immigrants now lived in enclaves and talked about going back to Mexico.

One very big difference though was that Okies were now assimilated into the larger society and were in all social strata. While California Mexican immigrants, even those that had been in California for three or more generations, remained for the most part in poverty and outside the mainstream. They still suffered from discrimination. That is ethnocentrism in action, Jimmy thought.

Dr. Suárez continued, and Jimmy jerked his meandering mind back to the discussion at hand. "So never mind what they say. We are going to Mexico for you and our teachers to be able to see the real Mexico, not the Tijuana, Mexico. In fact, you will find that Mexicans refer to the border towns, like Tijuana, as the *frontera* (the frontier).

"Now I want to speak to you about something else. *Hablando de otra cosa* (speaking of something else), as we say in Spanish. That 'something else' is your main assignment for this culture part of the institute. You are to write a paper on some aspect of Mexican culture as it exists in the United States, preferably as it is in California. You will then do an oral presentation of no more than ten minutes to the class. You will decide on your topic by next week, write a short paragraph describing it, and submit it to me. I may need to discuss some topics with you."

****

The days flew by, and soon it was time for the final classroom activities and preparation for travel to Mexico. The Spanish class by Señor Girón had been very helpful. The teachers and mono-lingual students could now articulate a few basic needs and utter a few pleasantries. Mostly it had taught them how difficult it is to learn a second language. For Jimmy, it had definitely increased his sensitivity to the plight of his non-English speaking students.

Now it was time to give the oral presentation. Jimmy wasn't thrilled about doing it, but he thought he had an interesting topic. Dr. Suárez thought so too. He had read Jimmy's paper and returned it with several thoughtful comments and an A.

Finally it was time for Jimmy's report, and he walked quickly to the front of the room with his 3"x5" cards in hand. He was a little nervous and launched right into describing his thesis: there are many similarities between the ill treatment of the Okies arriving in California and that of the Mexicans arriving in California. He listed and explained his points with great exactness and clarity.

When Jimmy was finished, Señor Suárez asked for questions   and comments from the class. A grossly overweight football player from Fresno State College was the first with his hand up.

"Yes, Fernando?" said Dr. Suárez.

"I think this whole thing he said is all wrong. I'm tired of people studying us and trying to make excuses for our treatment. The Okie kids didn't have the problems like we have. They don't like us just because we're Mexicans, not because of anything else," Fernando said.

As Jimmy started to reply, Dr. Suárez spoke up, "Excuse me, Jim. I appreciate your comments, Fernando, but I would like to put a word in here for the benefit of our college students. I would like to read something from a book titled *Children of the Dust Bowl* by Jerry Stanley.

"Mr. Stanley says, 'When one Okie family went to downtown Bakersfield, they saw signs on all business windows reading: *No Okies Allowed*! Okies stood out ... because they spoke differently and wore shabby clothes ... when a father identified a man in a field as an Okie cotton picker, his son said, 'Daddy, them things look almost like people when they stand on their hind legs, don't they?'"

Dr. Suárez looked up from the book into a room full of shocked faces. He said, "I won't read anymore, but I can tell you there is solid documentation here outlining the dehumanization and abuse which this group, called Okies, received. Some of them died because they were refused medical care. Many of the children were not allowed to attend school. Charges that the Okies were taking jobs from Californians and making their taxes go up were rampant. Sound familiar?

"I didn't read this to you for any other reason than to say perhaps some further study of the politics and economics affecting immigration to, and migration within, the United States would be helpful to our college students." Dr. Suárez finished, nodded to Jimmy, and sat down. After several more questions and comments, Jimmy was finished with his report and glad of it.

Since this was the last day of class before the Mexico trip, there was a small reception after class. Jimmy was busy gulping down boiled shrimp when one of the female college students approached him. "Are you learning a lot?" she asked.

"Yes I am. It's very interesting," Jimmy replied.

She pointed to Jimmy's bushy black mustache as she said, "I guess you grew that mustache because you are trying to imitate us. Well, you can't do it. We have a certain way of walking, a look about us, and you can never imitate it."

"Okay, thanks for the information," Jimmy said as he walked away. *Why would she think I want to imitate Mexicans? He wondered.*

Then Jimmy's thoughts went back to a few weeks ago. He'd had his eye on Sylvia ever since the time she had done the taco presentation. He liked her very direct and clear manner of speaking. He loved the cadence of her speech in accent-free English and the fact that she seemed genuinely interested in the teacher group. He also liked the fact that she was gorgeous with long hair that was black as a raven's wing. She was tall and athletic-looking with piercing dark eyes and mocha colored skin. She was more his age, having worked in the family restaurant in Los Angeles two years before entering college.

Jimmy had been chatting with her after class and just spontaneously asked her to dinner in the city. As she heard the question, she simply froze. There was a moment when Jimmy thought she had not understood the question. Her eyes looked back and forth between Jimmy and the floor.

Finally she replied, "I'm so sorry, Jim, but I couldn't possibly do that. My family would be very upset if they knew I went out with a white boy. I had a white boyfriend while I was in high school until my father found out. Then he told me I could never see him again or I would be kicked out of the family."

As Jimmy walked across the quad, past the library to his parking spot, he thought about both of his classroom encounters. Can't imagine why anyone would want to think I'm trying to be a Mexican, he thought, and Sylvia is 23 years old and still does what Daddy says. Very curious!

Jimmy thought, Sylvia's dad is a racist. And that Fresno State football guy, he didn't like me and I don't even really know him. It's just because I'm white. Wow, ethnocentrism is alive and well among the Mexicans.

Chapter 27

Finally, the big day came. It was time to go to Mexico. Jimmy had hardly slept the night before; he was up well before departure time. His dad agreed to drive him to Stockton to catch the bus to Mexicali with his classmates.

Jimmy's mom waved from the front porch as they drove into the rising sun. It was July now, and soon that sun would be blazing down on the valley. But for now, it was just peeping over the Sierra Nevada Mountains.

They reached the bus pickup point in time to see another of Jimmy's classmates being left there. As Jimmy lifted his one allowed suitcase out of the car trunk, he said, "Bye Dad. See you in a few weeks."

"Okay Son. Have a good time and take care of yourself," Dad replied.

The rented tour bus pulled up already half-full with all fifteen of the college students and five of the teachers. The remaining fifteen Stockton area teachers were greeted by Señor Girón and Dr. Suárez as they put their suitcases in the belly of the bus. Soon, they were on their way for the long drive to Mexicali.

After greeting his classmates, Jimmy slept for about four hours of the trip. The sleepless night of excitement he had just spent left him weary. He awoke to find his classmates sleeping, reading, or engaged in quiet conversation. The college students sat together and had little interaction with the teachers. The college students were housed in the dorms on the San Francisco State campus and had formed some tight bonds. Whereas the teachers had commuted and were less acquainted with each other.

After a long, uneventful, and frankly boring drive, the bus disgorged its passengers into a warm muggy night at Boarding Area #3 at the Mexicali Train Station. Two rest stops along the way had stretched the 11-hour bus ride to 12 hours. There was still plenty of time for Señor Girón and Dr. Suárez to hand out the tourist cards before departure. Proof of United States citizenship was all that was needed to enter Mexico.

Jimmy boarded the assigned train car with some trepidation, remembering Dr. Suárez's class warning to bring some canned food as the presence of a dining car was never a certainty. Jimmy knew that the first-class train accommodations could mirror the shabbiness of the only place he had seen in Mexico . . . Tijuana.

But a wonderful surprise awaited. Jimmy found his seat very quickly, suitcase in hand. His seat, as were all the others, was in a small room with a sliding door to the hallway. The "seat" was a wonderful easy chair the size of dad's La-Z-Boy. Situated in a corner was a commode and just above it a sink and mirror. Jimmy plopped down in the recliner seat and stared out the picture window which covered most of the exterior wall.

The dark gray on light gray color scheme of the upholstery and walls was nicely accented by the pearl-white bathroom fixtures. The room fairly screamed *luxury*.

Jimmy's fears of a donkey-cart-like ride went away. The long train ride to Mexico City with a change in Guadalajara would be a pleasure. Dining car or not, Jimmy didn't care. He had enough canned provisions in his suitcase to last the entire trip.

As the huge train station clock struck 11, and with a loud clang and several halting jerks, they were off. Jimmy sat in his oversized chair and watched the city roll by as they left Mexicali. There wasn't much to see after the lights of the city faded into the black inkiness of the desert night. Very soon after departure, there was a light tapping on his door. Jimmy tentatively opened it to find a porter in a starched white shirt and navy blue slacks.

Jimmy's Spanish lessons of the last few weeks had been helpful but had not prepared him to understand what this fellow was saying. Finally as the porter motioned for Jimmy to leave the room, he understood the word *cama* (bed). Perplexed but finally acquiescing to the porter's insistence, Jimmy stepped into the hallway. With a few deft moves, the porter transformed Jimmy's oversized chair into a bed which covered all but two feet of the entryway to the room.

With the assurance of a professional, the porter then reached into the sliver of a closet and brought out the sheets and blanket and made the bed. The bed fit nicely just above the sink and commode. Jimmy was thinking, what if I have to pee in the night? The porter motioned to a small lever under the bed and showed Jimmy how it easily became a chair again. With a final flourish, the porter fitted a two-step ladder to the bottom of the bed frame and bid Jimmy, "*buenos noches* (good night)."

It was a good night. Lulled to sleep by the slight rocking of the car and rhythmic clickity-clacking of the steel wheels on the rails, Jimmy drifted off to sleep. He was not aware of anything until he awoke with a start wondering where he was. That question was quickly answered by the view out the top half of his picture window. The sun was just rising over a striking desert landscape.

Within a few minutes of awakening, Jimmy saw a sign identifying the city of Benjamin Hill, and the train began to slow. They were exchanging some existing passengers for new ones. But what interested Jimmy most about this place was its name. Not a very Mexican sounding name, he thought.

Jimmy's curiosity was satisfied by Señor Girón, who explained. "Benjamin Hill was a hero of the Mexican revolution of 1910. He was a general in the forces supporting Madero, had studied in Germany, and was well-schooled in military strategy. He was appointed Governor of the State of Sonora in 1914, and this town was named after him."

"Yes, but why 'Hill?' That doesn't sound very Mexican," Jimmy said.

"You will find that not everyone in Mexico is descended from the Spanish. It is a much more diverse country than many believe. Look in the Mexico City phone book when you get there and see the varied ethnic surnames," Señor Girón further explained.

The desert-scape flew by as they left Benjamin Hill. Still no dining car, but there was rich, thick black coffee in the club car. Jimmy finished his second cup and arrived at his room to find it transformed again into a huge easy chair with a view out the picture window.

Jimmy sat down, retrieved his suitcase from the slender closet, and removed some of his food stock. Dr. Suárez was certainly correct in warning them to bring food. There was no dining car, and the club car only served beverages. So, he breakfasted on canned sausages and soda crackers, washed down with *agua mineral sin gas* (mineral water without carbonation). After a filling breakfast, he leaned back and watched Mexico roll by.

Eventually the landscape gave up its dry prickly look and took on a coat of green. They were passing Mazatlán through what looked to Jimmy like a jungle. A beautiful landscape appeared with lush greenery to the left, and the Pacific Ocean to the right. Jimmy was entranced; what beautiful country, he thought. He had never imagined seeing country so wildly different than anything he had ever seen before. He had seen desert before. The many trips back to visit relatives in Oklahoma had taken the family through the Mojave Desert. But this greenery was beyond his experience.

For the rest of the day, Jimmy watched the changing moods and look of Mexico. He watched from his room and from the outdoor platform between cars so he could smell the passing countryside. Late afternoon, he watched from the club car with a Modelo Negra beer in hand. He was amazed and engrossed with the countryside. He was startled to learn from Señor Girón that Mazatlán was founded in 1531, 76 years before the English planted a colony in Jamestown.

Once again, the porter arrived, but this time Jimmy knew to just get out of the way and let the man do his job. This time he tried some of his halting Spanish on the porter and was rewarded with a huge smile and a string of Spanish, to which Jimmy could only reply "*no entiendo* (I don't understand)." To that response, the porter stuck out his hand for a shake. "Have a good trip," he said in heavily-accented English. "Vaya Con Dios," he continued in perfectly accented Spanish which Jimmy still could not understand.

Jimmy jerked awake. The safety lights in the corridor were all he could see as he slid his compartment door open. There it came again … *Clunk! Bang!* The entire car shook. The train was moving backwards. What was happening? Jimmy stepped to the outside platform and saw row after row of train tracks, some with trains on them and some empty. Then he remembered that their car was going to be switched at Guadalajara and attached to a train going to Mexico City.

Jimmy peeked around the side of the car and watched the switchman giving hand signals to direct the engineer. The switchman's battery-operated lantern was a beacon to the engineer who watched it intently. The lantern was swung back and forth to tell the engineer to stop as the switchman uncoupled Jimmy's car and let it roll onto the new track he had just opened. Soon the cars with Jimmy and his classmates were attached to the train headed to Mexico City. The switchman gave the 'highball' signal to the engineer by swinging his lantern in a circle over his head. This was the engineer's signal that all cars had been securely attached to the train and it was time to leave. With a lurch and a rattle, the train began to move and was soon gliding along the well-maintained tracks.

A sea of lights was all Jimmy could see as they slowly moved through and out of Guadalajara. It was a large city, and he had been told, a beautiful city. Perhaps they would pass it in the daylight on the return. They were scheduled to reach Mexico City in the early morning, so Jimmy climbed back into his bed, and watching the night roll by, was soon asleep.

Jimmy awoke to the hissing sound of air-operated brakes as they pulled into Mexico City, the Distrito Federal (D.F.), equivalent to the United States' Washington D.C. He had overslept a bit, as the sun was well up and the city was bustling. He jumped out of bed, pulled the lever, turning his bed into a chair again. The train had slowed to a crawl when entering the city, giving Jimmy time to hurriedly brush his teeth and grab his suitcase.

All institute participants had been given instructions to meet on Platform 1 after departing the train, and Jimmy was ready. Soon he heard the hiss of air brakes, and the train came to a shuddering stop. People began to pour off the train like flour through a sifter. Jimmy, suitcase in hand, joined the flow of the crowd.

Jimmy had no trouble finding Platform 1. As soon as Señor Girón and Dr. Suarez had all of their ducks in a row, they and their charges walked out of the cavernous railway station. They were immediately hit by the overwhelming smell of car exhaust fumes. The sky above struggled to be blue and sunny but could only manage a slightly gray tint.

No wonder the travelers were greeted by such bad air quality. The city of nearly nine million was set in a deep bowl surrounded by mountains. Every bit of fume that billowed out of the hundreds of thousands of cars on the roads stayed in the city. The 80-degree temperature added to the discomfort. Jimmy's little group began to wilt a bit, buoyed only by their adrenaline rush over the excitement of this great city.

Dr. Suárez moved them along and soon found their chartered bus. Suitcases stored below, they headed for the Hotel Geneve in the Zona Rosa.

The ride there was comfortable in the air-conditioned tour bus. Jimmy looked at the congested honking traffic and thought, what a mess it would be to drive in this city. It reminded him of the chaos on the roadways in Rome minus the thousands of Roman motorbikes.

The grandeur of the city could not be diminished by smog and traffic. Soon they were on the Paseo De La Reforma. The broad tree-lined avenue brought up memories of Jimmy's walk down the Champs-Élysées in Paris. This grand avenue was crowned by the Angel of Independence known to most Mexicans only as El Angel. This grand gold angel was set atop a magnificent Corinthian column. It was inaugurated on Mexican Independence Day, September 16, 1910, to celebrate 100 years of independence from Spain.

Jimmy could hardly wait to get off the bus and hit the streets to experience this wonderful city, much as he had done in Rome, Paris, and the other great cities of Europe. He had found that the best way to know a city was to walk its streets.

He would have to wait for that. Señor Girón and Dr. Suárez had a schedule which would be reviewed shortly after checking into the hotel. Excitement rose as they pulled into the tourist bus waiting area in front of the Hotel Geneve. Jimmy saw with satisfaction that the hotel was only a short walk from the Angel.

Institute participants lined up at the front desk under the watchful eye of Señor Girón. Upon showing their tourist card, each person was given a key, a room number, and a schedule. A passport was not needed; only a tourist card was required. These cards had been issued by the Mexican consulate in San Francisco. All that was required for issuance was presentation of a document verifying legal United States citizenship or legal United States resident status. All participants had provided a birth certificate or voter registration card to the Embassy.

Since it was still early morning, all were allowed to go to their rooms and freshen up a bit. Jimmy was anxious after the long trip for a shower. He passed through the lobby with its elegant Louis XIV furnishings in utter amazement. He was expecting something more like the $5 a day hotels he had used in Europe.

He held his breath as he placed the large brass key into his second-floor room door. He feared that perhaps this was one of those hotels with a lovely lobby to offset the shabby rooms. He turned the key and tentatively pushed open the door to display a beautiful immaculate room, also with a Louis XIV dresser and side chair. The double bed looked comfy, and it was. Jimmy fell on its billowy comfort and just lay there looking at a beautifully textured and carved ceiling.

After a quick shower in the spacious bathroom, Jimmy slipped into the hotel robe, padded in his bare feet over the thick rich mahogany colored carpet to the side chair, and reviewed the schedule:

Institute of Mexican-American Education
Mexico City Schedule

Day 1:   9:00 a.m.   Arrive at Hotel Geneve.
            11:00 a.m.   Meet in Conference Room 2.
                            Orientation.

	12:30 p.m.	Lunch in the Green Room. This will be the main meal of the day.
	3:30 p.m.	Meet at tourist bus stop in front of hotel, board bus for tour of Mexico City. We will visit Chapultepec Park, Garibaldi Square, the Ballet Folklorico.
	11:00 p.m.	Return to the hotel.
Day 2:	Breakfast on your own. Free time.	
	11:00 a.m.	Meet in Conference Room 2.
	12:00 p.m.	Board bus for lunch at Reina Del Mar Restaurant, tour of City Center and Shopping at Sears.
	8:00 p.m.	Dinner in Green Room.
Day 3:	8:00 a.m.	Breakfast and meeting in Green Room.
	10:00 a.m.	Leave for individual placements with families.

The first-day meeting was a very short review of the schedule. Dr. Suárez described the three areas of Mexico City that would be visited and cautioned everyone that while they had time to roam in Chapultepec Park, not to stray too far from the group.

Lunch was an elaborate affair in the opinion of Jimmy and his fellow students. They were not accustomed to such a mid-day meal. It began with a chicken consommé, followed by a salad with light vinaigrette dressing. The main course was *huachinango al mojo de ajo* (poached red snapper marinated in garlic). This was followed by a dessert of very light fluffy pastry covered with strawberries and drizzled with cream.

The bus left at 4 p.m. for the very short drive to Chapultepec Park. After everyone was seated, Dr. Suárez again gave a last- minute warning to stick together. "This is a big city full of all kinds of people. And you, including you of Mexican descent, stick out like doves in a flock of ravens. Your clothing, your mannerisms, all mark you as foreigners and therefore potential targets. Any questions?"

A young teacher from the Central Valley raised her hand and asked, "Aren't we going to have Mexican food while we're here?"

"What do you mean?" said Dr. Suárez.

"You know, like tacos?" she inquired.

Dr. Suárez patiently explained, "The meal you just had was Mexican food. This is a very diverse country full of all kinds of people. Families all over this city just had a mid-day meal as large as the one you had. As in most countries of the world, the type of food depends on the income of the family. Your meal today was typical of an upper-income family. Usually, in the upper- income families, the meal is prepared and served by a servant who lives in the family home. However, you will find tacos here too, but they will not be Taco Bell tacos. They will be like the ones Sylvia presented at our buffet."

With that, the bus was off to Chapultepec Park. First stop, the monument to the Niños Heroes (Boy Heroes). Señor Girón explained, "This monument commemorates six teenage military cadets who died defending the Chapultepec Castle from invading United States forces during the Mexican-American War of 1847. This is where the line from the 'Halls of Montezuma' in the United States Marine Corp hymn originated. That line in the hymn refers to the battle of Chapultepec when the Marines stormed the Chapultepec Castle. As you can imagine, there are still some bad feelings from many Mexicans about that battle and the more recent incursions by the United States into Mexican territory."

In spite of the abrupt, somewhat negative, introduction to Chapultepec Park, all enjoyed the beautiful grassy spaces and small lakes and ponds. Chapultepec Castle was beautiful with its panoramic views of the city. Its rich history, having served as a military academy, the residence of Maximillian during the French occupation and more recently, as residence to Mexican Presidents, was intriguing to everyone.

Then it was on to the Palacio de Bellas Artes for the Ballet Folklorico. What an experience that was. The crowd was treated to a panorama of various Mexican regions and cultures through the medium of dance and music. Jimmy was particularly taken by one dancer's depiction of a deer. The dancer's alertness and movements of a deer were exactly those of a real deer that Jimmy had observed. As a whole, the experience gave Jimmy a new perspective on the rich variety of cultures and people in Mexico. He had never before envisioned Mexico being such a diverse and interesting part of the world.

Finally the evening wound down with a stop at Garibaldi Square. The square was named after Peppino Garibaldi, a Lieutenant Colonel during the Mexican Revolution.

Jimmy could hear the Mariachi music before they even exited the bus. Señor Girón was certainly right;

this is a gathering place for Mariachi music. They were ushered, among several roving Mariachi groups, to a small restaurant bar reserved for their use. As they were seated, a Mariachi group struck up the instrumental tune, "Jesusita en Chihuahua."

After several Mariachi performances and at least one Ponche de Granada (pomegranate punch), it was time to return to the hotel. The bus left the weary travelers in front of the hotel. They all trooped in, picked up their key from the front desk, and headed to bed.

Next morning, it was up and out again. This was their free half day, and Jimmy intended to make the most of it. For almost a year, Jimmy had wandered around the great cities of Europe and had no doubt he could navigate this one.

A restaurant for breakfast had been recommended by the desk man, and Jimmy headed for it. There was a wonderful menu and a young man waiting tables who was friendly and cracked a huge smile when Jimmy ordered *huevos revueltos, pan tostada y café* (scrambled eggs, toast, coffee). At least Jimmy had learned that much in his month long Spanish lessons.

Between the waiter's halting English and Jimmy's miniscule Spanish, they managed a small conversation in which the waiter indicated his pleasure that Jimmy was trying to learn Spanish. This was much unlike the incident Jimmy had witnessed in Paris when a young American tourist tried to speak French to a waiter. The waiter's response was, "I can't understand you. Please just speak English and don't butcher the French language." Jimmy, in many ways, found the Mexicans very welcoming and happy to help.

After breakfast, it was time to catch a taxi to Xochimilco. Jimmy was thinking of Señor Girón's advice on taxis as he stepped out onto the curb. "Remember that the Volkswagen taxis are much less expensive than the bigger American automobile taxis. And both of them are less expensive than the taxis parked in front of the hotels. The drivers will most likely not speak English, so just print the name of your destination on a slip of paper and hand it to the driver. When you arrive, pay the amount on the meter and a tip if you wish. Taxi rates are strictly controlled in Mexico City, so do not be worried about being overcharged."

Jimmy did as Señor Girón said and was soon seated in the passenger seat of a Volkswagen on his way to Xochimilco. When he arrived, he was astonished. It was everything Señor Girón had said it would be. Colorful barges floated down the last existing canals built by the Aztecs. Mariachi bands floated by in full voice. It was a carnival atmosphere not to be missed. Just think, these waterways were built over 500 years ago by a society as advanced as any in Europe at the time, Jimmy thought.

Jimmy spent a wonderful hour at Xochimilco. After a stop at the Angel monument of the Reforma, it was almost time for the 11 a.m. meeting at the hotel. Jimmy was feeling energetic, so he walked back to the hotel. He was entranced with watching the people and sights as he walked. He thought how beautiful this city is and how it is as interesting as any in Europe. He couldn't believe that he had thought that all of Mexico looked like Tijuana.

After a brief orientation, the group boarded the bus for lunch and another tour of the city. First stop, the Reina Del Mar restaurant. The reserved tables were laid out with white linen table cloths and napkins. A fixed menu was to be served. The first course was a ceviche of conch flown in daily from the east coast of Mexico. This was followed by a cocktail of extra-large shrimp in very tangy sauce. The entre was a choice of prawns or marinated and grilled sea turtle steak.

Jimmy chose the sea turtle because it sounded so exotic. It was as the waiter had promised, tender and delicious. There was no thought at that time of the ecological impact of killing and eating sea turtles. Turtles were a resource that it was thought would last forever. But only a few years later, the turtles were in rapid decline and soon protected by international law.

The meal was finished with an excellent flan, and it was time to board the bus. The next stop was the City Center or Zocalo. This main plaza of the city was built on the site that had been the primary ceremonial center for the Aztec empire. The major buildings of the Mexican Capital were packed into this plaza. On one side was a huge Catholic Cathedral. Just to the east was the National Palace with its Diego Rivera murals depicting the history of Mexico. The square was completed by more government and commercial buildings.

The tour started with the Cathedral. It was begun in 1573 by the Spanish, and placed directly on top of an ancient Aztec Temple. It was inspiring to Jimmy to see it. He thought it was as impressive as any of the European Cathedrals with its spires reaching to heaven.

The Zocalo inspired and haunted Jimmy. He was moved by a sense of loss at not having known that a culture able to build such a place existed at his back door, but he now exalted at having found it!

Back on the bus, Dr. Suárez promised that it would not be a proper trip to Mexico City without some shopping. "We will be going to a major and famous department store in the city. You may have heard of it . . . it's called Sayars. It's spelled Sears. That's right, the American company Sears has a major store here and it is quite an elite shopping venue. We will let you out at the back door and expect you back at the same door in two hours. Happy shopping!"

When released from the confinement of the bus, the students scattered like quail. Jimmy headed for the men's section. He was fascinated to see the beautiful clothing displayed in such artistic ways. It reminded him of a beautiful men's clothing store in Milan, Italy. Not that he had bought anything there, but he had looked at the window displays.

A young Mexican man dressed in a perfectly tailored blue pinstripe suit came over to Jimmy and asked. "May I help you?"

Jimmy stammered a reply, "No gracias."

The salesman responded in British-accented English, "Take your time. Call me if I can help."

Shoes made from the skin of the sea turtle, like the one he'd just eaten, were what Jimmy bought. They were a beautiful lustrous brown with the appearance of alligator. The young salesman explained that they were made from the sea turtle and were not only beautiful, but very durable. He told Jimmy that with proper care, the shoes would last for many years.

Too soon it was back on the bus and headed to the hotel. Sears had been a wonderland of beautiful and exotic products. Arrival at the hotel allowed for a short rest period before dinner. This was to be a typical Mexico City dinner and everyone knew it would be a small meal. They were not prepared for how small though. They were served a plate with a sweet roll, a slice of cheese, and a slice of brown bread. Chamomile tea, water, or Fanta soda were the beverage choices.

Jimmy heard one of his classmates ask the waiter if they had any tacos. "No sir," the waiter replied. "But if you would like some, there is a taco stand just down the block. We don't serve them here."

Dinner was a brief interlude in the day, leaving lots of time for the announcement they had all been anticipating, their upcoming travel location and partner.

Chapter 28

Dr. Suárez said, "I know you have all been waiting to know who your traveling partner is and where you will be going. Señor Girón and I have finished confirming placements. You will all be leaving at 9 a.m. tomorrow, so please be packed and at the bus by then. You will all be placed at different farming villages in the state of Guanajuato. The tour bus will take you to your sites, and Señor Girón will introduce you to your hosts."

With that, he began to read off the lists of travel partners and locations. Finally, Dr. Suárez called, "Jim Welch and Ramón Castro, you will be staying in Yuriria. In your packet there is some information about the town and surrounding area. There is also biographical information about the family that will be hosting you. Included is a map of the state of Guanajuato. I know you've all heard of the Mummies of Guanajuato. Do not be alarmed, none of you will be placed anywhere near where they are. We will not be going to view them before we return to the United States."

After a few more names were announced he said, "That completes the list. We have this room for another hour so meet with your traveling companion, get acquainted if you don't know each other, and discuss your placement. Señor Girón and I will be here if you have questions."

Jimmy knew who Ramón was but had never spoken to him. He was one of the college seniors, a tall guy with black curly hair, the build of an athlete, and an easy open smile. Jimmy walked over to Ramón, introduced himself, and they found a couple of chairs to sit and chat.

"Okay, let's take a look at the information in the packet," Jimmy said.

The material was very explicit, giving lots of information about the town and the family. The town is located in the southern part of the state of Guanajuato and was founded around 1540. The city center is very old and sparsely populated. The majority of the population is spread out over many miles. It is a farming area growing corn, wheat, broccoli, tomatoes, and several other row crops. There is a Catholic Church that dates from 1550 and is the largest building anywhere around. Remembering his history, Jimmy marveled at all this. Cortez had invaded Mexico in 1519 and as early as 1540, the Spanish were establishing villages, and by 1550, building huge churches and cathedrals.

As interesting as all this was, the family information was most interesting to Jimmy and Ramón. The García family owned a small farm on which the main crop was broccoli. There was a husband and wife and three children (20, 18 and 14 years old). There was also an eighty-year-old Grandmother in the home. No one spoke English except the 14-year-old daughter.

"Wow, this is going to be a trip," Jimmy remarked. "Do you speak Spanish, Ramón?"

"Only a little. My mom and dad told me we are never moving back to Mexico, so you need to speak English to be able to get a good job. They both learned English, and whenever I was around, they spoke English. I know they spoke Spanish when I wasn't around, but they never taught me any Spanish. My Grandad spoke to me in Spanish, so I learned a little from him. Now I have to go to school to learn it," Ramón replied.

The next morning they were all up and out on the bus by 9 a.m. Because Jimmy and Ramón were the furthest away, they were the last to be dropped off. It was 5 p.m. when they finally arrived. The trip had been generally uneventful, traveling through country that looked a lot like the farm fields back home. But there was one event that stuck in Jimmy's memory.

As he gazed out the window, he could clearly see a man and a horse plowing a field. This was not too unusual; he had seen several horse teams plowing fields on the trip. But what struck him about this scene was the plow. It was a tree branch. The fork of a tree about 6 feet long. The farmer held the two branches of the fork and drove the point into the soft earth as the horse pulled.

They had eaten on the way, so a 5 p.m. arrival was not a problem in that regard. They were now used to eating very little for dinner. The bus passed through the old section of town by the huge parish church and came to a stop just on the very edge of the town.

The house where they would be spending the next month was not visible from the road. The bus had pulled off the narrow two-lane highway onto a large dirt and gravel semi-circle in front of an enormous ten-foot, solid wood double gate set in an eight-foot concrete fence. The fence was topped by a concrete ridge in which broken glass was set. The wood of the gate was old and grayed but it still looked ominous and solid.

Ramón asked Señor Girón, "Why all the security? Is it dangerous here?"

Señor Girón replied, "There are many people in this area who have very little. Sometimes circumstances drive them to take what is not theirs. The most serious crimes committed here are burglary but never armed robbery or other violent crimes. Let's go meet the family."

They hopped off the bus with a mixture of excitement and anxiety. The anxiety was soon dispelled as they met the García family. Papa García was a sturdy well-muscled man of about 50, his hair and mustache streaked with gray. Mama García was a plump, round-faced woman of about 40. Boys, José (18) and Pedro (20), were younger versions of Papa. Daughter, Lucilla (14), had Mama's round face but not the round figure. Then came Grandma Doña Maria Elena García, the matriarch of the family. She was a small stooped little lady with gray hair and sparkling brown eyes.

Señor Girón made the introductions and explained that the two house guests were just learning Spanish and asked for the family's help to continue their learning. The family was instructed that they did not need to alter their schedule in any way. Jimmy and Ramón would participate in their family life and engage the townspeople as they were interested and able. With that, Señor Girón said goodbye, and Jimmy and Ramón sadly heard the bus release the brakes and pull away.

The García house was built in the Spanish style with rooms around a central square that served as the yard for children to play and where the family's beautiful flower garden was planted. As nearly as Jimmy and Ramón could calculate, the home had 8 bedrooms in addition to a living room, dining room, and kitchen.

What the house did not have was indoor plumbing. Jimmy and Ramón later learned that the house had been in the García family since it was built in 1850. It had been remodeled several times. In 1949, it was redone to add electricity. The 2-foot- thick Terra Cotta and plaster walls did not lend themselves to having wire pulled through them, so all of the wiring was in conduits attached to the outside of the walls. Installing plumbing in these walls was not possible, and opening the tile floors would have resulted in being unable to repair and match the 1850s tile.

The García family had developed a unique solution to the plumbing problem. They had built a toilet and shower house which did have running water. This building was 20' by 10' and located right behind the main house. It was a gray, steel-reinforced concrete house that resembled an ammunition bunker. In it were 3 separate rooms with a toilet and sink in each and 2 rooms with a shower in each — a clever solution to a vexing problem. To supply the kitchen with water, they had also run a water line along the base of the building, drilled a ¾ inch hole through the wall, and passed a line through to a huge 3' by 2' sink.

Señora García led them to a room along the south side of the square, opened the door, and flipped on the light. Inside were two twin-size metal-framed beds with thin mattresses rolled up and tied with a string. Jimmy and Ramón had brought their sleeping bags as instructed so no need for further bedding. With a smile, Senora García said, "***This is your room. Please make yourself at home. We will be having dinner at 8 p.m. in the dining room just across the yard.***" She pointed to the dining room and left.

"Wow, did you understand what she said?" Jimmy asked.

"Not really. I understood ocho (eight) and cena, which means dinner. I think she was telling us to come over there at 8 for dinner. Let's go over at 8 and see," Ramón replied.

At 8 o'clock sharp, Jimmy and Ramón went to the room across the yard and found it empty. As they stood there wondering what to do, the maid showed up. She spoke to them in words neither of them understood and then began to pantomime sitting down at the large oak table. They each took a seat and minutes later the food began to be placed on the table. By 8:30, everyone was seated and ready to begin cena.

When all family members were seated, the maid served sweet rolls of several types and chamomile tea. It was more than a little uncomfortable for Jimmy and Ramón as the family members spoke to them in Spanish and they did not understand. Jimmy thought of Jesús in his class and students like him who were in the same pickle they were in now. Jimmy realized that he had to do more for them when he got home.

Finally Lucilla intervened. The 14-year-old García daughter was a student in *secundaria* (high school) and was studying English. "Popi ask what work you do? Mama want know if bed okay?" Lucille said in heavily accented English. And so it went, getting acquainted as best they could. Jimmy and Ramón were content just to listen to the family chat with each other and to try to pick up a word here and there. Most of the conversation just sounded like noise to them.

Jimmy and Ramón returned to their room soon after dinner. It was already 10 p.m., and they were tired from their long trip. It was cool and dark in their room. They slid into their sleeping bags and were soon enveloped with the sleep of youth.

They didn't move until they heard the rooster crow the next morning. There seemed to be a lot of activity in the house even though the sun was just rising. Even young bladders can't go forever without emptying. They got out of bed, got dressed, then went down to the toilet building, as they called it. They washed their hands and face and were back to the dining room for a breakfast of scrambled eggs with green chilies, corn tortillas and cups of café con canella (coffee with cinnamon).

Now their work began in earnest. They were to go out into the town, observe life in a Mexican town, and talk with the residents. The observing part they knew would be pretty easy. It was the talking part that posed a problem. Ramón had a bit of an advantage having heard Spanish much of his life. But even though his comprehension was better than Jimmy's, his speaking ability was not much better.

After being let out of the compound by the maid, off they went to engage the town. It was a short walk from the García's compound to the city center. This was a bustling area that had existed for over four hundred years to support the agricultural production in the area.

Their first stop was at a small clothing store. "*May I help you?*" asked the proprietor.

Jimmy didn't understand exactly what was said, but he replied, "*Quiero camisa guayabera* (I want a guayabera shirt)."

Jimmy was gratified when the proprietor went immediately to a rack of guayabera style shirts. With their four pockets and pleats, these shirts were very stylish, especially in warm climates.

The guayabera shirt is Mexico's answer to shirts of Hawaii. Even though the guayabera originated in Cuba, they were widely adopted in Mexico. While not as colorful as the Hawaiian shirts, they were worn in the same fashion with the shirt-tail untucked. Jimmy had seen them displayed in Sears in Mexico City and had wanted one ever since.

Jimmy picked a light yellow one with long sleeves. It looked a little dressier than the short sleeves, and he liked that.

"*Cuanto* (how much)?" Jimmy asked. The shopkeeper replied, "*Ciento ocho* (one hundred eight)." Jimmy knew his numbers and retrieved a hundred peso bill and two five peso coins from his pocket. Jimmy accepted his two peso change and said, "*Gracias*" and he and Ramón left the store. Jimmy felt pretty happy about his first transaction entirely in Spanish.

They walked down the street observing everything. They saw how people greeted each other with a very brief handshake, how the colorful window displays presented products, some of which were made in the United States.

It was now lunchtime, and they looked for a place to eat. They knew they could make out the menu and were both emboldened by the successful shirt shopping. A little bit up the road, they found what looked like a restaurant, but it had a sign outside which said "*mujeres no permitidas.*" They knew the word mujeres and no and were pretty sure what permitidas meant.

"No women allowed," they both said. "Let's see what's

in there." They went into a small dark restaurant/bar and were seated at one of the four tables.

The place had the look of an old saloon from a Western movie. There were men occupying two of the four tables and eating. But the most outstanding feature of the place was a mahogany bar. It was a bar like neither of them had ever seen. There were no barstools; there was a brass rail in the floor on which patrons could rest a foot while they stood at the bar and drank. Between the bar and the rail there was a small trough, about 12-inches wide, filled with running water. The trough began somewhere outside the room, ran the length of the bar, exited through another opening, and ended somewhere outside on the other side of the building. The trough had about two inches of water running through it constantly.

The use of this little stream, running through the place, was soon made clear to Jimmy and Ramón. You could throw your cigarette butt into it, pee in it, spit in it. All these things could be done without ever leaving the bar. You could even drink beer while peeing as they watched one patron do.

Jimmy and Ramón both reconsidered eating there as they watched this display. Instead they stepped to the bar, put a foot on the rail and ordered Modelo Negras. This was just the first of almost daily Modelos that they would have at this little place. An excellent place, they said with a laugh, for men to have a beer and not waste any time going to the restroom.

After finishing their beer, they wandered on, still looking for a place to eat. Finally they found the perfect little outdoor café with six small tables covered by a kaleidoscope of huge colorful aluminum parasols. The waiter, a young man of about 16, welcomed them with a cheery greeting that neither of them understood. By now Ramón was remembering more Spanish than he thought he knew and greeted the waiter with *"Buenos Tardes. Tiene un menu? (*Good afternoon. Do you have a menu*?)"* As he held up a small chalk board, the waiter replied, *"Si señor aquí es (*Yes sir, here it is*)."*

The chalk board had two items on it, *mojarra con frijoles y arroz or tacos al Pastor* (mojarra with beans and rice or tacos made with spit grilled pork). Both read the menu and understood three words: tacos, frijoles, and arroz.

"Tiene burrito? (Do you have a burrito?)" Ramón asked.

"Oh no señor, aquí no comemos burritos, el animal es solo por trabajo. (No sir, we don't eat donkeys here; they are only for work.)"

The two understood three words: no, señor and burritos.

They understood they would not get a burrito, so they forged ahead to try to understand the menu. What they did not understand was the shock and disgust of the waiter at the idea of eating donkey meat. Jimmy pointed to the word mojarra and raised his arms palms up, in the universal sign, for *I don't know.*

At this point, the waiter immediately responded, *"Mojarra es un pescado así* (Mojarra is a fish this long)," as he held his hands out measuring about 10 inches. *"Preperada frito con frijoles y arroz* (Prepared fried with beans and rice)."

They understood frijoles and arroz and both gave the 'I don't know' palms-up gesture. At this the waiter made a swimming gesture and repeated the *pescado.* Still he saw no recognition in their faces.

"*Con permiso* (excuse me)" the waiter said and disappeared into the restaurant. He returned quickly with a beer advertisement in hand. A jumping marlin was superimposed over a beer bottle in the ad. Pointing to the marlin, he said *pescado*. Then pointing to the word mojarra, he held his hands out about ten inches and said, "*mojarra es un pescado, asi.*" At that, Jimmy and Ramón had an epiphany. A mojarra is a small fish! Jimmy quickly whipped out a small note pad and wrote down his new vocabulary words – pescado and mojarra.

"***Dos mojarra and dos Modelo Negra,***" they repeated in unison.

"Perfecto," said the waiter with a relieved expression on his face.

Soon the mojarra (small perch-like fish) were delivered head, fins, and all, fried and resting on a bed of lettuce with corn tortillas and a large portion of beans and rice on the side. It was worth the wait. The food was delicious. The smell of freshly cooked tortillas and the fish blended in a cloud of aromas that made Jimmy's mouth water, like his little dog Molly, when drool escaped her lips waiting for her dinner. Wrapping pieces of the white delicate flakes of fish in a corn tortilla with beans and rice was heavenly, washing it down with a Modelo Negra — divine.

After a wonderful lunch, they continued walking the city center fulfilling their obligation to observe and interact.

"There's Pedro and José," whispered Ramón.

"Who?" Jimmy replied.

"The García boys. I wonder what they're doing."

They both started walking in the direction Ramón had

pointed. The García brothers were seated at a restaurant sidewalk table with two men. Jimmy agreed with Ramón that they should go over and say hello. Jimmy thought that "Hello" was about as much as they were going to be able to say.

The smell of fresh bread wafted from the café to their nostrils as they approached the García table. As they neared the table, they saw the source of the aroma, a plate piled high with pan dulce. The aroma and sight of the gaily-colored pink and yellow baked goods made the two young men, who were not hungry, want a sample.

Pedro looked up as they approached, "*Hola. Como están hombres del norte* (How are you men from the north?)"

"*Bien* (well)," both answered.

"*Ven a ver estamos jugando domino.* (Come and see that we are playing dominoes.)"

The two wanderers didn't understand but knew that the brothers were motioning them to the table so they went.

"*Permítime presentarte mis amigos, Carlos y Tomás* (Allow me to present my friends Carlos and Tomás)," said Pedro.

"*Mucho gusto* (pleasure)," they both replied and rose to give a brief rather limp handshake.

Jimmy took particular note of the handshake. He had experienced this, what he would consider a "wimpy" handshake, from other Mexican men, but they were older and he had attributed the weakness of it to age. But now it was the same thing from two young men who seemed quite happy to meet them. Jimmy thought that he would check this out with Señor Girón.

Tomás knew a little English as he had lived in San Diego for a short while when he was a boy. "You want play?" Tomás asked.

Jimmy and Ramón replied in unison, "Sure."

It was an enjoyable hour of playing dominoes and communicating as best they could in broken Spanish and broken English. They learned that these four played dominoes almost every afternoon. Tomás nodded his head to Pedro and José and said, "They boss, don't have work." This peaked Jimmy's interest. He needed to learn more about the Mexican family roles.

The dominoes game broke up, and the six happy players went their separate ways — all to siesta except Jimmy and Ramón who were too excited to rest. They wandered down the side of the little two-lane highway and made an abrupt right onto a one-lane cobblestone street.

Even in this month of July, the weather was very temperate. They walked the old cobblestone lane through rows of two and three-hundred-year-old houses. The weather was very comfortable. Jimmy thought of the blazing heat that would be at home now. Yuriria rarely got above 90-degrees-Fahrenheit in the summer or below 40 degrees in winter. The bougainvillea plants were a sight to behold as they dropped themselves over ancient garden walls in all their pink and purple glory.

After walking some time, they were finally tired and were two or three miles from the García family compound, so they headed back. It was 6 p.m. when they arrived; all was well with los García (the Garcías).

Pedro had gone out to visit a girlfriend, and José was

staying at a cousin's house in the next village for a few days. It was Popi, Mama, Lucilla, Grandma and them for dinner. They had learned a few more words of Spanish during the day, and with Lucilla's help, were able to give at least a sketchy report of their day. The word mojarra was very prominent in their description.

****

Jimmy and Ramón slept well, and once again, were awakened by the rooster. This time there was something more, a strange click, click, click outside their door. They both jumped up and were dressed and out the door in minutes. The clicking was immediately obvious. A little white and brown goat ran up and down the terra cotta tile walkway. Click, click, click went hooves on the tile. They both laughed, the laughter of relieved tension.

After a quick breakfast of scrambled eggs, beans, and corn tortillas, Jimmy and Ramón were off. They felt confident enough after their encounters in the city the day before that they could deal with whatever the city had to offer.

Their first stop was at a hardware store, just because they were curious to see a Mexican hardware store. As they entered, there were plowshares, bags of vegetable seeds, and bags of nails all neatly stacked.

The proprietor came over immediately, "***Good morning. May I help you?***"

Ramón was emboldened from his positive experiences the day before, and he had begun to remember some Spanish from the early days when his grandparents spoke Spanish to him. "***Good morning. We here look see what here. We come from United States.***"

The proprietor said, ***"You look like a Mexican, but you sure don't talk like one. I suppose you learned that pocho Spanish in Los Angeles or somewhere, huh?"***

Jimmy understood not a word, but he could tell by the frown on the clerk's face that he wasn't happy. The only word Ramón understood from this rapid fire discourse was *pocho.* That was all he needed to understand that he was being insulted. He simply turned and said to Jimmy, "I'm leaving!" and walked out of the store.

Jimmy followed quietly behind asking Ramón, "What's wrong?"

Ramón responded, "Pocho is an insult. A lot of Mexicans don't like us because our family moved to the United States and we don't speak good Spanish. They call us pocho. They think we are low-class, that we're not even Mexicans. They know that most of us moved to the U.S. because we were so poor in Mexico and couldn't make it here. It's what Dr. Suárez was talking about when he told us to say if pups are born in the oven, are they pups or muffins. Dr. Suárez said that because he knows a lot of Mexicans don't like us."

"I'm sorry he insulted you; we won't be back there again," Jimmy said.

Jimmy thought about this as they walked. He remembered a similar incident in Oklahoma when his family had gone to visit. He was fifteen and curious as he wandered around the little town where his parents had grown up. He went into a pawn shop just to see if they had any guitars.

The proprietor came over and said, "Can I help you?"

"Well, I was wondering if you have any guitars for sale."

"No, sorry son, but I ain't had none fer weeks."

"How about guitar pickups," Jimmy said. "I'd like to find a good used DeArmond pickup."

"No, ain't got none of them either, but I'm fixin to get a couple from an old boy I know. He said he'd bring 'em in by next week."

As he was leaving, Jimmy heard the second man ask who the kid was. The proprietor said "Just some little prune picker. I don't know who he belongs to."

The word prune picker rang in Jimmy's ears still. The word, Okie, had been used with disdain to describe him in California, and now in a place where his relatives for at least three generations had lived and worked, he was called a prune picker.

Jimmy knew what the term meant. It was applied to those poor and dispossessed people who had to leave Oklahoma during the Dust Bowl or starve. Many had come to California and become migrant farmworkers, including some of Jimmy's family. Those who returned to Oklahoma for a visit were called prune pickers.

It is a sad fact of history that people uprooted and forced to move are usually not accepted in the place to which they move. And they are often shunned when they return to their homeland. Jimmy remembered his father's story of the Swede speaking broken English in California and talking about "damned Okies" invading the state. Okie children being allowed to starve or die of curable disease was not uncommon in 1930s California. Jimmy's parents weren't called prune pickers in Oklahoma because they still had the accent and knew the dialect. But Jimmy did not talk the talk or know all the social rules.

Jimmy felt deep empathy for Ramón. He was a nice guy trying to further his education and be a contributing member of society. And yet, he was called Mexican in California and pocho in Mexico. Ramón had told Jimmy tales of being teased in California, being called a Mexican jumping bean when he was little and a beaner or greaser when he got older. These hateful terms were as bad as prune picker.

Jimmy did see great parallels between their lives — families were dislocated, and forced to move to a strange new environment. Both families were insulted and disregarded when they arrived, and not able to fit in very well or even allowed access to basic health care.

Jimmy also clearly recognized that he had some distinct advantages. The primary one was that he was white and could blend in. He was no longer called "Okie" in the hateful way it had been applied to him as a child. He was white, did not have an Oklahoma accent, and he could blend in. His family maintained their accent but had dropped their Oklahoma dialect. They had moved into the middle class now. They were buying their own home, and his Dad had a great job.

Jimmy's folks had given up any interest in moving back to Oklahoma. They were Californians now, committed to this new part of the country. True enough, making a pile of money and moving back to Oklahoma was his parents' dream for a good many years. Many of the relatives were still in Oklahoma. All the grand times they talked of were in Oklahoma. The stories of their childhood were there; they just felt more comfortable there. But as job prospects and housing improved in California, thoughts of moving back faded and finally disappeared.

Ramón did not have some of Jimmy's advantages. He could never blend in with the dominant cultural group in California. His bronze skin announced his difference before a word was said. He spoke English without an accent, and his English was very good. His parents, like Jimmy's own, had harbored hopes of returning to their hometown in Mexico, but those hopes had faded. Their housing and job prospects were not the best, but they knew California had more opportunities for them than anywhere in Mexico. They knew that their children would have a chance for education in California that was not possible in Mexico.

Jimmy could tell Ramón was deeply wounded by the rejection in Mexico, even if he never planned to live there. As they walked and talked, Jimmy tried to gloss over what had just happened but it was no use. Ramón's speech was listless, and he finally said, "I'm going back to the house; I need to write some letters."

As Jimmy and Ramón parted ways, Jimmy continued down the cobblestone way leading to the church.

Chapter 29

In a few short blocks, Jimmy arrived in front of the *Iglesia de Nuestra Señora del Socorro y San Pablo* (Church of Our Lady of Help and Saint Paul). It was a magnificent stone building constructed by the Spanish in the 1500s. To Jimmy, it looked just like pictures of old castles he had seen with the turrets and spaces in between for archers to defend the castle. But this was a church and the center of communal life in Yuriria.

It was open, as were all churches Jimmy had encountered in Mexico. As he stepped into the vestibule, a hush and sense of peace descended on him. The sound of the traffic outside was immediately blocked by the thick oak doors and the stone construction. It was cool and dimly lit inside, and he felt an abiding comfort in being there. He walked through the nave and took a seat on a pew immediately in front of the sanctuary. As he walked, Jimmy heard the quiet slap of his leather-soled shoes and nothing more.

Jimmy sat for a long while staring at the statue of Our Lady of Guadalupe in the sanctuary. He remembered the explanation Señor Girón had given when someone had asked about Our Lady of Guadalupe. He explained that a shepherd named Juan Diego had seen a vision of Mary, and she had asked him to build a church in her honor. When Juan Diego took this request to the priests, he was rebuffed, and they refused to believe him. Juan Diego returned, and Mary instructed him to wrap some roses in his cloak and take them to the Bishop. Juan Diego complied and when he unfurled the cloak, the roses dropped out and an image of Mary was left on the cloak. Then the Bishop believed.

The Basilica of Guadalupe was erected, and the cloak resides there to this day. Mexicans travel great distances to visit and worship at the site.

Replicas of the image are seen everywhere in Mexico. Jimmy had even seen one on the face of an alarm clock. However, here he was not looking at a replica of the cloak; it was a statue of Our Lady of Guadalupe. She stood there in her white garment with a blue cloak and gold stars; she looked so serene. He didn't know if he really believed the story of Juan Diego and the apparition, but he knew he felt a strong sense of peace as he sat there.

After a time he began to pray. Jimmy was not Catholic, but he was Christian and believed all Christian churches were to be respected. Just as he was finishing his prayers, he heard the sound of quiet footsteps and looked up to find a priest in his brown cassock stepping down from the sanctuary.

"*Puedo ayudarte con algo mi hijo?* (Can I help you with something my son?)," the priest asked.

Jimmy replied, "Sorry but I don't speak Spanish."

"Oh well, fortunately I speak English," the priest replied in only slightly-accented English. "May I ask why you are here?"

"I'm here with a study group. We're staying with the García family," Jimmy replied.

"Yes, that's interesting, but I meant only why you are

here in this place. You are praying. Are you troubled?" the kind priest inquired.

"Not really troubled, but I'm looking for some answers to help my friend Ramón," Jimmy explained.

The priest said, "Tell me, perhaps I can help."

Jimmy looked at this small man in his brown cassock and shock of black hair and thought, maybe he can help.

"My name is Father Anaya."

"I'm Jim Welch," Jimmy said extending his hand. Jimmy was expecting the limp handshake, but he got a firm U.S.-style shake. The priest looked only a bit older than Jimmy but had an air of authority about him.

"You speak excellent English," Jimmy said.

"Thank you. It's easier for me to speak English because I was raised in the states. My dad was a career diplomat; I spent my first eighteen years living in Mexican consulates and embassies in the U. S. I went to school in American schools and was tutored in Spanish at the consulate. In my home, we always spoke English and Spanish. Both my parents speak fluent English. I feel very comfortable with either language," Father Anaya explained.

"When did you join the priesthood?" Jimmy asked.

"Right after high school I attended seminary in Mexico City. I was assigned right out of seminary to the diocese of Cuernavaca. There I met Bishop Arceo and his idea of Liberation Theology. It changed my direction as a priest. I loved the Mariachi masses that we had in Cuernavaca. In the years since I left, I have tried to emulate him. But enough about me, tell me about your quest for your friend."

Jimmy started to explain. "We're both from California. We're here trying to learn Spanish and about the culture of Mexico. I'm already a teacher, and he is studying to be one."

"What is your friend's name?"

"His name is Ramón Castro. I'm teaching in a school where almost all the kids are Mexican, and Ramón wants to be a teacher in Los Angeles in a school where most of the kids are Mexican too.

"Today we went to a store here; Ramón spoke Spanish to the owner and he called Ramón a pocho. It really hurt his feelings, I think. I was trying to think of how I could help," Jimmy explained.

"I'm not sure how you might be able to help Ramón except to keep being his friend. Just lend a sympathetic ear when he wants to talk. Let's talk a little about Mexico and the United States. I'm fortunate that I have seen both societies, learned both languages, and have thought a lot about the differences. I believe how most Americans form their opinions of Mexicans is from seeing the migrant farmworkers who come to the U.S. or by seeing an enclave, that you call barrios, of U.S.-born citizens of Mexican descent. In a few cases, opinions are formed by visiting some border towns like Tijuana. But they lump us all together as just Mexicans.

"In the case of the Mexican farmworkers, what they are seeing is a segment of the Mexican society that is at or near the bottom income level. They go to the U.S. not because they want to, but because it's the only way they can see to be able to provide for their families. There are no social programs that will help poor people in Mexico. The jobs available to them are few and very poorly paid. So, they go to the U.S. to work.

"Since the bracero program ended, they must enter your country illegally. Your country needs the hard labor that they provide, so there is a tacit agreement between big agriculture business and your government that the border won't be controlled as well as it could be. Farmworkers are *allowed* to sneak into the United States because you cannot do without their labor.

"These Mexican farmworkers are in a similar situation to the Okies during your depression. They don't want to leave home, but they are starving here, and the Mexican government will not help them at all," Father Anaya continued.

"Most of them do not like life in the U.S. It is too different, too fast, too much in pursuit of worldly goods. The women are considered loose and bossy, and the men have given up their role as head of the family. They see your country as morally bankrupt, and they just want to work to get some money and come home. The best way I can explain this is to say that they view the United States as a 'cesspool full of pearls.' The objective is to get the pearls and get home without being contaminated," the young priest smiled.

Father Anaya continued, "I know that I heard many complaints when I lived in the United States that Mexicans were not like other immigrants. They don't assimilate; they don't become part of the big American melting pot. They don't learn English and don't even try to fit in.

"I'm sure this is how it appears to many people in the U.S., but what needs to be understood is that many of the farmworker group don't want to fit in. They want to work, make some money, and go home. It is much easier for them to get home than for any of the other immigrants who came to the U.S. They are a bus ride away from home.

"To view them as dirty and stupid is also greatly in error. It is true that these farmworker families do not have facilities for clothes washing or bathing as readily as others. But they do quite well considering the circumstances under which they live: moving from place to place doing hard physical labor six days a week, dodging the immigration authorities and not knowing the language. And for the most part they have not had a chance for an education here in Mexico. Although, I can tell you that many of them value education highly. They know it is the way to a better life, but the demands of day to day living have prevented them from attending school. However, they do try to send their children to school.

"There are others in the U.S. who are of Mexican descent but have actually been born in the U.S. In some cases, their families have been in the U.S. for two generations or more and they are citizens. They speak English, have been to school at least through part, if not all, of high school, and are quite aware of the American world view. Many, if not most, buy into it and try to be part of the mainstream. Most of these families left Mexico to escape war and political persecution.

"So they like other immigrant groups left their country behind with no thought of return. They want to be Americans, but they are lumped with all other groups from Mexico, even though their purpose for being in the U.S. is quite different from that of most of the farmworkers. Some of these immigrants are actually from the upper income group in Mexico. But it is very difficult for them to fit in. They are too identifiable even after generations. Their skin color and their surnames identify them; they are called Mexicans and they face discrimination.

"This is so, even though many of them have never been to Mexico and don't speak Spanish. They are often taunted and called names. I know when I was in elementary school, people called me a beaner, Mexican jumping bean, and greaser. Perhaps your friend is one of this group.

"Sadly when they come to Mexico, we don't accept them either. They have lost their *Mexicaness*. They don't speak the language well or not at all. Those that have retained some Spanish speak a dialect of Spanish that we reject. Even though they are called Mexican in the United States, we don't accept them as Mexican. We call them *pocho*. In fact, you who are an American coming to Mexico trying to learn Spanish will be more accepted than they are.

"There are many people in the U.S. who have visited towns just over the border in Mexico. What they see is a variety of people trying to do what they can to make a living from the tourists. They are forced into this life because of the grinding poverty in Mexico. This results, in some cases, in catering to the more base desires of tourists. There are many bars, free flowing liquor, prostitutes, pornography, and generally vulgar entertainment. This results in visitors who see this, or worse participate, going home believing Mexican women are whores and the men are drunks. This is far from the truth. Observe while you are here. You will learn the truth.

"I know I have spoken at great length on this topic. It is only to try to help you understand and perhaps help to change things when you go home," Father Anaya concluded.

Chapter 30

Jimmy walked back down the narrow cobblestone lane to the highway and headed back to the García's. A two-mile walk was nothing for his strong frame. He had walked all his young life. In fact, the library was a mile and a half from his boyhood home, and he walked the three-mile round trip at least twice a week. In addition to this, he walked to school, to his friends, sometimes the seven miles to a fishing hole, and everywhere else he wanted to go. For him, two miles was just a warm up.

Jimmy arrived back at the García's just minutes before lunchtime. Ramón was in the room when Jimmy walked in.

"Where have you been, Jim?" he asked.

"Talking to the priest at the church," Jimmy replied.

"Confessing your sins, huh?" At that, they both laughed.

"No, getting dialed in to a whole lot of interesting information. Maybe you should go talk to him. He's got a lot on the ball. He grew up in the states and then moved back to Mexico to become a priest. He knows what it's like to be insulted about your background."

"I'll think about it," Ramón said. "Let's go eat!"

They arrived at the table just as the family was sitting. Pedro and José were just arriving from the fields where they had been supervising the workers harvesting broccoli.

The brothers' workday consisted of showing the hired farmworkers where and what to do and then leaving to do whatever they wished for the rest of the day, returning to check on the workers occasionally. Today, the work was in one of the four fields cutting and packing broccoli.

The brothers came to the table after having a shower and changing out of their work clothes. The rest of the family gathered around, and the maid was soon serving. Today it was chicken soup, veal cutlets, and flan for dessert.

Jimmy and Ramón were now used to the lunch hour menu but not to some of the customs. They were especially shocked when they saw Señora García cutting Señor Garcia's meat for him. What? They both thought, can't he cut his own meat? They later learned that it was a wife's duty to attend to and provide every comfort to her husband even as small a thing as cutting a piece of meat to save him the trouble.

Jimmy and Ramón had become accustomed to a short rest period after the meal — a siesta. Neither of them actually napped, being the strong active young men that they were. They lay on their beds and quietly chatted. "Sorry that guy in the store was such a butt," Jimmy said.

"Yeah, me too. Made me really mad," said Ramón. "I don't know where I have to go to be accepted. In the U.S. they call me a greaser, and here they call me pocho. I know it doesn't matter what other people think, but I would just like to be in a place where I didn't get insulted all the time. I thought maybe it was Mexico." With that thought, they both drifted off into their interior worlds, where no one could enter without permission.

The afternoon was spent around the house. Pedro and

José were off to their domino games and other pursuits. Señor García was off to the next town to inquire about buying some Brahman cattle. He thought they might do well in one of the pastures close to the lake. Señora García and Lucilla sat in the living room doing needle point.

As Jimmy and Ramón wandered by the living room, Lucilla waved them in. "How are you?" she said in halting English.

"We're fine," they both replied. It seemed that Lucilla wanted to practice her English.

"You go town yesterday?"

"Yes, we went and walked around the town. It's beautiful," Jimmy said.

"Yes, beautiful," she repeated.

Jimmy thought, here's my chance to learn more about Mexican life. The question and answer session began.

"Do you go to school, Lucilla?"

"Yes I go," she answered.

"Where do you go to school?" Jimmy asked.

"School is by church."

"Oh, it's a Catholic School?" Jimmy confirmed.

"Yes, Catholic. No school now, start Septiembre. How you say Septiembre?"

"September," Jimmy said. "Do you like school?"

Lucilla answered, "Yes, I like school mucho."

"Do you have a boyfriend at school?" Ramón asked.

"What is a boyfriend?" Lucilla questioned.

"Novio," Ramón offered.

At that exchange, Lucilla's caramel-colored face turned a dark shade of red. She looked quickly toward her mother who continued placidly doing needlepoint, paying no attention to the foreign noise called English.

"No, no boyfriend. No can be with boy. Popi say no," Lucilla said adamantly.

Jimmy and Ramón both realized they had hit on a sensitive subject and quickly headed for safer ground. "How many students in your school?" Ramón asked.

"We are two hundred veinte cinco? How you say veinte cinco?"

"Twenty-five," Ramón replied.

That evening as they were making up the beds, getting ready to sleep, Jimmy said, "I want to tell you something. That guy calling you a pocho has made me think about it." And he told Ramón his whole story of prune pickers and Okies.

When he finished, Jimmy said, "I know that it's not exactly the same because I'm still an Okie, but no one knows it. In my heart of hearts, I'm proud of being an Okie. My folks struggled to gain a place in society. No one gave us anything except a hard time. I know you can't blend in as I did, but I think better times are coming for you. You'll see." Jimmy did think better times were coming and was going to do all he could do to see that it became a reality.

****

The days passed more quickly than either of them could

have imagined. Day by day their worlds expanded, each learning more about the language and culture of Mexico and about each other. Jimmy realized that this was part of the plan. Pairing them so they could learn about each other. It was a good plan too. Jimmy saw the hurt, and the anger, that the idea of ethnic superiority created for Ramón.

All too soon, the day of departure arrived. Jimmy and Ramón said their farewells to the García's, with some tears and promises. In their newly improved Spanish, they promised to meet again. The bus carried Señor Girón to the front gate of the hacienda. Jimmy and Ramón stored their gear in the baggage area under the bus.

"Buenos días, estudiantes. Listos para regresar? (Good morning Students. Ready to return?)"

In his best newly-acquired Spanish, Jimmy replied, *"Bien Gracias. Sí estamos listos."* (Well, thank you. Yes, we are ready.)

"How was your stay?" Señor Girón continued in Spanish.

"Was good the stay here," Jimmy replied in his best Spanish, trying to mimic the accent of the García's.

"What did you learn while you were here?" Señor Girón questioned.

"Muchas cosas (many things)," Ramón replied.

"Such as what?" Señor Girón replied, testing their Spanish.

"We learned about family and town," Ramón replied.

"Very good," Señor Girón replied. **"Let's get on the bus. We have a long ride."**

Jimmy and Ramón were the first ones on the bus. Off they went, stopping at several little villages and towns to pick up classmates. Jimmy was glad to see Sylvia board the bus. He still had a little crush on her though she had made it clear she wasn't interested. "Buenos Dias (good morning)," he said as she passed his seat.

"*Buenos tardes* (good afternoon)," she corrected as it was three o'clock in the afternoon. "*Habla Español* (Do you speak Spanish)?" she continued.

"*Sí* (yes)" Jimmy replied with a smile. Sylvia chuckled and said, "*Felicidades* (congratulations)," as she continued to her seat.

At 6:00 p.m., they arrived once again at the Hotel Geneve for an overnight stay. Their arrival felt almost like a homecoming to Jimmy. The Hotel Geneve and the surrounding area were familiar now, and it seemed very comfortable to him. This would be a short stay though — breakfast at 6:00 a.m. and then on to the train station.

After a short night and a quick ride, they found themselves at the Mexico City train station ready to board for home. Jimmy felt a sense of sadness creep up that surprised him. He loved being in Mexico and was not ready to return. Even the ever-present smell of car exhaust in the air created a sense of longing to stay.

There was so much more he wanted to know about Mexico and the Mexican people. There was so much more fluency Jimmy wanted to acquire in Spanish. Father Anaya had suggested that if he wanted a deep immersion in the language and culture of Mexico, he should spend at least three months at a school in Cuernavaca called CIDOC. He made a note of this and planned to check it out. There were so many more conversations he would like to have with Father Anaya in Yuriria. Jimmy vowed he would take a Spanish class when he returned home.

Back on the train, it was another familiar and very comfortable experience. "*Muy buenos días* (very good morning)," Jimmy said with a big smile as he passed Sylvia in the corridor.

"*Buenos días Señor* (good morning, Sir*)*" she replied with a slight smile. "**How is your room**?" she asked speaking very slowly to enhance Jimmy's comprehension.

Jimmy understood the word room and guessing at the rest of the question, he replied, "*Bueno* (good)."

"**I'm glad**," Sylvia said with a smile and walked on.

The trip back to California was very much like the trip to Mexico. Jimmy greatly enjoyed seeing the panorama of Mexico flash by his window. He spent most of the day watching the view, studying Spanish, and trying to devise ways to accidently see Sylvia. Jimmy heard "Que Lindo Es México (How Beautiful Mexico Is)" from the vestibule one evening and looked to see three Mexican University students he had met earlier in the day.

Arrival back in California sent Jimmy into a bit of a funk, and he restlessly slept in his bus seat all the way home. He didn't even try to encounter Sylvia. Jimmy was full of questions about Mexico and Mexicans, and in his mind, challenging everything he thought he knew about them.

Chapter 31

After fond farewells to institute classmates and instructors and a brief time acclimating to the valley, it was time for Jimmy to start getting ready for the opening of school. Labor Day would be here soon, and with it the last day of vacation and the start to a new school year. For all his life, no matter where Jimmy went or what he did, summer would be bracketed by Memorial Day and Labor Day. Labor Day was now imminent.

September was here, another Labor Day, another eve of a new school year; Jimmy was ready. He had been in his classroom and gotten things ready for opening day of school. Books were all stacked neatly, and the bulletin boards were decorated. The number of children for the first day was only partially known. Some children from last year's fifth grade class would be back and were already registered. The major unknown factor was the migrants. No one would know until they showed up at school how many there were. That didn't matter to Jimmy; he was much more ready for them than he had been last year.

Ring went the 8:30 a.m. bell. Time for another McKinley School year to begin. The 32 chairs in Jimmy's classroom were all filled, and four kids were standing in the back. "Pablo and Ricardo, come with me please," Jimmy said as he motioned to the door. Down the hall they went to the cafeteria, picked up a table and four chairs, and were back before anyone in class could find a way to get in trouble. Having students like these two made Jimmy glad that he taught a multi-grade classroom. He got to see these young scholars develop over more than one year.

"Okay, let's set this table up, and you four grab a chair. This will have to do until tomorrow. We'll find some desks for you by then. I'm going to call roll now. Please answer here or present when I call your name."

Jimmy went down the roll all the way from Alaniz to Young. Thirty-six students, fifteen from last year. The rest were migrants who had arrived in town since school ended last year; most of them would be gone by Christmas.

Jimmy was pleased to see Jesús back in school and to hear that his English had improved. Jimmy liked Jesús' dad, Renaldo; he and his wife seemed to have a great deal of interest and concern for their children's welfare.

Jimmy was also pleased to welcome back his bilingual aide, Ofelia Sanchez. Her help was immeasurable; he relied on her in a great many ways. Although, his new found Spanish ability would somewhat reduce his reliance on her. He could make a few simple explanations for the limited and non-English speakers in the class. But conversations with parents and involved explanations to the kids would have to be done by Ofelia.

Class did go much more smoothly when Jimmy was able to give some individual help to the limited and non-English speakers. The more he communicated directly with them, the more he understood that what he had once seen as low ability was simply a lack of getting adequate information in a language they understood.

There were some new opportunities this year to help in that regard. The Bilingual Education Act had been passed in 1968 but had not yet been of great benefit. However, this year some new audio materials in Spanish had been received through funds from the act. In particular, a set of tapes explaining math functions in the sixth grade text looked to be potentially very useful.

There was another area of great interest to Jimmy. School districts could apply for grants for innovative methods of demonstrating bilingual language usage. Jimmy was very interested in this.

Day two of class began hot with the promise of more heat to come. The days of air conditioned school rooms had not yet arrived, and the San Joaquin Valley was hot and dry. On this September day, the temperature was expected to rise to a high of 101-degrees-Fahrenheit. Jimmy opened all the windows to catch what little cool air the morning afforded.

By 11 a.m. the heat was building to the point that the windows had to be closed. Unfortunately the push-out windows did not allow for window screens, and several dozen flies had come to school. The flies buzzed around like little fighter planes landing on this one and that one, causing a general disruption in an otherwise pretty placid classroom.

"Give me your attention, please," Jimmy requested. Everyone looked up with anticipation from the mixed fraction problems they were trying to solve. "We have a problem here, boys and girls. These flies have invaded our space and are being very rude. It's not enough that they have come in, but they insist on bothering you and me by landing on us. So, they must go. They have been given the chance to leave and have not done so. I'm afraid I must pass the death sentence on them. Those of you who wish to act as executioners, take out your rulers. No one is required to execute them, only those who want to, so take out your rulers."

The whole time this pontification had been going on, Ofelia had been translating for the limited English speakers but loud enough so others could hear. And it was a good thing, since the concept of execution was a stumbling block. In any case, all but three girls took out their rulers.

"Okay, now here are the rules. Not yet, but when I say 'go,' you may move about the room executing any fly that you see. However, you may *not* hit a fly that is on a person or on any breakable object. When I say 'stop,' you must stop executing flies and return to your seats. Any questions? No? Okay, ready, set, *go!*"

The clatter of wooden rulers hitting wooden desks was deafening. Flies lay mangled and flat all around the room. The carnage was awesome and terrible to behold. After about ten minutes there was not a fly left moving, and Jimmy said "*Stop!*"

"Now I need three volunteers to pick up bodies and one to do a body count. Three brave boys jumped forward, and within minutes the task was done. Seventy-four fly bodies were picked up with tissue and unceremoniously dumped in the trash. Hands were washed and everyone returned to the much less stimulating process of solving problems with mixed fractions.

****

The heat of September gradually melded into the cool mornings and pleasantly warm afternoons of October. Jimmy once again returned to thoughts of an innovative bilingual project. Then it hit him, just like the apple falling on Sir Isaac Newton's head — *a bilingual play*!

That's what we need to do. Jimmy would write the play in English, get it translated to Spanish, and have two performances, one in English and one in Spanish. The class will perform it and the whole school can come and watch. It will be *great*!

"Wow, this is quite an application form, Jim," exclaimed Principal Campbell. "Does it change your mind about wanting to do this?"

"No, it's just going to take a little longer than I thought. I'll take this and fill it out by next week and keep my fingers crossed."

That evening, working on the application, Jimmy got his first taste of federal bureaucracy, and it tasted a little bitter. Why ask the same question over and over in different ways, he thought? Oh well, if this what it takes to get the money to do the play, I'll do it. He labored long into the night and was ready the next day to put his application in the mail.

It was a modest proposal. Jimmy would write a script for the play on his own time. The budget request was for costumes ($150), translation to Spanish ($125), props ($75), printing ($80), and awards for actors ($25).

There was no requirement in the application to describe the content of the play, although Jimmy had an idea he was sure would work. It was tradition at McKinley School that a Christmas play in which all grades participated would be presented. The play Jimmy had in mind had a Christmas theme.

This year, in addition to making yards of green and red paper chains, his class would be practicing their parts. Jimmy knew that traditionally in Mexico the three kings brought presents to the children on Epiphany. But Jimmy also observed that it had not taken long before the children latched onto the idea of Santa Claus. Even in Mexico, things seemed to be changing. In Mexico City he had seen photographs of rows of brown faced Santa's in Chapultepec Park taking requests from children. That gave Jimmy an idea for a play that would not only use the two languages, but would also entertain and provoke some thought. Whether or not the federal grant was approved, he would find a way to do the play.

He began with the concept that a Mexican boy named Ricardo, whose family came to California, believed in Santa Claus, but he did not believe that Santa understood Spanish.

Jimmy knew very little about writing a play, but he had taken a drama class in his sophomore year of college. His final project for the class was to enact a scene from a play. He and his two partners choose Act 1 of *Death of a Salesman*. Jimmy still had the script in his papers somewhere. It took some time, but he finally dug it out of an old suitcase. He thought he would just use the format for the play, and he would name the new play, *Santa and Ricardo.*

The next day at the end of school, Jimmy was on his way. He was still living with his mother and father. After making his car payment, it was hard to have enough to pay rent also. He was saving and hoped to have enough soon to put a first and last months' rent deposit down on an apartment closer to McKinley School.

Fortunately, Jimmy had his old study area at home where he could work. He began to work on the play as soon as he arrived home.

Title: *Santa and Ricardo*

Act 1

Scene 1

Santa is at his desk reading letters from children. An elf enters in an agitated state with a letter in his hand.

ELF: (Elf trips then gets up) Santa, Santa! Look at this letter. You have to do something!

Santa takes the letter written in Spanish from the elf and reads it.

"Dear Santa, I don't think you know Spanish, but I want to send you this letter because maybe you have an elf who knows Spanish and can read it to you. I have been very good this year. I work in the field with Popi, and I do everything mama asks. I have been nice to my brothers and sisters, and I only want one thing. I really want a baseball glove. Please, Santa, I would be so happy to get the glove, so I can play with my friends."

SANTA: What? Santa doesn't speak Spanish? Whatever gave him that idea? Doesn't he know that Santa knows every language in the world?

ELF: I don't know, Santa. He moves around a lot with his family. Maybe he had left already when we left his present last year.

SANTA: Well, we will take care of this. I know Ricardo has always been a good boy. We will make sure he gets his baseball glove. Here is what we will do.

Santa devises a plan to be sure the glove is left where Ricardo is staying on Christmas. Santa leaves the glove and a note in Spanish that reads: "*Dear Ricardo, thank you for sending me your nice letter. I want to be sure that you understand that Santa does know Spanish. Santa doesn't care what language children speak; he only cares that they are good and kind. Santa knows about you, Ricardo. You are a good boy. Here is your baseball glove. Have lots of fun with it, Santa.*"

It took several after-school sessions, but within two weeks the play was finished. As fate would have it, the very next day a letter from the federal government arrived with approval for the funding. And just in time because there were only six weeks left before show time. Costumes needed to be made, the play needed to be translated, and most of all, auditions had to be held, players chosen, and scripts memorized.

Jimmy had mostly sixth graders, and most were eleven or older, so he doubted there were many Santa believers left but he wasn't sure. To find out, Jimmy devised a clever scheme. Among the multiple choice questions on the social studies test, he placed a statement: I believe in Santa Claus. True or False.

Jimmy just wanted to know because he certainly did not want to be the one to burst anyone's bubble. He remembered the nine-year-old boy next door who questioned his Dad about something he had heard at school. "Dad, is there really a Santa Claus? Billy said there isn't. Now tell me the truth; don't let me embarrass myself."

Jimmy was satisfied that they all turned out to be non-believers. Sad in many ways, but easier to deal with them in the play development. A jolly rotund boy named Carlitos got the part of Santa. José, because of his bilingual ability, became the head elf. Several students opted not to perform but to be the prop and scenery crew. Jesús took the part of Ricardo, and the rest of the fifth, sixth, and seventh grade classes were elves tinkering with toys and having a few lines of chatter.

The play was a smashing success. All the classes in McKinley School viewed it with great enjoyment. The players took at least two curtain calls each performance. Each class got to view the English version and the Spanish version and both were well received.

There were two evening performances for parents. They could choose the English or Spanish version or both. The Spanish version was most heavily attended, so a second performance had to be done to accommodate everyone. There was even a performance for the high school students held in the high school auditorium.

When the dust had settled, the play was considered one of the highlights of the Christmas season at McKinley School. Some migrant families even stayed over for a few days to see it. Jimmy was expecting nothing but good news when he was called into the school district superintendent's office.

"Hello, Mr. Welch. Please have a seat. I saw your play when it was presented to the high school. I must say, I'm impressed with the amount of work that went into it. It was a very polished and well-done production. I have just one other comment. The purpose of the Bilingual Education Act is to move students from their native language to English as quickly as possible. It's familiarity in English that will help them to prosper in this country."

Jimmy replied, "Yes, I understand that they need to learn English, but I don't think it is necessary to degrade their first language. My parents came here from Oklahoma, and people made fun of them for their accent and some of the words they used. They'll never lose the accent, but they have learned California slang. The negative reaction to their language use did nothing to help them. In fact, it made them just want to withdraw from people. I wasn't trying to help kids learn Spanish. I was just trying to let them know its' okay to speak Spanish, but you have to learn English too."

"I disagree with that message," the Superintendent said. "The more they think it is okay to speak Spanish, the less they are going to want to learn English. They have to become fluent in English if they are going to ever succeed in this society. Look at the turmoil in Quebec, Canada over French and English. You cannot have a cohesive society unless the people speak the same language."

"Yes, but don't you think it is okay for people to know more than one language?" Jimmy asked.

"Yes, it's not only okay, it's desirable, but English is the language of this country. It is and always will be the language by which we conduct business here. The ability to earn a good living here is contingent on the fluency one has in English. If a person knows another language, good for them. But English is essential. That's why it is incumbent on you and me to ensure that we teach them English first and foremost."

"Yes sir, I understand," Jimmy said as he went away from the meeting with lots of thoughts stumbling through his head.

Jimmy remembered his own days of being called an Okie and of trying to hide the facts of his background.

He thought of a particular day when he was listening to the Maddox Brothers and Rose. As he heard his friends walking up to the house, he quickly shut off the radio, not wanting them to hear.

He loved country hillbilly music. It almost always told a story. Jimmy liked to watch the Grand Ole Opry on T.V.; he even had a crush on little Brenda Lee. But he wanted no one to know for fear they would connect him to his Oklahoma roots. It wasn't until Bobby Dylan and the folk revival that he could listen to the kind of music he loved in public. He was determined that these kids should not be made to feel ashamed of their background.

But was it best to stomp out Spanish so the kids could focus on English? How would they talk to their parents? On the other hand, if they didn't learn English well, how could they ever hope to get a good job — a job where they didn't have to work in the hot sun all day? He had just learned in the Sociology of Education class that the purpose of the schools was to educate children to be able to participate in the *good life* as the society conceives of it. And the *good life* in the United States, at least in part, meant doing better financially than your parents did. It was clear that to be financially successful in the U.S., required English language ability. But what if you didn't intend to stay here? What if it was like Father Anaya said; they were just here to make some money and then return to Mexico? These and many other questions swished through Jimmy's head and screamed for answers.

Chapter 32

Daniel did well in the M.A. program. He was regularly at odds with his more liberal classmates, but he was quick and smart and most often came out on top of those seminar debates.

A classic example was the day they were discussing the politics of Manifest Destiny and how it resulted in the U.S. pushing relentlessly to the Pacific Ocean. Daniel was explaining his view that the move west had to happen; the growth and prosperity of the new United States depended on the continual move west. A student of Mexican descent challenged him by saying, "So it was okay that the U.S. took the whole southwest from Mexico?"

Daniel replied by saying, "I suppose it was just as okay as it was for the Spanish to steal it from the Indians and then the Mexicans to steal it from the Spanish."

Daniel then proceeded to chronicle the Spanish and subsequent Mexican abuse of Native Americans and takeover of their lands. "If we go far enough back, we can document the process of smaller Native American tribes being overrun by larger tribes. What is your point? That the thief twice removed from the owner is more honorable than the one three times removed? That's a bit of twisted logic."

After three grueling semesters of coursework, seminars, term papers, and thesis preparation, it was time for Daniel to begin his internship. The city and county of San Francisco had agreed to have Daniel serve as a policy analyst. As such, he would receive assignments to research topics of possible legislation for the city.

Daniel knew this would be a great experience for him for many reasons, but the paramount one was that San Francisco was both, and still is, a city and a county. The policy-making body, the Board of Supervisors, handled all of the city and county issues. He was pleased to know that he would get experience with both city and county legislative issues.

He knew his last semester would be a difficult one. His schedule would be to work at his internship from 8 a.m. to 3 p.m., Monday through Thursday. Monday and Thursday would be dedicated to meetings, and from 3:30 p.m. to 4:30 p.m., he would be with his advisor to discuss his intern experience. Friday, Daniel would meet with his thesis committee from 8 a.m. to 9 a.m. and would then have the rest of the day to work on the completion of his thesis. Of course, the weekend would, for the most part, be dedicated to his thesis.

Daniel's first day as a San Francisco Policy Analyst was one of those blustery, rainy days that occur occasionally during a San Francisco winter. He hoped that the fact that his umbrella blew inside out while he was running for the bus wasn't a portent of ill events to come. He arrived at City Hall in the Civic Center early, even with his umbrella mishap. As always, he had planned ahead and started out early.

He shed his London Fog trench coat as he came dripping through the door. The lobby directory was quite clear and led him without a hitch directly to the clerk of Public Safety and Neighborhood Services Committee.

"Hello. I'm Daniel Watson, the new intern from USF. Today is my first day, and I was told to report to you."

"Oh yes," the slight bespectacled man said as he rose from his chair, brushed his long thinning hair from his forehead, and stuck his hand out. "I'm Charlie Golden. Glad to meet you. Have a seat, Mr. Watson."

"Please call me Daniel," Daniel advised.

After a brief get-acquainted session, Charlie got right down to business. "Okay, Daniel, here's how it works. This committee keeps in touch with the various neighborhoods in the city, and we develop and present policies to promote appropriate services and needed safety measures tailored to the particular neighborhood. What you will do is gather, summarize, and analyze information needed to respond to issues as they come up. You will do your first assignment with one of our permanent analysts and then you will be on your own. Are you familiar with the city?" Charlie asked.

"Oh yes. I've lived here almost six years and have seen most of it," Daniel answered.

"Great! Here is a packet of detailed maps of each quadrant of the city. You will need these in making your reports. Any questions?" Charlie prompted.

"No, not now, but I'm sure I will have some later," Daniel said.

"Feel free to contact me any time. You'll be working with Alan Gering to start; let me call him in, and we will get you lined up for your first assignment," Charlie explained.

Alan Gering walked in and filled the room. His 6' 2" frame was topped by a jet black crewcut which served to enhance a pair of sparkling intense blue eyes. He walked directly to Daniel, stuck out his plate-size hand, and said, "So you're the new intern. I'm Alan Gering."

As Daniel's hand disappeared into Alan's, he managed to mumble his name.

"We're going to be working together for a while, so welcome aboard," Alan exclaimed. After the necessary volunteer paperwork was completed, Alan said, "Great! You're one of us now. Let's go down to my office and get started. See you later, Charlie," Alan shot over his shoulder as they walked out.

"Later," Charlie replied.

Alan led the way to his 8'x10' office, chatting all the way. "Okay, here's your work space," he said while pointing to a small, white table and a chair sitting against the wall. "We spend lots of time in the field talking to people, so we don't need a lot of office. This is where we do the analyses of the data we gather.

"Here's our current assignment. We're going to the Mission District to talk to some folks and then see what information we can find on the area. Most of the city and county data is kept here so we have ready access, but face to face interviews are also important.

"The supervisors have some questions about the population change in the Mission and if any changes in policy or property controls should be instituted. It seems that there is an influx of Mexican people coming to the Mission. There's even a nightclub called Mexico de Noche

(Mexico at Night). Police report that it's difficult to investigate a crime in the Mission because no one speaks English. We'll need to do a report for their meeting two weeks from now."

The report was ready well ahead of the two-week timeline. Indeed, it did verify what police officers had reported. The Mission District was a Spanish speaking environment. Whether by inability or refusal, very few residents spoke English. It appeared that the influx of population was a result of former farmworkers coming to the city to find work in hotels and restaurants. It was low-paying hard work, just like farm work but it was not seasonal and not as dusty and hot.

Daniel and Alan were all over the city in the six months of Daniel's internship. They witnessed and reported on the transition of the North Beach Italian neighborhood to a night clubbing area driven by the new topless craze led by Carol Doda. They saw China Town weather the push for modernization yet maintain its historical character. The ebbs and flows of city life were the constant topic of their daily work, and Daniel loved it.

Daniel loved it even more when a report of theirs resulted in positive change for city residents. Recruitment and placement of Spanish speaking officers in the Mission was one such result.   After the new officers began to work in the Mission, the crime rate dropped dramatically. Daniel was proud of this.

As Daniel walked to Market Street to catch his bus, he thought, this is what I want to do with my career. To be in a position to help people.

Alan and Charlie had both been very helpful to him.

They had taught Daniel a lot and given him good guidance. In fact, some of their comments would appear in his thesis: *Management of Local Government in California.* He was more than a little sad to say goodbye to them, but it was time. His time as a student was coming to a close. He needed to think about what was next.

Alan and Charlie had both assured him that if an analyst position were to open in San Francisco, he would be the top candidate. Unfortunately, nothing was moving with city or county employment, so he started looking.

Chapter 33

The school year went on somewhat normally but not uneventfully. The migrants came and went. It was spring, and Jimmy was feeling like a seasoned veteran. He thought often of his discussion with the superintendent, and he still had more questions than answers. The one thing Jimmy did know is that he was faced every day with a room full of children, at least a third of whom did not speak English. He was responsible to teach them; there was only so much he could do through a bilingual aide and his halting Spanish. One fine spring day, he came to the conclusion that in order to do his job, he would have to learn more Spanish.

The Spanish that he had learned at the institute and in Mexico was helpful, but he was still unable to give good instructions in Spanish to non-English speakers. Jimmy was always trying to be a better teacher. He took his responsibility very seriously.

He continued to study Spanish at the local Junior College, but he did not feel he was making much progress. The method of teaching relied heavily on reading and writing and making written translations. He had used a new method that relied more on listening, memorizing, speaking, and then reading and writing to teach Renaldo and Tiburcio. This method fit very well with what Jimmy had learned about language development in children. He knew that listening comprehension came first, then speech production, and reading and writing followed. He knew he needed immersion in the Spanish language, and he wasn't going to get it in college courses. Then he remembered Father Anaya telling him about Cuernavaca and CIDOC.

Father Anaya had explained that the Centro Intercultural de Documentación (CIDOC) had been founded by an Austrian priest. It was started for the training of Catholic clergy sent to work in Latin America. Father Ivan Illich started the center with the blessing of Bishop Arceo of Cuernavaca. Both were immediately accused of having leftist leanings and aligning themselves with socialists.

The center had begun in the early 1960s, and Father Illich had since gone on to other endeavors. The political overtones of the center had been abandoned, but the excellent Spanish language training component remained intact. In fact, now the primary mission of CIDOC was Spanish language training. Remembering this, Jimmy sat down and wrote a letter to Father Anaya explaining his situation and requesting information about how to enroll in CIDOC. He knew that mail traveled slowly in Mexico, but the cost of a telephone call was prohibitive. On a bright spring morning, Jimmy dropped his letter at the Perryville post office on his way to school with great hopes for an early answer.

Jimmy walked into his classroom that spring day with renewed hope that he could reach those limited and non-English speaking children in his class. They deserved to have an opportunity to learn, and they certainly couldn't do that with textbooks they couldn't read and a teacher they couldn't understand.

You only get to be eleven once, Jimmy thought, and some of these kids are missing out on an education because of this language barrier. Some might say that they were missing out also because their families moved so much.

That may be true, but Jimmy knew he couldn't do anything about that. He said to himself, I can do something about the language issue, and I'm going to do it. I'll learn to speak fluent Spanish one way or another, and I'll give these kids a first rate education.

With that thought in mind, Jimmy started his before-class tutoring session with Imelda. She was eighteen months older than the other students, and her size showed it. At least a foot taller than any boy in the class, she was a gangly thirteen-year -old. She was embarrassed to be there and told Jimmy she didn't want to come to school.

This delay in schooling was through no fault of her own. Her family had moved around Texas so much that she was never able to complete the sixth grade. Even with California's social promotion penchant and her age, she was still placed in the sixth grade. Jimmy had impressed upon her the need for an education, and made a deal with her that if she would come to school early, he would tutor her. She agreed, and they were now in week five of the tutoring sessions.

During the course of tutoring, Jimmy discovered that she was an extremely bright and eager student. It was a joy to watch her progress from the fourth grade reading level to sixth grade within five weeks. She was a fluent English speaker to begin with but obviously had not had much instruction in how to read.

"Good morning, Imelda. How are you today?" Jimmy asked.

"I'm fine. How are you?" Imelda replied.

"I'm great. It's a stupendous day," Jimmy exclaimed.

"What does that word, stupendous, mean?" she asked.

"You have your dictionary there. Look it up," Jimmy advised.

"How? I don't know how to spell it," Imelda said with frustration in her voice.

Jimmy explained, "Listen to the sounds. Stu-pen-dous. Do you know a word with the sound stu?"

Imelda thought for a minute. "Yes, student." She immediately started flipping through the dictionary. "Here it is!"

With a smile, Jimmy said, "Do you agree it's a stupendous day?"

"Yes, I do!" Imelda exclaimed.

"I'm glad because I have some news for you that will make it more stupendous! I talked to Mr. Campbell, the principal, and he agreed that if you can pass all the tests in reading, writing, and math for the sixth and seventh grade, then you can go into the eighth grade next school year. We will keep studying, and at the end of the school year, you will take the test to pass to seventh grade. Then, when you pass that, as I know you will, you will take the test to pass from seventh to eighth grade. When September comes, the rest of the class will go to the seventh grade and you will go to the eighth," Jimmy explained.

"But what if I don't pass the test?" Imelda said worriedly.

"If you keep studying as hard as you have these last few weeks, you will pass. Remember that saying a friend of mine told me, *'El camarón que se duerme se lo lleva la corriente'* (the sleeping shrimp is carried away by the current). So, keep studying, don't get lazy, and you will pass."

"Oh, thank you Mr. Welch. I will study very hard."

****

Within three weeks Jimmy had his answer from Father Anaya.

Dear Jim,

It was good to hear from you and to know you are educating our children. I still have friends at CIDOC and have made some inquiries for you. They would be glad to have you as a student. It is an individualized program, so you can start any Monday and end any Friday. They are primarily a language school now, but they do have some professors available who teach in other areas. The way it works at CIDOC is if you have an interest in a topic, you may hire a professor to teach you. If one is teaching a group and you have an interest, you may join. This is consistent with Father Illich's views on education. You may want to read his book, *Deschooling Society*.

If you want to attend the CIDOC language school, you should register now; any study you wish, in addition to Spanish, can be arranged after arrival. I have had a registration form for the school forwarded to you. Complete and return it with your registration deposit as soon as you can.

Please let me know your plans when you decide. Perhaps it will be possible for me to show you some of Mexico, if your schedule coincides with my vacation time.

Please be advised that this is a total-immersion language course. There are only two staff members at the school who are fluent in English. A few of the adjunct professors are English speakers, but you may or may not have contact with them.

Sincerely, Father Anaya

Jimmy was overjoyed to receive the CIDOC information. He was thrilled to think of going to a total-immersion Spanish course where in a period of months, he would learn enough to be capable of communicating well with his students and their parents. He answered Father Anaya immediately.

Dear Father Anaya,

Thank you so much for the arrangements you have made for me at CIDOC. I am eager to go and learn as much as I can. I find that my lack of Spanish fluency is hampering my ability to teach the non-English speakers here, and I look forward to correcting that.

My plan is to leave for Cuernavaca as soon as school is out on June 7th. My focus will be strictly on learning the Spanish language. Any other study I may be able to do while there will be a bonus. I am not sure how much travel I will be able to do. I will need to arrive back home by August 28th in order to be ready for school opening, but I will stay in touch.

Best Regards,

Jim Welch

****

A call to the principal's office from Jimmy's earliest days was usually a cause of angst. The next day when Jimmy answered the intercom in his room and Mr. Campbell said to please see him after school, Jimmy was a little worried.

At exactly 3:35 p.m., after all the children had left the classroom, he headed for the principal's office.

"Hey Jim, come in and have a seat. I've got some good news for you."

Anxiety leaving and curiosity rising, Jimmy said, "Okay, what is it?"

"Imelda passed all of her sixth *and* seventh grade tests with flying colors. She will be going into eighth grade next year. I thought you might want to tell her. I know you spent a lot of time tutoring her."

"Thank you so much, Mr. Campbell. Yes, I do want to tell her. She will be thrilled."

"Well, she should be. And I want to let you know that I'm thrilled to have a teacher that goes out of his way to see that his students learn all they can. This little girl was lucky to have you."

"Thank you, Sir."

The next morning at their regular 7:30 a.m. tutoring time, Jimmy waited with great anticipation for Imelda to arrive. His heart was filled with joy that she would be able to join her peers in the right age group. There would be no more teasing about how big or old she was; she would fit in, and that's all she wanted — just to be one of the group. As he watched her arrive, a tall thin girl with slumped shoulders, he was smiling as broad as a circus clown. "Good morning, Imelda. How are you?"

"I'm fine. Guess what? My Dad said that we are staying here all year this time. We're not going to Texas. A farmer he worked for gave us a house to live in and told my Dad he will have work for him all year. In the summer, he will irrigate, fix equipment, and watch over the workers. In the winter, he will prune. In the spring, he will plant, and in the fall, he will watch over the workers and help with harvest. We are all happy we won't have to move anymore."

"That's really wonderful, Imelda. I'm happy for you and your family. Now I have something to show you that I think you'll enjoy." With that, Jimmy handed Imelda her test results. She took a long moment staring at the paper than slowly raised her head to stare at him.

"What does it mean?" she asked.

"Well, it means that you passed everything with high marks and you will be going to the eighth grade next year," Jimmy almost shouted in an elated tone. "You're skipping seventh and going right to eighth grade when you come back in September."

"Oh!" Imelda said with a catch in her voice and tears welling up in her eyes. "Thank you. Thank you." The words poured out like water from a fire hose. "I will never forget what you did for me, *never*."

As the class began to filter into the room, Imelda took her seat and sat up very straight in her chair. No more slouching for her, Jimmy thought with a smile.

The rest of the day went very well for Jimmy and especially for Imelda. Her smile was plastered on her face permanently and her normally quiet retiring attitude had morphed into a bubbly talkative young lady. The song, *What a Difference a Day Makes*, kept running through Jimmy's head.

****

Spring had sprung, and the activity around McKinley

School picked up at a furious pace. Workers were busy planting everything from tomato plants to adding a new orchard. The small trees looked like tiny sticks. Oddly, all were planted at a slight angle pointing west. It had been explained to Jimmy that the prevailing winds in the area were west winds blowing from west to east. Thus the tiny orchard saplings were planted with a slight western angle to help them grow straight as the wind pushed them easterly.

The tomato planting was a thing of beauty and precision. The tomato planting and harvesting machines were, in part, a reaction to the attempt to unionize farmworkers. Big agribusiness had answered the union movement with redoubled efforts to mechanize farming. In 1965, the farmworker strikes were begun by a group of Filipinos in the Delano, California area. Mexicans and Mexican-American farmworkers cooperated and participated by refusing to cross picket lines.

By the end of 1965, Caesar Chavez had become the face and voice of the effort to unionize farmworkers. Under Chavez, the unionization effort grew and gained momentum. This effort was assisted by a documentary called, *Harvest of Shame* by Edward Murrow, which laid bare the reality of the backbreaking work being done by farmworkers for paltry wages.

The answer from some of the major agribusiness concerns in California was to try to further mechanize farming. Thus the tomato planting and harvesting machines were developed. Jimmy thought about this as he drove through the lush fields to McKinley and stopped to watch the tomato planting. Three workers sat on the machine. They planted tomatoes 24 inches apart in rows that were four feet apart. The rows stretched out over the rich tan loam until they converged in the distance then disappeared from sight. The work, this slow moving machine with a driver and three planters, was doing what would have taken ten workers three times as long to do.

That fact was not lost on Jimmy; he had heard enough talk around the school to know that farmers were trying to reduce the amount of human labor needed. The unspoken issue was that there would be little to unionize if machines did most of the work. It was also clear that there was just some work a machine couldn't do well. Picking the beautiful succulent apricots, plums, and peaches in this area was one task a machine would just mangle. That fact alone made it obvious that for the foreseeable future, a great need for farmworkers still existed.

****

Jimmy's adult class was going great, and his fifth and sixth grade class was learning and seemed happy. But Jimmy was a bit on edge; only three weeks left of school and he still hadn't heard from CIDOC. He was waiting for the letter of acceptance and needed to know what to plan for the summer.

After school, Jimmy pulled the CIDOC literature from his desk drawer and looked it over. Right on the first page was a series of numbers which appeared to be a phone number. He took it to the teacher's lounge and asked Ofelia. Yes, it was a phone number, and yes, she would make the call if Jimmy paid.

The very next day after school, Jimmy and Ofelia went to the phone booth in front of the McKinley grocery store.

Jimmy had $10 in quarters, and Ofelia had the phone number. She knew about calls to Mexico and told him it would be between $5 and $10.

The operator answered. Ofelia said she was calling Cuernavaca, Mexico and gave the operator the number. "Hold please," the operator said. There was a long pause while the operator checked the 'rate and route' information for the call. "That will be $5.50 for the first three minutes."

After several clicks and beeps, a voice answered, "*Hola, Centro Intercultural de Documentación* (Hello, Center for Intercultural Documentation)."

"Please deposit $5.50," the operator instructed. Jimmy started handing Ofelia the quarters. When the quarters had all dinged their way into the telephone coin box, the line was live and Ofelia began in Spanish, "***Hello. I'm calling about the registration for James Welch. He wants to know if he has been accepted and when he will get his letter.***"

"***Just a minute. Let me look.***" There was no sound on the line until the operator said, "Please deposit $1.25 for another minute." Five more quarters dinged their way down and CIDOC came back on the line.

"***Yes, he is accepted. His letter was mailed yesterday and should be there in about a week. It will have instructions for travel and housing.***"

"***Thank you very much***," Ofelia said and hung up.

Ofelia gave Jimmy the good news and they both cheered. Jimmy felt the adrenaline rush of excitement. He was going to spend the summer in Mexico learning Spanish. Ofelia was happy for him too. She had never seen a gringo that wanted so badly to learn Spanish.

Jimmy was walking on air as he went back to his car and began the drive to Perryville. All the way home, his head was full of plans — what to take, when to buy the plane ticket, how to get to the airport? It was three weeks before departure and he had lots to do.

After a restless night dreaming of Mexico and being a Spanish speaker, Jimmy awoke, jumped out of bed, dressed, and was out the door in 30 minutes. He was anxious to set everything right and finish up last minute projects before school was out. As he pulled into the school parking lot, he saw a car with U.S. Government plates parked in front of the principal's office.

Jimmy was curious — some would say nosey. So, instead of going into his classroom, Jimmy went to the teacher's room. As he entered the room, he saw a large blond-haired man in uniform, talking with the principal and some of the teachers.

"Jim," Mr. Campbell called out. "Join us. I want you to meet Mr. Claremont. Mr. Claremont is an immigration officer. He was just telling me that the schools may soon be required to check immigration documents of those parents who enroll their children in school."

Mr. Claremont chimed in, "Yes, that's what's being considered. I just wanted to give you folks a heads up in case the rule is adopted. It would start in September."

"What would happen if immigration documents aren't in order?" Jimmy asked.

Mr. Claremont explained, "According to the rule, you would have to see proof of citizenship or legal residency in the U.S. before enrolling the child. I'm not sure the rule has much of a chance because agribusiness' interests have a great need for workers. And now with the attempts to unionize farmworkers, they are lobbying even harder for less immigration control."

"What do you mean?" Jimmy said.

"If a farmworker is here illegally, he tries to stay under the radar, do his work, get paid, and move on. He's not going to be walking a picket line or going on strike. There's a whole army of strike busters out there ready to work — strike or no strike, as long as we don't control immigration. Agribusiness needs thousands of seasonal workers and most Americans are not going to do that hot, dirty, backbreaking work.

"After the bracero program ended in 1964, a call for workers went out when the strawberry crop was ready to be picked. Anyone who was receiving welfare payments could keep their allotment and also any extra money they made picking strawberries. Very few people responded; a large part of the strawberry crop rotted in the field that year for lack of harvest workers. The story that illegals are taking American jobs is not true. The illegal farmworkers however are driving down wages and preventing unionization of farmworkers," Mr. Claremont explained.

Jimmy asked, "What do you think of the proposed rule?"

"I'm not allowed to give an opinion one way or the other. I will tell you this though. I worked border patrol early in my career. I was tasked with trying to stem the tide of illegals flowing over the border. In those early years, right after the bracero program ended, the border became very porous because agribusiness needed workers and Mexican farmworkers wanted to work. A whole cottage industry of 'coyotes' transporting illegals has sprung up now. But at first, it was just individuals trying to get across to the United States."

Mr. Claremont continued. "One dark night I was on patrol down by Nogales, Arizona and I saw movement on my night scope. My partner and I drove out into that dark desert night and approached a Mexican man about 32 years old. He had no papers; he had nothing except 2 one-gallon plastic jugs filled with water.

"When we questioned him, he admitted that he had hopped a freight train in Hermosillo, Mexico, got off in Benjamin Hill and couldn't catch another freight, so he walked over 100 miles to Nogales and slipped across the border. He was planning to walk to Tucson and take a bus to the Imperial Valley to find farm work. Some friends had told him that Tucson was a Spanish speaking environment and he would be able to catch a bus.

"Now, I'm sure you know that a gallon of water weighs a little over 8 pounds. Here is this guy in *huaraches* (sandals) carrying over 8 pounds in each hand who walked over 100 miles in the desert before we caught him. He did all this so he could find a job doing backbreaking work in the hot sun. When we asked him why he did this, he told us he had a wife and three children and he could find little work in Mexico. The family was barely surviving.

"That is a long answer to your question about my opinion of this new rule. I have no opinion that I am able to state here. I will just tell you, a guy that would do what that man did to get here, be separated from his family, so he could do punishing work for low pay to take care of his family. I would be honored and proud to have that man as a neighbor."

Jimmy walked to his classroom with his head full of contradictions. An immigration officer, the '*Migra*' as the locals called them, admired those he was trying to apprehend and send back to Mexico. Maybe Mr. Claremont didn't have warm fuzzy feelings about all of them but at least he did about one. Then he freely admits that he loaded the guy up, and he was transported back to Mexico. "Doing my job," he said. "I will always do my duty, whether I like it or not."

Chapter 34

Juan was headed back to Perryville. He wasn't sure what he would do. He would work the farm this summer, and then, "We will see," he said.

MEChA had helped him develop a healthy respect for the role education can play in changing society, so he was thinking of teaching, although there were some significant impediments to becoming a teacher. California had changed the credentialing requirements to include a full year of postgraduate study to qualify for a credential. His scholarship had been used, and he could see no way to finance another year of college.

He arrived home to the welcome arms of his family and a party with the extended family. The first college graduate of all the family was a thing to celebrate, and they did. The festivities went on for a day and a night, then the family eased back into their lives with renewed hope for their children.

Juan was hoeing puncture vines from the watermelon patch one day when he remembered Jimmy Welch's offer to help. Yes, that's right, Juan thought. He said to call if he could help me with anything. Maybe he can give me some tips about how to finance my year of teacher education. That's really what I want to do — be a teacher!

At lunchtime, Juan came in, washed up, ate, and got out the telephone book. Sure enough, there was Jimmy's home phone number. Back to hoeing, he thought all afternoon about how to put his question to Jimmy.

After dinner that night, Juan made his call. When Jimmy answered, Juan said, "Hey, Jimmy. This is Juan."

"Oh, hi. How are you doing?" Jimmy asked.

"I'm doing great. I graduated from college, just got home last week," Juan replied.

"What are you doing this summer?" Jimmy asked.

"Just working on the farm," Juan answered. "What about you?"

"Well, I have a week before school gets out and then I'm going to Mexico," Jimmy answered enthusiastically.

"Wow, sounds great!" Juan exclaimed. "I called because I've decided that I want to be a teacher, but I'm having trouble figuring out how to pay for another year of school. Can you give me any ideas?" Juan asked.

"Well, what a coincidence," Jimmy answered. "I was just talking to my principal, Mr. Campbell, this afternoon and he was telling me that California has just started a teacher internship program.

"The way it works is a college graduate who wants to be a teacher can be placed in a classroom under the guidance of a master teacher. The intern must teach four days a week and attend college classes one day a week to complete academic requirements for the credential. At the end of a year, if the intern has successfully completed all classes and the master teacher has certified their ability to teach, the intern gets a provisional credential. After three years of teaching with positive evaluations, the intern receives a full credential. What do you think?" Jimmy asked.

"Sounds really great. Does the intern get paid?" Juan hesitantly asked.

"Oh yes. They get three-fourths of a regular teaching salary. Also, San Francisco State is providing an off-campus teacher training program in Stockton," Jimmy said.

Juan was perplexed, "Why is all this being done?"

"Because there is a teacher shortage in California," Jimmy replied. "We can't even get enough teachers by recruiting from other states. I'll get some information for you and drop it in the mail, or you can come by the school tomorrow and get it."

"Okay, I'll stop by tomorrow," Juan said. "This sounds exciting."

"Great. See you tomorrow!" Jimmy said.

Class was just being dismissed when Juan arrived. Jimmy had told him to come to Room 6, and he went directly there, just as the children were exiting. Jimmy and Ofelia were just finishing a discussion with a mother who had come to talk about her daughter. ***It will be fine; she just needs to spend more time doing the practice math problems in her homework,*** Ofelia said. Jimmy introduced Juan to Ofelia and Mrs. Sanchez.

"Are you going to be a teacher here too?" asked Mrs. Sanchez in very cultured Spanish.

Juan looked like a deer caught in the headlights, staring straight ahead, not knowing what to do. Ofelia quickly told him what she had asked.

"Oh, no. Please tell her I'm just here to get some papers," Juan explained.

Ofelia translated Juan's explanation and Mrs. Sanchez said to Ofelia, ***"He is Mexican but he doesn't speak Spanish?"***

Jimmy got the drift of the question and said to Ofelia, "Tell her his parents were born here."

"Oh, I see," Mrs. Sanchez said in response as she went out the door.

"What did she say?" Juan questioned.

"She wondered why you didn't speak Spanish. I told her it's because your family has lived here many years," Ofelia responded.

"Come over and have a seat. I've got some information for you," Jimmy said as he handed Juan a thick folder of papers explaining all the details of the new internship program.

After Juan looked the information over, he said, "I think this a great opportunity. I really want to do this."

"That's great, Juan. The principal, Mr. Campbell, has told me that we will be bringing two interns into our school. Would you like to be one of them?" Jimmy asked.

"I would love that. This is close enough that I could still help out on the farm on the weekends and all summer. And I see that most of the kids are Chicanos. The main reason I want to be a teacher is to help Chicano kids get a good education," Juan offered.

"That's great, but just a word to the wise — I would be very careful about using the word Chicano here. Most of the parents consider themselves either Mexican or Mexican-American. They don't seem to like that word, Chicano, so much," Jimmy explained.

"Oh yeah. Okay, I get it. My pop doesn't like it either," Juan confessed.

"But you are right; the best thing we can do is give these kids a great education that equips them to be successful in the world," Jimmy offered.

"Do the kids speak English?" Juan asked.

"The majority of them do, and we are getting more resources for those who don't. You know the Lau vs. Nichols case in 1974 resulted in legislation that requires schools to provide education in a language the children understand. We have money now for lots of bilingual instructional aides to help the mono-lingual teachers."

"I wish my folks had taught me Spanish," Juan said.

"Well, it's never too late," Jimmy replied. "But we can talk about that later. Meanwhile, if you want to be an intern here, take these papers with you, fill them out, and bring them to me tomorrow. I'll go over them with the principal. I need to do that soon though because I'm leaving for Mexico next week."

"Consider it done," Juan said. "I'll see you tomorrow."

Juan was true to his word. The dismissal bell rang and he was standing outside Jimmy's door. His papers were complete and looked very good. Graduating Magna Cum Laud was certainly a plus on his resume.

"Okay, this is very good," Jimmy said. "I'll take these to the principal today. I'm sure he will give you a call after he sees your paper work, and I'll put in a good word for you. I'll probably be out of town when he calls you, so just tell him what you told me about why you want to teach here.

He will love it. He loves these kids and does whatever he can to see that they get a good education.

"One other thing I'd like to talk to you about. I know you told me I could keep calling you Johnny because that's how we have known each other, but I don't want that. I was there on your first day of kindergarten, when you tried to tell the teacher your name was Juan. She just steamrolled you and named you Johnny. I hadn't thought much about that until I got here with these kids. We don't have the right to change their names. I want to call you by the name your parents gave you, Juan! Okay?" Jimmy asked.

"Yes, that's fine with me. I go by Juan everywhere now except to people from Perryville," Juan answered.

"Good! Well, good luck to you. I'll be back late August and hope to see you at new teacher orientation," Jimmy said.

Chapter 35

Finally the big day arrived. School was out for the summer. Jimmy had given his adult students directions about how to continue their learning by watching English language television and trying to speak English to the townspeople. He assured them he would start their classes again in the fall.

Jimmy had gotten his airline ticket; he would fly from Stockton to San Francisco to Mexico City. His CIDOC letter explained how to get the bus in Mexico City and take it to Cuernavaca. It also gave the name and directions to a four-room guest house where a reservation had been made for him.

Jimmy was engrossed in his thoughts as he and his dad pulled into the Stockton Airport. Jimmy's dad pulled right up to the departure door at the small airport, and Jimmy hopped out. He got his suitcase out of the trunk, waved goodbye, and walked with eager excitement into the airport.

The plane ride from Stockton to San Francisco to Mexico City was uneventful. The only unusual activity was the stewardess with a can of disinfectant. As they were on approach to Mexico City, the stewardess walked briskly down the aisle with a spray can of disinfectant pointed at the floor and operating at full blast.

Jimmy asked, "What is the purpose of that?"

The stewardess said, "Oh, it's a rule. The government here says they don't want any contaminants from the United States coming into their country. Just a jab at us for all the jokes about Mexico being dirty, I think. Do you speak Spanish?" she asked.

"A little," Jimmy replied.

"Well, here's a saying popular in Mexico City that sort of sums up their feelings about the United States: 'Pobre Mexico que es lejos de Dios y cerca de los Estados Unidos.' Did you get that?" she asked.

"Yes, I think so. Poor Mexico is far from God and something about the United States," Jimmy offered.

"Yes." she said, "Far from God and close to the United States."

"Whoa, I'm a little more nervous now about being here after hearing that," Jimmy exclaimed.

"Oh, not to worry. They will love you, especially since you speak some Spanish. It's the politicos that feel this way about the U.S. They don't like our government but love our people. You will be fine."

"*Gracias a Dios* (Thank God)," Jimmy said.

Entry through Customs was easy and quick, helped by the fact that Jimmy had renewed the passport from his European adventure. The presentation of a valid passport with an attendant photo seemed much more pleasing to the customs officers than the tourist cards most travelers presented.

Very soon, Jimmy was in a taxi headed for the Mexico City central bus station. The city of eight million looked gigantic and impressive from the air, a sight Jimmy had not seen on his previous train arrival. But the city was a maze of tangled streets and highways that made him glad he was not driving.

After a few near misses, a lot of horn honking, and hand gestures by his taxi driver, they arrived at the station. Jimmy had received written instructions from CIDOC about surface travel from the airport to Cuernavaca, and to CIDOC once in Cuernavaca. He now consulted the instructions again. "Secure a first-class bus ticket to Cuernavaca to ensure a seat for the two- hour ride," the instructions said. He found the ticket counter and was able to negotiate buying a ticket. He found his halting Spanish sufficient, although he was sure he sounded like a kindergarten child to them.

After a short wait, his bus arrived and he got in line. Asiento 5 (seat 5), his ticket said. But alas, when he found asiento 5, there was a gentleman seated there. Jimmy didn't have the Spanish to navigate this conversation, so he held up his ticket to the seated gentleman and pointed to asiento 5. The gentleman than withdrew a ticket from his pocket that also had asiento 5 printed on it.

Jimmy was perplexed as he looked around and saw the seats were now all taken and three people were standing in the aisle. The gentleman in seat 5 tapped Jimmy on the arm and pointed to a hanging hand strap, the type he had seen on the San Francisco streetcars. Jimmy didn't learn until later that if you wanted a reserved seat on the bus, you not only had to get a first-class ticket in advance, but you also had to get on the bus before the other person or people who had been sold the same ticket got on. This was a lesson learned for Jimmy as he grabbed the strap and prepared for two hours of standing in the aisle. Before the bus left, not only was every seat filled, but every spot where anyone could stand was filled. They were packed in like sardines.

Off they went with an overly full bus. Every curve and corner sent the standers swaying left or right. Every stop pushed them forward, and every acceleration backward. They were like a moving wave in the water.

After being jostled for two hours, Jimmy was very happy as the bus slowed and came to a stop and the driver called out *"Cuernavaca!"* Jimmy stepped off the bus, collected his suitcase, tipped the driver, and walked over to the taxi stand.

To say it was love at first sight is too mild a statement for how Jimmy felt about his introduction to Cuernavaca. Bougainvillea plants were everywhere, growing on ancient walls in this sixteenth-century city. Their rose, orange, fuchsia, and pink colors covered the city in a kaleidoscope of beauty. Their beauty was only enhanced by the urban forest that surrounded and shot through Cuernavaca. "The City of Eternal Spring," Jimmy had heard it called. The profusion of flowers and trees and the pleasant 70-degrees-Fahrenheit weather now verified how the city got its name.

Within a very short time, Jimmy and his brown Samsonite suitcase were deposited in front of what would be his home for the next 3 months. It was a French manor house from the time of Maximillian's domination of Mexico. The gorgeous stately whitewashed building was set among tall pines on a little knoll that ran down to a small outdoor swimming pool. One wing of the residence had been converted to housing for CIDOC students, four small rooms, each with its own bath.

The owners, the Fuentes family, had done a very nice job of providing pleasant rooms for rest and study. Adjacent to the rooms was a dining room where the main meal of the day was served from 1 p.m. to 3 p.m. Señora Fuentes now showed Jimmy to the room that had been reserved for him by CIDOC. She spoke softly to him in Spanish as they made their way to his room, and he was gratified to find that he understood most of what she said about the room and hours of dining.

Jimmy's room was bright and airy and looked out on a grassy decline to the swimming pool below. Surrounded by trees, the swimming pool area became a natural gathering place for the myriad of birds that populated Cuernavaca. He could hear them chattering in the trees now as he unpacked and placed his clothes in the small closet.

The two-hour time difference had little effect on Jimmy. The excitement generated adrenaline that coursed through his body; he was up and out of the room shortly after the sun was up the next day. The gentle breeze, the birds chattering in the trees, the smell of the many flower varieties and the pleasant temperature all served to remind Jimmy why this was called the City of Eternal Spring.

He could not go to CIDOC to register until 8 a.m. local time, so he wandered into the dining area in search of coffee. He was pleasantly surprised by a silver urn full of rich steaming black coffee, a pitcher of fresh squeezed orange juice, and a plate of melon slices.

The maid, Angelica, was there with a smile and said, **"Good morning, sir. May I pour some coffee for you?"**

"*Si gracias* (Yes, please)," Jimmy replied. The only

word he really understood was café (coffee), but the facts of the situation helped him to understand her meaning. This is how he would learn for the next several weeks, being immersed in the language and culture of the community.

After a leisurely coffee and melon for breakfast, Jimmy was off to CIDOC. He strolled the quarter mile to the town center, taking in the beauty of his surroundings. For the rest of his life, the sight of a bougainvillea plant would conjure up memories of Cuernavaca, *La Ciudad de Primavera Eterna* (the City of Eternal Spring).

It was not only the beauty of the natural surroundings that stuck in Jimmy's mind but the history and international flavor of the place that would entrance him.

Indigenous people had lived for eons in a place called Cuauhrahuac. When Cortez conquered Mexico, he established his summer palace there, and soon the city name became a perversion of Cuauhrahuac that, rendered in English, means cow's horn (Cuernavaca). When France ruled Mexico, Maximillian also established his summer palace in Cuernavaca. Mohammad Reza Pahlai, former Shah of Iran, lived in exile there after the Iranian revolution, and philanthropist, Barbara Hutton, had a home on the outskirts of the town. Over the years, the beauty, the friendly people, and agreeable climate had drawn people from all walks of life to this special place. Throughout his life, Jimmy would be glad for the time he had spent there.

But on that day, it was all new to Jimmy, and he absorbed it as he walked. His every sense was alive and alert. The natural and man-made beauty he saw was almost overwhelming. The fragrant smell of the flowers, the feel of the gentle breeze that caressed his face, the sound of the birds happily cavorting in the tree tops; it all combined to put his heart and mind at ease.   Jimmy could certainly understand why so many opted to avoid the Mexico City area and have their summer homes here. Jimmy only hoped his experience at CIDOC would be as pleasant as the city.

Jimmy arrived at the gate of CIDOC with a calm and relaxed demeanor and walked into the small office. *"Como puedo ayudarte* (How can I help you)?" the young man sitting behind a small desk asked Jimmy.

"I'm here to register for Spanish lessons," Jimmy answered.

"Oh yes. What is your name?"

"Jim Welch."

The young man went down his list and said, "Yes. Here you are. Your deposit has been paid for the first week. Welcome to CIDOC. My name is Alejandro García. I will be one of your instructors. Before we begin orientation, please tell me a little about yourself and why you are here." Jimmy gave him a brief resume and explained that he needed to speak Spanish in order to be able to speak with some of his students and their parents.   "That is very good, Señor Welch, that you take care of our people when they come to you. The poor people leave Mexico because they have no choice. We are a poor country, and they cannot make a living here. Thank you so much for wanting to help them.

"Let me tell you a little about CIDOC," Alejandro continued. "The school was started by an Austrian priest, Ivan Illich, as a training center for Catholic priests and nuns from other countries who were going to work in Latin America. He wanted to help them understand and fit in with the culture and of course to learn Spanish. They had to be fluent in Spanish and very familiar with local customs and culture in order to minister to the people.

"After several years of providing this teaching, the church withdrew support. When that happened, we transitioned to providing culture and language training to anyone, in or out of the church, who had a need to learn about Mexico and Latin America. Currently we have several French Canadian news reporters who will report for French language newspapers. We have some nurses who will do volunteer work in Mexico who have come here on their own. The rest are a mix of British and Americans who, like you, have some need to learn the language and culture.

"I should also tell you that there are adjunct professors here who can be hired to teach classes on the politics and history of Latin America if a small group wants to do that in the afternoon. They are Americans and will teach in English or Spanish. Three of them were previously instructors in the University of California system and came here over dissatisfaction with the politics of the United States.

"But let me get you registered and give you an orientation of the school. Please complete and sign these registration papers."

The paperwork was completed. Alejandro began, "Since today is Monday, we are taking in new students. You may start only on Monday but may drop out any day that you wish. However, fees for each week are paid on Monday, and no refunds are given for early departure. You may continue in the school as long as you wish. We are open Monday through Friday, year round, with the exception of a two-week break during the Christmas season, one week at Easter, and twelve additional holidays. You have chosen to stay in the manor house instead of with a family, so you will pay your lodging fee to them.

"Except in cases of extreme emergency, this is the last English you will hear from any of the staff at CIDOC. In fact, most staff do not speak English. Please ask any questions you may have as I go along. Class begins at 8 a.m., and please forget anything you may have heard about Mexicans not adhering to time schedules. Also, please disregard any other things you may have heard, like 'the clock doesn't run; it walks in Mexico.' Here it is not the land of mañana. At CIDOC, 8 a.m. means 8 a.m. *en punto* (sharp). The class schedule is as follows:

<u>8:00 – 10:00</u> Groups of four meet with their primary instructor. (9 a.m. on Mondays only.)

<u>10:00 – 10:15:</u> Morning break.

<u>10:15 – 11:30:</u> Groups of four meet with assistant instructor for guided conversation.

<u>11:30 – 12:30:</u> Groups of eight meet with primary instructor.

<u>12:30 – 1:00:</u> Entire student body meets with all instructors.

"Let me explain. At the 8 a.m. sessions, you will be required to repeat and practice the dialogue you have been given the day before. It will get progressively more involved. At 10:15, you will use your Spanish to discuss a topic given to you by the group leader at the time. At 11:30, your group and another at approximately the same level will meet and practice the dialogue of the day, first as a whole group and then in a round robin of pairs. At 12:30, the entire student body will meet with all instructors for group activity. We sometimes sing Mexican folk songs, have a lecture by an advanced student, or instructor, or are treated to a poetry reading by our local Poet Laureate. Occasionally one of the local painters will come and give a painting lesson. But remember, all of this is in Spanish. No English – no translation.

"When you see me later today, I will speak *no* English. When you leave here at 1:00, you will have approximately two hours of homework to prepare for the next day. And you should take advantage of this living language laboratory that is in the city. Walk the streets and talk to the people."

Jimmy sat there staring at Alejandro. He was excited, stunned, scared, and happy. He wasn't sure exactly how he felt, but he knew what Alejandro had described was what he needed. He resolved at that moment to participate in every way to learn the language and culture.

All at once, Alejandro stood and said, *"Son las nueve vamos a la clase* (it's nine, we're going to class)," as he gestured toward the door. Jimmy didn't know exactly what he said, but he got the idea — time to go.

Jimmy's group of four mirrored to a great degree the make-up of the student body of CIDOC at the time. Simon d'Armon was a 50-year-old French Canadian farmer from Quebec who planned to immigrate to Mexico when he retired. From England there was Charles Stuart, a 22-year-old Oxford literature student who spoke five languages and wanted to learn Mexican Spanish. And there was Margot deMer, a 24-year-old French Canadian reporter for a small French language paper in Quebec who wanted to be a Latin American reporter for the Canadian Broadcasting Company.

Chapter 36

Juan came in from irrigating the peaches, and Mom said, "A man called for you a little while ago. I wrote his name down with his number. He said he was calling about an interview; he wants you to call him back."

"Yes, I can be there tomorrow," Mom heard Juan say.

"I can't work in the morning tomorrow. I'm going to have an interview to see if I can get a job as a teacher in McKinley!" Juan exclaimed.

"Will you move there?" Mom asked.

"No, it's not that far. I can drive and still help out here," Juan reassured her.

It was decided. Mr. Campbell was very impressed with Juan, especially with his academic record. Juan was offered a job as a fifth grade teacher on the spot! The salary of $3,915 for a 9 month teaching year was three fourths of a regular teacher's salary. As soon as he got his credential, it would go up to $5,220, with yearly increases up to ten years and additional increases for college units earned past the B.A.

Juan was pleased with the arrangement. It gave him the opportunity to help kids like himself to get a good education.

It was more money than he had ever made. $435 a month, was close to the farm, and it gave him summers to work on the farm. Juan left McKinley School a very happy man!

****

Summer ended much too soon to suit Juan. He was used to a mid-September college start date. But K-12 schools all across California started on the very same day, the Tuesday after Labor Day.

Juan was reticent but ready. He wondered how he would be received, especially by the parents. He was a little anxious about his inability to speak Spanish. He also worried that he didn't know the first thing about how to teach children. He was enrolled in the required credential program courses, but they didn't start until mid-September.

The two days of teacher orientation had given Juan an opportunity to meet the staff members and get acquainted. He stood out; he was the only brown face in the group. But unlike his high school experience, he was welcomed warmly with many wishes for a good year.

And now he sat on the eve of his new venture, looking out over the watermelon patch. He was proud of his work there; not one puncture vine remained, and the melons were plump and green. A few had been picked and sold from the stand.

One long striped melon had been chilled, sliced, and eaten by the family. Juan thought of the feel of the sweet juice running down his fingers and the delicious crunch of the flesh as he spat the seeds onto his plate. He only hoped that his work with the children would go as well as his farm work had gone.

Chapter 37

The first day at CIDOC was a carbon copy of many days to come. The group of four included Simon who only spoke French, Charles who spoke British English and four other languages, Margot who spoke French and a little English, and Jimmy. Each day became a choral recitation.

Jimmy thought it sounded much like the choral speaking in an ancient Greek play. First the instructor, Alejandro, would repeat a word, and the chorus of four would mimic him. This went on, gradually working up to the repetition of phrases and then full sentences. The meaning was conveyed by Alejandro's body language and drawings interspersed in the text of their workbooks. As a last resort to catching the meaning, a glossary in English and French was included.

The repetition continued until Alejandro was satisfied they could at least approximate his speech. This was followed by each individual repeating the verbiage with corrections by Alejandro as needed.

The fifteen-minute break was a welcome relief after the difficult hour of tongue-twisting repetition. Not much talking went on among beginning students as even break time was Spanish only.

Jimmy did have a pantomime conversation as Simon pulled out a pack of Gitanes cigarettes. Simon inclined the pack toward him and motioned for him to take one. Jimmy was a very part-time smoker but did not wish to be rude, so he took the cigarette and lit up.

Jimmy took a pull of the cigarette and followed with a little cough. The rich, dark, French tobacco was something akin to a rough black Tuscan cigar he had once tried. Simon looked at him waiting for a response, and Jimmy, not having the Spanish words, flexed his bicep, pointed to the muscle, and pointed to the cigarette. Simon chuckled as he got the message of *strong*!

The second class was the guided conversation period. The question from period one, '*Cómo se dice*? (How do you say?),' came in very handy. Jimmy started out with *cómo se dice,* while feeling his bicep.

"*Fuerte,*" the discussion leader said.

"*Fuerte,*" they all repeated.

Jimmy pointed to Simon's pack and said "*cigarro fuerte,*" failing miserably to roll the double "r." To which the leader replied, "*Sí los cigarros Franceses son bien fuertes (*Yes, French cigarettes are very strong*).*" They all chuckled and proceeded to try out their miniscule store of newfound words and phrases.

The third period of the day was exhilarating with two groups of four beginners each and their instructors. Jimmy and the others found that they had already learned enough to know their fellow student's names and countries of origin. Counting Jimmy and his group, there was one American, three French Canadians, two British, one British Canadian, and one German.

The fourth and final period of the day was a gathering of the entire student body of eighty-five. They were treated to a Spanish language presentation by one of the advanced students. The student explained, in what sounded to Jimmy like flawless Spanish, about the nearby silver mining city of Taxco. What Jimmy understood was Taxco and *coche* (car). But it gave Jimmy hope to see that this American, now three months later, was fluent, at least to his ears.

The presentation ended day one. As Jimmy was walking to his room, he saw that Simon was coming along behind him, so he waited for him to catch up. As they walked, they discovered through hand gestures some French words, some English phrases, and some Spanish sentences that they were going to the same location. They arrived and just had time to put their books away and wash up before it was time for the mid-day meal which was just called *comida* (food) here.

The *comida* was a wonderful affair this day and every day thereafter. It always started with a soup of some kind, followed by a small salad, then a main dish. Today the entre was *pollo asado* (roast chicken). It was delicious! It was followed, very closely on the delicious scale, by a rich creamy flan.

After a very satisfying meal with little conversation, Simon and Jimmy retired to their respective rooms for study and siesta. There would be plenty of time to explore the city later in the cool of the evening. The evening would be a more interesting exploration as all shops were closed until about 4 p.m.

Jimmy was gratified to find that he adapted very soon and very well to the rhythm of life in Cuernavaca. His school days were very much the same as the first day, except with more involved and sophisticated language learned. He found he could master the art of rolling double r's as he repeated the practice phrase over and over each day:

"*r con r cigarro; r con r barril; rapido corren los carros en el ferrocarril* (r with r cigarette, r with r barrel, the railroad cars run quickly on the railway)."

Everything was new, and he had lots to see and do. Shortly after 4 p.m. Jimmy was out the door and on his way to the City Center. He had only gone a short way when he saw a man sitting under a huge shade tree painting. He stopped to watch the man apply several layers of very colorful paint to thick brown paper. The painter was working on a fantasy-like bird with flowing and colorful plumage in reds, yellows, and stark white.

The artist looked up from under a large panama type sombrero at Jimmy, and his dark brown face cracked open with a huge smile filled with brilliant white teeth. "***You like the amates?*** He   asked with a sweeping hand indicating the many completed paintings.

Jimmy didn't understand but could see this middle-aged man was proud of his paintings. He replied with the only words he could think of, "*Muy bonito (*Very beautiful)."

"***Ah, you are a North Americano***," the man continued in Spanish. "***They are 10 pesos for the small ones, 20 pesos for the big ones.***"

Jimmy understood that the paintings were for sale. He looked them over carefully and selected a red and yellow perched bird with a gracefully flaring tail. The artist quickly rolled up the 8" x 12" painting and tied it with a string. Jimmy did understand 20 and handed over four 5-peso bills, received his painting, and was on his way.

As Jimmy entered the city center, he saw a great open-air market stretched out for a long block before him. He was amazed at the variety of produce, especially the tropical fruits. He saw limes of every size and description from small green key limes the size of a marble to large yellow tinged limes the size of tennis balls. The avocados were a wonder to him. There were small purplish ones the size of golf balls, and huge green ones the size of softballs. There were many exotic fruits and vegetables that were completely outside Jimmy's range of experience.

As Jimmy stood staring at what he later learned were mangos, the vendor approached him. ***"Puedo Ayudar*** (May I help you)?" he asked.

Jimmy picked up a mango and said, "***Nombre*** (Name)?"

The vendor, who looked to be about 45, broke into a smile and said, "Oh, you from the states."

Jimmy, shocked at hearing English, replied, "Yes."

The vendor continued. "I work in the states. I bracero for many years. I work California."

"Where in California? What town?" Jimmy asked.

"Oh, I work San Diego, Monterey, McKinley."

"You worked in McKinley?

"Yes, yes," the vendor said eagerly. "You know McKinley?"

"Yes, I do. I'm a teacher there. I'm going to CIDOC now but going back to McKinley in August. Wow, what a small world," Jimmy exclaimed.

"Yes, the world small." The vendor then drew out a large folding knife from his pocket, picked up a mango, peeled the end a bit, and cut off a slice. Offering it to Jimmy, he said, "You eat mango." Jimmy took the slice and was delighted with the rich fruity flavor — unlike anything he had eaten before.

"You like?"

"Yes, it is very good," Jimmy replied. The vendor then took three large mangos, put them in a bag, and handed them to Jimmy.

"You take."

Jimmy asked, "Okay, how much do I owe you?"

"No, you take. No pay, you take."

"Thank you very much," Jimmy said. "My name is Jim. What's yours?"

"Okay Jim, my name Roberto. *Mucho gusto (It's a pleasure)*," he said and stuck out his hand for the limp shake Jimmy now expected and knew was polite.

"Do you own this stand?" Jimmy asked

"Yes, own this one, that one, and that one," as he pointed to two others. "When I bracero, send money to Mexico to wife. She buy, I come back. No more bracero, sell here. I have wife, kids, we are five."

It was beginning to be evening and Jimmy still had lots of studying to do, so he took his leave. "I have to go now. Thank you for the mangos. I will enjoy them," Jimmy said with a smile.

"You welcome. Okay, you go. You come back; I here *diario* (daily)."

It was true, thought Jimmy, some Mexicans were able to make money in the United States and return to Mexico and buy a business. Good for Roberto!

Jimmy walked back through the carnival atmosphere of produce stands, local arts and crafts, and every variety of Mexican fast food. There was a boiling pot of ears of corn for sale, a taco stand, sliced jicama, and horchata drinks.

It was becoming twilight as Jimmy approached the grassy, tree-covered knoll to his room. He heard what he thought were firecrackers, and suddenly the chatter of the birds in the trees stopped. All at once, the entire flock swirled in the air and was gone. As he approached his room, he saw a dark-skinned wrinkled little man loading a stainless steel revolver. He looked straight at Jimmy and shouted in violent-sounding Spanish, ***"Those birds make too much noise, and they shit all over everything. I'm going to shoot them all!"***

Jimmy wasn't sure what the old man said, but he saw him loading a pistol; Jimmy dashed into the house and went straight to Mr. Fuentes' door. "There's a man outside with a gun," Jimmy excitedly shouted. "A gun, a gun." Jimmy mimicked shooting a pistol with his hand.

Mr. Fuentes chuckled a bit and said, ***"Don't worry, that's my papa. He shoots up at the birds in the trees sometimes. It's okay."***

The only part Jimmy understood was the chuckle, papa, and *está bien* (its' okay), but it was enough for him to understand it was not a problem. He went in his room, locked the door, ate a mango, and went to bed.

The next morning Jimmy was up early. He drank a quick cup of coffee and was off for CIDOC. He arrived 30 minutes before class and went straight to the office and found Alejandro. "You told us English was only to be used in emergencies. Well I have one. There was a guy shooting a pistol outside the house last evening. I talked to Mr. Fuentes, and I think he said it was okay."

"Oh, yes," Alejandro replied. "That was Don Fuentes, papa of Señor Fuentes. Everybody knows about him. Sometimes the birds' bother him and he shoots at them."

"I thought Mexicans weren't allowed to have guns," Jimmy said.

"That's not true. We can keep a gun in the house. We are not allowed to have them in public. There are only certain kinds we can have. I'll talk to Señor Fuentes and ask him to lock the gun in his safe while you are here."

"Thank you very much," a relieved Jimmy replied.

"You're welcome. *Ahora vamos a aprender Español* (Now we are going to learn Spanish)," Alejandro said.

After the somewhat tense start to Jimmy's day, it actually went very well. He was intently pursuing learning Spanish and took every opportunity to practice. In his conversation class, he had learned how to say, "Your paintings are beautiful; do you come here every day?" Jimmy intended to have a brief conversation with the artist on the way home and to do that every day.

Before Jimmy knew it, the classes had ended for the day. Time to go to *comida*. As he walked, he passed by the amate artist. He stopped and said, "*Buenos tardes* (Good afternoon). ***Your paintings are very beautiful.***"

The artist looked at him with a smile and said, "*Gracias* (thank you***), I love to paint the birds.***"

Jimmy didn't understand the response but went right on with, ***"Do you come here every day?"***

The artist responded, "***Every day except Sunday.***"

Jimmy did understand the word *Domingo* and guessed that the sentence meant he was there six days a week. "*Hasta mañana* (until tomorrow)," Jimmy said.

The bemused artist responded, "*Hasta mañana.*"

Jimmy went on to *comida*, whistling a happy tune. He had engaged in a Spanish conversation, and that made him happy. The table was set and Simon was there when he arrived. Jimmy and Simon were becoming accustomed to the afternoon comida and siesta and found it very pleasant. Simon was in a talkative mood today and began to tell Jimmy a story in three languages. "Mi casa cerca la mer. See baleine to swim la mer."

Jimmy was at a loss but used part of their daily Spanish lesson, "*No entiendo.*"

Simon knew the sentence, "I don't understand," and redoubled his efforts. First he pointed to his eyes and said, "See baleine bleue." He made a spouting noise and fountain-like gesture with his hands, then a swimming gesture, then another fountain gesture.

Finally Jimmy put it together. The word bleue that sounded so much like blue in English tipped him off. Blue whale — he's saying he saw a blue whale. Jimmy knew that blue whales were sighted off the east coast of Canada where Simon lived, and he knew the word *casa*. He finally understood that Simon had seen a blue whale close to where he lived in Quebec. It was a little bit of a difficult discussion, but Jimmy vowed that he and Simon would be speaking a common language soon . . . Spanish.

****

The days rolled by like boxcars on a fast freight train. Jimmy was six weeks into his ten-week study and wondering where all the time had gone. The days were full; between class and homework, his studies took 7 to 8 hours, 5 days a week. He saw his ramblings in the city as a huge language lab, and he took advantage of every opportunity to practice his developing Spanish skill. His conversations with local citizens served to consolidate and extend what he had learned in his classes. His weekends were his own, but he felt that he learned something about the language and culture of Mexico with every interaction.

Even though Jimmy wasn't Catholic, he took the opportunity to attend the Mariachi mass at the Cuernavaca Cathedral. The venerable old building had been a place of worship since the sixteenth century. Jimmy went there for two reasons — to see Bishop Arceo celebrate the mass and to experience what was referred to, among his group, as the mariachi mass.

Jimmy could still hear the beautiful mass being sung by wonderfully talented musicians. "*Ten pieded de nosotros*," (Have mercy on us) they repeatedly sang.

Jimmy heard, understood, and agreed. Yes, we all need God to have mercy on us!

The love of the people for Bishop Arceo, who had instituted the mariachi mass and many other innovations, was evident. They related to him as one of their own. In return, Bishop Arceo was a comforting, loving presence in their midst. His homily was full of admonitions to love their neighbors and share worldly treasure with those less fortunate.

Like many great men, he was not universally loved.

Some saw him as a socialist and perhaps in league with the Sandinistas of Nicaragua. As it had for many years, religion in Mexico often collided with politics with a resounding boom!

The Bishop had even been criticized for allowing the Austrian priest, Ivan Illich, to start CIDOC in Cuernavaca. Illich took the stance that all, including the church and other nations, should cooperate with, not co-opt, Latin American nations. Thus some of the philosophy taught to the initial classes of priests and nuns was very controversial and smacked of socialism. The result was removal of church support and the transition of CIDOC to teaching strictly language and culture to paying customers.

****

Jimmy should have attended mass every Sunday. There was a Sunday activity two Sundays ago which caused him to lose two days of class time. It happened like this.

Fellow student, Charles, and Jimmy had been spending more time together and getting friendlier. Truth be told, they did engage in disobedient behavior by speaking English occasionally. One English episode was the time Charles told Jimmy about his experience bullfighting.

"Yes, when I was 21, I went to Spain on holiday. While I was there, I took bullfighting lessons. A matador showed me how to do the passes and then put me in the ring with a bull."

Incredulous, Jimmy interrupted. "With a real bull?"

"Yes, a real bull but a small one; it didn't have proper horns. Really they were just knobs. In fact it was probably just a bull calf."

They both laughed, and Charles continued. "But it was vicious. It kept coming at me, and I managed to make it go after the cape. But once it hit me in the stomach with its head and knocked the wind out of me. When I was down, it kept butting me until my teacher took its attention with his cape while I got out of the ring. I suspect this bull was only for practice, and when it grew, it was not going into the ring.

"I read a book about bullfighting later. It said that the bulls of the Iberian Peninsula are naturally very vicious. They raise them on ranches where they roam free and never see a man on foot until they enter the ring. They select the most vicious of them for the bull ring when they are small calves.

"A rider goes out with a long pole with a sharp end. He rides up to the calf and pokes it in the rear with the pole. If the calf turns and charges the horse, he is raised for the ring.

"They don't let the bulls see a man on foot until they enter the ring because they are very smart. When they get in the ring, they might go for the man instead of the cape if they have seen a man on foot before."

"So you had a short bullfighting career," Jimmy said chuckling.

"Yes, it lasted about 10 minutes but was quite eventful." They both laughed at this.

It was no surprise when Charles approached him one Friday after school. "Say old chap, would you care to join me this Sunday afternoon for a visit to the Pulqueria? It's a place where one goes to imbibe a beverage called pulque. I'm told it's quite delicious."

"What is pulque?" Jimmy asked.

"It's a beverage made from the fermented juice of the maguey plant. They cut the maguey bulb and remove the sap that seeps out and then ferment it. There are places where the only beverage served is pulque, and they are called Pulquerias."

"It's booze?" Jimmy inquired.

"Booze?" Charles repeated.

"Yeah, you know, alcohol," Jimmy clarified.

"Yes. I'm told it has a slightly intoxicating effect. Not to worry — it will be a learning experience, a chance to mix with the locals. We can soak in some of the local culture. And I do so miss my visits to the pub."

"Okay, sounds like it's worth a try. What time and where?" Jimmy said.

"Three p.m. I have taken the liberty of writing the directions on this paper in anticipation of your yes. Cheerio, see you *Domingo a las tres de la tarde* (Sunday at three in the afternoon)."

"*Hasta Domingo* (Until Sunday)," replied Jimmy as they parted ways.

Sunday at three p.m. Jimmy and Charles met right on time. The afternoon was like every afternoon in Cuernavaca — bright, sunny, around 75 degrees. It almost got boring; the weather was always so temperate.

The Pulqueria was a masterpiece of beauty in a rustic way. Over the front entrance hung a huge gold lettered sign announcing Palacio Pulque. Inside it was a perfect rectangle of narrow buildings surrounding an interior dirt floor patio set with small rickety tables and chairs. Overhead wires were stretched from building to building with multi-colored sheets of tissue. Each sheet had intricate designs cut into them and were called papel picado. The walls of the surrounding buildings were covered ground to roof with murals.

While not Diego Rivera quality, the murals were nevertheless very interesting. Each mural depicted a scene in the process of making pulque. In one scene, the maguey bulb was cut and began to fill with sap. In the next, a person sucked up the sap into a long gourd and deposited it into a vat. And so on it went through the storage and fermentation process, ending with a happy waiter delivering strawberry-infused pulque to some merry customers.

Jimmy and Charles seated themselves at a baby blue wood - slatted table surrounded by four bright yellow chairs. After allowing them time to make themselves comfortable, the white- shirted waiter arrived. ***"May I bring you something?"***

Trotting out his best Spanish, Jimmy replied, "*Sí pulque.*"

"What type of pulque? Today we have pulque with strawberries, with mango, or plain."

Jimmy answered, ***"I'll have strawberry."***

Charles said, ***"I will too."***

Both Charles and Jimmy had been warned not to eat any raw fruits or vegetables unless they could peel them. Oranges and mangos filled that description nicely. The CIDOC literature explained that fruits and vegetables were washed in local water, and tourists should not have even one drop of the water. It was not because the water was tainted. It was only because a foreigner's digestive system was not accustomed to it and might rebel. They had been told to drink only bottled water, *"aqua mineral sin gas* (mineral water without carbonation)." But this was different, they reasoned. The alcohol in the pulque would neutralize any impurities just like the ale of old had done for Englishmen.

The waiter soon brought two bright red strawberry infused glasses of pulque and put them before the two young adventurers. He then returned to his post beside the mural of pulque fermentation. He would wait there, never interrupting, until a patron signaled for service. Jimmy knew that, much like Europe, the wait staff in Mexico did not interrupt to ask if service was needed. Watchful waiting was their way.

Jimmy thought that this was a much more genteel process than the constant interruption of "How is everything?" in the United States. Or even worse, the question "Still workin' on that?" He had never experienced eating a meal as work and therefore was very put off by the question.

The signal to the waiter that service was needed was eye contact and a nod. Jimmy had been told that in some parts of Mexico, the way to signal the waiter was to kiss the air. He was glad they weren't in those parts of Mexico.

Charles and Jimmy watched patrons drift in and out. They were mostly men, but there was an occasional couple. There was never a woman or group of women alone. The young men drank the thick, viscous beverage and enjoyed the slightly sweet and sour taste. "Sour pulque, sweet strawberry, I presume," remarked Charles. "Well, I think we should test that theory by having a straight pulque, no berries." Before Jimmy could answer, Charles signaled the waiter and ordered. Soon two more half-liter glasses were set before them. This time they contained a milky, light green liquid. They both took a gulp. "Well old chap, what's the verdict?" Charles asked.

"You were right. The strawberry is the sweet part. This straight pulque is a bit sour, but I like it," Jimmy replied.

"As do I," replied Charles. "Even without the added strawberries, it's still very thick."

"Almost like drinking maple syrup," Jimmy said. They both agreed that they enjoyed pulque with or without the fruit. They went on to try it with mango, then back to strawberry, and through the flavors again.

Jimmy and Charles had a very pleasant afternoon at Pulque Palace exchanging stories, chatting as they were able with the waiter, and watching and listening to the conversations of the other patrons. They were gratified to learn that they could eavesdrop on the other patrons and actually understand some of what they were saying.

Finally Jimmy said, "Well my friend, all good things must come to an end. I have to get back and do some studying for tomorrow."

"Quite right. It's getting more involved with these reflexive verbs. I'll have to study a bit myself," Charles replied.

Jimmy knew that Charles would not be studying nearly as much as he would. Charles just seemed to have a gift for learning language.

After paying and giving a generous tip to the waiter, they walked out. Jimmy turned right, and Charles turned left with an "adios." Charles had taken a room at a nunnery and had a long walk up the hill. He reported the room to be sparse but clean and comfortable. Meals were plain but filling; he had no complaints.

As Jimmy walked, he realized he was a little buzzed. This was a natural effect of drinking several pints of a beverage that is about six percent alcohol. He felt okay, just a little light headed. He went directly to his room and got out his books. He was intent on learning all he could while he was in Mexico.

Jimmy was pleased that he and Charles had participated, and to a large degree, had fit in at a Spanish language venue. Even though their conversation had been in English, all interactions with others had been in Spanish. They understood and were able to respond, after a fashion, to all Spanish questions and comments.

Jimmy began to repeat and memorize the next day's lesson and a joke jumped into his head. *"No puedo nadar porque no traje traje."* The sentence definitely loses everything in the translation, he thought as he repeated it. "I can't swim because I didn't bring a suit" is not at all funny. *"No puedo nadar porque no traje traje,"* is hilarious — well, at least cute.

But that wasn't part of the lesson. Jimmy was having some difficulty concentrating on the lesson at hand, so he decided to take a walk. He went out the door and down the little grassy slope to the swimming pool. It was a gorgeous little pool in an oval shape, just large enough for four strong breast strokes end to end. It was blue, so blue he looked into it and thought of the deep blue ocean off the Pacifica City Pier back home. He realized he was getting a little maudlin, thinking of home and feeling a little homesick.

Snap out of it, Jimmy told himself. Then he went back up the hill and to bed.

It was 1 a.m., and Jimmy was lying in bed with a very queasy feeling in the stomach area. He was half awake wondering what was wrong. All at once, he knew what was wrong. He leaped out of bed and barely made it in time to get his head over the toilet. Once there, a boiling mass surged up from his lower parts through the esophagus and blasted out his mouth like a miniature fire hose.

That was just the first of many such episodes that some have described as "calling Ralph on the big white telephone." To add to his discomfort, he was soon presented with liquid material exiting at both ends, sometimes simultaneously. In fact Jimmy found himself sitting on the toilet holding a trash can in front of his face for a good portion of the night.

The next morning, Jimmy's fellow border and classmate, Simon, stopped by because he missed Jimmy at coffee. Jimmy weakly spoke through the door that he was sick and "wouldn't be at school."

"Can I help with something? Do you need some medicine?" Simon asked in their new-found common language, Spanish.

"No, thanks. I'll be okay," Jimmy faintly replied.

Jimmy made his way back to the bed and fell into a deep sleep. His active night had exhausted his body and mind. With the exception of one quick trip to the bathroom, Jimmy slept until the maid was tapping on the door to make up the bed at around noon. ***"Yes, who is it?"*** Jimmy weakly called out.

"It's me, Angelica, the maid. Are you okay?"

"I'm a little sick. I did not sleep last night. I'm going to stay in the room; I won't be eating," Jimmy said.

"Are you having stomach problems?" she asked.

"Yes, and I'm tired," Jimmy said weakly.

"Okay, you sleep."

And he did sleep; he woke in a fog about 3 p.m. to tapping on his door. **"Mr. Jim, I have something for you. Please open the door,"** the voice said.

Jimmy rolled out of bed and slipped on a pair of sweatpants and stumbled to the door. He was very surprised to see Angelica with a full tray. She stepped in and set it on the small dresser. She had two one-liter bottles of agua mineral sin gas, a medium- size bowl of boiled white rice, two pieces of toast, and two bananas.

"You have to drink lots of water or you will get dehydrated, very bad for you. If you can't eat, at least drink this water. I'll check on you later," Angelica said.

"I will drink, but I don't think I can eat anything," Jimmy replied.

"At least try to take some rice if you can," Angelica said.

"Okay, thanks."

Jimmy sat staring at the water bottle for a long time. His head was spinning a bit, his stomach ached, and his mouth felt like a sand dune resided there. He shakily reached for a water bottle and took a sip. Before he could reach the toilet, it came right back up along with some yellow bile. Frustrated and sick, Jimmy made his way back to the bed and immediately fell into a fitful sleep.

It was dark when Jimmy awoke to tapping at his door.

Again, Angelica was there to check on him. ***"Did you drink the water? You have to drink, very bad for you if you get dehydrated. Please take a drink,"*** Angelica begged.

"If I drink, will you leave?" Jimmy responded.

"Yes, until tomorrow." Jimmy picked up a water bottle, drank about 2 ounces, which stayed down this time, and Angelica left.

After Angelica left, Jimmy drank a little more and went right back to sleep. The next morning, he arose at dawn, ate about two tablespoons of rice, and went back to sleep. By the time Angelica was tapping on the door at noon, Jimmy had eaten the rice and drank a liter of water. She stood there holding two more liter bottles of water, smiling as he handed her an empty bottle. ***"At three, I will bring you some chicken soup. Very good for the stomach."***

"Thanks. I appreciate all your help," Jimmy said weakly.

With the help of Angelica's chicken soup and lomotil, by the third day Jimmy was back to school. He never understood whether it was the pulque, the water, the fruit, or another demon that had assaulted him at the Pulqueria. Charles reported a similar reaction, so they were sure the Pulqueria and bad judgement were the source of their discomfort. In any case, the Pulqeria was off limits to both for the remainder of their stay.

Charles said that Cerveza Modelo Negra would do nicely to quench his thirst in the future. Jimmy had learned during his pulque research, before their event, that pulque had a short shelf life and therefore could not be imported to the United States. At that time he was a bit sad at learning this. Now he thought to himself, thank God. I will never, ever have to even look at it again!

It was Wednesday back at CIDOC, and Jimmy was feeling thankful to be there. During the last period of the day, a student gave an announcement that he and four other students had hired a professor to teach them about recent history of Latin America. He explained that the professor had been a lecturer at U. C. Berkley but was asked to leave because of political activity. If others wanted to join, it would be a fee of $20 to $30 each for an eighteen-hour seminar. The cost would depend on how many signed up. The seminar would be in Spanish.

Jimmy thought about this during his walk home. The eighteen hours would be at CIDOC and over three weeks. There would probably be two 3-hour sessions each week. On the negative side, it would take away time from his study and language practice within the community. On the positive side, it would let Jimmy learn a little more about the history and culture of Latin America. The seminar was going to be in Spanish, so that would give him language practice. Before he reached home, Jimmy had decided to participate.

Jimmy's stomach was still a bit queasy, so he went to his room instead of comida. Soon there was a knock on the door. He opened it to Angelica and a beautiful little girl. *"You still don't feel well?"* she asked.

"I still have stomach pain, not feeling great," he answered.

"Okay, I will bring you some chicken soup when comida is over."

"Thank you so much. Who is this little doll?" he asked.

"She is the granddaughter of Los Fuentes. She is staying here for a few days and they asked me to watch her."

Jimmy looked at the chubby dark-eyed toddler with great interest. Actually, he focused on her beautiful frilly dress and her angelic little face but mostly, he was confused about her hair. She had been given a butch. Her hair was shaved down to a uniform one half inch all over. *"What happened to her hair?"* Jimmy asked.

"Mama cut the hair and then every three days she rubs a tomato on her hair. It will make it grow very thick and beautiful."

"Doesn't the little girl object to having a tomato rubbed on her head?" Jimmy asked incredulously.

"Oh, sometimes, but it's only for a while. When the hair grows out, they won't put tomato on any more. Lots of people do this to help the girls' hair grow to be beautiful," Angelica explained.

"Hm! Well, thank you again for checking on me. It's very kind of you," Jimmy smiled.

****

Ring, ring, ring went the portable fold-up alarm clock. It was a compact little device smaller than a pack of cigarettes. It had a tough main spring that could keep it ticking for twelve hours before being rewound.

At its jarring sound, Jimmy rolled out of bed feeling healed. He'd had a good night's sleep and was ready for the day. After a quick shower, he was out the door, ready for the day. He was gratified that his young body had overcome the evil he had brought upon it. He was thinking clearly and ready to learn.

The school day went well. Jimmy was pleased that he was now able to use full sentences in the guided conversations; this translated to better communication with the people of the town. He also now understood ninety percent of what was said to him.

Today was the first Latin American history and culture seminar. After a snack, the seminar participants met at 1:30 p.m. at CIDOC. The professor was young, perhaps 25–27. He introduced himself. "***Good afternoon. My name is Arnold Bonnie. We will be meeting here Tuesday and Thursday for the next three weeks. I want you to think of me, not as your teacher, but as the midwife of your ideas. This is a seminar. We will discuss facts and opinions, and you will form your own opinions. Let's get started.***

"You may have read in the newspaper that the CIA has been planting small bombs in seashells where Fidel Castro does his scuba diving. Without debating it, let's assume for the moment that this is true. The further information that we gather is that these are small explosives designed to maim, not kill. I will tell you that if all this is true, someone in the CIA understands Latin American culture very well."

And the discussion began. Would the United States really do that? Why would they try to maim instead of kill? The back and forth raged on with opinions and ideas flying, all in Spanish. Finally, Professor Bonnie brought it all together. "***Your discussions of Poncho Villa, Emilino Zapata, Benito Juarez, Miguel Hidalgo, and others in Mexican history has been very fruitful. Tell me, what do all these heroes have in common?***"

A quiet blanket fell over the group. Then came the statement from one of the students. *"They were all strong leaders. They were all charismatic leaders, therefore people were drawn to them."*

Professor Bonnie said, *"Yes. So, how does this relate to Fidel Castro and the CIA?"*

"Castro is very charismatic, and a strong leader," one of the students offered. Then there was a long silence.

"Yes, Castro is charismatic but how charismatic would he be with one eye, no nose and half a cheek?" Professor Bonnie asked. "Someone in the CIA knows that if he can be disfigured, it will greatly hamper his ability to rally the people. They also know that if he is killed, he will become a martyr and a rallying cry for the people. And finally, they are well aware that in Latin America, people will follow and fight for strong leaders as much as causes. I want to leave you today with a question. Does the U.S. intervene in Latin American affairs so forcefully and dramatically as to maim one of its leaders?"

With the seminar dismissed and Jimmy having missed comida, he started downtown. The open-air market was just opening after the mid-day break. Jimmy bought some small purple avocados and ate the rich buttery flesh on hot corn tortillas. He thought about the seminar and decided he would continue with it. He reminded himself that his purpose here was not to learn about relations with Latin America but to learn what would help him be a better teacher to a group of children who were not receiving a good education at that time.

****

The next Tuesday rolled around, and Professor Bonnie started the seminar with a story. ***"A woman I know was talking to her sister. The sister mentioned that her friend had just had a baby girl."***

"Is she beautiful?" the woman asked.

"Oh yes, a lovely child, only a little too dark," the sister answered.

"Why do you think she made the 'little too dark' remark?" Professor Bonnie asked.

This session, the students got it without much coaching. They discussed the fact that most of the low-level workers they saw in Mexico were dark skinned. One of the group knew a fact; she said, ***"Mexico spends more money cleaning the fountains in Mexico City than it spends educating all the indigenous people in the country."*** They all agreed that the indigenous people were dark skinned and on the bottom of the social order in Mexico.

It would follow then, that the darker the skin color, the more discrimination the person would face. They compared this to the plight of the black population in the United States. One member from Los Angeles said, ***"I was surprised when I got to Mexico City and saw all the light skinned people, even some with blue eyes. Every Mexican I saw in L.A. was dark. I thought all Mexicans were dark."***

Jimmy thought back on the contested social studies lesson about mestizos. He understood now why Carlitos' dad had wanted to deny that they were mestizos. Mestizo is a mix of indigenous people and Spanish blood and was indeed the ancestry of most of the Mexican population. But in the Mexico of the time, the less indigenous blood the better. Skin color was the barometer of Mexican society and fixed their place in the Mexican social order. Jimmy pictured his class; all his students were in hues of brown, from light caramel to very dark brown.

Professor Bonnie went on to explain that the Spanish intermarried with the native people much more readily than the English did in the colonies. He gave several reasons for this. One reason is the Spanish were not settlers; they were Conquistadors. They came to conquer and pillage and take riches back to Spain. As a consequence, when they invaded Mexico, they did not bring their wives or children with them. The soldiers, away from home for so long, began to have children with the native women. Many of them, being staunch Catholics, insisted on engaging in the sacrament of marriage.

The English did bring their wives and children to the New World. They came to stay, to make this new land their home. Thus they had no reason to intermarry with the natives.

Probably a more compelling reason for the difference was that the English saw the natives as a different kind of being, whereas the Spanish saw them only as lower on the social order. The English saw them as almost a different species, therefore any children that did result from dalliances with native women were not accepted into British communities.

"The Spanish saw them as simply of a lower social status," Professor Bonnie continued. ***"The result is that in Mexico, you have a new ethnic group that arises through the joining of Spanish and native Mexican DNA. As we have learned, those Mexicans in which the native genetic influence is strong, are at the bottom of the social***

order and, unfortunately, even today, face systemic discrimination.”

And so it went for six sessions. Jimmy found some of it useful, some of it not. His test for usefulness was if it was going to help him give his students a better education. He decided that the politics of U.S. and Latin America relationships were interesting but not very useful to him.

Jimmy understood that there were oppressed, abused, and neglected people in the world. He had seen them in Europe, in Mexico, and in McKinley. His own relatives were some of the abused and oppressed during the depression.

Jimmy knew that poverty was one of the chief factors that kept people oppressed. He believed that a good education was a way out of poverty. He knew that it had been the way out for his family. He knew he would not be where he was if his mom and dad had not insisted that he get an education. He was determined to pass that on and give the kids that came through his classroom the best education he could. They needed it, justice demanded it, and his conscience would not allow anything short of it.

All these thoughts raced through Jimmy’s mind as he walked back to his room. With every step he became more firm in his resolve. He reached the room in time to wash up and come to the table for comida.

Simon was at the table before Jimmy and wished him a hearty *“Buenas Tardes.”* He had missed Jimmy at mealtime for the last few days and was glad to see him. Now that they had a common language, they could have more prolonged conversations.

Simon asked, ***“You were sick the last few days, weren’t you?”***

"Yes, I was pretty sick. Guess I overdid it with the pulque," Jimmy answered.

"Yes, Angelica told me how sick you were. There must have been something more than just the alcohol?" Simon said with concern in his voice.

Jimmy answered, *"Maybe, but I won't be back to the Pulqueria."* They both chuckled.

Angelica, true to her surname, Papaqui, which means happy in the ancient Nahauatl language, came in smiling carrying the main dish. The whole red snapper looked delicious but difficult to eat. That is, until she deftly skinned, deboned, and put half a fish on each of their plates. *"Thank you,"* they both chorused. She was a wonderful help to them at all times, but especially to Jimmy in his recent illness.

As Jimmy watched her walk away, he realized for the first time that the indigenous part of her mestizo makeup was more prominent than the Spanish. Her short 5-foot frame, dark mahogany skin and black hair and eyes screamed *Aztec*. He thought back to the seminar in which they had learned that the majority of Mexicans were a mixture of Spanish and indigenous people, thus mestizo. But Angelica was more indigenous than light skinned Spanish and thus was assigned to the lower class of society. Jimmy thought, what a shame. She is such a kind, hard- working and considerate person.

The delicious smell of the roasted fish jerked Jimmy from his thoughts back to his plate. The savory white flakey fish was an experience in epicurean decadence. The fish, corn tortilla, black beans, and rice would stick in Jimmy's mind long after they were gone. He had learned to love the food of Mexico, the language and with it the people.

Jimmy turned to Simon and said, ***"You are lucky to be moving here. It's a wonderful country. The people here are nice. Why did you decide to leave the country where you were born?"***

Simon's ruddy face formed into a fearsome scowl. ***"It's because in Canada, we who speak French are on the bottom of society. We are treated like the Blacks are treated in the U.S.; except we have not been able to get the government to intervene for us the way blacks in the U.S. have. We have no hope of change, so I am leaving. My wife and I will move here and if we can arrange it, we will help our children and their families to move here. We are all farmers; we have no opportunity to change. They won't even teach our children in French, the only language we know. We are kept down with poor education and little job opportunity."***

The impact of those words were like a slap in the face to Jimmy. He thought, yes, we are doing the same thing at the McKinley School. This conversation only served to solidify his commitment to give his students the best education possible.

Once again, Jimmy thought, it is not only skin color that leads to societal abuse, but also poverty and being different from the majority. He would have taken Simon for an English-speaking person until he heard him speak. It's not only skin color that results in abuse; language and poverty do too. But skin color does not change. A person of color is easily identifiable. Even though they may change their speech and adopt the majority's cultural beliefs and mores, they still look different. That difference often leads to abuse. Ethnocentrism is unfortunately a fact of existence across all cultures and time.

As Jimmy's Spanish improved, his love of the community and people increased. The more he engaged in the life of the school and community, the greater his feeling of belonging grew.

Chapter 38

All too soon, Jimmy began to see his return date looming on the calendar. Just two weeks until he would go back home; he wasn't ready for that. He was bathed in the language and culture every day. He felt a part of the community. One night, Jimmy had a dream; when he awoke, he realized he had been speaking Spanish in his dream. As he thought about it, his thoughts were in Spanish.

Jimmy didn't want to go home just yet . . . he wanted more of Mexico. He ruminated on his situation for a couple of days, then it hit him. He could telephone Principal Campbell and ask for a two week extension of his summer break. The district had a great substitute who could get the class started until he returned.

He knew placing an international call would be expensive, but it was worth it. With another two weeks of instruction and practice, Jimmy knew he would be at a level of fluency where he could handle any teaching situation. His Spanish was at a level now that he could deal with the telephone transaction without assistance. He thought about this plan all evening. The next afternoon he made the call.

Principal Campbell was okay with it. In fact, he was happy that Jimmy was taking such an interest in making himself a better teacher. They had a very short, expensive conversation ending with Mr. Campbell saying he would check the availability of a substitute, and Jimmy should call back in two days. What good luck, Jimmy thought.

The time for his call came; he made it with fingers crossed.

"Hello Jim. How is it there?" Principal Campbell asked.

"Oh it's great. I'm learning a lot and doing pretty well with the language," Jimmy explained.

"That's wonderful, Jim. You'll be a great asset to the school. I got things squared away for you, and the two weeks have been approved. Give me a call when you get back to the states to confirm that you are able to start on September 16th."

"Great, thank you. I'll be starting on Mexican Independence Day," Jimmy said.

"I thought that was May fifth?" the principal asked.

"No, May fifth celebrates the Mexican Army's victory over the French at Puebla. I'll explain when I get there. Thanks again for your help. See you soon," Jimmy said excitedly.

****

Even with Jimmy's extension, time flew by. Sooner than he would have liked, it was time to go home. He had had a great awakening in Cuernavaca; he knew it had changed his life. He was not only better prepared to teach; he was better able to understand a people he once had disregarded. He was just better.

Jimmy attended his last class day at CIDOC with the same mixture of sadness and joy he had experienced at both high school and university graduations. All the same promises were made; we will keep in touch, here's my contact information, come and see me if you are in my area, and so on. They were all sincere statements, but if past life was indicative of the future, they all knew they would probably never meet again. And that was the sadness.

The joy? The joy of life to be lived was ubiquitous among them. Jimmy had much life to live and knew he was better equipped now to meet its challenges. That is the joy of any learning.

The parting from his living situation was a little more difficult. The Fuentes family was very nice but somewhat distant. Their maid, Angelica, however, was a friend to all. Jimmy and Simon had gone together and bought her a silver crucifix on a silver chain. When they gave it to her with their great thanks, she cried, ***"Thank you so very much. This is the most beautiful thing anyone has ever given me."***

It was with a heart full of excitement for the future and sadness for the present parting that Jimmy caught the bus to Mexico City. He had made sure this time he not only got a first-class ticket with a seat number, but he also got on the bus in time to actually get the seat.

Jimmy stared out the window wistfully as the bus pulled out. He had been happy here in this City of Eternal Spring. The rhythm of life here was more suited to human happiness than the frantic pace of life back home. He thought of the amate painter. ***"Why haven't you been on the corner for several days?"*** Jimmy asked him. He was startled by the painter's answer.

"I was not here because I had enough money. Now I need some more money, so I will paint more amates."

A startling answer to a young man immersed in the American ethos of work as a good thing in itself. The Horatio Alger stories, all with the same theme, ran through his head. Work hard, live a good life, and you will prosper. Work is a good thing. Those that prosper are good people, a theme left over from the Puritans. For most of the Mexicans Jimmy had met, work was the means to achieve a purpose; work was not their identity.

The bougainvillea-covered walls began to whiz by as Jimmy stared out the window. The bougainvillea would be with him for the rest of his life. They would be in his dreams and his waking hours alike, remembrance of a peaceful time among kind and considerate people.

The bus ride was pleasant enough, though the descent into the smog and congestion of Mexico City was disheartening. After the natural beauty and tranquil life of Cuernavaca, Mexico City was not as appealing as in his past trip.

Jimmy caught a taxi from the bus station directly to the airport; he was there on time to catch his 7:00 p.m. flight to San Francisco. He looked out from his window seat at the receding lights of Mexico City and muttered to himself, *"Voy a regresar a México* (I'm going to return to Mexico.)"

****

"How was the trip, Jim?" Principal Campbell asked.

"It was great. I learned a lot and saw a lot. I'm ready to get back to work. I'll be in Monday, the 16th, as we agreed. I'm here today because I'm moving into an apartment in town."

"Where is that? I didn't think there was much living space here," Principal Campbell said.

"Yeah, it's a small studio upstairs in the old hotel. I just want to get away from that drive and be more a part of the community."

"Sounds great. See you Monday," Principal Campbell acknowledged.

With still a few days to get settled, Jimmy went back to Perryville to his mom and dad's to get the rest of his meager possessions. The fold-up bed, kitchen table, and chairs they had given him would be all the furniture he would need to get started.

When Dad's pickup was loaded with furniture, Jimmy headed to McKinley. He had some trouble wrestling the bed and table up the stairs, but he was a strong young man and got it done.

Jimmy stood in the middle of his new place and looked it over. There was a small living area that would house the bed and table. A stove, refrigerator and small kitchen sink were located on the west end of the room. The bathroom was on the east side with a small window out to the street. He was happy; the three hundred square feet of his apartment would meet his needs nicely.

September 16th was the day Mexico attained freedom from Spain and the day Jimmy started school two weeks late. There was no big celebration, even at the migrant housing, because the big day of celebration in the U.S. was May 5th. Cinco de Mayo was a very minor holiday in Mexico. It celebrated victory over the French at Puebla.

However, May 5th was adopted by Chicanos in the states as a day to celebrate. This day of celebration for most U.S. residents of Mexican descent was adopted to celebrate their culture as it evolved in the United States. Because there was lots of drinking and partying associated with the holiday, many others outside the culture joined in. It was a big *pachanga* (party).

Jimmy was glad to be back. He felt more prepared to deal with teaching in this place now. The first person he saw at the school was his aide, Ofelia. Ofelia was now called an instructional aide, not a teacher's aide. *"Hola que tal* (Hi, how are you)?" Jimmy asked.

"Bien," she responded. ***"Do you speak Spanish now?"*** she questioned.

"Yes, I speak some Spanish. We will see how much, no?" Jimmy said.

"You sound like a native. Beautiful accent and choice of words," Ofelia praised.

"Thanks so much. I'm hoping it helps my teaching."

"Oh, it will. I think you may find you get more non-English speakers this year," Ofelia advised.

Jimmy exclaimed, ***"Bring 'em on! I'm ready."***

"Mr. Preciado has been asking for you. He was wondering if you were coming back. He and a couple of other guys are wanting to start the English class again," Ofelia said.

"Okay, I'll go see him after I get settled in a bit," Jimmy said.

"*Oh, you'll go see him? You don't need me now that you are a Spanish speaker, hm?*" Ofelia said teasingly.

"*Oh no. I didn't mean that, just didn't want to take your time.*"

"*I know.*" Ofelia chuckled, "*Just kidding.*"

"Hello, Mr. Campbell," Jimmy said.

"Hey Jim. Good to see you. I want to tell you what we've done with your class. We moved all the non-English speaking sixth graders there, and we moved a few non-English speaking fifth graders there too. So, you have 22 kids; ten of them speak little or no English. Sorry we had to do it this way, but you know the Lau vs. Nichols decision will change a lot of how we do things. It will be a challenge, but I heard you talking with Ofelia out there and sounds like you're up to it," Mr. Campbell explained.

"I am. I'm ready to do it," Jimmy exclaimed.

"Glad to hear it. It's good to have you back!"

When the dismissal bell rang, Jimmy went over to where he had been told Mr. Juan Martinez's classroom was. Sure enough there was Juan. Jimmy said, "*Hola Juan cómo va?* (Hi Juan. How are you doing?)"

"Hey Jim. Good to see you," Juan replied. "Yeah, I heard you were here."

"Glad to see the internship worked out. We'll have a good time working together this year," Jimmy said enthusiastically.

"Yeah, I hope so," Juan said. "I've been here two weeks

and still struggling. Mrs. Holiman has been helpful, but I've got 29 fourth grade kids. Six of them don't speak English, but they think I speak Spanish. They keep trying to talk to me, and I don't know what they're saying."

Jimmy said, "I'll be able to help. My Spanish is pretty good now."

"Yeah, I heard you went to some Spanish school in Mexico," Juan confirmed.

"Yeah, it was great. I learned a lot and had a good time." Jimmy went on to give a brief explanation of CIDOC.

Juan replied, "That's what I need to do. I want to learn Spanish."

"I have some contacts there now, so when you get ready, let me know. I'll get you hooked up."

"Thanks Jim. See you in the morning," Juan replied enthusiastically.

****

"Buenos días todos. Good morning everyone," Jimmy said in both languages. "I'm glad to see you. I know you've had a substitute for two weeks, but I will be your teacher for the rest of the year," Jimmy said and repeated it in Spanish.

Jimmy set up the class schedule in a way no one had ever seen before. In the morning, from 9 a.m. to noon, all the academic lessons were presented in English only. There was no translation or discussion in Spanish. In the afternoon, from 12:30 p.m. until 3:30 p.m., Jimmy presented the same content lessons but in Spanish.

Jimmy had learned the value and efficacy of language

immersion at CIDOC, and he brought the strategy into use with his students. As he explained to Mr. Campbell, the students were getting the content reinforced twice. When the year was over, they would speak English and retain Spanish. Plus, English speakers would learn Spanish.

Mr. Campbell said, "Well okay, we're going to let you go ahead with it, but I will want to see high quality test scores. Remember Jim, we are not here to teach anyone Spanish. Our job is to move them to English as soon as we can and to be sure they get the content."

"Yes. Got it," Jimmy answered. "You will see amazing results from these kids this year; I promise!"

"I'll hold you to it," Mr. Campbell smiled.

Jimmy's visit to Renaldo Preciado was a good one. As he approached the house, he saw Jesús in the yard. "Hello Mr. Welch," Jesús called. "You come back."

"Yes Jesús, I came back. I love this place. Is your Dad home?"

"I will get him," Jesús replied. Jimmy was gratified and cheered by Jesús' English ability in a short period of time. He had come from no English to almost fluent.

"*Buenos tardes*," Jimmy said as Renaldo came out of the house. Jimmy was a little nervous, but he continued in his best Spanish. **"I'm glad to see you. How is your family?"**

Renaldo replied, **"All good. Jesús talks and talks in English. I can't understand most of what he says."**

"We can fix that," replied Jimmy. **"Ofelia said you were ready to start English classes again."**

"Yes, I am ready. I want to learn English. Then Jesús can't tell secrets anymore to his friends. I will understand him." Renaldo laughed. **"And you learned Spanish, huh? Very good Spanish. I want to learn English like that."**

Jimmy was encouraged. **"Okay, you will, it just takes some time."**

"Okay, I'm ready," Renaldo said.

Chapter 39

Another school year almost finished. Friday evening Jimmy sat in his little studio apartment and thought about what to do for the weekend. I know, he thought, I'll go see Daniel. We haven't talked to each other in months.

"Hey, Daniel. It's Jim."

"Oh hi, it's been a while. How's it going?" Daniel asked.

"Great," Jim replied. "I went to language school in Mexico."

"Hey, I'd like to hear about it. Why don't you come to the city? I've got about three more weeks in this apartment and then I'm out of here. Don't know where I'm going yet; wherever I can find a job," Daniel said.

"Your M.A. in Poli Sci should be pretty marketable," Jimmy said.

"Hope so," Daniel replied.

"Okay, I'll be there tomorrow about noon!" Jimmy exclaimed.

****

They had a wonderful time all afternoon catching up. Jimmy was very impressed with all Daniel had done, especially the internship work. Early evening, after an afternoon of visiting, they decided to walk down to the beach, get some exercise and watch the sun drop into the

Pacific Ocean. There's nothing quite like watching that fiery, orange orb drop into the blue Pacific. No wonder the ancient ones were awestruck by it, Jimmy thought.

The day was a relatively clear day for May. The sunset was brilliant hues of red, orange, yellow fading to soft tones of gray then black. "Let's go to the Cliff House for a drink," Jimmy suggested. "I know you're still a starving student, so I'm buying."

"You said the magic words," Daniel replied. "I'm happy to drink whatever you're buying."

It was early in the evening. They were seated at a table for four looking out at the ocean through a magnificent wall made mostly of glass. The lights were on Seal Rock, and they could hear the barking sound of those beautiful sleek creatures.

After they had ordered drinks, a Manhattan for Jimmy and a dry Martini for Daniel, Jimmy said, "I'm going to be in Mexico when you walk the stage, so how about I buy you a graduation dinner here tonight and we celebrate now? Remember when we used to walk the beach and say, 'Someday I'll be able to afford to eat in that place.' Well, today is the day. This is your graduation present, anything you want. The sky's the limit."

Clinking glasses, they repeated their oft cited toast. "Up yours and down mine! Cheers!"

They feasted on Dungeness crab salad, freshly caught flounder washed down with champagne, and Crème Brule for dessert. It was everything their young student minds had imagined and more — delicious food, impeccable service, and quiet ambiance. They loved the sound of the waves gently lapping on the rocks below as they sat in their kingly seats on the cliff.

Over White Russians, Daniel said, "This was great. I can't think of a better graduation present. Thank you. Why are you going back to Mexico? I thought you finished your school there."

Jimmy began to explain. "I did finish my first course of Spanish, but I still have a lot to learn about Mexico and the people. A priest I met there is taking me on a tour of southeastern Mexico when school is over this year.

"The main reason I'm going again is that ninety-five percent of my students are Mexican nationals or at least of Mexican descent. I need to know more than I do about their culture and language in order to teach them.

"Also, in my teenage years, I had a very low opinion of Mexicans. Since then I've learned that the culture of Mexico is as rich and ancient as that of Europe. Are you aware that the Maya of Mexico were the first people to conceive of the concept of zero! Think about it; the complicated math coming out of the southern jungle of Mexico. They had a calendar that is more accurate than ours."

"Yeah well, that was a long time ago," Daniel said. "I don't see much of that today."

"That's why I go, to get the full story. The people we see here, that are identified as Mexicans are only one segment of the society. For the most part, they were dispossessed and marginalized in Mexico. They come here hoping for a better life," Jimmy explained.

"Tell me this: if they come here hoping for a better

life, why don't they try to fit into society better? Lots of ethnic groups have come here, and eventually they learn the language and the cultural norms and become Americans. When I was doing my internship, I saw all the neighborhoods in the city. The Italians in North Beach are doing very well. They all speak English and many still speak Italian also. They own half the city. The Chinese have their China Town, but they go to public schools; they fit in. They learn English, and many maintain their primary language. Their businesses are thriving.

"But when I went to the Mission District, where most residents are Mexican, hardly anyone speaks English. They're living two or three families in a two-bedroom house, and they don't send the kids to school half the time. I've seen people that have been here for twenty years and still don't speak English. Why is this?" Daniel questioned.

"I don't know all the answers, Daniel, but let me share some of my thoughts. First of all, I want to say right up front that it's not because they're stupid. I have a boy in my class who is a math whiz. He did two years of the math curriculum in about eight months, and I've seen numerous academic achievements in the short time I've been teaching.

"But they're different from any other immigrants who came here in many ways. They're coming to a place that was once part of Mexico and Spanish abounds. We are in San Francisco, not Saint Francis. The Mission, from which the Mission district takes its name, was originally *La Misión de Nuestro Padre San Francisco* and was founded in 1776, a year we all remember.

"When the Americans were breaking away from England, the Spanish were already founding cities throughout what would become the United States. The later revolution which broke ties between Mexico and Spain made the spot where we sit, and all of the southwest, part of Mexico.

"But probably more importantly, we are physically very close to Mexico. You can go right down to Third and Market and get on a Greyhound Bus and within ten hours be at the Mexican border. That's not true of any other immigrant group who comes here. When they leave their home, they know they are not going back. This will be their home, so they immediately start becoming part of the U. S.

"Many Mexicans I have met don't feel that way. They're here strictly because they can't make a living in Mexico. They go back to Mexico every chance they get to visit, particularly around Christmas. Some of them harbor the hope that they will earn enough here to move back and start a business in Mexico, a little store or something like that.

"In fact, the reason my family remained Okies so long was because of some of the same reasoning. My parents didn't like it very well in California. They both came from families that had deep roots in the south and mid-west.

"My granddad on my father's side was a coal miner in Muhlenberg County, Kentucky. You've probably heard the song *Paradise* by John Prine? It describes my family's journey pretty well. Grandpa married granny, who was from Arkansas. They had my dad in Tennessee and then moved to Oklahoma when he was three years old.

"My mom's folks were the first generation of non-Indians born in Indian Territory which was what it was called before Oklahoma was a state.

"California was a very different lifestyle than they were

used to. They only stayed because there was no opportunity to make a living in Oklahoma where they grew up. Until I was about twelve years old, we went to Oklahoma every year on Dad's vacation, and the folks continued to talk and plan about how to be able to move back there. Finally, we became Californians, but it took some years. And we had the advantage of speaking English," Jimmy concluded.

"So why do we let them come, if they don't want to be here and be Americans?" asked Daniel.

"Simple," Jimmy continued to explain. "American business wants the cheap labor, and agribusiness can't survive without their labor. Americans won't do the poorly paid hard work that the Mexican's do. We found that out when the braceros left.

"Shortly after the braceros left was when we began to allow workers from Mexico to slip across the border. Does anyone believe we couldn't shut that border if we really wanted to? All you would have to do is fine the employers who hired them, and the illegal immigration would stop.

"So while it looks like the illegal Mexicans are taking advantage of the U. S., it's really unscrupulous politicians trying to whip up hate by saying that they are taking advantage. The fact is that they are little more than indentured servants.

"They pick our crops, clean our hotel rooms, do all the grunt work for extremely low wages. They don't become assimilated because many of them don't intend to stay. Then the hate mongers, mostly politicians, whip up community sentiment against them by promising to deal with the Mexicans if the voters will just re-elect them.

"That was a pretty long-winded answer, but I want to

share what I've learned with you because I know you will be in some role where you will be able to influence public policy. I know you will use that Poli Sci degree and do well in politics. These people who come here from Mexico to do farm work and other menial jobs must be better treated. Purposely letting them slip over the border and then electing these two-faced politicians that demonize them is criminal. Not to mention that working them so hard for so little is simply not worthy of this great country and state.

"There's another group poised to take advantage of them — politicians of Mexican descent who are already citing what huge numbers of Mexican-American constituents they have. They are also very happy about the open border. Mexican-American politicians preach that no person of Mexican descent should trust anyone who isn't of Mexican descent. The logical extension, of course, is that the person of Mexican descent should be elected.

"So what you have, Daniel, is a toxic soup of some Anglo politicians preaching that Mexicans are taking American jobs while Mexican-American politicians are proclaiming to the high heaven that all people of Mexican descent should trust them, and only them, and reject and demonstrate against any Anglo candidate or incumbent.

"Meanwhile, every employer who can get some cheap labor from these farmworkers is only too happy to have them. And, now they are branching out from farm work to hotel, restaurant work, and even carpentry.

"You know the questions detectives sometimes ask when trying to solve a crime? 'Who profits?' Well, let me ask you; who profits from having a southern border like a sieve?

"I'll tell you. First and foremost, the employers do, especially in agribusiness. But also now other industries have caught on that there is a desperate hard-working pool of potential employees who will work for pennies on the dollar. And of course, the unscrupulous politicians on both sides who are able to whip up ethnic hate, always a sure vote getter.

"Once again, Daniel, I'm telling you all this because I expect you to be in positions where you will effect public policy. I hope you will remember that these Mexican farmworkers are the victims, not the perpetrators. They are a hard-working group of people who take care of their families. Many sectors of our society feed off them like parasites."

"Wow, pretty impressive speech, Jim. Maybe you should be the politician, not me," Daniel replied.

"Not hardly," Jim replied. "I'm a one-issue guy."

"Well, seriously," Daniel continued, "I'll consider what you have said."

Chapter 40

"Mr. Welch, please come to my office when the 3:30 bell rings." Jimmy heard over the intercom. All the kids began to twitter, "Oh Mr. Welch has to go the principal's office. What did he do?"

"Calm down. He just called me on the intercom because it's almost 3:30, and he wants to talk to me, probably about some of you," Jimmy said with a chuckle.

"Jim, come in and have a seat. I need to have a word," Principal Campbell said.

Jimmy's anxiety was raised a little by that invitation. "I have the second quarter test results here; the central office just sent them over."

Jimmy squirmed a little because the first quarter results were not so good. Was this a repeat?

"I have to tell you, Jim, I've never seen anything like it," Mr. Campbell said.

Oh, this is going to be bad, Jimmy thought.

"Your fifth and six graders have outscored every class in the district by twenty points. You know, I was a little skeptical of the setup you developed, but this is fantastic. I would never have expected anything like this. Congratulations and please congratulate your young scholars for me.

"You remember all the heat we took from those naysayers in the central office about teaching in Spanish.

Well, I'll be very happy to go over and review these results with them as soon as I can," Principal Campbell finished.

****

It was that time of year. With spring in the air, the wildflowers popped up, the birds began to sing, the migrants came back, and the teachers got their annual evaluations. It was a time of renewed hope on many fronts.

Jimmy was busy changing bulletin boards in his classroom. One of the bulletin boards displayed the cycle of water, the source of all plant growth. He displayed how water got from the snow-clad Sierra Nevada Mountains to the San Joaquin Valley through the irrigation system.

"Hey Jim, got a minute?" Juan asked as he stepped into the doorway of Jimmy's classroom.

"Sure. Come on in," Jimmy replied. "What's up?"

"Just wanted to thank you for your help this year. Look at the evaluation I just got. I think it's pretty good," Juan said with glee.

Jimmy took the single sheet Juan offered and reviewed it. "This is more than 'pretty good.' This is excellent. You really have a good way of relating to the kids. The fact that you took that Spanish conversation course shows initiative, and you're able to help the non-English speakers better now."

Juan explained, "Yeah, I learned some, and the folks have started speaking Spanish to me at home; that helps a lot. But I'm just not learning fast enough; I can't carry on a conversation. I want to talk to you about that school you went to in Mexico. Summer vacation is coming up, and the folks said they could spare me from the farm for about six weeks. Do you think that's enough time to learn anything?"

"Yes, absolutely. You're starting way ahead of where I was when I started. In six weeks, you could learn a lot from that intensive CIDOC program. I would think you could probably teach some subjects in Spanish after six weeks," Jimmy said encouragingly.

"That's good to hear. Can you help me get in touch with them?" Juan asked.

"You bet! I have several contacts there. I'm going to Mexico this summer too," Jimmy said.

"Maybe we can travel together if things work out," Juan proposed.

"Great idea!" Jimmy responded.

The very next day, after school, Juan was back in Jimmy's classroom. "Hey, Jim. I talked to the folks last night about Mexico again. They're okay with me going for six weeks. I'll have to leave right after school is out and be back by the last week of July. You know peaches and watermelon harvest is in August, so I gotta be home for that."

"Hey, that's great Juan. You won't regret it. I have an application for CIDOC at home — brought a few back with me in case anyone here was interested. I'll bring one tomorrow. We can also make a call, let them know you are coming, and that you will pay the registration fee when you get there."

"Thanks Jim," Juan said. "Oh, by the way, when are you going to Mexico?"

"I'll be going right after school is out," Jimmy replied.

"Would you mind if I get on the same flight you'll be taking? I'm a little nervous about this. I've never been out of the United States," Juan admitted.

"No, I didn't know that. I thought you had probably been to Mexico," Jimmy said.

"No, I haven't been there. When my family left, they left for good," Juan replied.

"Sure, we can book the same flight. I can go with you as far as Mexico City. I can even get you on the bus to Cuernavaca. In fact, if you would like, I can make a call and set you up to stay at the same place I stayed."

"That all sounds great," Juan responded.

"I'm meeting my friend Father Anaya in Mexico City. He's taking me on a tour of the east coast of Mexico. By the time you're ready to return home, you will have no problem getting back to the airport. Your Spanish and knowledge of the country will be much improved," Jimmy said.

Within a few days, airline reservations were made, Juan's application was mailed, and lodging was secured. Jimmy had spoken to Mrs. Fuentes, and she was happy to have Juan as a boarder. Jimmy's own reservation for the Hotel Geneve, where he was meeting Fr. Anaya, was secured, and both young men were excited for the new experience on the horizon.

****

It had been another great year in which Jimmy got more in touch with the community and more involved. His adult English class was a joy to watch. Renaldo, who had a third grade education in Mexico, was a voracious learner; he was already able to use past tense verbs. His vocabulary was enlarging, and he wanted to learn to read English. Jimmy started him with the Dolch Sight Word List, and he soon mastered 50 percent of the list.

Jimmy's classroom work with children was a tremendous success. His bilingual approach to instruction paid huge dividends in the children's progress. Evan, the dad of two little Anglo boys, thanked Jimmy for helping his sons learn Spanish. "The boys can help me give work assignments to the Spanish speakers now," he said.

Jimmy's students were some of the highest scorers in the district in all academic areas, including reading. Their performance helped him beat back the objections to so much Spanish being used in the classroom.

Even Jimmy's friend, Daniel, had objected when he described what he was doing. "You know one of the unifying aspects of a society is a common language," Daniel said. "You're not doing any favors by introducing so much Spanish in the classroom."

"We shall see," Jimmy had replied. Now we have seen, Jimmy thought, as he reveled in the grade reports.

A successful school year was finished, and now it was time for Jimmy to further his own education. He had arranged to travel with Fr. Anaya to see more of Mexico and to hone his already sharp Spanish skills. Jimmy's satisfaction with a job well done the past year was mixed equal parts with his excitement about the new learning opportunity.

Chapter 41

Jimmy and Juan met at the Stockton Airport on a hot June day. The valley hadn't flexed its real heat muscle yet, but that was soon to come. They took their seats for the short hop to their Mexico City connection in San Francisco, "Baghdad by the Bay," Herb Caen called it.

They boarded the American Airlines flight in San Francisco just in time to get seated, strapped in, and watch the beautiful young stewardess give the safety directions. "Wow! That stewardess is a looker," Jimmy said. "What do you think, Juan?"

"I guess I haven't told you, Jim, but I have a girlfriend."

"That doesn't keep you from looking, does it? But that's pretty interesting news, Juan. You have a girlfriend, but no one has ever seen her. Is this an imaginary girlfriend only you can see?" Jimmy said with a chuckle.

"Ha, ha," Juan replied flatly. "She's in San Diego. I met her at San Francisco State, but she's from San Diego. She's going to be a teacher too; she's just finishing up her student teaching. She'll be applying to districts around San Diego this summer; she wants to teach kindergarten or first grade."

"Is she bilingual?" Jimmy asked.

"No, she's like me, a Mexican-American who never learned Spanish."

"How serious is this relationship?" Jimmy asked.

"From her end, I'm not sure, but for me, I think she might be the one," Juan said shyly.

The ding of the 'release your seat belt' sign was the signal for Jimmy and Juan to order a beer and settle in for a long and comfortable ride. The coach seats were recliners. They were definitely big enough and reclined enough for a long nap.

Ding went the seat belt signal; Jimmy roused himself, fastened his seat belt, put his seat in an upright position, and closed his tray table. Juan was glued to the window *oohing and aahing* as the spectacle of Mexico City moved into sight.

"It's huge," Juan exclaimed. "How many people live here?"

"Last number I heard was eight million, but that was a year ago; it could be more now. People are coming in from all over the country; you'll see them. Lots of poor people from the countryside coming here with hopes for a better life. You'll see ladies they call the 'Marias,' poverty-stricken native people selling gum on the street corners, usually with a couple of little kids," Jimmy explained.

The plane had a perfect landing and touched lightly down, the roar of the engines quieting to a whine as they approached the terminal. Walking to customs, Juan looked dazed. "This is the most brown faces I have ever seen in one place," Juan whispered to Jimmy.

"Well, you're going to see a lot more before this trip is over. Remember what I told you? They will probably treat me better than you because of all the hang-ups about *Pochismo*," Jimmy warned.

"Yeah, I remember. That just gives me more ambition to learn perfect Spanish," Juan said.

Customs was a breeze. Bringing United States passports greased the skids. They were through Mexican customs and into a VW taxi, in record time.

"Señora Fuentes is expecting you today, and we're in plenty of time for you to catch the 1 p.m. bus. That will get you there by late afternoon or early evening. You'll like the place. The Fuentes family are nice people and they have the sweetest maid you've ever met. She is very helpful, and within a week or so of lessons, you'll be able to talk to her," Jimmy explained.

"I can't wait, Jim. I'll see Mexico City for a couple of days before I go back in July; right now, I just want to get there and get started," Juan said.

Jimmy pointed and said, "Here's the bus station. I'll get out here and show you where to get the ticket. I can get another taxi back to my hotel."

"Ugh, smells like gasoline spilled somewhere," Juan said.

"Unfortunately that's the air you're smelling," Jimmy said. "But never fear, in Cuernavaca you will smell only flowers and clear mountain air. And don't forget to get on that bus as soon as it pulls up if you want a seat. Remember the seat number on the ticket is only good if you're the first one in the seat."

Juan boarded the bus as Jimmy picked up his suitcase and walked to the taxi area. The trip to the Hotel Geneve was short in distance but made much longer by the traffic, the incessant horn honking, and breathing air that could probably fuel a bus.

Now it was time for Jimmy to get excited. He was meeting Father Anaya in the evening and leaving in the morning for parts unknown to him. The southeast of Mexico was very exotic and mysterious.

"Hello Jim. It's good to see you again. I was pleased to get your call. I'm always glad to show off this beautiful country." Father Anaya spoke English to Jimmy, and he responded in kind. Jimmy guessed that the Father probably had little opportunity to speak English, so Jimmy set aside his desire to use Spanish in favor of letting Father Anaya practice his English.

"It's really great to see you again, Father Anaya; I'm so grateful to you for showing me around," Jimmy said.

"It's a wonderful opportunity for me too; I need a vacation. Please call me Pablo. We are going to be seeing lots of each other the next few days, so let's get comfortable." Fr. Anaya said.

They chatted for a while during which Pablo showed Jimmy a map of Mexico and charted out where they planned to go.

"First stop is at Lake Catemaco, then on to the San Andrés Valley. We make an overnight stop at Coatzacoalcos so I can see my uncle; I haven't seen him in years. From there we continue to Mérida, Cancún and Isla de Mujeres; then we double back to Villa Hermosa and the Maya ruins at Palenque. Depending on time, you can fly home from Villa Hermosa or I will drive you back to Mexico City."

"Sounds great," Jimmy said. "I'm anxious to see everything. When do we leave?"

"I have my car here in the garage. We should leave about

6:30 a.m. so we can get out of the city before the major rush starts," Fr. Anaya advised.

"Okay, see you in the lobby at 6:30," Jimmy said excitedly.

After a brief dinner of sweet rolls and tea, they retired to their rooms. Jimmy was pleased to be at the Hotel Geneve again. It seemed like home, a very familiar place.

After a restful night, Jimmy said enthusiastically, "It feels good to be on the open road!" as they left Mexico City.

"Yes, it is some wonderful, beautiful country we will be passing through. This city that we are passing now is Puebla. You may remember that it is the city where the Mexican army defeated the French on May 5, 1862. That's the date your countrymen seem to think is Mexican Independence Day."

"Yes, lots of celebrations on Cinco de Mayo in California. Don't know if anyone really knows or cares what the reason is; it just seems to be a big party," acknowledged Jim.

They motored on in Pablo's VW Bug and after about six hours, began to descend in altitude. When, in another two hours, they reached Catemaco, they were only a little over 1,000 feet above sea level, down from the over 7,000 foot elevation of Mexico City.

As they pulled into the little resort on Lake Catemaco, the lush tropical vegetation surrounded them. Jimmy was amazed at the difference from the Mexico City plateau. They each grabbed their bag and headed for the small office to check in.

"Pablo, why aren't you wearing your collar or your priest clothes," Jimmy asked. It just occurred to him that he and

Pablo were dressed very much alike — jeans and a sport shirt.

"I'm not allowed to wear clerical attire in public," Pablo responded. "The church lost all authority after the 1910 revolution. The new constitution of 1917 took away church authority and prohibits public display of religious activity. Most Mexicans are Catholic, attend church, and we even have our festivals. But when I perform a marriage, it's not a legal marriage in Mexico. The couple then has to be married by civil authorities. Even so, the people remain loyal to the church. I still hear at least ten confessions a week, and baptisms and burials go on as before."

The boat ride on Catemaco Lake was interesting with its island inhabited by monkeys. The thick vegetation and oppressive humidity were not to Jimmy's liking, but he was young and strong; he could take it.

San Andreas Tuxtla was where Jimmy took up cigar smoking. The lush valley had been a tobacco growing region for many years. Its prominence was only enhanced by the arrival of cigar makers fleeing Castro's Cuba. Cuba was just a few miles across the sea but a million miles away from the freedom allowed by the Mexican government.

Jimmy and Pablo were both intrigued watching the rolling of cigars. Twenty small wooden desks were situated in a warehouse with a person reading while sitting on an elevated platform above them.

The rollers each formed the rich, loose strands of tobacco into a cigar shape, deftly using a half-moon shaped knife to cut the leaves into proper shapes for rolling. The knife was much like the Ulu knife, which is used by the indigenous people of Alaska. They added binder and wrapper leaves and rolled them all into a perfectly shaped cigar. All this was done very quickly, and with great precision, turned out uniformly shaped cigars.

As they worked, the reader on the platform entertained. He first read the headlines from the local newspapers. Following that, he gave a brief explanation of the work of an obscure Mexican poet then read several selections of poetry.

The supervisor of the rolling room explained that these expert cigar rollers could make a hundred or more perfectly formed cigars in a day. The reader was an innovation borrowed from Cuba. He found it true that the workers were more productive with the introduction of a reader.

Jimmy bought a box of Robustos in the showroom as they left. The cedar-lined cigar box was a work of art. The box was made of wood, aligned perfectly, and closed with a small brass clasp. He loved the smell of the cedar mingled with the earthy scent of the rich San Andreas tobacco.

"Do you see the irony on the box of cigars you bought, Jim?" Pablo asked. "There is a drawing of a matador at the moment of truth, getting ready to kill the bull. Underneath the drawing is printed the brand name Te Amo (I love you); those two don't seem to go together. Ironic."

There was an overnight stop at Coatzacoalcos for Pablo to visit relatives, then it was on to Mérida.

"Are you having trouble with the Spanish, Jim?" Pablo asked.

"Now that you mention it, I am. I thought I was pretty fluent, but I'm struggling. Didn't have any trouble in Cuernavaca or Mexico City or even back in California," Jimmy answered.

"Don't be distressed. The people in this area are some of the fastest talkers in the country. They clip their words off and run them together. Sometimes it's even hard for me to understand them. It's probably for you like it was for me when I traveled to Alabama. The English there sounds very different from other parts of the country."

The city of Mérida was like something from a fairytale to Jimmy. The sixteenth-century mansion, called Casa de Montejo, appeared to his eyes as a medieval castle of old. Jimmy could picture Spanish conquistadors riding in and out of its gates. He was enthralled with watching daily life in the Plaza de la Independencia.

Jimmy felt like Gulliver in Lilliput among the tiny Mayan street vendors. These descendants of the great culture that built the cities from Guatemala to Mexico, now had reverted to the jungle. They were residents of tiny huts who came to sell their wares in the city. Jimmy judged the tallest of the men to be about 5 feet 6 inches.

It was the rainy season and so hot and humid that two days was enough of Mérida.

"Let's move on to Cancún," Pablo suggested. "At least it's on the coast. Maybe we will get some breeze there."

They did catch a little breeze in Cancún. The temperature was still muggy and hot but a few degrees cooler. The small fishing village of Cancún held little interest for Jimmy.

"Not much to do here," Jimmy said. "I've walked the town twice today and pretty much seen everything here."

"Yes, you're right," Pablo acknowledged, "but I came here for another reason. This is the embarkation point for our trip to *Isla de Las Mujeres* (The Island of Women). But don't get too excited. The name comes from the many terra cotta figurines of the Maya goddess of fertility, Ixchel, found on the island by the Spanish. There is a small Maya temple on the southern tip of the island dedicated to Ixchel. You should visit it, but it will remind you of a little shack after you see Palenque.

"The island is 13 kilometers off the coast. I have made arrangements to leave the car at the hotel for a couple of days. We won't need a car on the island. It's only 7 kilometers long and 650 meters wide. There is a sea ferry we will catch at 7 a.m. tomorrow that will take us to the island," Pablo finished.

"Are my calculations correct?" Jimmy asked. "The island is about 8 miles off the coast and it's only a little over 4 miles long and about half a mile wide?"

"My mental math is not as good as yours, but yes, I believe your calculations are generally correct. But don't be concerned about the size of the island. The beauty of the place is the sea. The island is located where the Gulf of Mexico and the Caribbean Sea meet. We will rent some fins and masks and explore the coral reefs around the island. You'll see, it will be great fun," Pablo enthused.

It was exciting. After a pleasant boat ride over an only slightly choppy sea, they disembarked, found a hotel and immediately went to the dive shop and rented fins and masks.

As they approached the beach, Jimmy was startled to see schools of small brightly colored yellow and blue fish that looked like they were trying to get out of the water onto the beach. They struggled and fluttered their fins as they headed for the beach and pushed toward the waterline. Some dorsal fins were even out of the water.

"What's happening?" Jimmy exclaimed.

"Oh, the dive shop owner puts fish food right at the water line to bring the little fish up. He does this to encourage tourists to rent equipment and dive the reefs to see the bigger fish," Pablo explained.

"Wow! What a sight. It looks like a herd of cattle at the feeding trough, only smaller and prettier," Jimmy said. "You said 'for the tourists.' I don't see many tourists around. Most of the people I've seen are Mexicans."

"Well, yes Jim! I am a Mexican but also a tourist. This island is a tourist spot where Americans rarely venture. Almost everyone you see is a tourist," Pablo explained.

"Yes, of course. How could I be so silly? It's just that the Mexican people I know in California don't have money to be tourists like this," Jimmy said.

"I would judge that several of the Mexican tourists I have seen here have more money than most Americans will see in a lifetime. That's why they don't need to go to the United States. And if they did go there, it would be as tourists, and they would stay at the Biltmore, not the Motel 6," Pablo explained.

They snorkeled the reefs all afternoon. Beautiful blues, yellows, and reds adorned the reef fish. Jimmy had heard of the famous reef sharks; unlike other sharks, they have been documented resting on the sea floor and in caves. They don't have to keep moving in order to absorb oxygen in their gills. But they are still sharks and therefore predators.

With these thoughts in mind, Jimmy's heart started to pound as he saw a large fish streaking at him from the bottom of the sea. He felt helpless and very scared as he tried to paddle for shore. In seconds, the fish was treading water within five feet of Jimmy's face. Its yellow body gently undulated in the current and blue parrot-like mouth opened and shut, then the fish simply swam slowly away back to its reef.

Jimmy caught his breath and thought, to each his own — the fish to its reef and me back on dry land. One more of those incidents, and I'm afraid I'll need a new unsoiled bathing suit.

Pablo and Jimmy feasted late afternoon on conch cerviche and fish tacos with sides of black beans, rice, and corn tortillas. As they left the restaurant, Jimmy spotted a huge pile of large conch shells. The pink pearlescent interiors of the top shells gleamed in the sunlight, while those on the bottom of the pile were dull, crumbling, chalky shells.

"These shells are just being left to deteriorate," Jimmy said. "My grandma has one of those on her end table. They sell them in the states."

"Yes, I know," Pablo said. "But they are so plentiful here, they are like stones, just part of the landscape."

In the morning, Pablo announced, "Next stop, Villa Hermosa. It will be a long day, but we'll get there this evening." With that, he pulled onto the two-lane highway, and off they went.

"I'm loving every minute of this" Jimmy said. "Thanks for driving so I can see the country roll by."

"*De nada* (you're welcome)," Pablo replied. "I have reservations at the Hotel Manzur in Villa Hermosa. It's a great hotel, wonderful restaurants. We should spend tomorrow seeing the sights around Villa Hermosa. The next day, we go to Palenque."

They rolled into Villa Hermosa early evening and were up and ready to go early in the morning. "We are in the state of Tabasco now," Pablo said while they waited for the tour bus. "No relationship to your American hot sauce. The sauce maker is in Louisiana and just took our name and made it a brand of hot sauce."

The sights of Villa Hermosa were interesting, but the thing Jimmy would remember most was the dinner. The Manzur was a tourist hotel and therefore had a full menu for evening dining. "Try the pigua," Pablo suggested.

"What is it?" Jimmy asked.

"It is a freshwater lobster from the river here."

"You mean a crawdad," Jimmy said.

"What is a crawdad?" Pablo asked.

"A crawdad is about 4 inches long and looks like a lobster," Jimmy answered.

"Oh no, the pigua is twenty to twenty-five centimeters. Better yet," Pablo continued, "try the pigua and the filet mignon. The beef here is also excellent."

Pablo was right on both suggestions. The pigua was very lobster-like in size and taste. The filet was tender and cooked to perfection. As a four-piece combo played smooth jazz, they dined, surrounded by windows looking out on the lights of Villa Hermosa. It was a meal not to be forgotten!

Jimmy was very excited as they waited for the tour bus to Palenque. Mexico was full of ancient sites; Jimmy had seen a few, but this was special. He was soon to see his first Maya City.

The city was already abandoned and partially overgrown by the forest when the Spanish arrived in the 1520s. The tropical vegetation hid what once was a thriving city.

The guidebook Jimmy read had explained the fall of the mighty Maya empire. It had stretched from Guatemala to Southern Mexico in a series of powerful city-states and began to fall apart in the thirteenth century. The cities were abandoned, and the population returned to the jungle. Several theories for why this happened have been proposed. War, pestilence, drought — all were postulated as reasons, but none conclusively proven. How interesting that the fall of an advanced civilization is still unexplained, Jimmy thought.

The sight of the three Maya temples jutting up from the rich green jungle was Jimmy's first view of the ruins of Palenque. Jimmy mused, people built these spectacular structures over a thousand years ago. He was particularly impressed with the Temple of the Cross. Its delicate arched doorways and edifice with stone crosses caused him to wonder how they developed such architecture.

Most amazing of all was the Maya science. Their knowledge of the heavens was extensive. They could predict eclipses, and their calendar was more exact than any in the modern world. Art, architecture, mathematics, astronomy, agriculture — all had been brought to a very high level of excellence in the place called Palenque. It wasn't the most spectacular of the Maya cities but was definitely one of the most interesting.

Sadly, the next morning it was time for Jimmy and Pablo to part company. Pablo had to return to his priestly duties in Yuriria, and he had a long drive ahead of him. After another couple of days touring Palenque and the surrounding areas, Jimmy would catch a short flight to Mexico City and on to San Francisco. They said their farewells with some sadness in the front driveway of the Hotel Manzur. As Pablo pulled away, Jimmy wondered if they would ever meet again.

Jimmy was once again in a Spanish-only environment, but to his credit he had become accustomed to the cadence and accents of speech in the region. He knew he would be fine. Soon after Pablo left, it was back on the bus and across the river to the state of Chiapas and back to the city of Palenque.

Jimmy wandered aimlessly through the ancient ruins. He felt the oppressive humidity on his skin and wondered what it must have been like for the ancients in this city. He stood and stared for several minutes at the intricate stone carvings and the wondrous advanced architecture.

He called to mind the Roman Forum where he had also wandered. He had heard of the Romans since at least high school; he learned of their innovations in architecture, most notably the arch. But was any structure he saw in Rome more impressive than what he saw here? He thought, *no!*

Jimmy reasoned that the Maya were more obscure because their cities were lost to the jungle for centuries, and also because their culture was so very foreign to Western Civilization. Jimmy felt his spirit soar while standing among the ancient ruins. He knew that greatness had been here. He felt, in all his being, the joy of knowledge and wonder rising out of the jungle and bringing prosperity to the people. He felt connected in some strange way to those ancients who had lived, toiled, loved, argued, and flourished here.

Hours passed unnoticed as Jimmy wandered and ruminated about the past and its connection to the present. All at once, he realized that he was hungry, thirsty, and tired. Walking along a dirt road, he spotted a small whitewashed building with a thatched roof and a sign painted in bold red lettering '*Comida.*' He entered the open door to a cool dark interior with a hard- packed dirt floor. In the middle of the room, a black iron pot the size of two basketballs hung over a bed of glowing wood embers. The contents of the pot slowly bubbled and emitted a tantalizing aroma of seafood.

"Welcome, there are shrimp today," a man behind a small wooden bar said. *"Have a seat."* he beckoned to a small table with two woven chairs.

Jimmy's eyes had adjusted to the dim light now, and he saw three other small tables around the room with men clustered around them over plates of food. Jimmy sat as requested, and the man behind the bar stepped over to his table. The man Jimmy took to be the proprietor was dressed in somewhat soiled, loose fitting, white clothing. *"What can I get for you?"* he asked.

Jimmy replied, *"I'll have a cerveza Modelo. Do you have a menu?"*

"We have shrimp today," he replied.

"Okay, I'll have shrimp then," Jimmy said with a chuckle.

"Right away," the proprietor said as he opened a huge ice chest and extracted a short squat bottle of Negra Modelo. He then took a scoop the size of a small platter, dipped it into the pot, and brought out a pile of extra-large whole shrimp — head, tail, feelers, and all. He placed the shrimp on a plate and set the plate, beer, a fork, and paper napkin on Jimmy's table.

Jimmy stared for a moment at his plate. This was the first time he had ever eaten a shrimp that was looking at him; boiled or otherwise. What did you think, Jimmy thought to himself, that they were just tails swimming in the ocean? Well, when they come frozen, that's all they are.

These were not frozen; they were fresh out of the sea and delicious!

Soon the pile of shrimp was reduced to a pile of shells and heads, with little black beady eyes still staring at him. As the proprietor saw him finish, he stepped over to Jimmy's table to see if he'd like some more shrimp. Jimmy declined but declared that the shrimp were delicious.

"I do have a question about that bow and arrow you have on the wall. Is it real or just for decoration?" Jimmy asked. Jimmy pointed to a six-foot loosely strung bow of some hardwood variety. It was accompanied by six arrows with hollow reeds for shafts and several different tips. There was a serrated hardwood tip, three roughly made stone arrowheads, a round bulbous wood tip, and a slender straight hardwood tip.

"All for hunting a different type of game or fish," the proprietor said.

Arrows Jimmy had seen before, even those from Oklahoma had nondescript black or brown feathers. These Mexican arrows were fletched with brightly colored red, green, yellow, and blue parrot feathers.

"Where did you get this?" Jimmy inquired.

"I trade with the Lacandon Indians when they come into town," he replied. ***"They live out in the jungle in little huts. They hunt for their food with these bows but they come sometimes to trade for coffee and sugar; they love sugar. They bring bows and arrows, sometimes a tame parrot or a monkey, to trade. They are the descendants of the people who built the Palenque temples."***

"I see," Jimmy said. ***"I'd like to make a trade with you for that bow and set of arrows."***

"Oh no, Señor. I couldn't part with it. I love it."

"You can get another one," Jimmy pleaded, *"but I may never come this way again."*

"But maybe next time they won't bring a bow and arrows," the proprietor said.

"Well, some day they will bring one. Look what I have to trade," Jimmy said as he fished in his pocket.

Out in his hand came a nearly new Swiss Army knife. Jimmy opened the shiny three inch stainless steel main blade and then the inch and a half secondary stainless steel blade. He saw the interest in the proprietor's face increase as he opened the screwdriver. When he opened the bottle opener, wire stripper, and the can opener, he knew by the look on the proprietor's face that the deal was sealed! He went ahead and pulled out the tweezers and tooth pick and opened the cork screw and leather punch for good measure.

As the knife lay on the table, tools and blades protruding at every angle, its red handle with the metal Swiss cross glowing, Jimmy looked at the mesmerized proprietor and said, *"Do we have a deal?"*

"As you were saying," the proprietor answered, *"I can get another bow and arrows. Let me get it off the wall for you."*

****

Just after touchdown in Stockton, Jimmy went to the back of the plane where the stewardess was getting the bow and arrows from the closet where she had kindly stored them. Jimmy was very pleased that none of his homeward-bound flights had required him to check his precious and fragile souvenir. He was, as always, glad to be home and already missing Mexico.

Part III
1980s to Early 1990s

"Education is the most powerful weapon which you can use to change the world."

— Nelson Mandela

Chapter 42

The wedding was a gala affair. Juan's relatives came from all over California. Marina's relatives were fewer but were all in attendance. The rather sizable Catholic Church in Perryville had standing room only.

Jimmy was asked to be an usher. He and Juan had become close as the years of teaching together progressed. He was not surprised to be asked to be part of the wedding party but he was deeply honored when the invitation came.

Jimmy had thought many times while talking to Juan that things weren't going to work out with Marina. These long-distance relationships had a way of fizzling out over time. San Diego was definitely a long way from Perryville, at least an eight hour drive. Flying was an option but an expensive one which Juan took monthly.

What made a major change in their situation was that Marina snagged one of the coveted teaching jobs with San Francisco Unified School District. Her experience teaching in San Diego Unified served her well in the interview process, but her excellent recommendations from her principal and sparkling personality put her over the top.

Even at age 27, Marina's very traditional family would not hear of her living alone in San Francisco. But once again, her Tia came to the rescue. Marina considered it a homecoming of sorts moving back into her college room in Tia's Park Merced apartment.

Juan was overjoyed; instead of an eight-hour drive, she was now only an hour and a half away. At least one day a week, Juan pulled out of the McKinley School parking lot and headed west. He was at Marina's doorstep by 5:30 p.m. The three of them had a delicious dinner prepared by Tia. Following dinner, the two love birds would walk arm in arm down the block and across the street to the San Francisco State Campus. They would stroll and talk and revisit favorite campus spots. Then they would walk back, where Juan would say his good byes and be home to Perryville by 10 p.m.

On the weekends, Juan was welcome to spend Saturday night in Tia's spare bedroom. But she made it very clear there would be no late night bedroom calls in her house.

After six months of this courtship, Juan popped the question. Of course, the answer was a resounding yes. After three years of surviving a long distance relationship and six months of not wanting to be out of one another's sight, they were both pretty sure what the question and answer would be. The following June they carried out their commitment and then headed for a month-long honeymoon in Mexico.

"So how was Mexico?" Jimmy asked. He was delighted to see Juan back and ready for another school year.

"We had a great time," Juan replied. "Thanks so much for your travel tips. My Spanish was just fine — never had a problem. You were right; CIDOC did the trick!

"I took Marina to see Cuernavaca and the CIDOC campus, and now she wants to go. She still hasn't learned Spanish very well."

"You should take her. She will flourish like you did. I

know she's probably heard Spanish all her life. She knows more than she thinks she does," Jimmy said enthusiastically.

"Yeah, I would like to do that, but with the new principal job, I don't get as much time off," Juan explained. "It's an eleven- month contract."

"Take her there for a month; it will help. Do it before you have kids and get tied down. You are having kids, aren't you?" Jimmy asked.

"Is the Pope Catholic? Yes, of course we're going to have kids, but not for a while," Juan answered.

"Take her next summer," Jimmy urged.

"I'll talk to Marina about it," Juan replied. "How are things with you and Julie?"

"Oh, not good," Jimmy replied. "We parted ways last month. It's for the best. We finally figured out that we had pretty different ideas about how the future should be."

****

Hilario was so happy to be a staff member of Assemblyman Luis Padilla. His B.A. had gotten his foot in the door; his drive, aggressiveness, and smarts had kept him there. He loved the work and his surroundings. He would often just stand for a minute under the Capitol building dome, looking up through its beautiful stained-glass windows; he would marvel that Assemblyman Padilla's office was just down the hall and he had his own desk in the outer office. Hilario did good work and represented Assemblyman Padilla well at meetings of lesser importance.

This day, Hilario was sitting in a meeting of the Latino Caucus. The topic was school progress for Latinos; several school principals would be speaking. His only duty was to listen and report to Mr. Padilla. Hilario often covered these meetings where Spanish might be used because the Assemblyman spoke only a halting version of Spanish.

Hilario was just settling into his chair when he spotted his college acquaintance Juan at the podium. This was a surprise; he hadn't seen him in years. He wondered what Juan was doing here.

Juan was the first speaker on the agenda. "Good morning. My name is Juan Martinez. I'm the principal at McKinley School. We are a K-8 school in a very rural farming area. The student body is 95% Hispanic and 5% Anglo. I'm here today to ask for your help in getting more financial support for our bilingual program. We have a program in which each subject is taught every school day in English and again in Spanish. I can show you some statistics that verify that it is working. Our Latino students are on par with all students across the state, and our Anglo students are becoming fluent Spanish speakers. We have learned that studying the two languages, when done right, results in better reading scores in both English and Spanish. This is more expensive to do than a mono-lingual classroom. First, we must have two sets of textbooks, one in Spanish and one in English. More importantly, we need teachers who are bilingual. By bilingual, we mean a person who has done a formal study of both English and Spanish. It's important that when children are learning, they first learn formal language. They can learn slang later, if they wish. As you may imagine, bilingual teachers are hard to find. In order to attract them, our district adds 15% to their pay if they pass our bilingual language exam.

"This increased salary is a very large financial investment

and stretches our budget. When added to the additional materials needed, we are operating on a shoe string, and we're never able to develop a significant reserve. We respectfully ask that you take action to see that additional funds are allocated to schools in the state that have at least 51% Hispanic students and provide bilingual education. We would further like to suggest that as the percentage of Hispanic students rise, there will be a financial supplement beyond the base, which is equal to 5% additional funding for each 5% rise in Hispanic students. Thank you for your time. I'll take questions, if you have them."

Hilario was the first with his hand up, eager to grill Juan. Hilario thought, now is my time to fry this coconut.

"Señor Martinez, I have a question. How can you, a person who does not speak Spanish, be in charge of a bilingual school? How can you evaluate bilingual teachers?" Hilario asked in a very sharp tone.

"That's a good question. I do believe in the value of bilingualism, and for that reason, I have studied both languages extensively. But do you have a question about the content of my presentation. If so, you could perhaps ask in English because I believe that it is the only language that we all share," Juan answered pointedly in perfect articulate Spanish.

"No further questions," Hilario answered with an embarrassed grin.

The meeting ended with pledges from the caucus to work on getting items Juan and the other school administrators outlined. They all requested more money to support Latino students.

Hilario stepped up to Juan as he was exiting the room.

"Hola Juan. It makes me very happy to see you speaking Spanish."

"How have you been Hilario? I heard you were here working for Assemblyman Padilla."

"Yeah, it's good here. We get into a lot of interesting areas. Say, how about me coming to see your school? Then I can talk it up around the capital," Hilario offered.

"That would be great. Come anytime. Here's my number. Give me a call just to be sure I'll be there."

Within a week, Hilario was out to visit the McKinley School. Juan showed him around and spent a good deal of time in Jimmy's room.

"This is one of our best teachers," Juan said as they watched a Spanish math lesson for a few minutes. Hilario indicated he wanted to return to Juan's office.

"Have you seen enough to get a good feel for the school?" Juan asked.

"Yeah, I've seen enough," Hilario replied in stern English. "Why do you have a gringo teaching Spanish lessons?"

"Why do you ask that? Didn't you think his Spanish was good?" Juan wondered.

"Oh, the Spanish was fine, but he's a gringo," exclaimed Hilario.

"I wish you would quit saying that word. He's a teacher just like all the other teachers, except he's the best teacher in the school," Juan said sternly.

"But don't you think it's bad to have an Anglo teaching our *Chicanitos* (little Chicanos)?" Hilario asked.

"Well, first of all, if you asked the parents of these kids to describe their ethnicity, they would say they are Mexicano or Mexican-American. There's not one among them who would say he is a Chicano. Secondly, no, I don't think it's bad to have an Anglo teaching here. These kids need all the help they can get; he is giving them a first-rate education, and the parents love him!" Juan explained calmly.

"Does he get 15% more pay?" Hilario asked.

"Yes, he does. He passed the bilingual test with the highest score in the district," Juan answered.

Hilario was exasperated as he said, "Juan, he's part of the problem. His big, white, satisfied self; he's probably never had a day in his life when he took any of the kind of shit we suffered for years. How can he understand these kids?"

"Hilario, you don't know a thing about this guy except that you don't like him because he's an Anglo. I have to tell you that is racism just like the kind of racism we have had used against us. What I hope you will understand," Juan continued, "is that it's essential that these kids get a good education. In the long run, it's the only way they are going to get out of poverty."

"Yeah, I get that," Hilario said. "But they need to be taught by Chicanos, not Anglos."

"When you send me Chicanos who have the education, skills, and good heart that this guy has, I will hire them. Meanwhile, I would hire *blue* teachers if they could help these kids."

Hilario, rising from his chair and raising his voice a little, said, "I knew you were a coconut, Juan. I just didn't know how bad it really was. I think I'll just have to keep calling you Johnny until you decide which side you're on."

"See, that's the problem, Hilario. We shouldn't be choosing sides," Juan said as Hilario walked out the door.

"Yeah, right," Hilario said sarcastically. "See you around, Johnny."

Chapter 43

"Hello," Jimmy said while lifting the telephone handset off its wall base. He was proud of his new yellow wall phone. It dressed up his little apartment with a splash of canary yellow.

"Hey Jim. It's Daniel."

"Hey, good to hear from you," Jimmy said.

"Yeah, it's been hard to reach you these days. Seems like you're always in Mexico," Daniel said.

"No, just in the summer. What's up with you? Still teaching at the university?" Jimmy asked.

"No, that job as lecturer got a little boring. I've spent enough time in schools. I want to get into the real world where people do things," Daniel said enthusiastically.

"Okay," Jimmy said slowly. "You realize you're saying that to a teacher, right?"

"Oh yeah, sorry. I didn't mean anything by it. I just liked working for the City of San Francisco so much; I left the University for a short-term job with the San Francisco office where I did my internship," Daniel explained. "Anyway, I'm just calling to let you know my San Francisco job ends in a couple of weeks, and I'll be leaving town. I'm in the process of applying for a job with the Los Angeles Planning Commission. The job is as an analyst like what I did in my internship for San Francisco. Only Los Angeles is so big, I would be assigned to just a section of the city. It's an entry-level job. I think I have a good shot at it. My education, background, and my internship experience should put me at the top of the candidate list. That is, unless there is a far less qualified candidate from a protected minority who applies."

"What do you mean by that?" Jimmy asked.

"Come on, you haven't heard of Affirmative Action?" Daniel exclaimed.

"Oh yeah, there is that. Well, I'll keep my fingers crossed for you. I know you'll do well wherever you wind up." Jimmy spoke enthusiastically, "While we're just talking, I want to let you know I'm applying for a new job too, nothing as exciting as Los Angeles. It's right here in McKinley in the housing area next to the school. It's a federal program called the Child Home School Alliance (CHSA) funded by the federal Department of Labor. It's a cooperative venture with public schools to help families get out of poverty."

"I hope you get it, Jim. You should do well; you seem to have a heart for those Mexican people," Daniel said.

"Thanks Daniel. Let's get together before you go to Los Angeles," Jimmy offered.

"Good idea," Daniel said in agreement.

****

The debate in the Los Angeles' Personnel Committee meeting was heavy and immediate. "I want Daniel Watson," Councilman Jones stated firmly.

"Well Councilman, let me give you two reasons why you shouldn't have him," the personnel committee chair said. "First of all, we need another Latino in the management track. I know this Delgado kid is just out of school with a B.A., but he'll probably work out."

"That's okay for you to say, but Daniel Watson is just out with an M.A., an internship and sterling references from his intern supervisor and three of his professors. In fact, one of his best references is from a Poly Sci professor at University of San Francisco, Robert Leach; Leach says Watson is the best student he has had in twenty years of teaching. And by the way, this Leach guy is headed to the United States Senate in January."

"He's a Republican, so he's not going to help us," the committee chair said. "Let me give you reason number two why you want Delgado instead of Watson. You're up for re-election next year, and your staff is pretty lily white. That will be used against you in the campaign. You need to add some color to your group."

"Okay, I hear you. Bring Delgado in."

****

The day after he received his rejection letter from Los Angeles, Daniel got a call. "Hello, is this Daniel Watson?"

"Yes, this is Daniel," he replied.

"Daniel, this is Bob Leach from the University. I think you finished your M.A., didn't you?"

"Yes, I did," Daniel answered.

"What are your plans now, Daniel?"

"I'm putting out job applications now, just looking for a place to get started," Daniel replied. "I had a temporary job with the city and that has ended."

"That's why I'm calling. You may know that I was appointed to finish out Senator Lacy's term. I'll have a chance to do something about all the issues I've been preaching about for years.

"I've left the University as of June. I'm busy now recruiting staff and preparing to move. There is nothing certain about this. I've been given a leave of absence from the University so I can return if things don't work out. However, my intention is to stay and run for the office next election.

"So Daniel, having said all that, I'd like to offer you an opportunity to be a member of my staff. Now, before you answer, let me tell you that Alan Gering, your former supervisor at the city, is going to be my staff director. In fact, he's the one that reminded me that you finished your M.A. The job I'm thinking of for you is doing policy analysis and compiling data to give us some direction on various bills. I would need you to start right away doing some work here and then moving to Washington in July. We will take office after the August recess. Again Daniel, nothing certain beyond two and a half years. Why don't you sleep on it and let me know?"

"Professor Leach, I don't need to sleep on it. I'm honored that you thought of me, and having Alan there just makes it more appealing. I'm ready, willing, and able. When do I start?" Daniel said very excitedly.

The effort to get up to speed on issues and move to Washington D.C. was rapid and intense. Senator Lacy's heart attack was severe and rendered him incapable of continuing to fulfill the duties of his office. Professor Leach, now Senator Leach, went to D.C. to find housing for himself and his wife and to confer with senate colleagues. Daniel and Alan opened and staffed his San Francisco office until local office staff could be found.

In just three weeks, Daniel got the call that it was time to come to D.C. He had already given up his apartment and was staying in a hotel. His paltry possessions fit in one suitcase, which he checked on his United Airlines flight.

Even coach on the DC-10 wide body was comfortable and enjoyable. The ride to Dulles International was over before Daniel awoke from his post-luncheon nap.

Alan was already in D.C. or what they soon learned to refer to as "the district." Alan had booked a hotel for Daniel for two weeks in order for him to get to work and find permanent lodging.

Daniel caught the shuttle bus outside Dulles after a short wait for his bag. It was always a stressful time wondering if the luggage went to the same city as the passenger. After collecting his bag, Daniel got on the mini-van and headed for his first view of the Nation's Capital. As they approached Washington D.C., he was awe-struck to see the statue of the flag raising on Iwo Jima during World War II. Soon the mini-van was through the mid-day traffic and Daniel was being deposited in front of the DuPont Circle Hotel.

****

Meanwhile, back in McKinley a much different but no less important scenario was playing out

"What good news. We are going to have our own house right here in McKinley!" Renaldo exclaimed. *"Señor Holiman likes my work very much, he told me. He is also glad that my English is getting better and better, so I can*

talk to him without an interpreter. He's making me his foreman, and we will be able to live in the house on his property. The house will be a part of my pay, but he also will pay me more. And you know what else? He said I will have year-long work; he will pay me the same every month."

"Oh, my love. That is wonderful. We won't have to move anymore, and we will know how much money we will have each month. But can we go to Mexico for Christmas?" Conchita asked.

"Yes, I can take three weeks in December and still get paid the same for the month. But the best of all, my love, is he will sponsor us and help us to get our green cards. Then when we have the cards, no more worrying and hiding from the Migra."

"Oh, that will be so wonderful, my love. God has truly blessed us," Conchita said.

"Yes he has. We will light some candles in the church this Sunday and send our prayers of thanksgiving," Renaldo replied.

Chapter 44

Senator Robert Leach's office was located in the Russell Office Building, the oldest of the Senate office buildings. While some looked down on the Russell building accommodations, Senator Leach loved its 1909 architecture.

Daniel was very pleased with his little office, which was just outside the Senator's office. He was also pleased to be next to Alan Gering's plush office. Well, that's what the staff director gets, Daniel thought. He was sure he'd be there someday, if he survived in this town.

Daniel had already been involved in some of the policy wars and was a bit battered for the experience. He was a conservative in a liberal world. Daniel knew the conservatives would have their day. He thought, we're on the right side of history. People will recognize that capitalism is the only way, once they see how this pseudo-socialism flops.

Daniel was very much looking forward to his friend Jimmy's visit. Daniel knew the city well after his year-long residence. His little studio apartment on Connecticut Avenue afforded him easy access to many friendly bars and restaurants within walking distance. Even though he didn't care for the Adams-Morgan area, he knew Jimmy would love the international flavor, and he intended to take him there. What the heck? Beer is beer even if an Afghani pours it, he thought.

Daniel and Jimmy had over ten years of friendship. Even though they hadn't seen each other much the last few years, Daniel knew they would pick up right where they left off. That's how it was with good friends. He was excited to be able to show Jimmy around on his first trip to Washington D.C.

Jimmy had made an expensive telephone call to let Daniel know that he would be coming. He explained that his new job required him be at a Thursday meeting in D.C., and he was taking the following Friday and Monday off in order to see the city. Daniel was excited to be able to show Jimmy around but also to hear about his new job.

In attendance at a strategy meeting were Daniel, Alan Gering, and Senator Leach. Senator Leach began. "We've got to do something about the broken immigration system. Any thoughts on the subject?" he asked looking expectantly at Alan.

"Well Senator, we're in a bind here. Agribusiness needs the labor. The nation's crops wouldn't get harvested without the Mexican farmworkers," Alan began.

"Yes, I know. Go on," the Senator said.

"The best we've been able to do is just look the other way while they come across the border to do the work. But now things have changed. They're not going back to Mexico; they're staying! Illegally, yes, but they're staying in the country just the same! Some of them are getting green cards and becoming legal residents, but most just take up residence and live in the shadows," Alan continued.

"Okay, I get it. So what ideas can we put forth to correct this mess?" Senator Leach asked.

"How about a version of the old bracero program?" Alan suggested. "The program worked pretty well. It was controlled; only the workers came, no families. When the agriculture season was done, they went back to Mexico. No families came to burden our social services system, and there was little temptation to try to stay because their families were in Mexico. We could give it a better name, like say 'Guest Worker Program.' That says to the world, 'You workers are our guests.' What do guests do when their stay is over? They go home!"

"Okay. That sounds like a possible path to follow," Senator Leach said. "You and Daniel flesh it out and see if there's enough there to come up with some legislation that makes sense. We have got to stop this crazy backwater activity that's going on now. It's not good for the country, and it's not good for the workers. Let's see if we can clean it up," the Senator concluded.

"We're on it," Alan said as he and Daniel rose to leave.

"Okay, Daniel," Alan said after they were seated in his office. "Let's do a plan to get this together."

"I can track down agricultural crop production by state and estimate how many workers would be required to do the work. We'll also have to make some estimates of how many of those are illegals," Daniel said.

"Yes, I agree," Alan said. "But what I don't want is a S.W.A.G. report."

"What's that?" Daniel asked.

"A *silly wild-assed guess* report," Alan replied with a chuckle. "You know the results of a S.W.A.G. report can sometimes be a C.E.M.," Alan continued.

"What's that?" Daniel inquired.

"It's a *career-ending move*!" Alan said while looking at Daniel with a smile.

"I don't want either one of those things." Daniel chuckled. "I can get data with a sound factual basis. As always, with some unknowns, we have to do some extrapolation, but our report and backup for the legislation will stand up to scrutiny."

"Yes, I know. I was just funnin' ya," Alan said. "You work on that. I'm going to work the territory here and try to gauge how much support we might get for our legislation."

"On it!" Daniel said as he left.

****

"Hey, Jim!" shouted Daniel as he walked towards him. Jimmy had gotten off the shuttle at Union Station where Daniel agreed to meet him. "Welcome! Did you have a good flight?" Without waiting for an answer, Daniel continued. "Let's get your bag over to the apartment. The best way for regular people like you and me to get around this town is the Metro." Daniel started walking, and Jimmy grabbed his suitcase and followed.

Seated on the Metro, Daniel once again inquired about Jimmy's flight. "No bumpy ride?"

"No problem," Jimmy replied. "It was just a long time to sit without moving around much."

"Next time you come, fly into National. You can't get a direct flight from California to National. No flights over 1,250 miles are allowed in order to limit air traffic control near the capital. So, when you change planes, usually in

Chicago or Denver, you have a chance to walk around. I know going into Dulles is quicker, even with the van ride into town. But flying into National, in my opinion, is more comfortable."

"Good to know," Jimmy said.

"Here's our stop, Dupont Circle. We'll take a little walk to the apartment," Daniel said.

Jimmy was in awe of everything! His first time in his nation's capital was impressive. The efficiency and speed of the Metro was outstanding, clean and quick. He loved the funky little shops and restaurants as they walked up Connecticut Avenue to Daniel's apartment. Most of all, he loved the international look and speech of the people on the street.

"Here we are," Daniel said.

Jimmy walked into a compact studio apartment. One room had a bed, easy chair, and kitchenette with a small table and two chairs. The other room was a bathroom that contained all the necessary fixtures.

"I know it's small," said Daniel, "but the choice was small in a great part of town or large in a not so great part of town. And don't worry, I've got a blow-up air bed you're going to love."

"It's great. This is everything you need," Jimmy said.

"Yeah, it is. I'm not here much anyway. We're playing catch up trying to get good legislation out, so I'm working ten or more hours a day, five, sometimes six, days a week," Daniel explained.

"I know you have to be a busy guy and this is mid-week.

Are you sure you wouldn't rather have me stay in a hotel until the weekend?" Jimmy offered.

"Nonsense," Daniel exclaimed. "It'll be fine. What time is your meeting tomorrow?" Daniel inquired.

"It starts at 9 a.m. and is supposed to last until 5 p.m. I took Friday and Monday off. I plan to tour around the city on Friday, and maybe you and I can do something over the weekend. My flight on Monday is at 8 a.m.," Jimmy said.

"Sounds like a good schedule," Daniel said. "I know it's early for you, but its dinner time here. Let's take a walk; there's a great place right down the street."

They walked out into a chilly and cloudy evening in the nation's capital. The Timberlake was a dining event, unique in Jimmy's experience.

"You see those taps back there behind the bar?" Daniel asked as they grabbed two stools at the bar. "All eight of them have better beer than any of the swill we used to drink in college. I'm going to suggest for you a porter — you'll love it. Dark and rich, you can almost cut it with a knife."

"Sounds good," Jimmy said.

The Timberlake was indeed a wonderful dining experience. Everyone in the place was about Jimmy and Daniel's age, bartenders and waiters included. Just above the back bar were several televisions with every imaginable sporting event on them. The people were friendly, the beer was good, and the food was great. It was the kind of place that implants a message on the memory: *come back here!*

Daniel was right; the air mattress was very comfortable. Jimmy was not affected by jet lag; that would come in later years. Thursday morning, Jimmy was up and out, down the hill to the Dupont Circle Metro station. After a short ride on the red line to Judiciary Square, it was a couple of blocks walking to the Department of Labor (DOL) Francis Perkins Building at 200 Constitution Ave. N.W.

Jimmy entered through the Visitors entrance, was given a visitor pass, and was directed to his meeting room. There were directors of the Child Home School Alliance (CHSA) program from all over the nation in attendance; they were there to get their marching orders.

"Welcome," said the first presenter. "I'm so pleased to see you all here. You are the vanguard of a program that promises to change the future for the working poor. This first effort was assigned to DOL to administer. This was done because CHSA is, at its essence, an effort to help stabilize families with marginal incomes. If we do it right, it will bring them into more productive positions in the national work force. Yes, I know you are all engaged in education, child care, and social work programs. But make no mistake, the purpose of all of this from the DOL perspective is a better prepared work force."

There followed eight hours of orientation about program requirements, future meeting dates, and the like. Much to his surprise, Jimmy found it interesting and useful. He always thought that, 'I'm from the federal government and I'm here to help you,' was one of the three great lies. It was right up there with, 'The check is in the mail.'

Of the twelve geographic areas represented, Jimmy's was the only site funded to serve migrant farmworkers. After listening to the program requirements, he was sure it would be a challenge to do the kind of program reporting required, given the nature of the work done by farmworkers.

However, Jimmy knew that he and the staff were up to it; they would do whatever it took.

As the meeting ended, Jimmy met a colleague while getting his coat. "Hi, I'm Paul Strickland from Minnesota."

"Glad to meet you. Jim Welch from California, the central part of the state," Jimmy replied.

"Oh yes, you're the program for migrant farmworkers, right? What do you think about all this, Jim? Pretty overwhelming, huh?" Paul asked.

"Yes, I'm with the migrant program. It does sound pretty complicated, but it will all be worth the effort if we can give families a boost to a better life," Jimmy replied.

"Oh, for sure," Paul agreed.

"See you at the next meeting," they both agreed as they walked out of the building.

Jimmy was in awe as he exited onto Constitution Ave. I've seen many of the great cities of the world but I've never seen my own capital. What a magnificent city, Jimmy thought. The evening was coming. A slight breeze came up and carried a chilly hint of the winter on the way. The trees on the Capital Mall were beginning to turn beautiful colors; Jimmy admired them as he walked.

The sight of the Capitol building, on the east end of the Mall and the Washington Monument on the west, filled Jimmy with a breathless awe. He would be back tomorrow to see all of it; for now he just stood and stared as the sun slowly sank from sight behind the distant Lincoln Memorial.

Friday morning broke and Jimmy was up and out. Now it was time to explore. He took his time window shopping and reading menus all the way down to Dupont Circle; there he caught the Metro to Union Station. It is a beautiful place, Jimmy thought as he gazed at the life-size statues around the station's upper level. This reminded him of the photos he'd seen of crowds of soldiers in the station waiting for their trains during World War II.

Up across Capitol Hill, past the Library of Congress, past the Senate and Representatives offices, past the Capitol and down the hill to the Smithsonian Air and Space Museum, Jimmy went. There he lingered, amazed that he was actually seeing the Wright Brother's airplane, the Kitty Hawk, hanging from the ceiling.

The day brought Jimmy many sights that filled his heart with patriotism and pathos. Arlington Cemetery, with two of his childhood friends' names on Vietnam-era stones, was heart breaking. Jimmy walked for hours among those who had given their lives for the common good. He breathed deeply and sucked back tears. The Lincoln Memorial stood as a monument to a great president who died too soon.

Friday night, two young men were in a city full of exciting things to do! What could be better? Even though it was not his favorite place, Daniel had chosen the Adams-Morgan district to take Jimmy for Friday night festivities. He knew Jimmy would enjoy the international flavor of the area. Flavor was a good description of Adams-Morgan. It was filled with small restaurants with regional menus from all over the world.

With all the food choices available, Jimmy picked an El Salvadorian restaurant for dinner. He had heard of, but never tried pupusa from El Salvador. They walked in and seated themselves in the gaily-painted restaurant with five small tables. A raven-haired young woman stepped to their table; in halting English, she asked what they would like.

Jimmy listened intently as the waitress struggled to get Daniel's order of two chicken pupusas and a beer. When she moved to Jimmy, remembering his own language struggles, he began speaking in Spanish. ***"Good evening Señorita. I'll have two pupusas, one of chicken and the other cheese, and do you have beer from El Salvador?"***

"Yes, we have only pilsner beer," she replied.

"Is that the type of beer or the brand?" Jimmy asked.

"It's the name of the beer; it's the brand."

"Is it a pilsner beer?" Jimmy asked again.

"Oh, I don't know, sir. I just know it's the only beer that we have from El Salvador."

"Okay, bring me one please."

The waitress said, ***"Your Spanish is very good, sir. Where did you learn?"***

"I went to school in Mexico," Jimmy answered.

"Oh, I'm from Mexico," she said. ***"Where did you go to school?"***

"In Cuernavaca, at the Centro Intercultural de Documentación," Jimmy offered.

"Oh yes. I know Cuernavaca. I went there with my family on vacation once."

"Does your family own this place?" Jimmy asked.

"No, the owners are from El Salvador. I just work

here on weekends once in a while. I'm a secretary at the Mexican Embassy," she said.

"Very nice to meet you," Jimmy said, signaling that the conversation was over.

"Wow, Jim! I'm impressed. You've been making good use of your time in Mexico," Daniel exclaimed.

"Yes, I've definitely worked at it. It hasn't been easy." When she brought the beer, they could see that the Salvadorian beer was most definitely a pilsner. The pupusas were every bit as delicious as Jimmy had hoped they would be.

****

"So we've seen the funky side of the district. What say we go see a little of the up-side. Let's take a little walk over to Calvert Street and have a drink in the Omni-Shoreham lobby," Daniel suggested.

"Sounds like a plan," Jimmy said.

They walked through the cool night and chatted about old times and how different these new times were for them. As they approached the Shoreham, falling leaves showered down through the lights of the Rock Creek Bridge. Winter was on the way.

The lobby of the Shoreham was a step back in time. The elegant 1930s-era hotel had the expansive lobby of the times; it was still filled with gorgeous couches, tables, chairs, and settees of the period.

They passed through the outer lobby to the lower level, where the huge oval bar was located, and picked a small table for two. "Just want to warn you this is not a beer joint." Daniel said. "They do have beer, but mixed drinks are the specialty."

"Got it," Jimmy nodded.

When the elegant blond waitress in a sequin dress glided up to the table, Jimmy ordered a sweet Manhattan, up. Daniel selected a very dry Martini with two olives. When the drinks arrived, "Up yours and down mine," they both intoned.

"So what have you been working on this week? That is, unless it's top secret," Jimmy asked.

"No, no secret. The Senator wants to introduce legislation to bring back a form of the bracero program."

"How would that work?" Jimmy asked.

"The United States would set a number that was needed, of what we would call 'guest workers' for each agricultural season. Mexico would screen and recruit potential workers, and the United States would select from the labor pool provided. They would be given temporary work visas and would return to Mexico when the work season was over. That way they would be here only when working and would not stay and overburden the social welfare system. Also, they would not bring their families to flood the school and welfare systems. You've worked with migrant farmworkers quite a bit. What do you think about this idea?" Daniel asked.

"My first reaction is that there were lots of political forces lined up against the bracero program; that's why it ended. You know, the effort to form a labor union for farmworkers is still ongoing. I can't imagine union organizers would take too kindly to your proposal. They would see it as just another "rent a slave" program that would prevent them from bargaining for better wages and working conditions. And as I'm sure you know, they have a pretty powerful political organization," Jimmy explained.

"But all that aside, I don't care for the idea because it would break up families just like the bracero program did. And it's not worthy of the U.S. to have a "rent a slave" program, which is what it would be," Jimmy said.

"I've been doing some research on this, Jim, and the situation right now is pretty bad for the workers. We let them sneak in, and they often sneak in with their whole families. Farmworker unions are neutralized because so many 'illegals' are here working; they'll take whatever the employer offers. They only have fake, if any, documents, so they try to stay in the shadows. Some won't even go to the doctor for fear of being deported. And it's true that on occasion the dad gets deported and the family is left behind to fend for themselves. When that happens, their only hope is for help from friends and neighbors," Daniel offered.

"You're absolutely correct about what you've said," Jimmy replied. "I've seen it up close and personal. The illegals take a lot of abuse. I know of at least one case where a farmer worked a group for two weeks, didn't pay them, and then called immigration. He turned them in and they were deported. Admittedly that is an exception. Most agriculture business employers know they can't survive without migrant farmworkers, so they don't overtly abuse them. But even in the best of circumstances, the illegals drive wages down because there are so many of them looking for work. They will take whatever working conditions and pay is offered," Jimmy finished.

"So why don't we fix the immigration system by closing the border and only allowing the workers we need and their families to come in?" Jimmy asked. "Seems like that would be a better area for legislation."

"Yes, in theory it would," Daniel agreed. "Except there are very powerful political forces lined up against that happening. In order for that to occur, we would have to admit publicly that we can't get along without foreign workers.

"Then we would have to issue papers giving the workers permanent, or at least, long-term visas and treat them not as guests but as an integral part of society," Daniel explained. "The farm labor unions would form, prices of fruits and vegetables would rise, and agribusiness would make less profits. Think of it, Jim. The price of all produce you buy goes up dramatically because the farmworkers now have a union and negotiate higher wages and benefits. Agribusiness makes a smaller profit because there's a cost threshold after which people won't buy the product. They can't just keep passing higher costs on to the consumer."

Daniel further explained, "The public outcry would be immediate; the problems are because of all these foreigners who have come in. This would then be coupled with accusations that our taxes go up because these foreigners get on the welfare system. A whole cascade of charges would follow until Congress would begin to introduce legislation to undo the immigration change. You know this is true. There's a huge furor every time any discussion of immigration change begins; this is precipitated by those who have a financial stake in seeing no change to the current structure.

"And let's not forget those politicians who see more population from Mexico as adding to their political base, even though the immigrants can't vote. They anticipate many more illegal immigrants entering the U.S. under the current system than would come under a legal entry system. Therefore, their political base would grow larger under the current system because we count everyone in the census whether they're here legally or not. I believe they are correct in this assumption. Also, higher union wages would force more mechanization of agribusiness and thus fewer workers needed.

"These politicians who want illegals to come, posture and preach and quote the abysmal living situations of many Mexican immigrants. They are quick to add that only they, because they are of Mexican descent, can help these poor down-trodden people. Then the ultra-liberal contingent of our society does what the illegal immigrants can't do. They vote these charlatans into office, where time and time again, they help to torpedo any effort to fix our broken immigration system."

Daniel got more excited the longer he talked. "Even worse, we have politicians on the other side who use the tactic of whipping up hate against Mexican immigrants; whether legal or illegal, they don't care. They get votes every time they promise to stem the rising tide of Mexican immigrants. The immigrants are easy targets because they are so slow to assimilate. I know you've told me all the reasons for the slow assimilation, but the fact remains. As a group, they don't adapt to English as quickly as other immigrants. They retain the Spanish language and customs."

"I know you probably don't want to hear this, but there are some Mexican customs that would benefit us if we adopted them," Jimmy said.

"Like what?" Daniel asked with force.

"Like families sticking together and watching out for each other. Like not making a job the center of your life and your identity. If we did at least these things, I have no doubt the incidence of teen suicide would drop and heart attacks among adults would be fewer," Jimmy explained.

"Well, be that as it may, I still believe they are making themselves big and easy targets. I've even seen them waving the Mexican flag around. I saw a group in San Francisco, half of them carrying the Mexican flag and protesting because a group of illegals had been deported. Like I said, they make themselves easy targets!" Daniel explained.

"They play right into the hands of the hate mongers in Congress. They promise that they will pass legislation to ensure sanctions against the illegal population. As the influx of illegal immigration grows, so does their ability to get votes by stirring up sentiment against the immigrants." Daniel continued.

"The situation is that currently, we see no chance for immigration reform. Too many politicians and business people profit from the increased illegal Mexican population and cheap labor that the current system provides. These politicians and business people have powerful lobby groups and political connections. They will prevent any change to the system that will diminish the personal advantages that illegal immigration provides to them.

"We recognize that the legislation that the Senator is

about to propose is not perfect, but it is better for the United States and the immigrants than the current situation."

Daniel finally concluded.   "Okay, enough of my pontificating. What's up with you, Jim? I heard something about you getting an award for innovative teaching."

"Yeah, that was a while back," Jimmy replied. "I was teaching a dual language system, so all the kids learned both English and Spanish."

"I heard you got an award and a lot of flak from some in the community," Daniel remarked.

"Yeah, I got both. I don't see what the problem is. I know that I certainly understand English better after I studied Spanish. But the main reason I taught in both languages was that the majority of kids I was teaching weren't getting an education — because of their lack of English skills. After we started the dual track, they did better in all areas of school," Jimmy said.

"Knowing you, I know your motives were good. But from a political viewpoint, I also know that one of the primary factors that holds a society together is the use of a common language. My hope is that your teaching method ensures that all those Spanish speaking children learn English," Daniel said.

"Yes, that is certainly the goal. I love the Spanish language and Mexican culture, but I also realize that English is the language of this country. To be successful here, you must have English proficiency.

"My new job will help me to press that point even better," Jimmy continued. "It's a project funded by the DOL. The purpose is to move the working poor to higher paying jobs and to move them out of poverty. It's a multi-pronged approach that provides pre-school and adult education, job counseling, health assessment and remediation for the family, and some job placement."

"You're doing this with the migrant farmworker population?" Daniel asked.

"Yes," Jimmy replied.

"You know many of them are not here legally, so why are they being included?" Daniel questioned.

"The federal government doesn't require a check of immigration status in order to participate in the program," Jimmy replied. "We don't know which are here legally and which aren't. We are directed to enroll participants in the program without verification of legal status, and I think we both know why, right?"

"Yes we do," Daniel replied. "The government is complicit in what we have just discussed."

"What I say to myself is that if any of these enrollees are illegal, they still deserve to participate as partial payment for the grinding hard work they do for such low wages. We've been through this discussion before, and I'm still of the opinion that the farmworkers are the ones getting shafted by our society, not the other way around," Jimmy finished.

"Yes, I know you are, and to some degree, you've convinced me. That's why I'm working hard trying to get this guest worker legislation research done for the Senator," Daniel said. "Say, how about we take a walk down Connecticut Avenue. At this time of night, you can usually see some interesting characters and maybe some street musicians," Daniel suggested.

"Let's do it!" Jimmy replied.

Chapter 45

It was a wonderful visit with Daniel and so inspiring to see the nation's capital. Even so, Jimmy was glad to be back at his new office in the Housing Authority building in McKinley. He was only half a block from the McKinley School and kept in constant contact with Juan. The two of them formed a great team and were putting together an exemplary program.

Juan had agreed to have two portable buildings moved onto the campus of the school. They housed pre-school programs during the day and converted to adult education in the evening. Jimmy still taught the adult English as a Second Language (ESL) class and there was a thriving adult basic education class next door to his office.

Jimmy had a vacant building in the migrant housing area remodeled and negotiated with the county public health officer to locate a clinic there. He kept a quote from a book entitled, *Children of the Dust Bowl* by Jerry Stanley on his desk blotter:

". . . disease broke out in the Okievilles scattered throughout the San Joaquin Valley. The bad sanitary conditions and inadequate diet led to epidemics of dysentery, tuberculosis and pneumonia . . . one squatter said 'we lived like animals.'"

Below the quote, Jimmy had penciled, "We will not let this happen again."

According to the book, some Okie children had died of curable health conditions because no medical care was available to them. Jimmy was determined that these migrant workers would not suffer the neglect and abuse that his extended family, and others like them, had experienced.

Jimmy was a teacher to his core, and the project reflected that. He instituted an after-school program for elementary children in need of English language practice. He taught part of it but recruited local high school students with good English skills to serve as language models for the younger students. This English tutoring was only part of the center program. Two tutors were available for three hours after school to help in any academic area from first through twelfth grade. Math was the one area where high school students generally needed help.

Attending to the political aspects of the program was also Jimmy's responsibility. It suited the current federal administration's populist view to have a program board of directors comprised of adult program participants. Jimmy was one hundred percent in agreement. It was in constituting this board that a great deal of teaching was done. Board training consisted of budget review, using parliamentary procedure in the conduct of the meetings, the structure and purpose of the program, and the DOL program review process and schedule. A tremendous learning opportunity, Jimmy thought.

The program was moving along nicely. Juan and Jimmy were happy with the progress. The participants were happy, the federal reviewers were pleased with what they saw, and the community was in support. What could possibly go wrong?

****

"*Buenos Dias*, Renaldo," Jimmy said.

"Good morning," Renaldo replied in his best English.

"How are you?" Jimmy switched quickly to English wanting to support Renaldo's continued learning.

"I am fine. I am very happy today! I get my green card. Mr. Holiman, he help me so I keep work for him."

"That's really great, Renaldo. Getting your green card is a real accomplishment. I'm so happy for you and your family," Jimmy exclaimed. "I wanted to talk with you today because the program needs some help. The government requires the program to have a board of directors to work with me to help make decisions about managing the program. For example, each year we do a budget to plan how to spend the program money. Staff members would write out a budget and then give it to the board to review. Any changes would be put in before the budget was sent to Washington D.C. for approval."

"Oh, I will help," Renaldo said emphatically. "You need, I will do it. You teach me English, and that help me so much. I get green card, better job, better house, all because I can talk English," Renaldo said.

"The English helped," Jimmy said. "But your hard work and being reliable is the main reason you got all those things."

"What is 'reliable'?" Renaldo asked.

"It means you come to work on time, get the work done, don't miss work unless you're sick, and you take care of your family, reliable." Jimmy answered.

"Thank you," Renaldo said.

"No, thank you, Renaldo," Jimmy said. "There will be a meeting on Thursday at 7 p.m. I will explain about the board of directors again, then we will have an election later for board members. I just want to be sure you would agree to serve if you are elected."

"Yes, I will help always," Renaldo said.

Renaldo was elected to the Board of the Child Home School Alliance program (CHSA). He was a well-respected member of the community; people relied on him for many things, not the least of which was English translations. Between Renaldo and Jesús, English could be quickly translated to Spanish.

Chapter 46

"Antonio, I've been hearing lots of noise about a great program for Latinos going on in McKinley. I want you to go out there and find out what it's about. Maybe it's something we can use other places. My old friend, Juan Martinez, used to be a school principal there. Find out if he is still. Today is Tuesday; I want your report by Friday," Hilario directed.

"Yes, Assemblyman Jiminez. I'll get right on it," Antonio said. As staff director, such investigation fell squarely into his sphere of responsibility.

The year had been good to Hilario. The Sacramento State opportunity had set him on a course to reach his goal, the California State Assembly. In the first year of his two-year term, he did little in terms of legislation. In his second year, he was looking for something to get his name in front of his constituents and help get him re-elected. His primary concern now was to get re-elected. He knew he would be challenged and that crying racism and bad-mouthing gringos was not enough to get him re-elected. He was hoping to find some program, maybe in McKinley, that he could bring to his own district. He was well aware that he had two possible challengers, both Chicanos and both very capable. He would have to do something substantial to get his name out there and be re-elected.

Thus as Friday rolled around and he waited for his 8:30 a.m. meeting with Antonio, Hilario was hoping for good news. He didn't like Juan Martinez's politics, but he knew Juan was very smart and competent; Hilario was expecting to hear something he could use.

"What did you find out?" Hilario asked.

"They have a great program for Latinos in McKinley. The elementary school and this federal pre-school and family support program work together to help families. The pre-school program is located at the school. They enroll kids from three years to school age and have space for sixty kids. They keep them all day so parents can go to work. Most of the parents out there are farmworkers, so the school keeps the kids eight to twelve hours a day, depending on the season and work load for parents. While the kids are in the child care center, they get meals and snacks, and they give them learning activities so they do better when they start school.

"They also give classes for the parents in the evening and on weekends. They used to do the adult classes at the school; now they have a building right in the housing area where they do the classes. They teach all sorts of things — nutrition, GED prep, and English. I brought a schedule so you can see. They have a group of parents that make decisions about the classes they want and many other things.

"The school and this program cooperate on lots of things. They have joint staff meetings. Staff from both the school and the program meet with parents when their kids are having a problem. Also, they are working to get everyone to be bilingual. Kids, teachers, and parents. It's a great program. We should look into starting one," Antonio said excitedly.

"Does this program have a name?" Hilario asked.

"Yes, it's called Child Home School Alliance (CHSA)," Antonio replied.

"Is it a state program? Where do they get the funding?"

"The school, of course, is state funding based on attendance. The other activities are funded by the federal Department of Labor."

"How do we get this program in my district? And remember, it has to be done well before the election," Hilario commanded.

Antonio thought for a minute, then replied, "The federal part of it is granted through a competitive application process. The applications are open now, so we would have to get a school that wanted to cooperate and then write an application."

"Okay. Is my friend, Juan Martinez, still there?" Hilario inquired.

"Yes, he remembers you very well."

"I bet he does," Hilario chuckled.

Antonio was no sooner out of the room than Hilario was on the phone. "Hello Juan. It's Hilario. Remember me?"

"Yeah, you're kinda hard to forget. What's up?" Juan said.

"I've been hearing about that program you have and want to get one started in my district. You know I was elected to the Assembly, right?" Hilario said.

"Yes, I'm aware of that," Juan acknowledged. "Congratulations."

"Thanks, Juan. I was wondering if you are willing to help get one of those programs started up here."

"For you Hilario, *no*, but for the kids, *yes*. What do you need?" Juan asked.

"I need you to tell us how to do it and help us do the federal application for funding," Hilario responded.

"Okay. I can meet with the school people and give pointers on how to do it. But I don't do the federal application. You'll have to have help from Jim Welch on that."

"Jim Welch, is he that gringo you had teaching there?" Hilario asked sarcastically.

"Yes, he is the gentleman who has taught here for years. He's now the Director of the Child Home School Alliance program. He writes the funding application and administers the program," Juan explained.

"What is going on down there, Juan? You have a gringo administering a program for Latinos," Hilario said with venom in his voice.

"Yes, we have a person of Anglo-Saxon heritage administering a program for children and families and doing a damn fine job of it too," Juan said pointedly.

"Okay, okay. Don't get all in a huff about it. I have a school in mind. How about you come up here and tell them how to do it?"

"Sure, I'll do that. Now do you want me to ask Jim to help with your application or not?" asked Juan.

"No, we don't need help from a gringo. Antonio can write the application," Hilario said smugly.

"Okay, set up the school meeting," Juan advised.

The meeting with the school went well. They were excited about developing a closer relationship with families and helping kids succeed. The writing of the application didn't go so well. After a week of struggle and strife, which produced two of the thirty-five pages required for the application, Antonio called Jimmy.

Antonio knew better than to let Hilario find out that he asked for help from Jimmy. He signed himself out to do a field review of a state water program and hightailed it down to McKinley. The afternoon with Jimmy was very productive but not enough.

"Okay Antonio, we need more time. Tell you what, I'm pretty busy the next few days, as you can see lots of people in and out. I'll come in on Saturday, and we can spend the whole day with your application."

"Thank you so much. I'll be here at your office at 8 a.m. on Saturday. Is that ok?" Antonio exclaimed.

"That'll work," Jimmy said as he rose and headed for the door.

"See you then, and thank you, Jim."

"You're welcome," Jimmy answered.

Saturday was a very productive work day. Antonio was quick on the uptake, and Jimmy was willing to write most of the application for him. "You'll be able to do this yourself next time," Jimmy told him.

"Yes, I get it now," Antonio answered. "I heard you

speaking Spanish to one of the staff last time I was here. I didn't think you were Latino."

"No, I'm not Latino," Jimmy said. "I'm an Okie."

"Your Spanish is just about perfect, better than most of my friends. How did you learn it?"

"I went to school in Mexico, and the kids and parents here help me a lot," Jimmy replied.

"You also seem to know the customs of Mexico. I saw you with the parent group last time," Antonio said.

"I don't think you can learn a language without learning the culture of the people who speak it. The language and customs are all tied together. The words people use in any language tell you what is important to them. For example, a matador I met in Mexico told me that there are twenty-six words in Spanish to describe the horns of a bull. One word tells you length, color, curvature, and so on; everything you need to know about the horns of your opponent. An extreme example, I know, but clearly this tells you what is important to that group," Jimmy replied.

"Okay, I think we're done here," Jimmy said. "You've got a nice tight application, and that should get you the program."

"Thank you again, but can I ask you, why do you do all this work with these people who are not your own?" Antonio asked.

"Simple. They are my people. They're in this country, and they need the help that I have to give," Jimmy said.

Incredulously, Antonio asked, "Yeah, but what if they just take all this education and go back to Mexico?"

"Then they will have a better life there and help the people around them. Speaking English will get them a good job in Mexico. I don't want the neglect and abuse that happened to my family when they came here to happen to these folks.

"Alright Antonio, you're good to go. I expect to hear that you got this funded. Please let me know, will you?" Jimmy asked.

"For sure. Thanks again," Antonio said in parting.

Antonio thought about how to present this to Hilario. He knew Hilario would be furious if he found out that an Anglo helped on the application. Antonio would have to present it as his work and hope Jimmy's help never came to light.

Chapter 47

The CHSA Board meeting was another great success. Renaldo had been elected Chairperson for the second year, and he proved to be very effective. He moved the meeting along, gave ample time for discussion, and was fair and equitable in his decisions. Jimmy thought, this is a good man. We're lucky to have him. Just then the meeting ended.

"Señor Jim. I have something to tell you," Renaldo said. "Mr. Holiman is help me start a place grow trees."

"You mean a nursery?" Jimmy asked.

"Yes, yes, that what he call it. He is grow lots of *almendras* now . . . I don't know the word," Renaldo inquired.

"Almonds," Jimmy supplied.

"Yes, almonds. He is grow lots of almonds. He say to me that he will give me the twenty acres free for three years. After, he will charge me rent. He say that I grow the almond trees and sell to him the first crop of trees. After that, I sell him two more crop of trees. Then I can sell to who gives me the best price. That is what he say to me. What do you think?"

Jimmy acknowledged, "That sounds like a great deal for you, but how are you going to do that and do your job also?"

"Oh, Jesús will help me. He work hard; he a good son. He going to the college school in Stockton, and when not in school, he help me. He want to be a *contador*. How you say in English?"

"Accountant," Jimmy responded with the English word.

"Yes, accountant. He good with numbers and will help me in my nursery business," Renaldo beamed as he spoke.

"That sounds like a wonderful opportunity for you and your family. I'm really happy for you to be starting your own business. I'm so glad to hear Jesús is going to college. He's a smart young man; he'll do well."

"Yes, he a good boy," Renaldo confirmed. "I teach him always be good worker and to be proud that he work hard." Here Renaldo's English would no longer suffice to tell the story, so he switched to Spanish. ***"One time, we were working in the fields and I drove to the store at lunch, told Jesús to go in and buy some food. He said he didn't want to go because his hands were dirty from picking tomatoes. I told him to go. Be proud of your hard work. When he came out, he said the man in the store said, 'I can see by your hands you are a hard worker. Your family must be proud!' Jesús always remembers that lesson,"*** Renaldo finished.

"Yes, I'm sure he does. How's the rest of your family?" Jimmy asked.

"Oh fine. My daughter, Andrea, want to go to college, but Conchita not like the idea much," Renaldo said.

"And what do you think, Renaldo?" Jim asked.

"Oh, it's okay. Jesús is there, he will protect her. Conchita will let her go," Renaldo said. "And Conchita is very happy. We are bring Uncle Gustavo here to live. We sold house in

Mexico and he comes to live with us. Government lets us bring him."

"Great news," Jimmy said. "I'll look forward to meeting him."

****

Antonio got the call from the Principal of Lincoln School. "We got it! Just got a call from one of the feds at the DOL. We will be funded for two years. He had lots of accolades for the proposal, and said we would get a funding letter authorizing us to begin within two weeks. I want to thank you and the Assemblyman for your help with this. We have lots of kids and families out here that really need help."

"Don't mention it," Antonio said. As he hung up, Antonio thought, yeah, don't mention it either, Jim Welch.

"We got the program," Antonio said to Hilario with elation.

"Great. When does it start?" Hilario asked.

"They'll get funding authorization in two weeks, so they can start spending then. But they can start interviewing and detail planning today," Antonio explained.

"Excellent! You be sure they understand they hire only Chicanos for the program," Hilario said smugly.

"I'll remind them," Antonio replied.

"Is that gringo still running that program down there with my coconut friend, Juan?" Hilario asked.

"Yes, he is," Antonio answered.

"We've got to get him out of there," Hilario proclaimed.

"Why?" Antonio asked.

"It doesn't look good for a gringo to be running a program for Latinos. It looks like we can't handle our own business. But most of all, it's just because he's a gringo."

Chapter 48

Renaldo had done well. He was in the right place when the "almond rush" occurred. The international sale of almonds boomed, prices skyrocketed, and farmers responded. Less profitable crops were abandoned, and almond orchards replaced them. Land previously left fallow now sprouted almond trees. Even land in the foothills, previously deemed unfit, was treated and amended until it grew almond orchards.

Renaldo was there to supply the increasing need for almond tree saplings. His twenty acres of rented land had become forty. Within two seasons, he was able to make a substantial down payment on the purchase of another 100 acres. Business was good. Even so, he continued his employment with Mr. Holiman.

Renaldo and Jesús, with an occasional hired hand, were able to manage the 140 acres of almond saplings. But they needed to have a talk. Jesús wanted to leave the junior college and get his B.A. degree at Stanford University. He had been offered an academic scholarship; he would be ready to go in September. He needed to explain to his pop and make him understand the long- term benefit of a college education.

That night after dinner, Jesús said, ***"Pop, I got this scholarship that will pay for me to finish school at Stanford University. I only have two years to go."***

"Will you have to move there?" Renaldo asked.

"Yes, I have to live there," Jesús replied.

"What about the trees?" Renaldo wondered.

"School only lasts from September to the first week in June, and I have two weeks off at Christmas and one week in the spring. I can work all summer with the trees and help with planting in the spring. If there's pruning, I can do it at Christmas time. You said Uncle Gustavo was coming to live here; he can help," Jesús explained.

"Uncle Gustavo can help, but he's too old for doing hard work like we do," Renaldo said.

"Yeah, but you can hire a guy to help. Roberto does good work. He would work for you full time, and I know how to do the taxes and everything to pay him," Jesús said.

"Yes, you do know. I thought that's why you were going to school to help me with the business," Renaldo said.

"That's true, but now I have a chance to finish my degree. I can be a C.P.A. instead of just a bookkeeper," Jesús said with a pleading voice.

"Alright my son, let me think about it."

"Thanks Pop!"

Renaldo went to bed with a troubled mind that night. He wanted the best for his children, and he knew how much Jesús wanted this — he wanted it for him. Imagine, Renaldo thought, my son, who didn't even speak English when we came here, graduating from a college in America.

"Conchita," Renaldo said the next morning, *"Jesús has to go to the far away college in September. He has to do it."*

"You are right, my love," Conchita said. *"I'm glad you decided that."*

"He's a good son. He will come back and help me when he is finished with school," Renaldo affirmed.

"Yes, he will. And something else to think about, my love; Andrea wants to be a teacher, and she will have to go away someday soon too," Conchita said sadly.

"Yes, my love, I will think about that. Now I have to go to work."

That evening, Renaldo called Jesús into the yard and said, *"Your mama and I are very proud of you, and we want you to go to college. I've decided that I will hire Roberto full time. Uncle Gustavo will help, and you will help when you can. Between all of us, we will keep our tree business going, and maybe even increase it."*

"Wow, thanks Pop. Yes, I will help on all my vacations from school. When I get finished with school, we will increase the business. We will have a great business. Thanks Pop!" Jesús exclaimed.

Chapter 49

Riiiinnnggg! The wall phone in Jimmy's little studio was urgently calling. "Bueno," Jimmy said into the hand set.

"Whadda ya mean, Bueno? Don't you speak English anymore?" Daniel spit into his handset.

"Oh, hi Daniel. Good to hear from you too!" Jimmy responded.

"How's the world treating you, Jim?"

"All good, just working and trying to avoid polluting the environment," Jimmy replied.

"Oh no! Don't tell me you're not only a do-gooder but you're a tree hugger too?" Daniel said with a laugh.

"What got into you?" Jimmy asked. "You seem pretty feisty tonight."

"Well, I have to admit, Jim, I've been doing a little celebrating tonight, and that's why I'm calling. I just announced my candidacy for the House seat for District 12, California," Daniel exclaimed.

"Whoa, that is big news!" Jimmy replied.

"Yeah, you know when Representative Ramirez announced her retirement? I talked to Senator Leach about it. He was very supportive. He said that he thinks the district is ready for a big change. It's been moving our direction for a while now. Senator Leach has lots of contacts with big money people. He has promised to endorse me and help with campaign fundraising. He's even assigning his campaign manager to run my campaign. Good thing he's not up for re-election or he would need him," Daniel said.

"Congratulations, Daniel," Jimmy said. "I think you would be a great addition to the House."

"I know I would be a good steward of the public trust. I'm just not sure how good a campaigner I will be," Daniel worried.

"I think you'll do fine. You're a good debater and you've never been afraid of public speaking," Jimmy said.

"Yeah, what I'm concerned about is the sleaze factor. I don't do mudslinging," Daniel replied.

"I know that is the modus operandi of lots of politicians. But maybe people are ready to just consider and discuss ideas and good plans for the future," Jimmy responded.

"I hope you're right about that because that's the kind of campaign I want to run. In fact, I have one idea I want to pass by you now. You remember the guest worker plan Senator Leach proposed?" Daniel asked.

"Yes, I do. I understand it went nowhere," Jimmy answered.

"That's right, and the reason is that too many people profit from the way things are. I'm sure you remember our discussion about fixing the immigration system. Well, I think I have some ideas about how to fix it. I'll be proposing an amnesty program for those Mexican nationals who are here now without papers. They'll be able to apply and work toward getting permanent resident status. Coupled with that, I'll have a plan to close the border to illegal crossing. Here's the kicker — we would fine employers who knowingly hire undocumented workers. The third phase would be to introduce a revised version of Senator Leach's guest worker program. What do you think, Jim?"

"Wow, that's a big idea. My first inclination is that it will be well received by the farmworker unions because illegal immigration is one of the things that constantly stymies their organization efforts. The guest worker part will bother them, unless you put in language that says workers will only be brought in when a shortage of workers can be verified. And you must put a strong verification process in place." Jimmy further offered, "The agribusiness interests will probably be alright with it if you can get the guest workers piece done to ensure them adequate workers. Although, they will be concerned about the possibility of unionization and wages going up. The politicians will be against it because it's a no-win for them. Latino politicians won't be able to point to the poverty and abuse of the increasing Latino population. Anglo politicians won't be able to whip up sentiment against Latinos and claim that they are taking all these jobs that Americans want. On balance, probably a good plan if the nuances are handled delicately," concluded Jimmy.

"Well, thanks very much, Jim. That's a very insightful analysis. I couldn't agree more with your thoughts on it. I know you are not a politician and you don't like this whole nasty business, but will you help talk up this immigration reform idea?" Daniel asked.

"I think it's a good plan, and as long as it helps make people's lives better, then yes, I will do what I can to help."

"Thank you very much, Jim. I'll let you know. I'm going to be very busy during the run-up to election but I will be in touch," Daniel promised.

"Alright, I'll be looking forward to seeing how it goes for you. Best of luck. I know you will provide good leadership."

Chapter 50

"So Antonio, I just saw a review of all the CHSA programs in California. Please tell me why our program is twenty points lower on the scale than that coconut and gringo's program?" Hilario said.

"Well, they've had it longer and know the regulations better, is all I can say," Antonio replied.

"Starting the program did help in my re-election. But we can't have the highest scoring program in the state be the only one where a gringo is in charge," Hilario complained.

"What do you want me to do?" Antonio asked.

"I'll think of something," Hilario answered.

****

"Hello Juanita. I have a little job for you," Hilario said. "I want you to go to McKinley and get acquainted with the parents there. Get a job as a preschool teacher; you've got the credentials. Then start bad-mouthing that gringo director there, Jim somebody. Convince them we need a Latino in that job. Talk about how he doesn't understand us; you know, how he's not bicultural. Get the parent council to ask for his resignation. If he doesn't resign, set up a protest accusing him of racism. You know the drill," Hilario said with a sly chuckle.

"Okay, yeah, I get it. What's in it for me?" Juanita asked.

"Keep the money you'll make as a teacher plus a 25%

bump from my office fund as a consultant. When he's out, they'll be looking for a Latino, or should I say 'Latina,' to be the director."

"Ok, I'll do it," Juanita said confidently.

****

And she did it! It took about six months of whispered innuendo and rumor. "Jim comes to work late. Jim has an eye for the ladies; he actually propositioned a teacher. She told me this before she moved back to Texas. He really doesn't like Mexicans or Latinos, he just used us to get this big job." On and on, Juanita went spreading her venomous stories.

This talk over months resulted in a parent council meeting where Tomás Alaniz repeated all these rumors in closed session and proposed asking for Jimmy's resignation. There was a low rumble of murmuring in the room, seeming to indicate general acceptance of the idea.

That is until Renaldo Preciado stepped forward. "*I don't know where you got all these ideas, but I know they are all false. I have known this man for years, ever since he was teacher of my children. He taught my son and me English. He's the reason I was able to get my green card. Whoever has the bad heart to say these things about him is a liar, a fool, or both. If there is proof of any of this, Señor Alaniz, bring it here. No, you can't, can you? Because there isn't any. I say no, we do not ask for his resignation. No, instead I propose we get a certificate made for him and present it at our next meeting to thank him for all his help to us.*"

There was silence in the room. Everyone looked at the table except Renaldo, who stared intently at Señor Alaniz.

Finally Renaldo said, ***"There have been proposals made, Mr. Chairman. We should vote."***

"Yes," the newly elected chairman said weakly. ***"All in favor of asking for Mr. Welch's resignation, raise your hand."*** The hand of Señor Alaniz went slowly up and stood there wavering like a willow tree in the breeze.

"All those opposed?" Every other hand in the room shot up and stayed there. The Chairman announced, ***"We will not ask for his resignation. All in favor of giving him a certificate at our next meeting?"*** All hands were raised except for that of Mr. Alaniz. ***"All who are opposed?"*** Mr. Alaniz raised his wobbly hand. ***"Renaldo, will you take care of getting the certificate?"***

"Yes, with great pleasure," Renaldo replied.

****

"Look Hilario, I did my best," exclaimed Juanita. "I had it all set up. This Alaniz guy swallowed the whole story and took it to the parent council. If it hadn't been for Renaldo Preciado, the gringo would be looking for another job right now."

"Okay! I hear you. Don't worry, I'll get him out of there yet!" Hilario vowed.

Chapter 51

"I'll be home late tonight, honey," Juan said as he gathered his briefcase. "I have to go to Sacramento today and don't know how it will be getting back through all that traffic. Don't wait dinner for me; you and the kids go ahead and eat."

"Okay dear. Drive carefully," Marina said.

Driving up the freeway, Juan had plenty of time to think about yesterday's talk with the superintendent. "I'm not going to be your token Mexican," Juan had said.

"What do you mean?" the superintendent asked.

"Every time there's some hearing in Sacramento, you send me. Why don't any of the other principals go?" Juan blurted out.

"Did it ever occur to you, that just maybe your ethnic background has nothing to do with why I send you to Sacramento?" the Superintendent asked.

"What do you mean?" Juan responded.

"I mean that I send you to Sacramento because you're the principal who understands California politics best. Also, I know you will keep a cool head and not make some remark that would embarrass the district."

"Oh, I guess I misunderstood your reasons," Juan said. "I apologize."

"No need," the superintendent replied. "I know there are some businesses and schools that always send an ethnic minority person to represent them just to imply how liberal they are. That is not the case here. You're the best person for the job."

"Thank you," Juan said and left. As he thought about the exchange he was embarrassed to a degree by his verbal attack on the superintendent. But he was also pleased to know that he was seen as a valuable employee because of his intellect and work unrelated to anything about his ethnicity.

"Sacramento traffic," Juan groused to himself as he pulled into the L street parking garage. He was accustomed to country driving and liked it. Years of living in McKinley's wide open spaces had spoiled him for city life.

Today he was to give a short testimony to a hearing committee. Over the years, the bilingual approach to educating children that Jim Welch had first used had proved very effective. Juan's testimony was in support of the state funding bilingual education programs in all schools serving language minority children.

Juan found the committee room easily; the hearing was conducted very efficiently. Consequently, he was out the door in just over two hours, a record for one of those events. As he was preparing to exit the Capitol building, he heard his name being called.

Juan turned to see a grayer, plumper Hilario in a blue pinstripe suit bearing down on him. "Hey Juan, it's been a long time. How is it with you?" Hilario asked.

"Oh, all is well. Doing great," Juan responded.

"Are you married yet?" Hilario asked.

"Yes. I'm married with two kids, an 8-year-old boy and 6-year- old girl. How about you?" Juan asked.

"Congratulations," Hilario said. "I'm divorced, no kids."

"You seem to keep getting re-elected, so I assume your constituents are happy," Juan said.

"Yeah, I keep things moving and ensure that the Chicano population gets their fair share, and maybe a little more," Hilario chuckled.

"What will you do when your time is up because of the new term-limit law?" Juan asked.

"Oh, not to worry. There are many appointed positions in Sacramento. Maybe I'll be the chair of the Tea Quality Tasting Board," Hilario said with a smirk. "What brings you to Sacramento?"

"I just finished providing testimony to support Assembly Bill 162 on bilingual education," Juan answered.

"Oh, how did that go?"

"It went fine. You know one of our teachers was one of the first in the state to try bilingual education, even before equal language access was mandated by Lau vs Nichols," Juan said.

"You mean that Spanish speaking gringo?" Hilario responded.

"I mean Jim Welch. One of the best teachers that has ever been in my school."

"Yeah, I heard about him with that CHSA program," Hilario said sarcastically.

"Yes," Juan said. "He directs that now, and it has a national reputation as being one of the best in the country."

"Yeah, I heard," Hilario said with a downcast look. "I guess he did okay for the people there. Too bad he's a gringo."

"Did it ever occur to you, Hilario, that you calling him a gringo like that is no better than someone calling you a beaner?" Juan asked.

"Oh, don't get on your high horse, Juan. I know he has done a little good work, but you know, he's still a gringo," Hilario said with a sneer.

"Good bye, Hilario," Juan said and walked out the door shaking his head.

Chapter 52

Jimmy picked up the ringing telephone. "Bueno," he answered.

"Hey Jim, its Juan."

"Hey Juan, how is it with you?" Jimmy asked. "Are you getting used to that rarified atmosphere up there in the Superintendent's office?"

"Somewhat," Juan replied, "but I still like to get out where the people live and see the world, which is why I'm calling. How about giving me a tour of the CHSA program, then we can have lunch from the taco truck?"

"Sounds great. How about tomorrow?" Jimmy asked.

"Okay," Juan said. "I'll just move a couple of things around. It will be fine. 10 a.m. okay for you, Jim?"

"It's good for me," Jimmy replied. "I'll see you here at my office at 10."

It will be nice to get together with an old friend, Jimmy thought. We are getting pretty old. We're both past 40; we've been through a lot together and always had each other's back. With that thought, Jimmy turned and went back to work at his desk, glad to be where he was doing his work.

****

Jimmy could tell by the heavy rapping on his office door

that Juan had arrived. Juan walked in looking every bit the school superintendent that he was. His gray sharkskin suit was offset by a paisley tie with just the right shades of blue and light gray.

"Come in, come in," Jimmy said. "Have a seat. Before I forget, are we still playing this Saturday?"

"Is the Pope Catholic?" Juan replied. "We've got a 7:30 a.m. tee time. I wouldn't miss it."

"How are Marina and the kids?" Jimmy asked.

"All great. Kids are doing well. Marina took a part time teaching job so she could spend more time with them. Now that they are teenagers, they need a little more supervision," Juan responded.

"And of course, with your big-time job now, you don't need the money," Jimmy teased.

"Well, yeah, that too!" Juan chuckled.

"Have you learned anything new since you've been the superintendent?"

"Yes I have. I've learned that people are going to get mad at you about some of your decisions; it's inevitable. The key to survival is not to get all of them mad at you at once," Juan said with a laugh.

Jimmy chuckled at that comment and said, "Come on. Let's go see the people."

With that, they began their walk around the CHSA site. There were a number of new activities since Juan had left as principal. They began in the computer room. Two of the very first personal computers were available. Class instruction in their use was done once a week for parents and twice a week for children ten and older. Then they toured the book mobile which was housed in a motor home and sent to the CHSA site three times a week by the County library.

Juan enjoyed seeing the program he had helped to start, but most of all he loved seeing the children. Even though he was doing a great job as superintendent, he would always be a teacher at heart.

"Okay, it's taco time," Jimmy announced as he saw the food van pull into the housing area. Juan and Jimmy were the first customers of the day and were gone with their tacos before the rush hit.

Returning to Jimmy's office, they popped open their containers and without a word, began to eat their chicken taco and cheese enchilada with beans and rice.

As they finished their meal, Jimmy refilled their coffee cups.

"Juan, I'm glad you came today. There's something I want to discuss with you. Remember that I told you I was considering taking a job in D.C.?" Jimmy asked.

"Of course I remember. How could I not? I've been thinking about how it would feel to lose my best professional colleague and my friend," Juan replied.

"Worry no further," Jimmy said. "I'm not going."

"Why, I thought you had decided on it," Juan exclaimed.

"They turned me down, Juan. They told me they needed a Latino in the position," Jimmy explained.

"I'm sorry for that happening, Jim. I know you understand it's not about you. It's the political climate.

I'm also sorry for the Latino that gets placed in the job solely because of ethnicity. I hope he or she does well. Failure in the job would just perpetuate the myth of Latino ineptitude.

"I hope this doesn't make you bitter, Jim. I know it isn't fair to you, but society is trying to make up for many years of unfairness to Latinos," Juan replied.

"No, I get it," Jimmy said. "I think that a period of preference for minorities is needed as an adjustment. After a time, we will have no need to use race or ethnicity as a criterion for job placement. It may take a whole generation, but then it will be done," Jimmy acknowledged.

"Meanwhile, I am very sorry for you, Jim. I know you would have done a great job. But I'm glad for me and the community. We are sending lots of kids into the world that are equipped to make it a better place to live, and we will continue to do so," Juan proclaimed.

"I'll drink to that!" Jimmy said as he raised his coffee cup.

Chapter 53

Jimmy picked up the office phone on the second ring. "Good to hear from you, Daniel. How goes the campaign?"

"It's going," Daniel replied. "I'm sure *getting there* is one of the hardest parts of being a member of the House. But we're doing okay, just exhausted. What I really want to know is are you taking the job in D.C.? You know, it sure would be nice to have a real friend here. President Truman was right when he said that if you want a friend in Washington D.C., get a dog. It's definitely survival of the most devious here."

Jimmy paused and then answered, "I'm not coming to D.C. I'm going to tell you why because I know you'll keep it to yourself. You and Juan are the only ones who know it wasn't just because they found a better candidate.

"Like I told you before, the boss at DOL, Odessa, called me into her office when I was there for a meeting. She told me that the CHSA program had grown, and they were going to hire a national director for the program. She also said that they wanted to increase the number of farmworker families enrolled in the program. She told me she thought I would be great for the job and asked me to send her my resume. She said it was going to be an appointed position, so no application process was needed.

"As you know, I wasn't wild about going to D.C. It's a wonderful city to visit but I wouldn't want to live there. As I thought about it though, I decided it was a great opportunity to help more families. I would have the authority to push program operators to enroll more farmworker families to meet the DOL mandate. So, I sent my resume.

"About two weeks later, I got a call from a secretary at DOL. She asked to schedule a meeting with Odessa. When I got there, Odessa and I talked about the goal DOL had to enroll more farmworker families. We also talked about other DOL program objectives. I was very comfortable with my ability to do all she was asking.

"The more we talked, the more I warmed up to the idea of taking the job. By the time I left, I was ready to do it. She called in two of her Latino assistants before I left, and we just talked for about an hour and a half.

"Two days after I got back, Odessa called. She said that she was withdrawing my name from consideration for the position. I didn't even have to ask why; she was very honest.

"Odessa said, 'I'm sorry Jim; this was my mistake. I thought you were Latino. I heard you speaking Spanish when we were at the meetings here and I knew your program was for farmworkers — I just assumed you were Latino. I know your good reputation. Your program is known for excellence. I thought you would do a great job as our director like you have done for your local program. I still think that, but I have to be honest. We have to hire a Latino for this position. I know you speak the language, know the customs, get along well with the farmworkers, and all that. But I'm getting heavy pressure to get a Latino in a management role here. They use the term bicultural for the acceptable candidates, which means a Latino and no one else is eligible for the job. I'm sorry, Jim.' I told her not to be sorry and that I was alright with the decision; I am alright with it," Jimmy finished.

"Well, you shouldn't be alright with it. That's the same kind of discrimination that the minority groups have said society uses against them. It's not right! You don't cure racism with more racism," Daniel responded.

"I believe in what I'm doing here, Daniel. We're teaching these kids to compete with anyone out there. And if it takes a period of having racial discrimination turned in their favor, then so be it. Things will level out after a time, maybe as long as a generation, but then there will be no further need or desire for racial discrimination by or against minorities. We will level the playing field," Jimmy said passionately.

"That's a nice thought, Jim," Daniel began, "but do you think people like that guy Hilario that you told me about will ever believe we have done enough to level the playing field? No, they will find reason after reason to continue racial preference for school and jobs.

"This business of affirmative action is bullshit. It diminishes the person who receives anything through racial preference. It makes them and everyone else unsure if they are capable or just the right color. Hilario and his kind will continue to plead the case that society owes them. The tribalism we see developing now is nothing! You said 'maybe a generation!' I promise you they will demand preferences for minorities as long as society will put up with it. If this polarization continues, it will tear this country apart.

"If we allow this institutionalized racism by the minority to be turned against the majority, it will destroy this country. We are forgetting a very basic aspect of a democracy, and that is that it should promote the greatest good for the greatest number. Make no mistake, Jim, there are lots of members of minority groups out there that hate us just because we're white. I've encountered a great number of them here in D.C. They don't want the playing field leveled. They want a hill built and given to them so they can stand on it and spit on us. They will generate all kinds of twisted data to show how they deserve preference," Daniel concluded.

"Daniel, I hope you're wrong about the widespread nature of this ill will. As a society, we can withstand a period of reverse racial discrimination. If it should continue into another generation, I might be inclined to accept your opinion, but for now, I think it's just a course correction on our journey to a better future where we don't use race or ethnicity to make any decisions about a person. Like Dr. King said, we should judge each individual by the content of their character, not the color of their skin. We have to work to see that everybody gets an equal opportunity, no matter how many tricks the manipulators of the world pull or how much bogus data they generate. We have to promote peace," Jimmy said.

"Jim, you have a much more optimistic view of people than I do," Daniel said.

"Let me tell you a little about myself that you probably don't know. Maybe it will explain a bit about my optimism. I'm ashamed to admit it, but I was just as bad as the people you're describing. I didn't want to be around Mexicans, didn't think they were good people. I threatened a Mexican guy one night with a two-by-four. I never actually did anything to anyone because they were of Mexican descent, but I just didn't like them for no reason other than their ethnicity. And I, of all people, should have known better. I have heard stories from my own family of how they, and our extended family, were abused. I have experienced some abuse and disregard myself because we were Okies. We were not a different ethnic or racial group. We were just poor and powerless," Jimmy said.

"What made you change? You've been a bleeding-heart liberal all the time I've known you," Daniel chuckled.

"Education changed me, Daniel. My grandad told me something just before I left for college. He said, 'Son, a man needs an education to get along in this world today. There's two ways I know to get it. There's *book learnin'* and there's *life learnin.'* Now you're goin' away to get some *book learnin'* and I'm glad. The world is a lot more complicated now than it was when I was a young man. You need to study on some of these new things. But don't neglect your *life learnin,'* son. If you pay attention, the world around you will teach you some things you may not learn from them books.'

"You know, Daniel, he was right. I learned a lot in college; we both did. But I got a lot of *life learnin'* in Europe. The minute I stepped onto the McKinley School campus, my *life learnin'* really accelerated. My *life learnin'* lined up with my *book learnin,'* and the change that had started in college expanded. I say again, education changed me.

"I'm a behaviorist devotee. So, I'm a believer that a change in behavior is the best evidence that learning has taken place. I know my behavior has certainly changed as

I learned more about the people I thought I didn't like," Jimmy concluded.

"Yeah, I get that," Daniel replied, "but remember the old proverb, 'You can lead a horse to water, but you can't make it drink.' What made you want to learn, and how do you think learning will happen for others?" Daniel asked.

"Well, Grandpa was right. The *book learnin'* piqued my interest about different ethnic groups but the *life learnin'* helped to further my education; I'm still learning. I have had lots of good life learning teachers. The people in Europe and a little Mexican boy with blue eyes were probably the first. My friend Juan, who has weathered all the insults and become a force for good in the community, has taught me a lot. The farmworker families who struggle to make a living, face gross abuse and yet, for the most part, maintain a happy outlook have also helped. I have a friend, Renaldo, who I want you to meet someday. He has overcome some awful circumstances, and he has been one of my greatest teachers.

"The Mexican people, especially Father Anaya as I traveled in Mexico, have been very gracious in dispensing their lessons to me. Of course the kids at McKinley school have been some of the best teachers I have known.

"What all these good teachers have taught me, in a nutshell, is that when we have personal relationships, we find that we have at least similar views of the world. We still may not like each other when we get acquainted. It might be because of some personality clash or other cause, but most times it won't be because of race," Jimmy continued.

"We don't like each other's groups sometimes, because we don't take the time to understand each other. Then sometimes we don't like each other because we do understand each other. But more often than not, when we get up close enough to smell each other's garlic, we find a sense of our common humanity and we can get along," Jimmy said emphatically.

"My education isn't done yet, but believe me, Daniel, this is one gringo that is very thankful for the education he has been given!"

Acknowledgements

Special thanks are due to my wife, Janette, for her reading, typing and editing of the manuscript. Her constant encouragement and support kept me going when the road got rocky. Without her, the book would not have been completed.

Thanks to Michael A. Tabangcura for sharing his first-hand knowledge and personal experience of farm work in the San Joaquin Valley.

Thanks to Hannah Neeley for her helpful and conscientious copyediting.

Many thanks are due to Carl Baggese for his patient persistence in completing the layout of the book.

I am grateful to Ken White for his guidance in getting the book published.

Finally, thanks to the many colleagues, friends and students I have known over the years who would describe themselves as Latino, Hispanic, Mexican, Mexican-American, Chicano, Filipino and just plain American.

Study Questions

1. The author mentions ethnocentrism several times in the book. What point is he trying to make by doing this? Do you agree or disagree with his premise?

2. Jimmy travels to Mexico in order to learn both the language and culture of the Mexican people. He states that he does this in order to become a better teacher. Do you think that the study of culture and language in Mexico would make him a better teacher of children of Mexican descent in the U.S.?

3. Jimmy compares his own background with that of Mexican farmworkers. Do you agree that his comparisons are accurate?

4. Jimmy says that the Okies and Mexican farmworkers were abused primarily because they were poor and powerless. Do you agree or disagree?

5. Jimmy makes the point that he could blend in with society, whereas Juan and others in the story could not because of skin color. Do you agree or disagree?

6. The author makes the point in several places in the book that Mexican farmworkers are used and taken advantage of by politicians. Do you agree or disagree?

7. Daniel proposed a plan to control the southern border by allowing Mexican farmworkers and their families to immigrate based on the need for workers. He includes a mechanism to allow temporary "guest" workers into

the U.S. when agribusiness and farmworker unions certify that workers are needed. Is this a workable plan? Why or why not?

8. Are the characters in the book believable?

9. What caused Jimmy's change in attitude toward Mexicans?

10. Did Daniel have a change in his attitude toward Mexicans? If so, what caused the change?

11. What was your favorite part of the book?

12. Which public figures do you think would benefit from reading this story?

13. Was Juan's patience, persistence, and eventual success believable? Why or why not?

14. Did you empathize with Hilario? Why or why not?

15. Have you ever known anyone like Hilario?

16. Which character did you relate to most, and why?

Photo by James A. Ewing

ABOUT THE AUTHOR

H.R. DeArmond has been a teacher and administrator at all levels of the California public school system. After attendance at Modesto Junior College, he received his B.A. from San Francisco State University followed closely by an M.A. from California State University, Stanislaus and later an M.A. from the University of San Francisco. He was born in Oakland, California and spent much of his youth in the San Francisco Bay Area before moving to the San Joaquin Valley. He lives with his wife, Janette, among the verdant fields of the valley.

www.ingramcontent.com/pod-product-compliance
Lightning Source LLC
Chambersburg PA
CBHW061216190726
48288CB00001B/200